Waller Ashe

Personal Records of the Kandahar Campaign

by officers engaged therein

Waller Ashe

Personal Records of the Kandahar Campaign
by officers engaged therein

ISBN/EAN: 9783337423322

Printed in Europe, USA, Canada, Australia, Japan

Cover: Foto ©Andreas Hilbeck / pixelio.de

More available books at **www.hansebooks.com**

PERSONAL RECORDS

OF THE

KANDAHAR CAMPAIGN,

BY

OFFICERS ENGAGED THEREIN.

EDITED AND ANNOTATED, WITH AN INTRODUCTION,

BY

MAJOR ASHE

(Late King's Dragoon Guards),

AUTHOR OF 'THE STORY OF THE ZULU CAMPAIGN,' 'THE MILITARY
INSTITUTIONS OF FRANCE,' ETC. ETC.

LONDON:

DAVID BOGUE, ST. MARTIN'S PLACE, TRAFALGAR SQUARE.

1881.

DEDICATION.

To the Right Hon. the Earl of Lytton, G.C.B.

ETC. ETC.

My Lord,

IN venturing to dedicate to your Lordship these fugitive Records of the Kandahar Campaign, I believe they contain the recorded opinions and conclusions of many of my friends and comrades, who, like myself, have served amongst Asiatics, and studied the question of our Indian North-western Frontier—not, I trust, in a party, but in a purely impartial spirit—and whose views are based upon some experience of the Afghan character and the social features of the race.

At the present moment it would seem as though the chief end and aim of the Administration which rules our policy in 1881 were directed to the iconoclastic measures of undoing, with the hammer and the hatchet, whatever structures the calm and deliberate intellect of the late Cabinet thought fit to carry out. The triumphant response to your Lordship's vindication of your frontier policy, while acting as Her Majesty's representative in the Queen's Asiatic Dominions, given spontaneously in the House of Lords, is, I venture to believe, but a reflex of the sober and honest opinions of all civil and military authorities who value England's honour more than party prejudice.

The bright heritage of your Lordship's name, while recalling noble thoughts clothed in pure and polished phrase, in the pages of one whose intellect and powers were without equal in his day, has suffered no diminution in its halo at your hands; and in letters, diplomacy, and the Senate, your countrymen recognise a worthy successor to one whose pages contain no mean or ignoble sentiment. As a poor tribute to your Lordship's literary and diplomatic labours, I am asked by the writers of the following letters to offer you these 'Records of Kandahar;' which city, if now surrendered, we must at no future date, I believe, again fight for!

Your Lordship's most obedient Servant,
WALLER ASHE
Major (Late King's Dragoon Guards).

PREFACE.

FROM the days of Alexander to those of Napoleon
Military Fame has been one of the sweetest, if
not the most coveted, of human distinctions; and
although we read of

> ‘The shepherd kings of patriarchal times,
>   Who knew no brighter gems than summer wreaths,
>   And none but tearless triumphs,’

such potentates belong, I fear, but to a fabled
age—that Arcadia which is born only of the
poet’s inspiration. From the commencement of
authentic or reliable history, battle and conquest
have ploughed the soil where civilisation and
progress have subsequently reaped a fair and
goodly harvest. From the loftiest monarch to
his meanest subject war has ever been one of the
fatal penalties imposed on life ; for, as long as the
present world shall last, there will be, I opine, not
wanting those who covet their neighbours’ lands,
and, consequently, owners who object to the sur-

render of their inheritance. That *pax perpetua* of which Leibnitz speaks, but which is, alas! found only in 'God's acre,' will never, I believe, dawn upon this earth until our human nature shall change into Utopia, and until the ideal of a Sydney shall be found.

From the dark and awe-inspiring Presence that overshadows the realm of the Czars, to the paltry, yet subtle venom of the reptile crew, who, usurping the name of Patriot and of Irishman, crawl over the sister kingdom with a track of seditious slime, there will be incentives to possess *le bien d'autrui* which can only be met by armed defence and the antidotal remedies of lead and steel. Happily, however, for England, the growth of our vast empire has been like that of the forest oak—the dowry of generations; while, certainly of late, annexation and confiscation of territory have been, with few exceptions, more thrust upon us than coveted; while

> ' The big wars
> That make ambition virtue '

have for many years found little favour with our kings, our ministers, or our people.

But the Conservative patriotism, which, with all deference to Iconoclasts of the Parnell and

Bradlaugh type, still, as of old, animates the heart and the honest intelligence of these islands, teaches us to maintain the unity, as well as the honour and dignity, of this great empire—won by the courage and enterprise of our forefathers, and bequeathed to us as a heritage, of which, as a nation, we may well be proud.

Our Indian Empire, if commenced and founded in invasion and conquest, was a necessity of the time, and the choice of rule lay only between France and England—between Lally Tollendal and Clive—between the Courts of Versailles and Saint James ; and, in fact, became simply a question whether Paris or London should give laws and civilisation to the greater part of Asia. If most of our Colonies have grown up in peace and prosperity, they have, even now, to claim very frequently the protection of the mother country ; and our men and ships are a necessary part of our integrity of empire. It is not by the holy Gospel alone, nor by the missionary zeal and self-abnegation of our pioneers to remote and savage places, that the barbarian can be tamed into the shepherd or the dweller in cities. He will, even in his gentlest moments, occasionally dine off his missionary, and too often gives a decided preference to the 'fire-water of the pale faces' rather than to the abstemious teachings of Sir Wilfrid!

If, then, we may admit that war is sometimes a sad necessity, it is well to know that our defenders have not, in our time, become degenerate or unworthy of the old days, when England meant but one small island, and our forefathers' only boundary was the sea that washed our cliffs. The unhelmed front of Harold was pierced by the barbed Norman shaft at Sanglac; but his spirit and Saxon soul hovered over the adamantine squares that held the bloody slopes of Mont St. Jean. Drake, Frobisher, Hawkins, Howard, and Raleigh, come back to our Navy in such sea-captains as Nelson, Hood, Collingwood, and Jervis. The prototypes of Rupert's fiery Cavaliers gallop again with that *beau sabreur*, Cardigan, in the 'Valley of Death' at Balaclava; while Cromwell's 'Ironsides' live once more in the British 'Heavies' that followed Scarlett, and burst like an avalanche through the Ruski's squadrons. To remind us of Créci, Poictiers, and Azincourt, have we not Blenheim, Ramilies, Oudenharde, and Malplaquet, renewed again in Talavera, Salamanca, Vittoria, and Thoulouse?

It cannot, therefore, but be satisfactory to see that our military history repeats itself in the exploits of, and the reputations won in the field by, the leaders that we now possess; and we may remember, not without pride, that India and our first Eastern Empire were alike the schools and training-ground of Clive, Napier, Hardinge, Gough, Rose, Colin Campbell, Outram, Havelock, Michel, Hope Grant, as well as of their successors, Mansfield, Chelmsford, Garnet Wolseley, Evelyn Wood, and, last not least, Frederick Sleigh Roberts, whose deeds find passing record in these pages.

Having many relatives, friends, and former brother-officers, among the staff and regiments lately or still serving at the front in Afghanistan, and with whom I have maintained a constant and uninterrupted correspondence since the war operations commenced at the mouth of the Khyber, I have felt considerable interest in noting the varied phases of the campaign; and have been enabled to collect such material details as only eye-witnesses can give. From the letters, journals, chronicles, and sketches, sent to me from the scenes of action, and aided by such poor experience as twenty years' regimental and staff service allows to me as a soldier, I have essayed to write a History of the present Afghan War, which, I trust, will shortly be in the publisher's hands. But as it seems to me that the Kandahar episode forms a complete act and chapter in the drama now continuing, I have placed together these fugitive records of General Roberts' great march and victory while the interest is yet warm, and while the question of the Durani capital and its retention or surrender are before the Parliament and the public.

Some six years' service with my late regiment in India, and a personal acquaintance with many officers of note or standing serving now or lately at the seat of war, gave me opportunities and channels of information of which I gladly availed myself in following the fortunes of the campaign, and in watching the distinctions won by regiments and individual officers with whom I had marched and lived under Sir Frederick Paul Haines, and last served in India; and the names of Generals Primrose, Hills, Roberts, Biddulph, Browne, Gough, and Gordon; and of Colonels George Luck, Galbraith, Macpherson; Majors Oliver and Ready, and all the 66th ('Old Berkshires'); and lastly, not least, the comrades of my first corps, the 85th Light Infantry, recall pleasant memories of a soldier's life.

The following records relate only to the Kandahar episode of the war, in which I was particularly interested, having many old friends in the 66th and other regiments therein engaged, whose picturesque letters were, as I received them, by their permission, transcribed by me, as nearly as possible without curtailment or alteration, and handed for publication to my friend, the Editor of a leading London paper, while I retained the originals to assist me, as an · *aide mémoire* towards my forthcoming Afghan History.

Many of these letters were not only quoted but copied *in extenso* in various London, provincial, Irish, Scotch, and even Indian journals. As I had merely to arrange them, and, with care, place them in due order of date and locality, I can claim no merit save that which a military experience of twenty years may give; but I may be perhaps excused in believing that, in completeness of detail, graphic and picturesque description, and technical professional knowledge, they were not excelled by any contemporaneous correspondence from the seat of war; and such, I am glad to know, was the expressed opinions of English and foreign officers of high rank, whose letters to me were most gratifying. The letters dated Kandahar, July 30–31, if compared with the official despatches published months after, will be found to be singularly minute and correct in all matters of detail. *Vide* the description of the defence at the walled enclosure at Maiwand, and other episodes of the battle.

Certain critics, however, who carefully concealed their identity, chose to question the validity of the letters in question, on the grounds, firstly, that the letters dated Kandahar, July 30–31, could not have arrived in London (from Kandahar) at the date of their publication ; and, secondly, that the battles therein described were not like any battles seen by the critic !

To the first of these objections I have to say, that the battle of Maiwand was fought on the 27th July, and the British army was routed and flying on the afternoon of that day. Survivors of that engagement—Major Oliver and others, to wit— reached Kandahar on the morning of the 28th, and sent despatches to England on the 30th, which despatches, making every allowance for disturbed roads, &c., could find no difficulty in reaching London on 29th August ; while the letter I received first was not published till 7th September, and the same mail brought me Indian newspapers of a much later date than my letters.

To the anonymous ' Moltke,' who finds fault with my friend's descriptions of battles, I can only say, that the account was penned by spectators, or rather, I should say, actors in the scenes described ; and written by officers whose services and professional knowledge are justly appreciated by the military authorities, although they, unfortunately, failed in writing to the taste of their anonymous critic, and have not described the fight at, and retreat from, Kushk-i-Nakhud, as the critic would have done !

The moment I read the letter of the masked slanderer who questioned the authorship of the letters I had received and sent for publication, I wrote to the journals which had inserted his communications, giving my name, army rank, address, and vouchers for my correspondence, and demanded the name and rank of the person who signed himself ' Soldier,' and who, under that disguise, assailed me and my friends. I stated my willingness to place the original letters I had received in the hands of any responsible gentleman, on condition that ' Soldier ' would unmask.

As my challenge remains unaccepted, I conclude that 'Soldier' possesses no right to that honourable title, but has his own reasons for 'keeping dark,' while I may justly, I believe, apply to him the fable of the ass who assumed the lion's skin, but was discovered by his bray.

WALLER ASHE,
MAJOR (late K.D.G.).

BALNACREE HOUSE, TIPPERARY,
March 1881.

CONTENTS.

	PAGE
DEDICATION	v
PREFACE	vii
INTRODUCTION	xix

CHAPTER I.

IN GARRISON WITH GENERAL PRIMROSE	1
ON RECONNAISSANCE WITH GENERAL HILLS	11
KANDAHAR 'GUP,' ABDURRAHMAN, AND AYUB	17
WITH GENERAL BURROWS—OPINIONS OF THE WALI	23

CHAPTER II.

CONDITION OF KANDAHAR AFTER BURROWS' DEPARTURE	34
WITH GENERAL BURROWS—MUTINY OF WALI'S TROOPS	40
IN KANDAHAR AFTER THE MUTINY—MILITARY SITUATION	53
WITH GENERAL BURROWS — CAVALRY RECONNAISSANCE BEFORE THE BATTLE	60

CHAPTER III.

THE BATTLE AND DEFEAT OF MAIWAND	69
AFTER THE BATTLE—HORRORS OF THE NIGHT RETREAT	85
STATE OF THE KANDAHAR GARRISON AFTER MAIWAND	98

CHAPTER IV.

VALEDICTORY VISITS IN CABUL—ABDURRAHMAN	112
IN CABUL—THE NEWS FROM KANDAHAR—THE RELIEVING COLUMN	120
BANQUET TO GENERAL ROBERTS—THE NEW AMEER—THE MARCH	130

CHAPTER V.

ON THE LINE OF MARCH WITH THE RELIEVING COLUMN   144

THE SORTIE FROM KANDAHAR—VILLAGE OF DEH KWAJA   159

CHAPTER VI.

WITH GENERAL HILLS IN CABUL—INTERVIEW WITH THE AMEER—EVACUATION OF THE CITY BY GEN. STEWART   170

WITH SIR FREDERICK ROBERTS—ARRIVAL AT KANDAHAR   178

CAVALRY RECONNAISSANCE BEFORE THE BATTLE   188

CHAPTER VII.

THE VICTORY OF BABA WALI   198

AFTER THE BATTLE—CAVALRY PURSUIT—BURIAL OF THE DEAD   212

AFTER BABA WALI—A NIGHT-RIDE WITH GOUGH IN PURSUIT OF THE ENEMY   224

THE SITUATION IN KANDAHAR—PEACE, HONOURS, AND REWARDS—BREAKING UP OF THE KANDAHAR FIELD FORCE—RETIREMENT TO INDIA   241

INTRODUCTION.

THE Afghan war, which commenced on the 20th of October, 1878, may be divided into three distinct periods: namely, 1, From the expiration of Lord Lytton's Ultimatum on the above date, and the advance of our troops, up to the signing of peace at Gundamuck on May 27th, 1879; 2, From the outbreak at Cabul and the massacre of Sir Louis Cavagnari on Sept. 3rd, 1879, to the entrance into the Afghan capital by Sir Frederick Roberts on October 12th following; and, 3, From Ayub's advance from Herat to the Helmund on June 7th, to his defeat by our troops at Kandahar on Sept. 1st, 1880. These 'Records' deal only with the latter episode.

That we must be prepared for a fourth period and further episode of this war I believe to be inevitable, and I can scarcely doubt that Ayub will neglect the opportunities our present Government have given him, and the temptations we have offered by the ridiculous haste with which Cabul and our garrisons were evacuated, and the country denuded of troops, before Abdurrahman was well seated on the throne. The extraordinary policy which dictated what may, without exaggeration, be termed an ignominious flight from all those coigns of vantage won with our blood and treasure, and by the heroic self-sacrifice of our troops under Generals Roberts, Stewart, and Browne, must, in the eyes of impartial England, be alone held responsible for whatever further bloodshed may result. The same fatuity which hurried our victorious soldiers from the plains of Ulundi to those of Aldershot, leaving Zululand, Basutoland, and the Transvaal, in a fermenting and feverish unrest; the same inaction and want of purpose which has encouraged rebellion in Ireland, and which has, as it were, offered a premium to violence and murder; now impose a tax upon the energy and purse of all our public departments of this Empire, in a manner and to an extent never before paralleled. Who can possibly deny that the blood of our soldiers shed at Kushk-i-Nakhud and Deh Kwaja, and our terrible loss of prestige at those affairs, were not the immediate and swift retributions of the *quieta non movere* policy, which left our most important conquest, Kandahar, with a garrison one half its proper strength, and which compelled General Primrose to still further deplete the same, by detaching General Burrows to the Helmund, to be cut up in detail by Ayub Khan? Fortunately for us, the Afghan Prince was precipitate and rash in his advance from Herat, for if he had waited another month, the splendid force collected by Sir Frederick Roberts at Cabul would, in accordance with the behests of the Home Government, have been on its way to England, and Kandahar, unhelped and unrelieved from Cabul, must have fallen.

What has been the course pursued by the Government since? Having, by the outlay of a vast sum, and by the splendid march achieved by our most successful General, saved Kandahar from massacre, anarchy, and the hireling swords of Ayub's soldiers, it is gravely announced in Parliament that England will, in a short time, renounce the bulwark and the defence we have won, and restore to an uncertain dynasty the prize which forms the natural key to the most important portion of our Indian frontier, and which can, at any future time, be readily unlocked by Russian gold, if not by Russian steel and lead.

When the people of England learned, from a passage in the Queen's speech at the opening of the present Parliament, that it was the intention of our Government to withdraw our forces from Kandahar, they naturally were led to believe that such a course must have been advised and dictated by the judgment and opinions of the most competent authorities, namely, our best and most experienced Indian administrators, and our military advisers on this particular subject. Of course, to the great mass of the British public, the vast magnitude of the issues involved by the retention or evacuation of the Durani capital would scarcely be realised, and they naturally felt assured that the measure contemplated would not have been thought of, unless the opinions of the most competent authorities in India and England had been taken. But gradually it has been found that such has by no means been the case, for neither the Government of India, which, it may be allowed, is the authority most responsible for the integrity of our Eastern Empire, and its immunity from invasion and conquest, nor our best Indian military authorities, have been at all consulted in the matter.

If we may allow that the subject must be looked upon and discussed purely upon political and military reasons, let us by all means obtain and be guided by those political and military authorities whose honour is known to be above party feeling, and whose expe-

rience and knowledge of Indian history are worthy of
reliance. That having been compelled and forced, most
unwillingly, into this Afghan war of 1878, and having
won such a position of advantage as Kandahar, we
should be acting with deliberate and suicidal policy
were we to abandon it, I venture to maintain, knowing
that I am merely asserting the opinions and convictions
of ninety-nine men out of a hundred who, like myself,
have served in India, and look with utter astonishment
at the present attitude of the Government.

If we are to look upon history as a guide in matters
of this kind, we have only to remember that nearly
every invasion of India from the north-west, in ancient
or modern times, has been preceded by an advance
upon, or towards, Kandahar. From 536 B.C., when
Afghanistan formed the eastern portion of the Medo-
Persian empire founded by Cyrus, down to 1878, when
Chamberlain's mission was rejected by Shere Ali, the
western capital has been the *point de mir*, and one of, if
not the most coveted coigns of vantage. Alexander,
Salukas Nikator, the Parthians, the Sassanides, the
Saracens and Arabs, the Tartars, Mahmood, Genghis
Khan, Tamerlane, Baber, Nadir Shah, Ahmed Khan,
and the numerous other rulers who have attempted to
gain a footing in Hindostan, have nearly always made
the district of the Helmund their principal attack.

The experiences of the late as of the former wars we
have had with Afghanistan show plainly how difficult
is the march from Quetta to Kandahar, and how useless
would the former be as an outpost were the latter held
by an enemy. General Roberts marched more quickly
from Cabul to Kandahar than did General Phayre to
the latter place from Quetta.

Let us examine briefly, but in detail, the reasons which have been set forth by those who advise the abandonment of this strategic position :—The disinclination of our native troops to serve in Afghanistan, and the difficulty of recruiting ; the injustice of possessing ourselves of a district which forms part of a neighbouring and independent country; finally, the expense involved, and the difficulty of supplying and maintaining our garrison. In the first place, in regard to our native troops, I believe, and, indeed, have reason to know, that our Sepoys feel most acutely the disgrace of retiring from our conquest, and would most willingly serve in Afghanistan if periodically relieved and allowed to return to their families. The difficulty of recruiting is purely imaginary, and we have only to seek in the proper sources to get together as fine a frontier native army as can be formed anywhere amongst the Sikhs, Goorkhas, and other races who are hereditary foes to the Afghans proper. As to the injustice we commit, we need only to read the honest and impartial statements of officers who have lately returned from the Durani city, to see and acknowledge that it is the Kandaharis themselves who are the most anxious for us to remain—those very people who dwell in the Pishin Valley, on the slopes of the fertile Kojak Kotal, in the country between Kandahar and the Helmund, and in the city of Kandahar itself, and who dread our departure as the greatest calamity that can befall them !

Are those advocates of evacuation aware of whom and what the Kandaharis are, and come from ? They are certainly *not* Afghans ; and a study of any of the old chronicles of the district will show that they are descended from the Turkis, the Kizilbashis, the Tajiks, and the Khorassanis, who lived in or near the city in prosperity before the Afghan spoilers came down upon them to rob and murder from the hills around. How have the Afghan rulers treated Kandahar and the Persian element since? In 1709 the Persian Governor and his nobles were treacherously murdered at a banquet by the chief of the Ghilzai tribe, and since then years of oppression, tyranny, spoliation, and devastation of commerce and agriculture, have been the unhappy lot of these people, until our troops have given them that protection which they now ask us to continue, but which Mr. Gladstone wishes to take from them!

For more than a century and a half, and I have the authority of Colonel Malleson, Sir Richard Temple, and other experienced officers and historians for saying this, barbarism has oppressed and ground these people to the dust. Each successive Governor has ruled on the same lines—namely, to tax and impose to the utmost, and to drain all the industry and wealth of Kandahar, as a means whereby treasure might be transmitted to be spent at Cabul.

Finally we come to the question of expense, and here we have only to remember what vast changes a railway, in part completed, would effect. It has been estimated that the retention of Kandahar would cost us 2,000,000*l.* per annum, and, even allowing such a sum to be correct, what would such an outlay be compared with the peace and security of our vast Indian Empire? But with our occupation and the consequent security to life and property; with roads and steam, and those improvements which follow in the footsteps of civilisation, trade and commerce would increase with rapid growth, and the surrounding districts, which are now half desert and wild, would teem with agriculture and riches. What portions of our Indian province were self-supporting when we first annexed them? Certainly not Scinde, nor the Punjab, nor Burmah, but all of these are now a source of revenue rather than an expense. What better authority can we have on this subject than Sir Richard Temple, a financier of experience, one acquainted with Kandahar, its people, and its undeveloped sources of wealth, under a wise and civilised rule? Sir Richard has not long returned from the Durani city, and knows the feelings and the aspirations of the inhabitants. He is well acquainted with the people and their disposition towards us, which he assures us is most favourable, while in the surrounding districts he describes the occupiers of the soil to be industrious and peaceable, wanting only a firm and good rule to make the districts as prosperous as any we possess in the East. With Kandahar in our possession, we can make it the mart and emporium for Central Asia, a vast bazaar of trade, commerce, and agriculture, a landmark of progress and civilisation, and the finest bulwark England can hold against the inevitable, but dark and sinister, designs of Russia.

Although this little book refers only to the Kandahar episode of the campaign, I have thought it not out of place to offer in the Introduction some data which may serve as a reference to those who have not paid attention to the history of the Afghan power and its varied peoples and nationalities, and who have not followed the political phases of our Indian north-western policy. In this view I have sketched briefly the origin and growth of the Afghans as a power, and given a summary of our former wars with them ; while I have added a short notice of the geographical features of the country and a description of our line of frontier, together with a synopsis of the events which, year by year, led up to the Ultimatum of Lord Lytton and our invasion of the Ameer's territory.

In his admirable work on Afghanistan, Colonel Malleson tells us that the oldest European authority on the subject of Afghanistan is Hanway, and according to him Mahomedanism was introduced into the country towards the end of the ninth century. At this time Afghanistan formed part of the dominion of the Somani Princes, who ruled over a great part of Central Asia, and whose capital was Bokhára. During their sway, which lasted 120 years, Afghanistan first came into notice. On the death of Abdul Melek of the Somani dynasty in 961 all the high officers of State assembled to elect a successor. With the exception of Alptegin, who, originally a Turki slave, had risen to be Governor of Khorassan, they voted for Moursun, a member of the royal house. To punish him for his conduct, Moursun deprived Alptegin of his governorship. On his being subjected to further persecutions, and finding his life in danger, Alptegin rebelled, and escaping to Ghuzni, proclaimed himself independent. Balkh, Seistan, and Herat adhered to the Somanis ; but Eastern Afghanistan favoured Alptegin, who succeeded in consolidating his power and founding the celebrated Ghuznivide dynasty. The most remarkable member of this family was Mahmud, the son of Alptegin's daughter. He made eleven incursions into India, annexed the Punjab to his dominions, occupied several districts, sacked many towns in Hindostan, and extorted tribute from numerous Rajahs. He also conquered Samarkand,

Bokhara, and Persia. In 1187 Khusru, the last of the Ghuznivide dynasty, was deposed, and soon after murdered by Ghyas-u-Din, Chief of Ghor, who had for some years previously been gradually stripping that prince of his dominions. Ghyas-u-Din associated with himself his brother Mahammad Ghari, who, on his death, became sole ruler. That prince invaded India, and, conquering Delhi and the surrounding country, left as his viceroy a favourite slave, Kutb-u-Din. On Mahammad Ghari's death, Kutb-u-Din extorted from Mahammad's son and successor, Mahmoud, the empire of Delhi ; Mahmoud retiring to his ancestral home in the mountains of Ghar, retaining, however, ' the overlordship ' over Afghanistan. Taj-u-Din, in the last days of Mahammad Ghari, whose slave he was, had seized and proclaimed himself King at Ghuzni. He and Mahmoud combining conquered Herat and Western Afghanistan, but failed to recover from the King of Kharism Afghan Turkestan. The latter monarch, indeed, soon made himself master of all Afghanistan.

About 1219 Genghiz Khan subdued the kingdom of Kharism and its independency, Afghanistan. Under the rule of this monarch and his successors Afghanistan remained until 1251. In that year the Governor of the Punjab for the King of Delhi seized upon Ghuzni and Cabul. It would seem, however, that they were speedily recovered by the Maghols, for in 1336 we find a Ghorian Prince seated on the throne of Ghuzni and acknowledging the suzerainty of the Maghols of Central Asia. The fourth of this second Ghorian dynasty asserted his independence, but in 1383 the dynasty itself came to an end, the redoubted Timour Leng having conquered Afghanistan. On his death Afghanistan was broken up into provinces ; Herat, the then capital of Khorassan, being governed by one and Ghuzni by another prince of his family. Timour's great-grandson, Abusaid, reunited the scattered portions of the great conqueror's dominions into one empire ; but on his death they were again partitioned.

At the beginning of the sixteenth century, Baber, after many alternations of fortune, succeeded in building up an empire which comprised Afghanistan, Central Asia, the Punjab, and India. When he expired in 1530 his eldest son, Humayun, mounted the throne of Agra ; a younger son, Kamran, being the semi-independent sovereign of Cabul, Ghuzni, and Kandahar. A few years later Kamran extorted from his brother the cession of the Punjab and the territory south of the Sutlej as far as Hansi and Hissar. Humayun, driven from India by a competitor for the throne, after a prolonged struggle succeeded in subduing Kamran and rendering himself master of Afghanistan, and subsequently invading India reconquered the latter.

He was succeeded in Hindostan by his son, the famous Akbar ; and in Afghanistan by his youngest son, whose mother was the Regent. Akbar was during the early part of his reign only the nominal suzerain of Afghanistan, his attention being taken up by other parts of his vast empire. Eventually, however, on account of his brother's misconduct towards him, the suzerainty was enforced. On his brother's death, in 1585, Akbar nominated a viceroy to rule at Cabul. Kandahar had, soon after the accession of Akbar, been conquered by the Persians, but it was recovered in 1603. In 1622 it again fell into the hands of the Persians. Fifteen years later it was traitorously surrendered to the Emperor of Delhi. In 1647 the Persians once more captured Kandahar, and the Emperors of Delhi this time lost it for ever.

In 1709 the Ghilzai tribes in the neighbourhood of Kandahar, weary of the tyranny of Persia, were induced by one of their chiefs, Mir Vais by name, to shake off the yoke. By treachery Mir Vais and his adherents assassinated the Persian Governor and his principal officers, and by stratagem obtained admission into the town. Elected King by the assembled chiefs, he succeeded in maintaining his position ; and may be said to have been the person who consolidated the scattered atoms of the Afghan race into one nation. His son, Mahmud, conquered Persia and was crowned Shah. On the death of Mahmud in 1725 Kandahar became virtually independent of the Afghan Sovereign of Persia. A few years later Nadir, a Turki adventurer of mean family, rose to power; and on the 13th of January, 1730, he annihilated the Afghan army, and replaced the son of the deposed Shah on the throne. In 1736 he himself assumed the crown. In 1737 Nadir advanced, by Herat and Farrah, which submitted without resistance, on Kandahar ; and after a year's siege induced it to surrender on honourable terms. In the following year he captured Ghuzni and Cabul. In 1747 Nadir was assassinated by his nobles, when Ahmed Khan, one of the officers of the Afghan contingent, having vainly attempted to avenge his sovereign's death, proceeded, accompanied by the whole contingent, to Kandahar. On arrival at that city the chiefs of the principal tribes of Afghanistan assembled to deliberate on the course to be adopted.

The result was a determination to throw off the

yoke of Persia, and the election of Ahmed Khan as King of the Afghans. Changing the name of his tribe from Abdali to Durani, he was the founder of the dynasty of that name. Hastening to extend his power he marched on Ghuzni, which surrendered without a shot, and on Cabul, which he easily captured. Invading then the Punjab, he crossed the Sutlej and reached Sirhind, where he was defeated by the troops of the Emperor of Delhi. Hastening back, he had reached the Indus when he heard of the Emperor's death. On this he retraced his steps, marched on Lahore, induced the unsupported Governor to submit, and then appointing him his Viceroy of the Punjab, returned to Kandahar. His next exploit was the conquest of Herat, which he annexed to the Afghan kingdom. He then invaded Khorassan, but was worsted and forced to retreat. He compensated himself for this disaster by the conquest in 1752 of Kashmir. In 1756, on the death of Ahmed Shah's Viceroy, the Mogul Emperor sent an army to reoccupy the Punjab and establish his own nominee as governor. Ahmed soon drove him out, and, his demands for compensation being refused, crossed the Sutlej, and occupying Delhi that place became a scene of plunder and massacre at the hands of his insubordinate soldiers. Marrying, and causing his son Taimur to marry, princesses of the royal family, Taimur's bride brought as her dowry the Punjab and Scinde. Leaving as Vizier at Delhi one of his adherents, Ahmed returned to Kandahar. He was at once called on to subdue the Governor of Scinde. Him he defeated but gave him honourable terms, granting him semi-independence, only requiring that his suzerainty should be acknowledged, and that a Belooch contingent should be furnished in payment when needed. He then marched to India, which had fallen under the sway of the Mahrattas. These, in 1761, he utterly defeated at the battle of Paniput. Replacing the Mogul Emperor on the throne of Delhi he returned to Kandahar. In 1762 he was summoned to the Punjab to put down the Sikhs, and had scarcely overcome them in a decisive battle at Sirhind than he was informed that his capital was in revolt. Hastening back by the Girnal Pass to Ghuzni, he soon re-established his authority in Kandahar. In 1767 he again drove the turbulent Sikhs from the plains of the Punjab to the hills. In 1773 he died from a cancer in the mouth.

Of this remarkable man it has been said : ' The chief merit to be ascribed to Ahmed Shah is undoubtedly the consolidation of the Afghan tribes. He made of them a nation. The chiefs whom he failed to conciliate he reduced. Forming a council composed of a leading chieftain of each tribe, consulting with its members and often adopting their advice, he was able to concert measures which commended themselves to the general body.'

His son and successor, Taimur, had not the character and energy of Ahmed, and he was frequently harassed by rebellion. During his reign Scinde and Balkh became virtually independent of him, and the seeds of further dismemberment were sown. Zaman Shah, the fifth son of Taimur, was elected, on the death of the latter, his successor. Of his elder brothers, Humayun was Governor of Kandahar and Mahmud of Herat. Marching against Humayun, Zaman Shah defeated him and drove him from the kingdom, but patched up an accommodation with Mahmud. Rebellion having shown itself in the Punjab, Zaman Shah marched to quell it. Recalled by tidings of risings nearer home, he retraced his steps ; but to follow his career would be profitless. It is sufficient to say that in 1799, being at Lahore with a view to invading India, he was recalled by the tidings that the Shah of Persia, instigated by the English, who were alarmed at the idea of an invasion of India, was threatening Khorassan.

This was the first occasion that Afghanistan came within the scope of Anglo-Indian politics. At the close of 1799 a conspiracy to depose Zaman Shah, whose tyranny had become unbearable, was betrayed. The leader of the conspiracy, Payandah Shah, the chief of the Barukzyes, and several of his associates, were executed, and Payandah's eldest son, Fathi Khan, receiving timely warning, fled to join Mahmud, who was striving to induce the Shah of Persia to espouse his cause. Urged by Fathi Khan, Mahmud appeared at Farrah, and issued an appeal to the natives. The Barukzyes and other Durani tribes flocking to his standard, he besieged and took Kandahar. He subsequently captured Cabul, and Fathi Khan, having gained over Zaman Shah's principal supporters, Zaman was seized and blinded.

Under Mahmud's lax rule the empire soon began to diminish. Khorassan was seized by the Persians, and the Punjab south of the Indus threw off his yoke. At length his brother, Shah Sujah, rebelled against and displaced him.

The new monarch having, however, failed to conciliate Fathi Khan, who had submitted to him, that chief caused constant rebellions against him, which were with difficulty suppressed. In 1808 the English, for the first time, entered into direct relations with the Afghans, Mr. Mountstuart Elphinstone being the envoy. That gentleman was well received, and succeeded in concluding at Peshawur a treaty, of which the principal article was 'that neither the French nor any other foreign Europeans should be permitted to have a footing in his dominions.' Mahmud and Fathi Khan, taking advantage of the King's absence, seized Cabul, met Shah Sujah near Gundamuck and completely defeated him. Shah Sujah, nevertheless, continued the struggle for several years, but with constant ill-success, till in 1811, seized by the Sikh Governor of Attock, he was sent a prisoner to Kashmir, when he was shortly afterwards allowed to join his family at Lahore. Escaping in 1815, he sought an asylum at Loodiana, in British territory. On Mahmud's restoration to the throne all real power was assumed by Fathi Khan, and one of the first acts of this Afghan king-maker was, aided by Runjeet Singh, to bring back Kashmir to its allegiance. In every way he displayed the utmost vigour and capacity, and the kingdom had never been so prosperous. He had, however, a cruel and remorseless enemy. Mahmud's son, Kamran, having under the most cowardly circumstances murdered his cousin, Fathi Khan declined to give him any public employment. At length Kamran found an opportunity for revenge. Mahmud's brother, Feruzudin, Governor of Herat, having refused to admit the Vizier into the town, the latter succeeded in making him a prisoner, and sent him off under an honourable escort to Cabul.

The day after his departure Dost Mahomed, contrary to the express commands of his brother, plundered the seraglio and offered a gross insult to Mahmud's daughter, who had married Feruzudin's son. Dost Mahomed was at once disgraced and placed in confinement by the Vizier. This was not, however, enough to satisfy the malice of the enemies of the latter, and Kamran extorted from the King an order that Fathi Khan should be blinded. Kamran, keeping this order secret, proceeded to Herat, dispelled Fathi Khan's suspicions, and one morning, when Fathi Khan paid Kamran a visit, that prince caused him to be seized and deprived of sight.

This atrocity caused the downfall of the Sudozye dynasty. The brothers of the Vizier at once collected forces, which were placed under the command of Dost Mahomed. Cabul was occupied by the Barukzyes after a victory, and Dost Mahomed and his brother, Mahomed Azim Khan, Governor of Kashmir, marched with 4000 men to meet Mahmud and his son Kamran. Mahmud had, on the approach of the Barukzyes, fled to Ghuzni, where he was joined by Kamran, who had hastened from Herat to assist his father. Altogether they had 12,000 men, but these all went over to the Barukzyes as soon as the latter appeared, and Mahmud and Kamran fled to Kandahar. They, however, halted on the way to wreak a last vengeance on Fathi Khan, who was murdered in the King's presence, Kamran striking the first blow. After numerous wanderings they reached Herat, which still remained faithful to them, and thereby acknowledging the suzerainty of the Shah of Persia they succeeded in establishing themselves.

In 1829 Mahmud died, at the instigation, it is said, of Kamran, who himself was assassinated by his Vizier, the infamous Yar Mahomed, who had dethroned him the previous year. A few years later Yar Mahomed was himself murdered. A period of anarchy and confusion followed the dethronement of Mahmud ; the Barukzye brothers, each governing different districts, worked without concert. At length Azim Khan established himself at Cabul as chief administrator of the kingdom, but he was not readily obeyed by either the tribes or his brother in the Afghan Turkestan, and Badakshan having recovered their independence, and Runjeet Singh having conquered Kashmir, Moolta Dera, Ghazi Khan, and Attock, was threatening Peshawur. Azim Khan, taking with him Dost Mahomed, marched to meet the Sikhs, and was utterly defeated at Noushera. Azim Khan died shortly afterwards, bequeathing to his son, Habib Ulla, the Cabul district.

Of the Barukzye brothers, Dost Mahomed was at Ghuzni, Purdel Khan and two of his brothers were at Kandahar, while Sultan Mahomed was at Peshawur. A civil war broke out among the brothers, the upshot of which was that Purdil Khan remained in possession of Kandahar, while Dost Mahomed was ruler of Cabul, Ghuzni, and Jellalabad, Sultan Mahomed being obliged to content himself with Peshawur.

In 1834 Shah Sujah, who had, a few years after Mahmud's flight from Cabul, made a futile attempt to gain the crown, traversed the Bolan, entered Afghanistan, and besieged Kandahar. Anxious to ascertain whether Shah Sujah would be supported by the British, Dost Mahomed sent an envoy to Loodiana to inquire. The answer seems weak and ambiguous. It was to the effect that the British would not support Shah Sujah, but that he had their best wishes. How history repeats itself! Reassured, Dost Mahomed marched against Shah Sujah, and in a desperate battle defeated him. Shah Sujah fled, and after some wanderings regained his old asylum at Loodiana. After this victory Dost Mahomed, feeling himself virtual sovereign of Afghanistan, resolved to establish this fact formally in the eyes of the world. The Duranis had called themselves kings, but then they had a kingdom. A practical man, Dost Mahomed, condemned titles indicative of a state of affairs which did not exist, saying, 'I am too poor to support my dignity as a Sirdar; it would be absurd for me to call myself a king.' He decided, in consultation with the chief, to assume the modest title of Ameer-ul-Momerin — Commander of the Faithful. Dost Mahomed announced his elevation to the Governments and of the States bordering his own, the Sikh and the British Governments excepted. Thus, through their injudicious treatment of Dost Mahomed, the Indian Government took the first step towards alienating the Afghans.

Runjeet Singh had taken advantage of Shah Sujah's invasion to add Peshawur to the Punjab, and though the Afghans made several attempts to regain their lost dependency they never succeeded. In 1837 the Persians laid siege to Herat. Dost Mahomed sought, by means of a British alliance, to check Persia and recover Peshawur. Taking advantage, therefore, of the arrival in India of a new Governor-General, Lord Auckland, he sent him a complimentary letter, and mentioned his grievances against the Sikhs. Lord Auckland declined to interfere, but announced his intention of sending a mission to Cabul to discuss commercial topics.

In the meantime Dost Mahomed's brother at Kandahar, dreading the strength which he would gain by an English alliance, sent applications for support both to Persia and Russia. Persia gave a favourable reply, and

Russia sent an envoy, Captain Vikovitch, to Kandahar. Captain Burnes, the Envoy of the British Government, was well received at Cabul, which city he reached in September 1837. He had, however, no power to deal with political matters. The Ameer opened his heart to him, and did all he could to secure the friendly aid of the British, abstaining so long as the matter was doubtful from any intercourse with Vikovitch, who had arrived from Kandahar. When, however, he saw that Lord Auckland was not to be moved, he threw himself into the arms of Russia. Vikovitch promised money, the restoration of Herat, and to negotiate with Runjeet Singh. He also, with the Ameer's consent, brought to a conclusion the treaty between the Kandahar princes and Persia, by which the latter promised to aid the Afghans with troops. This close connexion between Afghanistan and Persia, with the shadow of Russia in the background, alarmed the Indian Government, and they determined to take vigorous action. The Liberals were then in power, and Colonel Malleson, one of our best authorities, scathingly deals with the deviation from their cardinal principles on this occasion. He says that their policy was at all events remarkable :—

'They proposed to depose the ruler who, out of the chaos resulting from the expulsion of the Sodozyes, had evoked at least a semblance of order, a form of good government, and most certainly a respect for authority . . . and to replace him by a prince who had already enjoyed under, for Afghanistan, favourable circumstances, the opportunity of ruling and had failed; who, when subsequently treated with as to the conditions of his return by the Barukzye Chiefs, had acted in a manner which plainly showed that he had learnt nothing and forgotten nothing. . . . The subsequent conduct of the Government was still more extraordinary ; with the raising of the siege of Herat

all pretext for interference had disappeared. The Russo-
Persian-Afghan alliance had collapsed. The dangers with
which it was suffered to be fraught had been proved to be non-
existent; their very shadows had disappeared. A Lieutenant
of Artillery had made the political situation in Western Asia
more favourable to England than it had been at the time of
Burnes' mission, for he had caused the Russo-Persian bubble
to burst under the very nose of the Ameer of Cabul and his
brothers.'

The project of re-establishing Shah Sujah was,
however, persevered in, with what disastrous results we
all know.

It would have been superfluous to write a detailed
history of the first Afghan war, for the subject had been
ably and exhaustively treated by Sir John Kaye. I
give, therefore, a mere outline, and this outline demands
no notice from us. I therefore pass on to the period
between 1842 and 1869.

In 1854 Dost Mahomed, alarmed at the intrigues of
Persia, determined to seek support of the English, and
the same year concluded a treaty of alliance with them.
The result was, in 1856 the Persians besieged Herat.
England declared war against the Shah, and in the early
part of the following year another treaty was concluded,
by which we engaged to aid the Ameer, to defend his
dominions, and to grant him during the war a subsidy
of 10,000*l.* per month. It was also provided that the
Ameer was to send a Vakil to reside at Peshawur, that
during the war English officers were to reside at Kandahar, Cabul, or Balkh, or all three places, and that on
the conclusion of peace they were to be replaced by a
native Vakil, who was to reside at Cabul. Colonel
Lumsden and two other officers were in consequence
sent to reside at Kandahar.

On the determination of the war with Persia, Ahmed Khan, a nephew of the Ameer, became ruler of Herat on a quasi-independent footing; but, intriguing with Persia, Dost Mahomed besieged and took Herat, he himself expiring in the moment of victory. At his death the whole of Afghanistan acknowledged his rule, for Kandahar had some time previously recognised him as Sovereign. The events which followed are, thanks to the recent debates and Parliamentary papers, fresh in the memories of all. It is needless, therefore, to recapitulate them. It need only be said, that even before Lord Lytton arrived in India we had by our stolid policy thrown Shere Ali into the arms of Russia, and that we might easily have secured him as a firm ally.

As regards Shere Ali personally, there are no grounds for the most unpatriotic doctrinaires and humanitarians considering him an interesting victim. He has been spoken of as 'cruel, ungrateful, and self-seeking,' and draws attention to the treatment which he accorded to those who were most instrumental in establishing him on the throne. The three adherents who had rendered him the greatest services were his son Yakub Khan, his brother Aslam Khan, and his nephew Ishmael Khan. Yakub Khan he enticed, under the most solemn promises of safety, from Herat to Cabul, and then threw him into the dungeon, in which he lingered until his father's flight; Aslam Khan he caused to be strangled; Ishmael Khan he drove an outlaw to Lahore, where he died.

Nearly forty years have elapsed since the last British expedition to Afghanistan took place. With its policy and its general results I do not now propose to deal. I will only say that the British advance upon the Afghan capital was a complete success, and that its object—the overthrow of Dost Mahomed—was easily accomplished. It was after the occupation of the capital that the struggle commenced which is associated in the public mind only with the greatest disaster that ever befell our arms in India ; and it is of that struggle that we now propose to give as detailed an account as our space will allow.

It was on the 13th of January, 1842, that from the ramparts of Jellalabad, a fortress garrisoned by a brigade under the command of Sir Robert Sale, there was observed a fugitive British officer bending over his horse's neck, making his way to the fort. That officer was Dr. Brydon, the solitary survivor, as we supposed for many months, of the British army occupying Cabul. Dr. Brydon, who had received several wounds and lost one hand by a sabre cut, had managed to escape by the stoutness of his horse. Of 16,000 men, women, and children, who had left Cabul with him on the 6th January, he alone was there to tell the melancholy tale, although it subsequently became known that a few officers and soldiers, and Englishwomen, were detained in captivity.

This is the disaster which has thrown into oblivion all the glories of the Afghan campaign, and which Lord Carnarvon and Mr. Baxter lately held up to us as a warning against any further intervention in the affairs of Afghanistan. And this is how it came about. After the dethronement of Dost Mahomed and his deportation to Loodiana as a State prisoner, Shah Sujah, a creature of the Indian Government, was placed upon his throne, and a British force remained in occupation of his capital, under the command of General Elphinstone, an officer of no experience or capacity, and a confirmed valetudinarian. With him were associated the British Envoy, Sir William Macnaghten, and Sir Alexander Burnes, a civilian of great promise. The British force occupying Cabul consisted of 4500 men all told, inclusive of one English regiment (H. M. 44th Foot) ; some 12,000 camp followers were attached to the force. On the 2nd November a rising took place in Cabul, and an attack was made upon Sir Alexander Burnes' dwelling, in which he and his brother were killed. General Elphinstone withdrew all his troops into the cantonments, leaving the commissariat fort, containing all his supplies, to be guarded by a few troops, who speedily abandoned their post. From this moment the resistance of the British troops was only a question of time, as every day brought them closer to starvation. After a month of spiritless defence, during which the numbers of the enemy had enormously increased, negotiations were resorted to. But it soon became clear that Akhbar Khan, the leader, was only trying to gain time ; and still no active steps were taken by the British Commander to confront the difficulty. To add to the miserable prospects of the garrison, a heavy fall of snow covered the ground. Six weeks after the rising a pretended programme was submitted to the British Envoy, to which he assented, and in accordance with which, unaccompanied by any escort, he went to meet Akhbar Khan. Sir William Macnaghten paid with his life for his credulity. He was shot through the head by Akhbar Khan, and his body was exposed in the principal bazaar of Cabul.

General Elphinstone, not even yet convinced of the depths of Afghan duplicity, again opened negotiations, instead of endeavouring to cut his way through the enemy; and finally, on the 6th of January, he marched out with upwards of 4000 fighting men and 12,000 camp followers. Almost immediately the massacre commenced; the rear guard was attacked, the guns captured, and every mile the army traversed had to be won with the sword. Want of food and excessive cold paralysed the native troops, so that they were cut down without any attempt at resistance. The soldiers of the 44th Regiment were destroyed almost to a man. General Elphinstone surrendered to Akhbar Khan, and eight ladies, including Lady Sale and Lady Macnaghten, put themselves under his protection.

At Jugdulluck, only thirty-five miles from Cabul, there were, with the exception of a few prisoners, 300 survivors out of the 16,500; and of these the only one left on the 13th of January, seven days after leaving the capital, was Dr. Brydon, who died about four years ago.

Sir Robert Sale, commanding at Jellalabad, had received an order from General Elphinstone in captivity, authorising him to evacuate the fort and retire into British territory. But his answer was to prepare to defend it to the last extremity. For three months the fort was besieged by an immense Afghan force, who were repulsed at every assault, and finally, on the 7th of April, severely beaten and driven off with heavy loss by the garrison. Had Sir Robert Sale been in command at Cabul, we should not have to record the disastrous retreat of the British force. On the 16th of April the advanced guard of the avenging army under General Pollock came in sight of Jellalabad, and the heroic garrison was finally relieved.

As soon as intelligence reached the Indian Government of the destruction of the Cabul army, it resolved on prompt measures for the relief of General Sale at Jellalabad, and the punishment of Akhbar Khan's treachery. Accordingly a strong force was immediately pushed up to Peshawur, and on the 5th of April General Pollock, without waiting for his full strength, marched upon the Khyber Pass with 8000 men. The Khyber was then, as it is now, in the hands of the Khyberees, who exacted a heavy toll from all who desired its passage, whether Afghan or English, and an attempt was made to purchase their neutrality. But General Pollock could not brook delay, and as the negotiations were necessarily protracted, he determined to force the Pass. He found the entrance fortified, and held by a considerable body of the enemy. His dispositions were soon made. Detaching two strong columns by a circuitous route to clear the heights to right and left, he held the main body of his army at the mouth of the Pass, ready to storm. But the two columns having once reached the heights, drove the enemy rapidly before them, and the entry was unopposed.

Discouraged by this first success, the enemy retreated along the Pass, not even occupying the fort of Ali Musjid, which commands a formidable defile in the Khyber. Within ten days General Pollock had emerged from the Pass, and on the 16th of April had effected a junction with the brave garrison of Jellalabad. Having so far successfully effected his object, the British General rested his force in order to give time for supplies and reinforcements to come up, the intense heat of the weather rendering active operations in the field impracticable.

On the 20th of August he began his march upon Cabul with a force of about 8000 men, including two

English regiments, and three days afterwards completely defeated an Afghan army of 1000 men near Gundamuck. But now began the chief difficulties of the expedition. From Jugdulluck to the end of the Khoord Cabul Pass —the scene of the massacre of the Cabul army—there was a distance of some forty-two miles to be traversed, in which deep ravines, rocky watercourses, and narrow defiles, closed in by perpendicular heights, had to be traversed. The cliffs were lined by bodies of the enemy, and one after another had to be cleared as the British army moved forward. At the valley of Tezeen he halted his troops, and the Afghans, under the command of Akhbar Khan, coming up in great force, attacked and drove in his pickets. The following day General Pollock commenced his attack, and a pitched battle of a most desperate character took place, cavalry and infantry taking part in it. In the end the enemy, numbering 16,000 men, were defeated with great slaughter, and the Pass was forced.

By the 15th September General Pollock had crossed the Khoord Cabul Pass, and pitched his camp on the racecourse of Cabul. On the following day the British standard floated over the Bala Hissar, the citadel, and within a week all the prisoners taken from the Cabul army were restored. So much for the difficulties of a direct advance from Peshawur upon Cabul when conducted by a resolute and capable commander.

In the meantime a rising, akin to that which had resulted so disastrously to our arms at Cabul, had taken place in Kandahar. General Nott was in command there with 10,000 men, and, like Sir Robert Sale, refused to obey General Elphinstone's orders for withdrawal. But it was thought prudent to reinforce his command,

and for that purpose General England marched up from Scinde through the Bolan Pass to Quettah; but at the Kojak Pass his advanced guard met with a disastrous repulse, and was compelled to fall back.

Whilst these operations were proceeding the British garrison at Ghuzni had been compelled to surrender from starvation. General Nott thereupon determined to make a simultaneous movement upon Cabul, and on the 7th of August he started with a view, if necessary, to reinforce General Pollock. The country through which he had to pass, though not so difficult as that on the Peshawur route, still presented very great natural obstacles, and afforded more than one stand to the enemy. On the 29th of August the Afghans gave battle in a well-chosen position, but were defeated with great loss. On the 5th September he reached Ghuzni, and made preparations for attack upon the fortress, which, like ·the surrounding hills, was held in considerable strength by the enemy. In the night · the fortress was captured, and General Nott, as a punishment for Afghan treason, razed the fortress and the city to the ground. From Ghuzni the British force moved on to Cabul, and fought one more battle with complete success, finally effecting a junction with General Pollock at the Afghan capital.

When the work of punishment had been completed, the three armies—General Pollock's, General Nott's, and General England's—evacuated Afghan territory in compliance with orders from Lord Ellenborough, but not before they had exacted a terrible vengeance for the Cabul massacre, and achieved a series of brilliant successes, which, but for the memory of the disaster to General Elphinstone's army, would have been remembered always amongst the greatest triumphs of the British flag.

I have contented myself with a bare recital of facts, because the Afghan war of 1841–2 is almost invariably spoken of as if it had begun and ended in shame, and because there is a disposition in some quarters to magnify the difficulties of an Afghan campaign. But the narrative I have given affords its encouragements as well as its warnings. We have not gone backward within the last forty years in military organization. We have better arms, more knowledge of the country, readier means of reinforcing and supplying our troops. Above all, we are not likely to make the mistake of appointing an incapable man or creating a divided responsibility. The story of the Cabul massacres is one of overweening confidence in Sir Alexander Burnes, extreme credulity in Sir William Macnaghten, and absolute weakness in General Elphinstone. The combination was enough to have ruined an empire—it actually lost an army. But the splendid achievements of Pollock and Nott restored the honour of our flag. It is treason to their memory to croak over the earlier disaster.

The north-west frontier of India may be said to commence at the Guntrab Pass, in the uppermost corner of Kashmir, whence, running in a south-westerly direction, it strikes the Baroghil and Kamarbund roads, entrances from the Pamir steppes to the British dominions. It then, generally speaking, follows the course of the river Indus to Torbela, a few miles north of the junction of the Cabul river with its parent stream. As far as this point there are no roads worthy of the name between Afghanistan and India.

From Torbela the frontier line takes a sweep round the Peshawur Valley, and, to avoid the Afridi lands, juts back to the river at the Narai Sir. It now bears westward to Thull, on the Kuram river, and then runs parallel to the Indus until it reaches the sea, the watershed of the first low ranges of the Sulimani range being the actual recognised official border-line between Cabul and British India. To protect this line we have military stations of greater or lesser strength, guarding, as it were, the entrance of the main thoroughfares between the two countries, such as Hoti Mardan and Peshawur in Yusufzae; Kohal, at the eastern extremity of the Kuram route; Bunnoo, opposite the Dawar Valley road; Dera Ishmael Khan, in front of the Gomal; Dera Ghazi Khan, conveniently near the Sakhi Sarwar; Rajanpore, near the Dera Bugti road; and Jacobabad, at the mouth of the Bolan. Connecting the military posts is a road, unmetalled and unbridged, running the entire length of the border; whilst similar roads, useless in rainy weather, are constructed to the mouths of the various passes. In advance of the larger stations enumerated, there are close on a hundred small outposts (garrisoned either by detachments of regular troops or else by local levies), for the purpose of watching the lesser passes and preventing the irruption of these and other raiders.

The British cantonment, Jacobabad, the eastern extremity of the Bolan Pass, was built by General John Jacob, the founder of the Scinde School, which has produced a body of men who have never ceased to press upon Government the necessity of extending our borders to the westward. It is a small but thriving place, the centre of a flourishing trade .between Scinde and

Kandahar, and is the head-quarters of a very fine body of irregular soldiers, the Scinde Frontier Force, which, although it has never had the opportunities of seeing service, like its Punjab comrades, would doubtless work well if called upon. The main frontier road runs north from this, connecting all the stations we have described with Peshawur. The population is about 5000. In pursuance of the policy which he had been sent to India to inaugurate, Lord Lytton, in October 1876, threw forward the southern frontier a distance of 202 miles to Quetta, at the western end of the famous Bolan Pass. There were commercial as well as military reasons for this step, owing to the powerlessness of the Khan of Khelat to exercise authority over the Belooch chiefs of that part of the country. These had been in the habit of harassing the whole district, and thus interfering with the large trade between Scinde and Kandahar.

It has ever been our object to encourage the Pourndah merchants, who carry the goods of the English and Indian markets to the bazaars of Central Asia, and it was deemed advisable to locate a British force at the further extremity of the Pass, in order to keep it clear for traffic. Undoubtedly the military reasons for this step were equally grave. Russia, ever since the Crimean War, had been slowly, but none the less surely, pushing her way southward and eastward in the Steppes. Turkestan, Tashkand and Samarkand, Bokhara and Khiva, had been incorporated into her empire; Merv even was threatened. Under these circumstances it was necessary for our Government to make a decided move in order to secure thoroughly the main roads leading to British India. Quetta consequently was garrisoned, and the Bolan Pass sealed. As this Pass is now in British dominion, and is one of the roads to Kandahar, a brief description of the road between Jacobabad and Quetta will suffice.

As far as Dadur, at the foot of the mountain ranges, the road is across a sandy desert, intersected here and there by very deep nullahs and dry watercourses. In the immediate vicinity of Dadur, which is 114 miles distant, there is a great deal of fine cultivation, and this might, and probably will, be made the site of a strong position.

Leaving Dadur the road drops into the bed of the Bolan stream, which it ascends for forty-four miles. The hills on either side are bleak and bare, their summits often inaccessible. At some places they open out to the distance of nearly a mile, at others they close to within fifty yards. The roadway is over loose boulders, very trying to man and simply killing to cattle. From the Sar-i-Bolan, or head of the stream, the path-way, for it is little more, descends into the Dasht-i-Bedoalat plain, and thirty miles further Quetta is reached.

It is but another instance of our national dilatoriness in military matters, that although years have elapsed since we occupied Quetta, avowedly for the purpose of establishing a military position to flank our present frontier, no steps have been taken to improve the road, which formed such a serious obstacle to Sir John Keane's advance in 1839.

At the distance of a few miles beyond the Bolan Pass stands this small town of Quetta, the capital of the district of Shawl, in latitude 30° 11′. Its height above the level of the sea is 5500 ft. It is a poor, miserable town, consisting of a sort of mud edifice called a fort, built upon a mound of earth, and having about 400 wretched mud hovels, with flat roofs, clustered around its foot.

The district of Shawl is situated between the 29° 50′ and 30° 50′ of N. latitude, and the 66° 4′ and 67° 20′ of E. latitude, and is bounded on the north by the Takht-a-Pul mountains, on the south by the Bolan range, on the east by those of Zingoon and Tharkoo, and on the west by Chuhultan. The general aspect of this country is hilly, rocky, and sterile, particularly on the south side, but where mould exists (which is the case on many of the northern faces) vegetation is luxuriant, and a variety of English trees, shrubs, and herbs, are to be found ; such as cherry, almond, hawthorn, carberry, &c. &c., also the juniper, which grows to a height of from 18 to 30 feet.

Within eight miles of Quetta there is a forest of the above description on a piece of table-land, which affords an inexhaustible source of fire-wood, and also rafters for building. The wood of the juniper is exactly similar to that used in cedar pencils, and the scent equally aromatic. The assafœtida grows in abundance on these hills, many of which are composed of mica and chalk. Coal of a uniform description is found in the Bolan Pass. Around Quetta are numerous orchards filled with apricots and almond-trees, peaches, apples, and fine poplars, with vines trained up their limbs.

Since our occupation its defences have been improved, barracks built for native troops, and a strong garrison thrown into it, from its position as a natural support to Kandahar, or even the Pishin Valley. Quetta is now likely to become a military station of great importance.

Intervening between our own frontier, the main features of which were described in the foregoing pages, and the eastern borders of Afghanistan, lies a broad belt of rugged, inhospitable mountains, bounded on the north by the semi-independent khanates of Central Asia, on the south by the Bolan Pass, on the east by the British outposts, and on the west by the imaginary line drawn from Jellalabad, through the Shutargardan Pass, to the Khojak, between Quetta and Kandahar.

Putting aside any consideration of the tribes dwelling to the north of Torbela, because the country is quite impracticable for military operations, it will be necessary merely to enumerate those lying within the boundaries we have just described. It is through this tract of land that the many roads between Cabul and British India run, and therefore our intercourse with the tribes inhabiting it will be far more constant, and, let us hope, of a far more amicable nature, than it has been hitherto. It is a stain on our national character for geographical enterprise that we are so profoundly ignorant of this border-land of ours. A glance at most of the maps shows that they have been filled in by conjecture, and that with the exception of those small patches traversed by our troops in the many frontier expeditions, we know no more of the Suliman and Sufaed Koh ranges than we did forty years ago. The line of the Indus is delineated by a series of vague dots, between Skardo and Tahkote, although in its entirety its left bank is within British territory. How is this? Simply because each successive Government of India has stifled the spirit of adventure, and the thirst for knowledge so deeply implanted in the minds of our countrymen have forcibly prevented non-officials from crossing the border, and threatened with dismissal any Government servant offending in like manner. The consequence is, that no Englishman has visited the majority of the country inhabited by these border tribes since Masson fearlessly travelled in Afghanistan in the early part of this century, and our information is necessarily vague, incomplete, and often inexact.

This rugged tract of mountainous country is peopled by a series of wild, fanatical, and mountain tribes, who defy the authority of their nominal ruler, the Ameer of Afghanistan, and resent equally strongly any interference by us. The tribes of the north are fiercer, more untamable, than those of the south. Accustomed, from the early period of their history, to dash down from their mountain fastnesses and ravage the plains stretched out, rich, smiling, and fertile, at their feet, they have ever harboured feelings of animosity towards the strong hand which took those plains under its protection, and the Government of India have never hesitated to follow up and punish marauding bands which entered British territory. It is said that these tribes can turn out a quarter of a million of fighting men, and this is doubtless well within the mark; but it should be borne in mind, that until we reach the Beloochis, south of Dera Ismail Khan, who generally own loyal obedience to their hereditary chief, there is not a single instance of a clan that is not divided against itself, so that spontaneous action on the part of the northern sections need not be assumed.

It may be well to group these tribes geographically, placing in the first section those Pathans, or Pushtu-speaking classes, who dwell north of the Khyber Pass; in the second section, those inhabiting the lofty ranges intervening between the Khyber and the Kuram; in the third, those who live in the heart of the Suliman ranges, between the Kuram and the Gomal route ; and, lastly, those Belooch tribes which lie between that road and the Bolan. Before entering into a detailed description of these tribes, it may be well to mention that the Mahabun mountains, north-west of Peshawur, and the Bozdar country, north of Dera Ghazi Khan, the ranges immediately contiguous to our frontier, are peopled by thirteen different clans, whose conduct has necessitated no fewer than thirty separate punitory expeditions.

Commencing, then, with the first section, we have the Jadoons, the Bonairs, the Swatis, the Ranazais, and Mohmands, lying along our border ; in rear of them are the Bajawaris, the Ningraharis, and Shinwarris : in the aggregate these muster no less than 60,000 fighting men. Against the five first we have undertaken nine separate wars.

Between the Khyber and the Kuram are the Afridis, the Orakzais, the Turis, Zaimukts, Jazis, Chamkanis, Mangals, and Ghilzais; these latter, indeed, form a backing to all the clans from Jellalabad to the western end of the Gomal, and can probably put 50,000 men in the field, the remaining five being of about the same strength.

From the Kuram to the Gomal lie contiguous to our frontier the large Vaziri tribe, which numbers at least 40,000 men, indifferently armed, but dashing, gallant fellows. Behind them lie the Jadrans, Khostwals, Dawaris, Gurbuz, numbering perhaps 30,000, and in rear again the Ghilzais.

South of the Gomal we have the various Belooch clans of Bozdars, Kasranis, Sheoranis, Osteranis, Ketrans, Lagharis, Maris, and Bugtis, and behind them the large Afghan tribe of Kakars : these may be computed at

d

100,000 men. All these tribes are nominally subjects of the Ameer, but there are few from whom he collects revenue, none whose territory he dare enter for that purpose unaccompanied by a powerful force. He has fortified posts in the Mohmand, Shinwarri, Khost, Kuram, Ghilzai, and Kakar territory, the residences of Deputy-governors, who annually, at the head of a force, perambulate the country, screwing out the taxes from the scowling Pathan.

These tribes differ but little in their natural characteristics; the northern clans are fairer in complexion and more powerful in build than the southern. They are also, as a rule, more friendly to our rule, and at first sight more open-hearted, frank, and honest. It is, however, impossible to trust any one of them, and a description of one suffices for all. They are, as a rule, fine athletic men, whose springy steps and proud, defiant mien, denote their mountain origin; lean, hardy, and muscular; they have long gaunt faces, high cheek-bones, prominent noses, and dark complexions. They are brave in action, fearless in the defence of their homes, make as a rule good soldiers, though, in common with all Orientals, are apt to break away directly a flank attack against them is developed.

Such, then, is a brief description of the tribes, and of our connexion with them. Since we first became neighbours, the whole of these, if the scheme of rectification of our frontier be carried out by the retention of Kandahar, will be swept within our boundaries, and become subjects of our own. Whether a closer acquaintance with us and the justice of our rule will lead them to tolerate or even welcome us as conquerors, or whether it will convert them into more inveterate foes, is still an open question ; but the balance of opinion inclines to the fact, that ere we persuade them to enlist in our service they will learn to know the difference between our justice and the tyranny of their former oppressors.

Kandahar is the ancient capital of the Durani Empire and the burial-place of their kings, and is situated between the Argandab and Turnak rivers, 89 miles south-west of Khelat-i-Ghilzai, and 144 north-west of Quetta. It is built on a level plain well covered with cultivation. The town is surrounded by lofty mud walls, with large circular towers at the flank, a deep and wide ditch adding to its strength. Though nearly four miles in circumference, it is stated by Bellew, who lived there nearly six months, and has twice visited it, to contain not more than 20,000 houses. These are generally built of sun-dried bricks and have flat roofs, though some of the dwellings of the richer classes are covered with chunam—a glistening white plaster, which in the distance gives them the appearance of marble. The tomb of Ahmed Shah, an octagonal structure overlaid with coloured porcelain bricks and surmounted by a golden dome surrounded by small minarets, is the most striking building in the city, and attracts the eye of the traveller from afar.

The trade between Kandahar and Herat is carried on by Persians, who bring down silk, copper, weapons of all sorts, horses, and carpets, taking back felts, skins, and camels'-hair cloaks. The Povindahs, or nomad Ghilzai tribes, carry on the trade with Hindostan by the Gomal and Bolan Pass.

From the latest accounts we have of the city given in the following letters it cannot be considered a powerful fortress ; the weakness of the parapets and small dimensions of the ditch would cause a besieger provided with a siege train but little trouble. Its strategic value, however, is great : being the first and only place of any strength, or where supplies in any quantity could be obtained between Herat and the Indus, it naturally is regarded with a jealous eye by all who look upon an extension of our frontier as desirable. Sir Henry Durand drew up a very able memorandum connected with the defence of this city.

Cabul, the capital of Afghanistan, is 103 miles from Jellalabad, 88 from Ghuzni, and 318 from Kandahar ; it is situate near the junction of the Cabul and Logar rivers, at the western extremity of a spacious plain, in an angle formed by the approach of two ridges of hills ; these completely encompass it on three sides, the fourth only being open, whence the roads from Ghuzni and Jellalabad approach the city. Its elevation is 6396 feet. The hills completely overlook the city, there being only a narrow path between the city wall and their base. These hills are steep, bare, and rocky, and crowned with a long line of wall, having round towers occurring at regular intervals, which is carried up their nearly perpendicular sides, along their summits, and across the narrow entrance that lies between them. This wall was intended as a defence against the Ghilzais, and shut up all entrance from the west ; but it has been allowed to fall into ruin.

The town of Cabul is in length, from east to west, about a mile ; and in breadth, from north to south, half a mile. It is surrounded by a high but weak mud wall, and has no ditch. East of the town, and separated from it by a ditch, on the top of a rocky eminence, stands the fortress of Bala Hissar; and on the slope of this acclivity are situated the king's palace and gardens, with an extensive bazaar, surrounded by a wall and ditch, and separate from the city. Above the fortress, upon an eminence overlooking not only the fortress itself, but the level all around it, is the citadel, and within this fort a brother of Dost Mahomed built a palace which he called Koolah-i-Feringee, or the European Hat; and which, very curiously, became, during the British occupation in 1839, the hospital of the 13th Light Infantry.

The population, according to Burnes, consists of 60,000 souls. The Cabul river, which enters at the north of the gorge from the west, flows eastward, close under the northern wall; and a rich slip of meadow land, covered with gardens, rises up from its northern bank to the base of the hills on that side, increasing in breadth as the river flows eastward.

Herat, the capital of one of the most important, and certainly the richest, district in Afghanistan, is commonly called 'The Key of India.' It is situated in a fertile and well-watered valley, about thirty miles in length and fifteen miles in breadth. The city is nearly square in shape, surrounded by a lofty mound of earth from forty to fifty feet in height, and of immense thickness, surrounded by a brick wall about twenty feet high. Outside all is a wet ditch. Each face is about a mile in length; thus the city occupies nearly a square mile of ground, and its population is estimated at 50,000 souls, who are mostly Shiahs. Vambery gives an amusing account of the various races to be seen in the bazaar—Afghans, Hindoos, Tartars, Turkomans, Persians, and Jews. Every one carries weapons, and to be in the fashion it is necessary to take a whole arsenal about with you.

Herat is essentially a city of trade, being the emporium between Cabul, Kandahar, Hindostan, Persia, and Turkestan. Its chief manufactures are carpets, which are renowned in Asia, and fetch high prices. Varieties of the most delicious fruits are grown here, and the ordinary necessaries of life, such as bread and meat, are cheap and plentiful. The climate is healthy; though for two months in the year the heat is excessive, for the remaining ten it is delightful. Its history is one long tale of wars, sieges, and rebellion. In 1157 it fell into the hands of the Turkomans, who completely destroyed it. In 1232 Jangiz Khan besieged it for six months, and on its capture massacred 160,000 of its inhabitants. In 1398 Miran Shah laid the place waste and decimated the inhabitants. In 1477 Jehan Shah once more destroyed it. In 1554 and 1607 the Uzbegs twice sacked it. In 1370 Nadir Shah besieged and took it; and twenty years later Ahmed Shah Durani, after a siege of fourteen months, gained possession of the place. Zaman Shah, in 1805, carried the place; and in 1816–19–21–22–23 the Persians made various efforts to seize it. In 1824 the ruler, Kamran, after a temporary absence, returned from Farah and found the insurgents had gained possession of the place; after a short and bloody encounter he recovered it. In 1837 Yah Mahomed, assisted by Eldred Pottinger, drove off the Persians, after having been closely besieged for over six months. In 1836, in spite of previous treaties, the Persians laid siege to it once more, and obtained possession of it in October of that year: they abandoned it, however, at the close of the war with England in 1857. Dost Mahomed, in May

1863, after a siege of ten months, captured the city, which has since remained a portion of the Afghan kingdom.

Its occupation by the British has been the dream of our anti-Russian party, and there are many reasons to be urged in favour of such a course. Herat is a point which must necessarily be seized by any army invading India. It is a fruitful district, and affords a favourable spot for the concentration of troops prior to an advance eastwards towards the Indus. The roads are easy, provisions for an army to be found in plenty *en route*, and the means of transport abundant. The tribes in the immediate neighbourhood are powerful and warlike, and, as we have lately seen, are capable of turning out 50,000 horsemen and 25,000 foot: these, under European training and guidance, might be converted into an admirable irregular force. These reasons apply equally well to the construction of a defensive post at Herat to bar the invasion of India, as they do to its importance as a point of concentration to an army advancing eastward.

The letters and telegraphic despatches which during the Conservative Administration passed between the India Office at home and the Viceroy in Calcutta or Simla are, I believe, a full vindication of the policy the Government was compelled to adopt, and the theory of *quieta non movere*, or 'masterly inactivity,' so pertinaciously urged by Lord Lawrence and his school, finds a complete answer in the pages of those blue books which record our ineffectual endeavours to conciliate the late Ameer Shere Ali Khan. How these pacific overtures were rendered abortive by the headstrong monarch who fled from his throne and his kingdom at the approach of the British army, and the manner in which events were hurried on by the circumstances connected with the reception of a Russian mission in July 1878, and the rejection by the Ameer of the special embassy accredited to his court by Lord Lytton, are points to be duly and impartially considered by those who take any interest in the honour and the welfare of our Indian dominions.

The various communications which from time to time passed between the Government at home and that of India, ending with Lord Salisbury's despatch of the 4th of October, 1877, contain a complete exposition of the general policy of the British Government towards Afghanistan, and set forth, I venture to believe, the considerations which then induced Her Majesty's Government to endeavour to place their relations with the Ameer on a more satisfactory footing.

In order, however, that the reader may have no misapprehension on this subject, I deem it necessary to recapitulate some of the more salient features of that policy, and to have the progress of events which have led to the present condition of affairs in Afghanistan. It is almost needless to recall the differences of opinion which have for years, and under various governments, existed, and indeed still exist, among the most eminent authorities on the subject of the frontier policy to be pursued by our Indian Government. These differences, I maintain, have had reference rather to the methods to be followed than to the objects in view. The consistent aim of the British Government during a series of years has been to establish on its north-western frontier a strong, friendly, and independent State, with interest, as far as possible, in unison with those of the Indian Government, and ready to act in certain eventualities as an auxiliary in the protection of our frontier from foreign intrigue or aggression. The treaty of 1855, negotiated by Lord Dalhousie with the approval of Lord Aberdeen's Government, and still in force, bears witness to the importance then attached to friendly relations on our part with Afghanistan. To quote one phrase will give an idea of the whole : ' The treaty gives to the Government of India on its western frontier as complete security against a foreign and distant enemy as it is possible for us in the nature of things to compass.'

Since the period, however, of the transfer to the Crown of the direct administration of India the question has assumed a special prominence, and this growing interest in the subject has been the result partly of the increased responsibilities assumed by Her Majesty's Government in maintaining her Indian Empire, and partly of the intestine disorders to which Afghanistan became a prey after the accession of Shere Ali Khan in 1863. Upon Lord Lawrence devolved, at that time, the direction of the policy to be adopted in this new state of affairs, and that statesman, it is well known, considered that the objects of the British Government would be best obtained by abstaining from active inter-ference in the internal affairs of Afghanistan, and by the friendly recognition of the *de facto* rulers of that country, or of portions of it, without undertaking inconvenient liabilities on their behalf. On this basis Lord Lawrence considered that the British Government would have the greatest chance of gaining the permanent friendship and alliance of the Afghan people.

The outposts of Russia were at that time distant from the borders of Afghanistan, and his Lordship's Government attached no special importance to the probability and danger of the growth of the former Power in the direction of India, which they considered would, in any case, best be restrained, or at least rendered innocuous, by a friendly understanding on the subject between the English and Russian cabinets. I need not say that the views of that day were, on the subject of their relations with Afghanistan, in complete harmony with those of Lord Lawrence. They had no desire to exercise active influence in Cabul, nor to interfere in the conflicts then rife between contending parties in Afghanistan, so long as those conflicts did not jeopardise the peace of our frontier. This policy was therefore adhered to, although, it must be allowed, not without a certain amount of inconvenience during the civil war which raged after Shere Ali's accession to the throne, and perhaps might not have been unsuited to the exigencies of the time. But the final and unaided success of the Ameer in regaining his throne in the autumn of 1868 in some measure changed the position of affairs, and, in the opinion both of Lord Lawrence and of Her Majesty's Government, justified some intervention in his Highness's favour, and the grant to him of such assistance in money and arms as appeared conducive to the maintenance of his authority.

The policy followed by Lord Mayo's administration in its dealings with Afghanistan was, to a considerable extent, in accord with the course of action thus finally adopted in the autumn of 1868 by his predecessor. While, however, Lord Mayo did not deviate in any material degree from the attitude of non-interference in the internal affairs of Afghanistan, which had been so long maintained, he recognised Shere Ali as the *de jure* as well as the *de facto* ruler of that country, and, in a letter addressed to that prince, engaged to view with severe displeasure any attempt on the part of his rivals to disturb his position. This step, added to the marked personal influence obtained by Lord Mayo over the Ameer, was sufficient at the moment to remove a certain feeling of resentment which had been generated in his mind by the apparent indifference shown by the British Government to the result of his struggle for power, and, at the same time, rendered his Highness's position at Cabul more assured than that of any previous ruler.

It must be remembered that the advances of Russia in Central Asia had not, up to this period, assumed dimensions such as to cause uneasiness to the Indian Government. Lord Mayo agreed, therefore, to the views of his predecessor, inasmuch as he considered that the best means of averting interference on the part of Turkestan in the affairs of Afghanistan would be by a frank interchange of views on that subject between the Government of Her Majesty and that of the Czar. Her Majesty's Government had independently arrived at the same conclusion, and, early in 1869, initiated friendly negotiations at St. Petersburg, which terminated in a very distinct understanding on this subject, and in the recognition by the Czar's Government of the limits of the Ameer's territories in complete accord with the wishes of Shere Ali as well as those of our Government.

The policy of his predecessors was in nearly all respects followed by Lord Northbrook, although the rapid development of events in Central Asia was gradually compelling our Government to closer relations with the ruler of Cabul. Then came the capture of Khiva by the army of the Czar in the spring of 1873, and the total subordination of that Khanate to Russia caused Shere Ali considerable alarm, and doubtless led him to question and consider the pledges with reference to his kingdom which had been given to him by England and by his Imperial Majesty the Czar. Actuated by his fears on this score, his Highness sent a special envoy to Simla in the summer of that year, charged with the duty of expressing his anxieties to the Government of India.

Finding that the object of the Ameer was to ascertain definitely how far he might rely on the help of the British Government if his territories were threatened by Russia, Lord Northbrook's Government was prepared to assure him that, under certain conditions, the Government of India would assist him to repel unprovoked aggression. But it so happened that Her Majesty's Government at home did not share Shere Ali's apprehension, and the Viceroy ultimately informed the Ameer that the discussion of the question would be best postponed to 'a more convenient season.'

This announcement, although conveyed in the most conciliatory language, was received most unfavourably by his Highness, and the policy which dictated it was unintelligible to his mind, while he received it with feelings of disappointment and perhaps resentment. His reply to Lord Northbrook's communication was accordingly couched in terms of ill-disguised sarcasm, and he took no notice of the Viceroy's proposal to depute a British officer to examine the northern frontier of Afghanistan. The Ameer then showed his displeasure by refusing permission to Sir Douglas Forsyth and Colonel Gordon to return from Kashgar to India through Cabul, while he left untouched a gift of money lodged to his credit by the Indian Government, assuming at the same time a general attitude of sullen reserve.

Such, then, was the aspect of affairs when the Conservatives came into office in 1874. The maintenance of Afghanistan as a strong and friendly power had at all times been the object of British policy, although the methods adopted in attaining that object had not always met with such success as was desirable. Its accomplishment was nevertheless a matter of grave importance, and had now to be considered with reference to the rapid march of events in Turkestan. It was impossible for Her Majesty's Government to regard with indifference the probable influence of those events upon the character of an Asiatic prince whose dominions were brought within a steadily narrowing circle between two great military empires, and, although no immediate danger appeared to threaten British interests on the frontier of Afghanistan, the situation in Central Asia had undoubtedly become sufficiently grave to suggest the necessity of timely precaution. Her Majesty's Government, therefore, considered that the first step necessary in this respect was the improvement of their relations with the Ameer himself. With this object in view they deemed it expedient that his Highness should be invited to receive a temporary mission at Cabul, in order that an accredited British envoy might confer with him personally as to the events which were then taking place, might assure him of the desire of the British Government that his territories should remain safe from external attack, and, at the same time, might point out to him the extreme difficulty of attaining that object unless it were permitted by him to place its own officers on its frontier to watch the course of events beyond it. True it was that the relations of the Ameer with the Russian Governor-General of Turkestan had of late become more intimate, and that a correspondence with that official had commenced with the Cabul durbar in 1871, and which at one time had caused serious disquiet to the Ameer, was being carried on with increased activity, while his Highness's original practice of consulting the Indian Government as to the replies to be sent to General Kaufman's communications had been discontinued. Nevertheless Her Majesty's Government were willing to believe that Shere Ali, if his intentions were friendly, would be ready to join them in measures advantageous to himself and essential for the protection of common interests.

Few will deny that these interests and responsibilities had morally devolved upon England on behalf of the safety of Afghanistan as a friendly and independent Power, and of the protection of our Indian north-west frontier. Looking, therefore, to the imperfect information available in regard to the country ruled over by the Ameer, and to the responsibilities we had incurred in its behalf, the Government of Lord Northbrook had in 1873 expressed an opinion that the temporary presence in Afghanistan of a British officer, as then suggested by them, would go far to allay any feelings of mistrust lingering in the minds of the Afghan people, and might, at the same time, prepare the way for eventually placing permanent British representatives at Cabul, Herat, and elsewhere. Encouraged by this opinion our Government arrived at the conclusion, that although Lord Northbrook's efforts to attain the desired object had not met with the success they deserved, the time had come when the measure thus indicated could no longer be postponed.

The Indian Council had, indeed, while fully alive to all the advantages likely to eventuate from the measure, frankly represented to Lord Beaconsfield's Government the difficulties attendant to its initiation, while Lord Lytton's predecessor believed the time and circumstances of the moment to be anything but opportune for placing British agents on the Afghan borders, he being of opinion that such a step should be deferred till the progress of events justified more specific assurances to Shere Ali, which might then possibly be given as a treaty, followed by the establishment of agencies at Herat, Kandahar, and other places.

Her Majesty's Government, however, were unable to agree in this view. They deemed it probable that, if events were thus allowed to march without measures of precaution on the part of the British Government, the time would have passed when representations to the Ameer could be made with any probability of a favourable result, and they considered it important that the actual sentiments of his Highness, in reference to which so many different opinions were held by various authorities, should be tested in due time.

When, therefore, Lord Lytton left England to assume the Viceroyalty, our Home Government instructed his Lordship to offer to Shere Ali the same active countenance and protection which he had previously solicited at the hands of the Indian Government. It was clearly impossible, however, to enter into any formal engagement in this sense without requiring from the Ameer some substantial proof of his unity of interests with the British Government. Our Secretary of State, therefore, authorised the Viceroy to concede to his Highness substantial pecuniary aid, a formal recognition of his dynasty so far, indeed, as it would not involve England in active interference in the internal affairs of Afghanistan, and an explicit pledge of material support in case of unprovoked foreign aggression ; but Lord Lytton was at the same time directed not to incur these heavy responsibilities unless Shere Ali, on his part, was prepared to allow a British agent, or agents, access to the positions in his territories (other than at Cabul itself) where, without prejudicing the personal authority of the ruler, they could acquire trustworthy information of events calculated to threaten the tranquillity or independence of Afghanistan.

The measures which the Viceroy adopted on his arrival in India to give effect to the explicit instructions he had received were, I believe, undoubtedly framed with much discretion, and in a spirit of consideration towards Shere Ali. Lord Lytton's native aide-de-camp, Ressaldar Major Khanan Khan, was sent to the Ameer, charged with the duty of informing him of his Excellency's desire to depute temporarily to his capital, or to any other point in Afghan territory agreeable to his Highness, a special Envoy, whose mission was not merely to be one of compliment but one for the discussion of matters of common interest to the two Governments ; and his Excellency took care to convey to his Highness verbal assurances of the friendly character of his advances to him. What then followed is a matter of history—Shere Ali positively declined to receive any envoy, and distinctly rejected all overtures !

Lord Lytton's next step was to exhort, in a serious but most temperate manner, the Ameer to consider well the consequences of an attitude which might end in compelling the British Government to look upon him thenceforth as a prince who voluntarily desired to isolate his interests from those of the British Government. In a most conciliatory spirit Lord Lytton abstained from pressing upon the Ameer the reception of our Envoy, and his Excellency at the same time acceded to a suggestion made by Shere Ali, to the effect that his Vakeel at Cabul should make personal representations to the Viceroy on behalf of the Ameer. These representations proved eventually to be merely a recapitulation of grievances dating from 1872, and it may not be out of place to enumerate them :—(1.) The communication which the Ameer had received from the late Viceroy in 1874 on behalf of his rebellious son, Yakub Khan, whom he had imprisoned. (2.) The decision on behalf cf the Seistan boundary. (3.) The gifts sent by the late Viceroy direct to the chief of Wakhan, who is a tributary to the Ameer. (4.) The repeated rejection of his previous requests for an alliance, and a formal recognition of the order of succession as established by him in the person of his son, Abdullah Jan.

These grievances would seem to have weighed heavily on the prejudiced mind of Shere Ali, and Lord Lytton did not lose a moment in assuring the Ameer, through the Vakeel, that it was the sincere desire of England to cultivate a friendly feeling towards him, and on his part as Viceroy it was his wish to remove, by a frank exchange of views, all causes of irritation on the Ameer's mind, while at the same time his Excellency was most willing to receive an Afghan Envoy at Peshawur, in lieu of our sending Sir Lewis Pelly to Cabul. Lord Lytton's Vakeel thereupon returned to Cabul, charged with the duty of explaining to the Ameer, with the assistance of a clearly worded *aide mémoire*, the very favourable treaty which the British Government was prepared, upon certain conditions, to negotiate with him, and its desire to heal up all differences with him. But his Highness manifested no cordiality in his reception of the Vakeel ; and he deputed to Peshawur his Minister, Synd Noor Mahommed Shah, there to carry on, with Sir Lewis Pelly, the negotiations with Her Majesty's Government—the negotiations which the Viceroy had deemed of sufficient importance to be undertaken on Afghan soil, and with the Ameer himself.

Although the Ameer had been informed in writing both of the concessions which the British Government was ready to grant to him, and the conditions thereunto attached ; and although it was signified to him, at the same time, that it would be useless for him to send his Envoy to Peshawur, unless his Highness was prepared to agree to these conditions as the basis of the proposed treaty, it became apparent in the course of the conference that the Minister had received no specific authority to accept them. Moreover, the language and general demeanour of Shere Ali, which had for long been dubious, now became perfectly inimical, and the Viceroy, therefore, judiciously took advantage of the sudden death of the Envoy to discontinue the negotiations, the basis of which had been practically rejected.

From the outset of these complications the whole conduct of the Viceroy, in his dealings with the Ameer, met with the entire approval of Her Majesty's Government. As Lord Lytton's predecessor observed, in a despatch dated October 4, 1877, Her Majesty's Government had been in hopes that the advantages they were willing to render would have been accepted by the Ameer, would have been accepted in the same spirit in which they were offered. At the same time, we cannot but remember, that the attitude assumed by Shere Ali for some years past had been so ambiguous and eccentric, that we might have been, to a great extent, prepared for the results. Still, the failure was not held by Lord Lytton as a ground for total inaction and continued acquiescence in the existing state of relations with the Ameer ; and the conclusion was arrived at, that while the prevailing uncertainty as to his Highness's disposition rendered caution necessary in their advances, it was in itself a reason for adopting steps which would elicit the truth. From this point of view Her Majesty's Government could not regard the result of the Peshawur conference as altogether unsatisfactory, inasmuch as they were no longer left in doubt as to the reality of the Ameer's alienation, which, up to this time, had been a matter of speculation. On the other hand, the proceedings at the conference, and the previous negotiations, had placed before the Ameer, in a clear light, the views of our Government as to our existing obligations towards him, and had, at the same time, informed him of the terms, so favourable to his own interests, on which they were willing to draw closer the bonds of union between the two countries, and to place the mutual relations on a footing more advantageous to both.

The overtures of our Government having been thus slighted, it was held that no course remained open but to maintain an attitude of vigilant attention and reserve, until such time as Shere Ali could be brought to realise his own position and his own interests. This was the opinion of the Viceroy, and had been conveyed to the Afghan Envoy by Sir Lewis Pelly ; and Lord Lytton, since the close of the Peshawur conference, adopted a policy in accordance with this view.

While carefully watching the progress of events in Afghanistan, so far, at least, as our imperfect means of obtaining information existed, Lord Lytton carefully abstained from all interference in them, in the hope that time would enable his Highness to realise the dangers accruing to himself by the rejection of our friendly advances. That hope was not, however, destined to be realised. Shere Ali, as we have seen, persisted in his unfriendly isolation, and ultimately, having two years before declined to receive a British Envoy, even temporarily, within his territory, on the ground that he could not guarantee his safety, nor thereafter be left with any excuse for refusing to receive a Russian mission, welcomed with every appearance of ostentation an Embassy from the Czar, despatched to his court at a time when there were indications that an interruption of friendly relations between this country and Russia might be imminent.

Under these circumstances, the Viceroy represented to Her Majesty's Government that a policy of inaction could no longer be continued, and that the reception of the Russian mission, at such a time and under such circumstances, left him no further excuse for declining to receive at his capital an Envoy from the British Government.

Lord Lytton proposed, therefore, to demand the reception of a mission to Cabul, headed by an officer of rank in the person of Sir Neville Chamberlain, whose name and family were held in high esteem by the Ameer. This proposal was agreed to by the Home Government, for it was self-evident that a potentate who willingly admitted to his capital at a most critical period Envoys of a Power which at the moment might be regarded as making its advances with objects not friendly to the British Government, could not reasonably refuse to receive a mission from a Power with which he had been in continual alliance.

In the Council of the Governor-General, Lord Lytton did not anticipate any such refusal, and Her Majesty's Government saw no reason to question the soundness of his Excellency's opinion on this point, based as it must have been on the best available information.

The anticipations of both the Viceroy and the British Government were, however, disappointed by the event. In a friendly letter carried to Cabul by the Nawab Gholam Hussein Khan, Lord Lytton informed the Ameer of the date on which Sir Neville Chamberlain was to leave Peshawur, and ample time was given to Shere Ali to issue orders to his local officials for the reception of the mission. It was also intimated to the Ameer that a refusal to accord a free passage to the mission would be regarded as an act of hostility. The orders, however, sent to the Afghan officials at Ali Musjid were the reverse of what our Viceroy had a right to expect, and Major Cavagnari, who went in advance of our Envoy, was distinctly informed that any attempt to enter Afghan territory would be resisted by force, of which an ostentatious display was at once made.

This conduct on the part of the Ameer was in all respects without justification. He was aware, from various communications addressed to him by the former Viceroy, that the Russian Government had given assurances to Her Majesty's Government to regard his territories as quite beyond its sphere of action; he was also aware that the whole policy of the British

Government, since his accession to power, had been to strengthen in every way his authority and his power, while protecting him from foreign aggression. Although the methods adopted by our Government may not have been at all times in accordance with his own, he had received since his accession abundant evidences of good will, manifested by large gifts of money and arms, as well as by its successful efforts in obtaining from the Czar's Government its formal recognition of a fixed boundary, agreeable to himself, between his kingdom and the neighbouring khanates; his subjects had been allowed to pass freely throughout India, to the great benefit of the trade and commerce of his country; and in no single instance had the Ameer himself, or any of his people, been treated unjustly or inhospitably within British jurisdiction.

By every bond of international courtesy, as well as by the treaty engagement of 1855 existing between the two countries, binding him to be the friend of our friends and the enemy of our enemies, the Ameer, Shere Ali, was bound to a line of conduct the reverse of that which, to his cost and destruction, he adopted.

Lord Lytton, in reporting the slight which had been put upon our Empire by Shere Ali, expressed his conviction, and that of the Indian Government, that this act deprived the Ameer of all further claim upon the forbearance of the British Government, and necessitated instant action. Her Majesty's Government, however, were unwilling to accept the evasive letter brought from Cabul by our messenger, Nawab Gholan Hussein Khan, as the final answer to our Government, and it was accordingly determined to give the Ameer a short time for reconsideration.

Although our Government fully acknowledged, as binding on them, the pledges given by Sir Neville Chamberlain to the friendly chiefs and people who undertook the safe-conduct of his mission, they decided to make one more effort to avert the calamities of war, and with this object the Viceroy was instructed to address the Ameer a demand, in temperate language, requiring a full and suitable apology, within a given time, for the affront which he had offered to the British Government, the reception of a permanent British Mission within his territories, and reparation for any injury inflicted by him on the tribes who attended Sir Neville Chamberlain and Major Cavagnari, as well as an undertaking not to molest them hereafter. These instructions were promptly carried into effect by the Government of Lord Lytton, and the Ameer was distinctly informed that, unless a clear and satisfactory reply were received by the 20th of November, the Viceroy would, in Her Majesty's name, be compelled to consider his intentions as hostile, and to treat him as an enemy. A *précis* of the above facts was written by Lord Cranbrook (at that time the Secretary of State for India), and was not only sent to India for the Viceroy's information, but was published, by Her Majesty's command, for the general information of the public, who might certainly, on its perusal, have reason to say, ' Thrice is he armed that hath his quarrel just.'

The ultimatum having been allowed by Shere Ali to expire on the 20th November, war was declared, and the frontier crossed on the 21st by three columns, acting on the Khyber, the Kurram, and the Quetta lines of attack. The objective point of the two northern columns was Cabul, that of the southern Kandahar.

Ali Musjid, at the mouth of the Khyber, fell on the 21st, and the Kurram stream was crossed at dawn on the same day. The Peiwar Kotal was stormed early in December; Jellalabad was occupied, and General Donald Stewart was pushing on through the Bolan, the Pishin, and the Khojak, towards Kandahar, when the arrival of winter frost and snow caused a pause in operations.

Meanwhile, the death of Shere Ali caused his son Yakub to treat with us, and the peace of Gundamuck was signed on May 27th, 1879.

Then came the massacre of our Embassy, and the taking of Cabul by General Roberts, and other operations which led up to the Kandahar campaign of 1880, the records of which are here given from the rough jottings of officers engaged therein.

WALLER ASHE.

PERSONAL RECORDS OF THE KANDAHAR CAMPAIGN.

CHAPTER I.

IN GARRISON WITH GENERAL PRIMROSE.

Kandahar, June 27.

SINCE I last wrote to you from this ancient capital of
the Durani Empire, and where are buried the kings of
that race, many changes have taken place in our garrison,
which, I frankly confess, is considered by many of us as
far too weak for the duties we may yet have to perform.
Built on a level plain covered with cultivation, surrounded by lofty mud walls, with large circular towers
on the flanks, and deep and wide ditches, having a circumference of nearly four miles, this place should be
held by a much larger force than our General has now
at his disposal. The city itself cannot at present be
considered a powerful fortress, and although Colonel
John Hills, our commanding Engineer, has considerably
strengthened some of the outworks, there remains much
to be done to render the place secure against such troops
as we understand Ayub has collected during his advance
from Herat. Thirty-six guns and fifteen strong regiments of infantry, together with a formidable cavalry force,
are, it is reported on the best authority, under the Herat
ruler; while an advanced brigade, under a good and

experienced soldier, Luinob, formerly Governor of Turkestan, are known to be *en route*. With the force under
General Primrose, weakened by numerous detachments
at Khelat-i-Ghilzai, Thall Chotiali, Gatai, Melkarez,
Kushdil-Khan-Ka-Killa, Chaman, the Sangan Valley,
and along the Bolan, we are beyond all question too
small a garrison for the size of the defences. Ayub, by
the most recent accounts, is well aware of these facts,
and is not the man to neglect the opportunity he now
holds with the means at his disposal. His proclamations
to the soldiers have reached some of the rich merchants
of this city, and have caused no inconsiderable uneasiness,
and indeed consternation, amongst those of the inhabitants who have been friendly to us since our entry here.
The Prince is playing a bold game, and holds out hopes
to his mercenaries of plunder and loot, which have irresis-
tible attractions to such soldiers. He impresses upon
them the fact that we have spent millions of rupees in
payment of supplies since our occupation of Kandahar,
and that property of all kinds will be the reward of the
brave men who help him to chase away the hated
Feringhi from the capital of the Durani kings. All these
items of gossip come to us daily through the medium of
the Persian traders who come from Herat with silk,
copper, horses, carpets, cloaks, and ornamental weapons,
taking back felts, skins, camels'-hair garments, and
British rupees; while along the Bolan, Gomal, and
Khojak, the Povindahs, or nomad Ghilzais, make known
all our deficiencies and weak points. Colonel Hills and
all our best engineer authorities are of opinion that this
place cannot be considered by any means a powerful
fortress, inasmuch as the weakness of the parapets and
small dimensions of the ditch would cause a besieger,

with even a moderately powerful train, but little trouble, were his guns properly served ; and as we are tolerably certain that Ayub does not depend solely upon native artillery officers, we have every reason to wish our ordnance to be at least double its present strength. But, independently of its capacity as a fortress, we must remember that its strategic value is very considerable, being the first and only place of any strength, or where supplies in any quantity could be obtained, between Herat and the Indus. Some considerable time back Sir Henry Durand drew up a very able memorandum connected with the defences of the city, and it is much to be regretted that since our occupation some of his suggestions were not acted upon, as recommended by Colonel Hills.

In 1824 the ill-fated Shah Sujah marched against Kandahar, but, after displaying great bravery, was defeated by Dost Mahomed and compelled to raise the siege, with a loss of 2000 men. He retired on Shikapur, but in 1839 once more entered the city accompanied by Lord Keane, when no resistance was offered. During the rebellion of Cabul, thanks to the good management of General Nott, in spite of numerous attempts to gain the city on the part of the Ghilzais, the British remained masters until the end of August 1842, when, in obedience to instructions from home, Nott evacuated it and marched on Cabul. Since then it has often changed hands, but was finally captured for Shere Ali by his then gallant though unfortunate son Yakub Khan, after the severe battle of the Helmund on the 1st of April, 1868, since when it has remained the capital of Southern Afghanistan. You will remember, in my former letters, how I told you of General Stewart's entry into Kandahar, on the 9th January last year. The importance of holding the second city of the empire since then can scarcely be over-estimated in either a political or a military point of view. The possession of Quetta and 65 miles of the Bolan in its rear gave us an overwhelming advantage in this in comparison with other Afghan wars, and we shall indeed be most remiss should we not take advantage of this weak point in our enemy's line of defence. In 1839 Sir John Keane took 23 days in covering the distance between Quetta and Kandahar, and the further march to Ghuzni occupied him 24 more days. From Kandahar to Cabul is about 200 miles by the road which passes by Ghuzni, and our generals commanding at these points can easily join hands by the Logar Valley, taking the comparatively strong fortress of Ghuzni as a *point d'appui*.

In spite of the weakness of our force at Kandahar it has been decided, not by General Primrose, who is too prudent a leader to incur needless risks, but by what is pleasantly called 'higher authority,' to despatch General Burrows to Girishk, on the Helmund river, to effect a junction with the Wali Shere Ali, our new ruler, in order to check the advance of Ayub Khan, who, as I have already stated, is advancing in force from Herat. The strength of Ayub's force has, I venture to state, been considerably underrated, as, since he left Herat, he has been continually reinforced by adherents and by deserters from the Wali's troops. General Burrows received his instructions a couple of days back to take with him for the above duty a force of 2270 men, made up as follows :—E B., R. H. Artillery, 6 guns ; 6 companies 66th, or the 'Old Berkshire' Regiment, 500 bayonets ; the 1st and 30th Bengal Native Infantry, 1000 bayonets ;

a company of Native Sappers, 70 men ; the 3rd Bombay Cavalry, 350 sabres ; the 3rd Scinde Horse, 200 sabres. Yesterday, at daybreak, this force was paraded and addressed by our chief, after a long consultation had been held with General Burrows and the officers commanding corps.

I need not tell you how many years I have had the pleasure of knowing and serving under General Primrose, and I do not suppose any of those who have appreciated his talents as a staff officer will deny to him those qualities which make up a good leader in the field. His untiring energy, fertility of resource in moments of emergency, invaluable forethought, and invariable consideration and courtesy towards those under his command, have made him one of the most esteemed as well as most popular generals in our service. Since General Stewart's departure for Cabul his successor has had no easy time of it. Notwithstanding the optimist platitueds uttered by the supporters of the Liberal Government, and the assertions that the war is over, the General and those of his staff known to be in his confidence are of strong opinion that dark and dangerous clouds, although at present no bigger than the proverbial 'man's hand,' are gathering in the south-westerly portions of Afghanistan. The announcement so prematurely made upon assuming office by the Gladstonian Cabinet, of their anxiety at all hazards, and at almost any price, to withdraw our troops, has had the effect of a spur upon the ready imaginations and energies of the disaffected factions of this sadly divided kingdom. Latent ambitions and dormant hopes of power and aggrandisement have been fired by the change of policy. Each pretender to the succession has redoubled the promises formerly made to his adherents, and none more vigorously and steadily than Ayub Khan, who, with his partisans, sees that the time is now opportune to strike a blow at our irresolution. While we daily receive instructions in regard to preparations for our diminution of military force in this part of the country, we are not without intelligence from the camps of our enemies, who see in our preparations for departure not a sign of good will, but an evidence of a prudence bordering on fear. Only two days ago, General Primrose gave audience to some wealthy and friendly citizens of Kandahar, who asked to be allowed to deposit the bulk of their property in our treasury. These men showed letters to our chief from persons in authority at Herat, advising them of Ayub's determination to march with all speed upon the western capital, where plunder and rapine would reward the devoted band who drove out the English dogs. With the arrival of the new Viceroy, the departure of Lord Lytton, and the reductions which are on all sides ordered under the new *régime*, we have given causes for grave anxiety to those portions of the Afghan nation who would prefer the just rule of England to the exactions and confiscations of their own princes. By our negotiations with Abdurrahman, and our contemptuous disregard of Ayub, we are fast alienating the confidence of the Kandaharees, who have no wish to be left to their fate when we evacuate their territory. In the interviews at which I have been present between General Primrose and some of the chief men of this city, the arguments I have cited above have been most ably set forth by men whose influence and experience of native feeling well entitle them to be considered authorities. When General Primrose announced to our visitors that Mr. Lepel

Griffin had been summoned to Simla to a conference with the Viceroy on the claims and merits of Abdurrahman, one of the citizens remarked in Persian that the subdivision of the country, and its being handed over in separate governments to different Walis, would, in his opinion, be a course more acceptable to the majority of the well-disposed population than the complete cession of Afghanistan to one ruler, who would be certain to meet determined opposition from his rivals. Abdurrahman has, he added, certain claims which are not to be disputed; but the strong partiality he is known to possess for Russia, and his slowness in showing his hand to our Viceroy, make him altogether a dangerous selection.

'What do you consider of the other candidates?' asked the General, after he had listened attentively to the arguments adduced by the speaker.

'Failing the nomination of Abdurrahman, there would be the young Musa Jan, who, with a regency chosen from among his own relatives during his minority, would have the strong support of the Ghuzni people and those of Kohistan,' replied the Sirdar, who was evidently no admirer of either Abdurrahman or Ayub Khan.

'I believe,' added the other chief, 'that any member of Dost Mahomed's family would be acceptable to the Cabulees, who are by no means pleased at the present negotiations with Abdurrahman.'

The parade of General Burrows' small force for the support of Shere Ali at Girishk was a smart affair, and came off under the critical eyes of General Primrose on a piece of ground admirably suited for the purpose. A wide plain, stretching away to the banks of the river, and here and there intersected by small canals and watercourses, over which our active Engineers and Sappers had erected temporary cask and plank bridges, strong enough for the passage of field artillery, afforded plenty of space for the troops. On the General's arrival the troops were wheeled from column into line, and were formed up as follows :—On the right and left flanks were half-batteries of the E B., R.H.A., looking in splendid condition, the guns, harness, men, and horses, showing admirably the care bestowed on this branch of our little force; next, on the right, came the 3rd Bombay Cavalry, admirably horsed and commanded ; on the left flank the two squadrons of the Scinde Horse, dressed in that most picturesque of military costumes, the thick turban and loose collarless shirt, with smart cummer-bund round the waist, their arms being the long and deadly bamboo lance which has lately proved such an admirable weapon. The 66th, or 'Old Berkshires,' with six strong companies, occupied the centre of the line, commanded by as gallant a soldier as we have in the service, Lieut.-Colonel James Galbraith, with Majors Oliver and Ready as his seconds in command. The native regiments were on either flank next to the cavalry, while the camels, elephants, and baggage-carts, were formed in rear. With General Primrose rode Major Burnett, 2nd battalion 15th Foot, his assistant adjutant-general ; Major Adam, assistant quartermaster-general ; Colonel French, commanding Royal Artillery ; Lieut.-Colonel Hills, commanding Royal Engineers ; the two brigade majors, and Deputy Surgeon-General O'Nial, principal medical officer. This brigade is under the command of Brigadier-General Burrows, and is under orders to march towards Girishk, on the Helmund river, where the Wali Shere Ali will join us with his troops, and where the combined force will be used to hold in check the troops of Ayub advancing from Herat.

Meanwhile these preparations in no way interfere with our usual garrison amusements ; and under our excellent chief we have theatricals, racing, polo, cricket, and all the usual *délassements* peculiar to Indian cantonment life. Our little garrison is in excellent health and spirits, supplies are plentiful, and the people apparently quiet and friendly. From Cabul our news is not quite so satisfactory. General Hills is about marching with a brigade to disperse a gathering in the Logar Valley, and writes to his brother, who commands the Engineers here, to say that Mir Batcha holds a strong position near Farrah, while his cavalry pickets prowl along the roads between Cabul and Kohistan. He is forcibly collecting revenue, and his people have carried off a number of horses belonging to Sirdars friendly to our rule. Bahadur Khan Abdul, Gholam Hyder Charkh, and two thousand Jadrans and Mongals, are plundering the district ; the Ghazais in Maidan are daily becoming more audacious, and several encounters have lately occurred between them and the villagers of the Logar. The supplies are becoming scarce in Cabul, and the poorer classes of the population are suffering bitterly. Such are the prospects so glowingly foreshadowed by those who have already discounted the promises of ' peace at any price' for this poor country. Meanwhile our *protégé*, Abdurrahman, has taken advantage of our overtures to send a circular to the Sirdars announcing that the English Government has offered him the sole Ameership of united Afghanistan ; meaning, of course, to include Kandahar. This has so disconcerted and alarmed Hashim Khan that he has fled from Cabul and established himself at Cherki, near Khurd Cabul, where a large collection of Yakub's Sepoys are daily flocking in to his colours.   In deciding the future of Afghanistan we cannot forget those who have thrown in their fortunes with us, nor can we leave, by the too hurried withdrawal of our troops, these unfortunate people to be plundered and massacred.   Afghanistan has been for years the hardest problem Indian statesmen have had to solve.   It would scarcely seem that the recent change of politics and Ministry at home has strengthened our position in the country, or improved our *prestige* amongst the people.   I sincerely hope that my forebodings may be eventually cleared away by the course of events ; but, being on the spot, we who are actors on the scene have more opportunities of forming opinions than those whose wish is father to the thought, and who tell us in print that the present war is over.

Girishk, towards which General Burrows is ordered, is a village situate on the right bank of the river Helmund, 73 miles west of Kandahar, and 290 south-east of Herat.   Its strategical value is great, and, guarding as it does the high road to Merv and the fords on the Helmund, its possession is of vital importance.   Conflicting opinions are held as to its strength, but as none of these are of modern date they are comparatively valueless.   There is no doubt it might, with the expenditure of labour and money, be made an admirable advanced post for an army occupying Kandahar, and its occupation at a future time will be an earnest that we intend to delineate our new frontier on truly strategical grounds.   But with our small garrison I cannot but consider that we should not divide our strength, and repeat the errors which led to Isandwhlana.

ON RECONNAISSANCE WITH GENERAL HILLS.

Cavalry Camp, Zurgun Shahr, July 2.

FIFTEEN hours in the saddle, forty miles' ride, and as pretty an affair, won almost entirely by *l'arme blanche*, as we soldiers can ever hope to get, must be my excuse for a short despatch by this mail. And all this it was my good fortune to share in but yesterday. When, not many years back, as I remember, under the last Gladstonian Ministry and Cardwellian *régime*, Sir William Harcourt and Mr. George Trevelyan talked of our military dandies, who preferred to hard knocks the 'sweet shady side of Pall Mall,' I opine we did not much care for such a sneer, and since then we have had, I venture to say, sufficient examples to show that the hard fare and hard knocks of camp life are more envied by our *jeunesse dorée* than the club and drawing-room luxuries enjoyed by our brethren in your little 'village' on the Thames. Such are our egotistical reflections, and to such conclusions did we arrive when last evening the 'calumet of peace' was smoked around the camp-fire in front of my tent; and when we were honoured, when the fight was over and our horses and wounded cared for, by the presence of two of the most popular men in our service—General ('Jemmy') Hills, V.C., and his dashing brigadier and *beau sabreur*, Brigadier Palliser.

The affair came to pass in this wise. Towards the end of the last month General Hills was told to organize an expedition for the purpose of dispersing a somewhat threatening gathering in the Logar Valley, and for this purpose he took with him a small force of infantry and

Palliser's cavalry brigade, consisting of the 1st and 2nd Punjab Cavalry and the 10th Bengal Lancers, making at most not more than 550 sabres and lances. Meanwhile, on the afternoon of the 28th, Major Evans Smith, General Hills' chief political officer, came into camp with news to the effect that our old enemy, Mahomed Hassan Khan, had instigated a large number of the Zurmuts to gather under his command in the fastnesses of the valley. It would not be easy, nor even will it be now necessary, for me to describe the variety of scenery, of rock, vale, hill, mountain, forest, and stream, of this beautiful portion of the Ameer's dominions, inhabited, however, by as troublesome sets of clans as this country of clans can produce. Imagine Scotland—say a portion of the Trossachs—combined with a little of Norway and a *soupçon* of the tropical features of the West Indies, where alternate sunshine and snow, fertile corn-field and palm-grove, are neighbours to, and overshadowed by, terrific crags and inaccessible peaks, over which the savage beast of prey ranges and the leaping torrent foams—then perhaps you can, in 'your mind's eye,' picture the scenes through which good steeds carried us during our late expedition.

But on service the soldier, and above all the cavalry man, has but little time to linger over the beauties of river or tree, of stream or mountain; and as our advanced pickets and flankers felt their way with stealthy caution by the fertile plain, through the dense groves of date and palm, and as we watered our horses in each rippling stream, a vigilant look-out was kept by our vedettes in front and rear. I rode with General Palliser part of the way, and afterwards with Major Atkinson, 1st Punjab Cavalry, and with Captain Bishop, 2nd

Punjabs, and I am glad to let their friends at home know—what they, perhaps, would omit to state—that they both displayed such cool and steady courage, as well as conspicuous valour, that they have both been mentioned for the Victoria Cross.

About noon on our second day's march our scouts brought us in intelligence that the enemy's pickets were in force along the three converging roads leading from Padkhao to Altimore. Their main body of cavalry, acting as an advanced guard, held the large village of Padkhao, which is situated on a small stream about twelve miles south of our present camp at Zurgun Shahr. I was allowed to go out at 3.30 a.m. on the 1st with our advanced guard, consisting of detachments from our three corps, numbering fifty sabres, and commanded by my friend Atkinson, who had with him young Leslie Bishop as second in command. About four miles from Padkhao Shana I rode with a couple of files, both good shots, to a small rocky eminence upon our right, and where we noticed the ruined walls of a dismantled fort. From this coign of vantage we could see without being seen, and, with delight, we observed a column of some thousand or twelve hundred infantry moving parallel to us and on our right flank in the direction of Altimore.

Leaving my men to watch, I galloped back to our Brigadier, who was most anxiously waiting my return; and he at once, seeing the ground was fairly practicable, ordered our whole line to form to the right, and charge! Never was any movement better timed. As our well-drilled squadrons swung round at a canter into line, not a man was out of place; not an interval was lost! Our first line consisted of the 1st Punjab Cavalry on the right and the 19th Punjab Cavalry on the left, with the 2nd Punjabs in rear as support. The Brigadier, upon a splendid grey Arab of great substance and speed, rode ten horse-lengths in front, with his A. D. C., young Barrow, close on the right rear, both keeping the line as steady and as straight as on parade. The ground at first was sloping downwards, intersected by several small watercourses, and here and there some awkward boulders, over which my horse twice or thrice nearly came to grief. The men, however, were steady, kept their horses well in hand, and took the time from their squadron-leaders. After we had gone about six hundred yards the ground became more level, more free from obstacles, and our chief allowed us to improve the pace. When we were within half a mile of the enemy his cavalry—apparently about 700 sabres—broke and fled, leaving the unfortunate footmen to their fate.

We were now cantering at an easy pace across a level and open plain, rising slightly as we advanced, the best possible ground for a charge of cavalry; and when we came within about three hundred yards of the Afghan infantry their generals managed to rally them into some kind of separate squares to receive our shock. They were, however, too late, and our fellows in the front line got in amongst them before they were quite formed. Never did I see such a *déroute*. Never did I hear such a clash of horse against man, of sabre against shield, of lance against foeman's breast. Palliser, Barrow, and Atkinson, were in front, with Gordon, 19th, on their right flank. The squadron and troop-leaders came next, and our long, unbroken line of turbaned squadrons behind, with lance and sabre at the engage. 'Well done, the 1st!' 'Steady, my lads!' 'Go it, Bob!'

' Bravo, Jack ! ' Such were the European exclamations from officer to officer along the line while we broke the half-formed squares, and engaged hand-to-hand with our foe—surprised, but, for a time, at bay.

The ground now became more broken, and as our formation was, in a measure, gone, the footmen were enabled for a short time to hold their own against the sowars, whose horses were somewhat blown. Had the Afghan cavalry at this juncture been at hand, and taken us in flank, we might have lost severely; but they did not return, while our second line of reserves and supports coming up completed the route of our antagonists.

The pursuit was continued for more than five miles, and until the fugitives who survived managed to obtain some shelter from the hills which bounded the plain, which, when we recrossed it, we found was strewn with arms, standards, and all sorts of *débris*, amongst which were many guns of English make, including Martinis and Sniders. Two hundred and fifty bodies of the enemy, I am told, were counted on the plain; but I will not dwell on such ghastly details, which are the necessary consequences of human battle.

Our loss was wonderfully small, considering the stand made by our enemy. Burrows had a narrow escape, and would have been speared had not one of his jemmadars pinned the man with his lance. Three of our men killed, and only some twenty-two wounded, made up our casualties. Mahomed Sultan and Mahomed Synd Khan were the principal Afghan leaders, while the rank and file were nearly all Zurmuts.

We reached our camp at Zurgun Shahr about seven the same evening, having, as I have said, been some fifteen hours in the saddle, and covering some thirty-five or forty miles!

Meanwhile coming events are already casting their shadows before, and certain engineering operations are on the *tapis* at Cabul, which to an observant mind seem to point to a change of masters in the city. Mahomed Jan has made overtures, and purposes, we hear, writing to our authorities to announce the possibility, under certain conditions, of his adhesion to the rule of Abdurrahman as Ameer. But Abdurrahman is as reticent as was General Monk at the time before Charles II.'s restoration, and although he is marching towards the capital he is taking a long time on the road. Should we withdraw our troops from Cabul as soon as we have sanctioned the proclamation of the new Ameer? Most of us, as you must know, are anxious to get away, but the time is not yet come for the abandonment of this place ; nor should we, in justice to the friendly portion of the population, leave them to rapine and plunder as once before we did. However, as we hear rumours of orders to the Engineers to undermine the forts and other defences we built around the city, we must assume that orders of some sort have been given from home. Letters at the same time come to us from Kandahar and the West which cause no inconsiderable excitement here, and it is more than whispered that Ayub Khan, with banner and drum, is already on the march from Herat to the Durani capital. If this be true, and we retire from here, we shall have the whole country once more in arms against us, and all our work will have to be done over again. Even these vague rumours of Ayub's advance have made the people here assume an insolent and defiant attitude. To make matters worse, in case of a march with any large force from Cabul, provisions and forage are becoming very scarce, so we should have infinite difficulty in providing supplies, and much more in carrying them.

KANDAHAR 'GUP,' ABDURRAHMAN, AND AYUB.

Kandahar, July 3.

LITTLE did I imagine, when, in a somewhat idle hour and mood, I sat upon a stool in front of my comfortable tent, and called to my faithful native for 'brandy pawnee,' and my pens, ink, and paper, to send you home the 'short but simple annals of the poor' English soldier, who does his sultry campaign in what they term at home the 'Gorgeous East,' that events would have so rapidly marched towards the *dénouement* of the present 'situation.' A celebrated English general officer, more renowned for a good seat in the saddle and a sonorous word of command than for writing in the Addisonian style, once immortalised himself in his comments upon a court-martial by observing that 'the president of the said tribunal had seemed to have lulled himself in a conviction.' Here we who are in a measure behind the scenes, and who, I may at once allow, neither take too pessimist nor too favourable a view of our present *status quo*, are unwillingly impelled to the strong belief that a third campaign is upon the eve of commencement. The parade of Burrows' small brigade, less than 2500 men, of which I gave you a description in my last, the denuding of our already attenuated garrison in this to my mind most important of our frontier bastions against

Russian advance; the irresolution of our new *protégé*, Abdurrahman; his doubtful popularity; and, above all, the vigour and boldness of his rival, Ayub Khan, who we know is marching in force *viâ* Girishk upon Kandahar, all point to more serious fighting in the south and west of this most unhappy country.

'I want a hero!—an uncommon want, since, I own, each day brings forth a new one,' was said of yore by the author of *Don Juan*, and might be aptly quoted by those of the new *régime* in your Indian Councils at home, who wish to find a safe and reliable successor to poor Yakub Khan. Abdurrahman, I suppose, is considered our trump card, but as General Primrose said to me the other day, 'We might as well place the country under the protectorate of a Kaufmann, or any other Russian friend of our new Ameer!' Hashim Khan, as we heard, and as I told you, fled from Cabul with most of his treasure on the night of the 25th ult., the moment he heard of Abdurrahman's probable advent to the northern capital, and we now hear from reliable sources that his object is and has been to make a strong party with the Ghilzai faction, with whom he has been long coquetting, against our proposed negotiations with the man he dreads. Abdurrahman, meanwhile, with all the will and art of his father, has, I find, been carefully misrepresenting the tenor of the proposals made to him by our trusting officials, whose promptings come as we know from home. Hashim Khan is now at Cherki, near the Khurd Cabul, and has with him more than 5000 Sepoys, disbanded from the late Ameer's mercenary army. He has, I know, listened to the flattering overtures of Abdulla Khan, and their united action may cause our rulers much trouble. We now come to a still more troublesome factor in the settlement of the new dynasty, and this is Mir Batcha, whose pickets are now holding the roads between Cabul and Kohistan. He and his myrmidon, Mir Said, have forcibly collected the revenue on the present harvest, and are therefore equipped with the sinews of war and ready at a moment to take the field. To gain additional adherents this most bitter enemy to the English has, I find, been travelling from village to village and from house to house preaching a sort of Jehad, or religious war, with the Koran in his hand, and adjuring the people to rise, when the time shall come, to sweep the Feringhi into the sea! Baba Kushkar, Dakre, Furseeh, and places near Kariz Mir, are now the hotbeds of discontent, where the Kohistanis, under Mirzoo-shah, the brother of Mir Batcha, are armed and drilled. Letters from Maidan tell us that the gathering daily swells to large proportions. Five thousand infantry and fifteen hundred sabres are, we are told, ready to march, and amidst the villages at night are to be seen watch-fires and other signals. To-day we hear that Mahomed Jan has arrived as far as Killar Amir, in the Logar Valley, and that he has with him no less than 3700 men, whom he is leading on to Chark, where Yakub's old Ghuzni faction has promised to rise in support. Five thousand well-armed men are collected at Killaishakaga, where Tarakis, Wardaks, and Tayaks are daily arriving to serve under Mahomed Jan.

All these items of menace, however, fade into insignificance when we look to Herat and the armament now being collected, organized, and disciplined under one of, if not the best of Afghan generals, Ayub Khan. This man has shown such evidences of military skill that he should by no means be despised, and were he to gain a point or two In the impending game, our situation here would be more than serious. All the best authorities, upon whom we depend for information, assure our chief that Ayub's artillery and cavalry are highly disciplined by leaders not taught in native wars, and that the calibre and working of the guns are far different to the weapons we encountered at Ali Khel and on the Peiwar Kotal. We received some valuable information yesterday from two of the most unmitigated scoundrels I ever beheld, and these were a couple of the Wali's Sepoys who deserted from Kandahar some months ago, served under Ayub at Herat, and returned as spies to our head-quarters. As I was sent for to the General's quarters the other morning to interpret the tale they had to give, I may describe to you what happened, remarking, however, that their story must be accepted, as Afghan information generally should be, with considerable caution and many grains of salt. To those who do not know General Primrose I may describe him as a well-knit, middle-sized, middle-aged, and most soldier-like man, of about sixty years of age. Long staff service and native experiences of the Indian Sepoy have given him an intuition into the Asiatic character, which comes in most usefully in cases like the present, where we have to deal with a cunning and duplicity seldom to be equalled in other armies. The General is a fair Hindostani scholar, but has not had sufficient practice to master the local idioms of the Afghan tongue, and he did me the honour to allow me to translate for him. The two troopers brought before us were certainly fine specimens of savage humanity, and their mien and bearing were in keeping with the daring adventures they had courted and gone through. The taller and elder sowar, who was clad in the ragged remains of what was once a picturesque and workman-like uniform, consisting of the dark purple turban, grey tunic, and well-worn knickerbockers, was the spokes-man, and answered my questions with an apparent frankness which made it difficult to separate fact from fiction.

'What have you to say to prevent your being tried by court-martial and shot as deserters?' said the General, as he fixed his eyes full upon the men, who stood firm and uprightly at attention at the foot of the table at which we sat.

'We did not desert, Sahib,' said the tall soldier, as he saluted in the most graceful manner. 'We were in the village near here one afternoon last year, and were taken prisoners and sent away to Herat, where we pretended we were glad to escape to our own people.'

'And then,' asked our chief, 'what did you do?'

'We drilled with Ayub, and were promoted as non-commissioned officers, but seldom received any pay, unless our money was taken from the villagers around the city. For six months we served, until we were sent with the advanced guard of Ayub on the march towards Kandahar, and one night we saddled our horses and came away, travelling only by night and resting while the sun was high.'

General Primrose now suggested that the men should be examined separately, and this was accordingly done, the result being that both their accounts tallied to a certain extent, and confirmed in a great measure the reports we had previously received of the drill and equip-ment of Ayub's levies, and the foreign organization we had long suspected.   The younger of these deserters was a mere lad, and made a more favourable impression upon us than his more truculent comrade. He had been, from some previous knowledge and aptitude, drafted into the artillery, and from his accounts we are led to the strong conviction that Ayub is tolerably well supplied with breech-loading guns, as well as with small arms of that description. The Prince's popularity amongst his men was much emphasised by our interlocutors, who were evidently anxious to let us know that he was an enemy not to be despised. His cavalry, they also assured us, was formidable, both in numbers and discipline, and was daily gathering recruits from numerous desertions from the troops formerly in Yakub's pay. While the examination continued, one of our staff came in to announce to the General that the father, mother, and two sisters of the young soldier, all Kandaharees, craved an interview to become hostages for his safety, as they were under the impression that, as appearances were against him, he would be tried by drumhead court-martial and shot. I need scarcely say that assurances were given that no such summary conviction or punishment should take place, and that, conditionally upon the statements we were told being found to be true, reward and promotion, instead of death, would be given by our chief.

According to the information given to us by these men, it would therefore appear that Ayub Khan marched from Herat some five weeks back, about the 9th of June, and that he had with him on arrival at Farah, from where these men deserted, some 5000 infantry, 2500 cavalry, and five batteries of artillery. His first encounter should be, we think—that is, if he means fighting—with the Wali, who is somewhere on the Girishk road on the look-out for him. I know the country about there tolerably well, as I was with Colonel Malcolmson in the smart little affair we had with the hillmen last year. Ayub would probably at this season be able to ford the Helmund at or near Hyderabad, and would then move by the valley of Maiwand, where supplies of all kinds for his troops would be abundant. When I rode through Maiwand with Malcolmson last year the fort was half tumbling down and the village in ruins, but I hear it has since been rebuilt. I need not tell you that Kandahar is somewhat excited at the present time, and that many of the richest merchants are leaving with their wives and treasure, not feeling at all secure or comfortable at the menaces sent on by Ayub, whose emissaries are promising unlimited loot and vengeance to those who will help to drive us out. The defences of the town of Kandahar leave much to be desired, but General Primrose has already made some well-planned additions to the works, while he is collecting supplies to provision the citadel in case of a siege.

WITH GENERAL BURROWS—OPINIONS OF THE WALI.

Singuri (12 *miles from Kandahar*), *W.*, *July 6.*

As one of your friends at Kandahar tells me he wrote to you on the 27th ult., giving you details of General Burrows' small force, destined for Girishk and the Helmund, and to try conclusions with Ayub Khan, known to be advancing in force from Herat, I need not enlarge upon these matters, but merely state that at a final parade of all ranks, previous to our march, our field state was as follows :—1 battery, 6 guns, E B., R.H.A., 220 men, Major Blackwood; three squadrons, 300 sabres, 3rd Light Cavalry, Major Currie; 2 squadrons, 220 sabres, 3rd Scinde Horse, Colonel Malcolmson; 6 companies, 512 bayonets, 66th Regiment, Colonel Galbraith; 6 companies 1st Bombay Grenadiers, 515 bayonets, Colonel Anderson; 6 companies 19th Bombay Native Infantry (Jacob's Rifles), 512 bayonets, Colonel Mainwaring; 40 sappers : making a total, irrespective of officers, of 740 sabres and 1579 bayonets, or in all 2319 men. Brigadier-General Reynolds Scott Burrows, Bombay Native Infantry, is in command of our force. Although he obtained his first commission as ensign as far back as 1844, he has, I am told, never, till now, seen any active service, but has held the reputation of being a capital staff officer. Our brigade-major is Captain Percy Heath, Bombay Staff Corps. Of the composition of our force, I may say that Major Blackwood's battery is as smart and well-ordered as such officers as Captain Slade and Lieutenants Maclaine, E. G. Osborn, and N. P. Powell, can make, and the horses are in fine condition. The old 66th, or Berkshires, have not, perhaps, the stamp of men they paraded the last time they left India, in 1865; and it must be allowed, in all honesty, that short service has not improved the appearance of our companies, to say nothing of the extreme youth of our non-commissioned officers. But the regiment, though lacking its former physique and inch measurement, is, under its present leader, rapidly improving. Our native regiments are good specimens of such troops. The 19th Bombay N.I., better known as 'Jacob's Rifles,' have always held a high position in the opinion of old Indians, and are at present fairly efficient. But having said all this, it is impossible not to allow that the native regiments are most imprudently and injudiciously under-officered. In the corps I have named, the full complement, small as it is, of commissioned officers is never with the corps, and the consequences are, that in moments of emergency or danger the men are left to themselves, and lose their cohesion as a body.

We received our orders to take part in this expedition some ten or more days ago, and since then have looked forward with some excitement to the campaign before us, with every confidence in the result, but with a full conviction that ours will not be a mere *promenade militaire*. Kandahar we regard as a place we are not likely to return to, as our movements will probably be towards the Indian frontier should the campaign be successfully closed before the winter sets in. Meanwhile let me give you a sketch of the movements of our opponent as reported to General Primrose by the most reliable authorities. Ayub Khan, we know, left Herat on or about June 19, having with him 4500 regular infantry, 1500 regular cavalry, and 36 guns, together with a force of irregular but most efficient horsemen, drawn from the fiercest and most warlike of the western tribes—fellows whose desire and hope to kill an infidel lead them to look upon danger and death as but the prelude to Paradise. This latter force forms his advanced guard, and is supposed to be one day's march in front of the main body. Of the Khan's artillery we know that it consists of almost every species and pattern, some of English, but most of Afghan make. His proclamations to his troops reached us by spies in due course, and therein Ayub tells his soldiers of the wealth and plunder to be gained when the English are slaughtered in or before the western capital. As soon as this news was confirmed, Wali Mahomed, the native governor, volunteered to go forth as far as the Helmund and drive back the invader. He was accordingly allowed to march westward with 4000 men, chiefly Afghans, recruited near Kandahar. The Wali, however, soon after he had marched, sent us word back that he was more than doubtful of the fidelity of his men, and his application for immediate reinforcements was doubtless the cause of our expedition being organized. I applied for, and obtained permission to accompany the Wali, who is an old friend of mine, for a couple of days' marches on his road to Girishk, and found him an intelligent and most agreeable companion. He is an admirable genealogist, and told the many points of relationship regarding the various pretenders to the Afghan throne, of which before I knew but little. Ayub he considers one of the most talented of Shere Ali's sons. His mother was the daughter of that same Mohmund chief who was so civil to us at the commencement of the war at Lalpura. He was born in 1851, and consequently is now but thirty years of age. He was first prominently noted in the campaigns of 1867 and 1868, when the exploits and successes of his brother, Yakub Khan, placed their father, Shere Ali, on the throne. When Yakub and Shere Ali quarrelled, in 1871, Ayub would not give up his friendship for the former, and joined him with his adherents in attacking Herat, and in expelling the Ameer's Governor; and up to the end of 1874, when Yakub ruled there as an independent Prince, Ayub assisted his brother in the government. When, under British advice and the promise of safety from Shere Ali, Yakub Khan was lured to Cabul, he left Ayub in charge of Herat; but the skill of the Ameer's general, Omar Khan, and the prompt measures taken by him, were too much for the young prince, and he was compelled to fly for safety from his father's vengeance to Persia, where he was well and honourably received by the Shah, who granted him safe residence and a handsome pension to uphold his rank. Here he lived until the British power made the Afghan kingdom crumble away, and until he saw in the march of events the opportunity he had waited for to restore himself to power. Appearing suddenly before Herat, the Governor there gave him welcome and refuge as the son of Shere Ali, his master; but Ayub soon so far consolidated his power in the west that he was enabled to send troops against us to the north. These, however, arrived too late, as the Treaty of Gundamuk had been signed.

After we had withdrawn our troops from Cabul last year Ayub did not leave Herat, doubtless preferring his independence there to the subordinate rank he would have held under his brother's rule. From the commencement of the present campaign Ayub has not been much heard of, but he has evidently not been idle, if the organization and efficiency of his troops are as stated to us.

'Abdurrahman,' said I; 'what is his lineal descent, and what do you think of him, Wali?'

'He is the lineal descendant beyond all doubt, and the senior representative of Dost Mahomed, the great Ameer, who died in 1863, just a fortnight after he captured the city of Herat. Abdurrahman is the eldest son of Afzul Khan, who was himself the eldest son of the Dost, and he is therefore nephew to Shere Ali, and first cousin to both Ayub Khan and Yakub Khan. He was born in 1830, and is now consequently fifty years old. When the Dost Mahomed died he nominated his favourite son, Shere Ali, and the latter succeeded, but Afzul Khan, the father of Abdurrahman, was at that time governor of Balkh, and ruled in his capital of Takht-i-Pul, and with his younger brother, Azim Khan, and his son, Abdurrahman, he joined in a conspiracy against the new Ameer. During the civil war which followed Abdurrahman evinced much military genius, and in 1865–6–7, he gained some great victories, amongst others, those of Shaikhabad and Khelat-i-Ghilzai. A year later, however, he was completely defeated by his nephew, Yakub, at Bamian and at Tinah Khan. He fled to Russian territory, was hospitably received by General Kaufmann, received a pension of 25,000 roubles a-year, and was allowed to reside at Samarcand. He remained an exile and a pensioner of the Russian Government till 1879, when he suddenly left, and came *viâ* Balkh towards the Cabul frontier.'

On the second day's march I left the Wali at Singuri, where we now are, and came back much pleased with my ride with so intelligent and well-informed an Oriental. On Saturday last, the 3rd, we received our final order of the route, which was that the cavalry and artillery would parade for march under Brigadier Nuttall, with Major Hogg as brigade-major, on the following Sunday morning, and that ours and the main body would follow the next day.

In making my farewell to Kandahar I determined to take a valedictory ride round the town, to correct one or two sketches I had made of the surrounding country, and I had the good fortune to secure General Primrose, who is anxiously watching the progress of the defensive works, as my companion during my *promenade à cheval.* The city of Kandahar, I may tell you, has considerably increased in size and prosperity since our advent, and if our occupation is to be permanent its progress will be proportionate. The town itself, I need scarcely say, is situated at the foot of the Tarnak Valley, and separated from the river of that name by a low range of hills, which divide the valley and run almost parallel to the river for about eighteen miles. Rising defiantly from the plain on three sides are lofty rocky cliffs, while on the fourth side there is an open space leading along the valley, the greater portion of which is now well cultivated and fertile. In our early morning's ride, on the western side of the town, we passed by gardens, orchards filled with rich fruit-trees, and fields of clover, barley, lucerne, and corn, bounded in the distance by bright green meadows and luxuriant palm and cocoa groves. All these are irrigated by canals, many in number, and fed through the gap in the hills by the Arganda Hab, a tributary of the Helmund. Away to the east we saw but the commencement of a sun-dried, or, rather, sun-baked, inhospitable desert, covered with large boulders, and most scantily supplied with water.

The town is, as I said, now becoming larger and daily more populous. It is in the form, as my sketch will show, of an oblong, 2000 by 1600 yards, and is surrounded by a poor and weak wall of sun-dried bricks, rubble, and mud, thirty feet high, and flanked here and there by bastions and semicircular towers. The walls are not revetted with stone or brick, but are defended by a ditch ten feet deep and twenty-four feet wide, which, as General Primrose has arranged, can be filled in a few hours by water from the canals which run through the city.   In this great city wall are four principal gates ; the northern, or Eedgah ; the southern, the Shikapore; the eastern, the Cabul ; and the western, the Herat.   The parapet, here and there in ruins, was once battlemented, loophooled, and pierced in the Oriental style with apertures for the purpose of casting boiling oil and other missiles into the ditch.   There are no less than sixty-two towers, including those over the gates and at the four principal angles of the *enceinte*. The gates are of rotten timber, and had they not been strengthened by the clever engineering skill of our popular 'sapper and miner,' 'Jack,' otherwise Colonel John Hills, they would have afforded small defence against an ordinary battering-ram such as we read of in mediæval wars.   It was not without a curious feeling of interest and even regret that I looked at the place and its surroundings, where, when we are gone, the General, whom we all like so well, and whose consideration, tact, and complete kindness of heart have endeared him to all ranks, may, with his strangely weakened garrison, be compelled to hold an absurdly weak citadel against a foe whose whereabouts is seldom discovered until he strikes his blow.

There are, you may not be aware, three roads almost parallel to each other from the Helmund to Kandahar, and as our numerical strength only permits us to go by one, nothing could be more easy for Ayub than to make a feigned advance by one path while he struck a desperate blow by the other.

On Saturday evening the 66th mess, always re-

nowned for its hospitality, its *cuisine*, and above all for
its cellar, presented a semblance of its former glory,
even in the wild capital of South-western Afghanistan.
No gorgeous service of plate, it is true, adorned our.
sideboard, for the simple reason that no such luxuries
had we ; but a comfortable marquee, and stout wooden
forms whereon to sit, a table made of unplaned wooden
planks, and a select company of chosen guests to partake of a repast duly appreciated even by those who
would find fault at the Madras, the Byculla, or the
Calcutta clubs, made up an entertainment that few
who were present will forget ; for it was, as the President well remarked, a parting banquet, to the like of
which some of us might never return. Amongst our
most distinguished guests were, *facile princeps*, the Commander-in-Chief, Brigadier-General Burrows, our special
commander ; my friend, Colonel J. Hills, a name now
identified with the Indian army ; Lieut.-Colonel Galbraith, 66th ; Majors Oliver and Ready (three insepara-
bles for many a long year) ; Major Burnett, our assistant
adjutant-general ; Major Adam, assistant quartermaster-
general ; and Brigadier-General Brook, commanding the
other brigade.

On the following morning, at daybreak, the whole
garrison was voluntarily present to give a *vale* to the
cavalry brigade under General Nuttall, consisting of the
regiments and artillery I have mentioned.

Monday came, and with it the turn of the main body,
consisting entirely of infantry ; and after a very short
but minute inspection we managed to get upon the road
soon after daybreak. The morning was glorious in its
Oriental splendour, and as we moved westward through
the gap in the hills, of which I wrote above, the grey

mists of the night seemed lifted like curtains from the
earth, and the most glorious tints of colour met the eye.
Our fellows, as the post of honour, led the way, the
drums and fifes giving music to the measured tread of
our 500 youngsters, all marching, as soon as we were
clear of the cantonment, at ease—pipes, stories, songs,
and laughter being the order of the day. In front rode
the Colonel, renowned as having been in the old corps
from boyhood, and on his right and left the two majors,
Oliver and Ready. The General and his staff had
ridden on an hour previously to see about our first halt,
and in what state the roads were after the passage of
cavalry and guns on the previous day. On arriving at
the gap in the hills we entered a sort of covered way,
where, with a well-placed fort on either side, an enemy
might for long be held in check. This passed, the river
appeared, and along its banks birds of variously coloured
plumage were sailing, uttering the signs so peculiar to
Indian wild-fowl. After a short halt it was deemed
advisable to send on a portion of our native infantry to
act as a sort of advanced guard, and for this purpose the
grenadiers were sent to the front at the double, while
flanking parties along the hills were furnished by
'Jacob's Rifles.' As soon as we recommenced our
march we were met by a couple of orderlies with
despatches from General Nuttall, and they passed us
at a gallop, merely saying that as yet no enemy had
been seen. We came in about an hour to some rocky
and difficult ground, and saw the *débris* of an ammunition waggon which had rolled over, and, after being
cleared of its contents, had been abandoned. No
ammunition, however, had been lost, and the state of
the roads fully accounted for the mishap.

The country as we advanced became more wild and picturesque, and on the crags and hills above our flankers were seen driving away some scattered hill men who ventured within range, presumably scouts sent out from the villages to watch our movements and to note our strength. These bodies never appeared in force, but were all armed with the long Afghan smooth-bore and flint-lock, which at short range can still hold its own when in the hands of a Pathan fighting for his land. As the day wore on some of our camels began to tire, and we had to make a second halt to get their loads lightened. Your camel is of all animals the most patient, but he has a shrewd knowledge of when he is overworked, and experience tells him that a silent protest by a timely halt will usually have its effect, and cause his load to be lightened. By noon we were marching on to our camping-ground, whence I date this letter, and our men and horses were soon enjoying their mid-day meal ; satisfied, I believe, that, taking the heat and the state of the roads into consideration, we had done a fair day's march, and were twelve miles nearer to our enemy. The day after to-morrow we hope to reach Kushk-i-Nakhud, which is thought by many to be the key to Kandahar. Here we shall get certain news from both the Wali and from Ayub. Here it was that in 1879 General Biddulph, retiring from Girishk, was attacked by some 2000 of the Alizai Durani tribe, fanatics of desperate courage belonging to the Zamindawur region. Though they outnumbered our troops ten to one they were thoroughly beaten, and chased from the field by the 3rd Scinde Horse, now with our advanced column. May the omen be propitious !

CHAPTER II.

CONDITION OF KANDAHAR AFTER BURROWS' DEPARTURE.

Kandahar, July 10.

SINCE I wrote to you on the 3rd events have marched at a rapid pace, and I shall not be very rash if I hint that the clouds now menacing dark and threatening upon our horizon are likely soon to burst into a storm. Since I last took pen in hand in your regard, Burrows and his handful of men have left us, and, I cannot but opine, most unwisely was the order for the departure given. The Brigadier took with him, as I notified to you in my last, a force which consisted of but 740 sabres and 1579 bayonets, or, in all, 2319 men. Now, this column, weak in itself, still more weakened our small garrison, where we have left not more than 1700 men to defend a place whose *enceinte* is no less than 2000 by 1600 yards, or about a mile square. It is true, indeed, that the Wali has promised to effect a junction with General Burrows on the Helmund; but it is more than doubtful whether his troops can be relied upon, or even whether his authority over them will prevail when in proximity to Ayub and his army. Upon whose responsibility rests the order for this extraordinary march? Such is the query propounded from morn till eve, as we sit and scan the horizon, and wonder when reinforcements will arrive.

Meanwhile, I have had more than one long conversation with General Primrose, who is by no means satisfied with matters as they stand. We have carefully reckoned up the state of our defences, and the nature of our supplies, as the General is not one of those men who wait till the last moment to prepare. Bygone times have seen Kandahar beleaguered by an Afghan enemy, and successfully held by a British garrison. A citadel without glacis, ravelin, or flanking defence to defend a long line of curtain, was strong enough in 1842 to resist with as weak a garrison as we now possess an Afghan army of 10,000 men. If General Nott could achieve this, we need not apprehend that our General will fail against similar odds. Our entire force consists of four guns, C battery 2 brigade R.A., and the whole of 5 battery 11th brigade R.A., or 10 guns; the Poona Horse, three squadrons, the 7th Royal Fusiliers, the 19th and 29th Bombay N.I. With the gallant Fusiliers are Lieut.-Colonel Alfred Daubeny, in command, an old Crimean and Redan hero, Major Vandeleur, Captains Keyser, Graube, Manning, Conolly, and Adderley; Lieutenants Rodick, Thunder, Anderson, Galt, Porter, Graham, Drummond Wolff, De Trafford, Moss, Wood, Marsh, Barttelot, and Forbes; Paymaster G. Moore, and Quartermaster Clowes. Our gunners are Major Grey, Captain Law, Lieutenants Barry and Smith (C 2nd), and Major Clennel Collingwood, Captain Hansby, Lieutenants Fowke, Bell, Irving, and Fox.

As I told you something about the city and its defences in my last, I will only add that since General Primrose took over the command here in April from General Stewart, much has been done by Colonel Hills and those under him to strengthen the place. The walls have been repaired, the ditches widened, and arrangements made to fill them from the neighbouring canals at an hour's notice. The defences of the city are uniform on all sides ; the walls are of mud hardened in the sun, and mixed with chopped straw. They are 33 feet in height, but without stone *revêtement*, which could be easily added were it our intention to permanently hold the place. The *enceinte*, 2000 yards by 1600, is divided into curtains and semicircular towers, 62 in number, and guns could easily be mounted on these ; in fact, such will, I believe, be done at once. The *enceinte* is defended by a low *fausse braye*, with a ditch 10 feet in depth and 24 in width. The southern front is 1300 feet, the northern 1100 feet, the eastern 1600 feet, and the western, which is really two sides meeting at an angle, 1900 feet in length. The citadel, or *arg*, consists of an inner quadrangle of 200 yards, entrenched in the centre of the northern face. It is protected on one side by a tolerably good fosse, with a large bastion on its southern face, and four towers respectively on its eastern and western faces. Our city, as doubtless you may know, stands on the western side of a huge plain, having towards the south as a boundary an almost impassable desert, and to the north the branches or offshoots of a mountainous range. Exactly opposite the city, and about two miles to the west, there is a sort of a natural gateway formed by a gap in the hills, through which leads the road to Herat, and through which gap come the canals and watercourses taken from the Argandab to supply the city and irrigate the fields around. On three sides of our city we have smiling villages, clustering orchards, gardens, vineyards, cornfields, and groves of palm.

As I have lately returned from Girishk and the Helmund, I may give you some idea of the country where General Burrows is now operating. From the small post at Girishk the road crosses over the Helmund, usually in the dry season about four feet deep at the fords, and from 90 to 120 yards in width; but having a separate channel, it presents a formidable obstacle to the passage of guns and cavalry. During the rainy seasons and the floods, the river would be quite impassable without a bridge. The fords in the dry season are numerous, but the principal one for the two northern roads is at Girishk, where the castle of that name stands at a point where the road leaves the valley and winds towards the plain westward. The country from the Helmund on to Kandahar is in its configuration a strip or band of verdure, and cultivation bounded on either side by two sterile borders. This cultivated and alluvial tract is dotted here and there with woods, meadows, and cornfields, and around the numerous villages in the valley there is, I noticed, an elaborate system of cultivation. Grass and wood are both abundant. Coming to the great bend of the Helmund, where it starts along the desert, the valley is equally cultivated and productive, and seems green and smiling on either bank, while the most sterile wastes and deserts lie beyond. Bost, once a fortified town, commands the entrance from the Gurmsir and the valley of the Helmund into the Doab and on to Kandahar. At Kushk-i-Nakhud, Kila Saidal, and indeed all along the banks of the Helmund, remains of fortifications show how highly these strategic points were estimated. At Sung Hissar I saw the ruins of what must once have been an important work, standing on an isolated hill commanding the valley below; and at Alla Karez there is a site which sweeps the elevated open plain, and dominates the valley of the Argandab. These points, no doubt, we shall utilise before long.   From Girishk I crossed the river and followed the road due east right up to Kandahar.   For some miles after leaving the river the ground on either side is a wide stony plain, bounded northward by a considerable chain of hills, running parallel to the road, from which several spurs trend outwards towards the valley of Kushk-i-Nakhud, on the east and west. From the Helmund to Kushk-i-Nakhud the plains become more and more undulating, until the elevation becomes abrupt and difficult, and although not actually impassable for any arm, yet would be sufficient to prevent cavalry or artillery passing except at a walk. I gave my notes of the topographical features of the route to General Burrows on my return, and trust he may find them of use where he now is.

Since the departure of General Burrows and his brigade the inhabitants here have been in a most nervous and unsettled state.   Beyond all doubt our rule has been exceedingly popular, and the change in appearance of the streets and bazaars would alone prove this, did we not possess the assurance of all the wealthy and well-to-do sections of the population.   During the *régime* of Shere Ali, every rupee of the revenues, amounting, I am told, to about 65,000*l.* annually, was sent direct to Cabul, not one penny being spent upon the city or its institutions.   All this has been altered by our government, the city has been partly rebuilt, the streets cleaned, the fortifications placed in repair, and the gardens placed under cultivation, while the supplies furnished to our troops have proved a source of wealth and prosperity to the inhabitants.   A small tax levied upon the shops in the bazaars for the purpose of cleansing the city has been willingly paid, and the result has been that our sanitary arrangements have prevented disease amongst our troops. Since our advent the older inhabitants say the whole place teems with life and bustle, commerce thriving in the mart, and money rapidly changing hands in the bazaar, women moving about freely and unmolested at all hours, children playing in the streets, gardeners working at their plots, merchants conversing upon their exchanges, droves of camels, donkeys, and oxen moving along each highway, and, in fact, all the signs of a prosperity usual to our British rule.

Kandahar is supposed to have been one of the seven cities built by Alexander the Great, and was originally known as Iskandahar, having been called after him. At his death it passed successively through the hands of the Parthians, the Sassanides, the Arabs; it was conquered by Mahmood of Ghuzni, by Timurlane, by Baber, and by the Persians, until, at the commencement of the 17th century, it fell into the hands once more of the Mogul dynasty; but in 1650 the Persians again captured it, and though Arungzeeb once besieged it in person, and made several attempts to gain possession of it, the Persians retained it until a revolt of the Ghilzai Governors forced it from their hands. In 1737, Nadir Shah determined to recapture it, and, after a siege of nearly two years, compelled its Governor, Meer Hoossain, to capitulate; at the death of Nadir, Ahmed Shah Durani was crowned in the mosque, and made it the capital of his kingdom. His successor, Timur Shah, changed his capital to Cabul; the Sadozai branch of the Duranis retained possession of the place until Purdil Khan Barukzai seized it. In 1824 the ill-fated Shah Sujah marched against it, but, after displaying great bravery, was defeated by Dost Mahomed, and compelled to raise the siege with a loss of 20,000 killed. He was compelled to retire on Shikarpur, and, in 1839, once more entered the city, accompanied by the British army under Lord Keane. No resistance was then offered. During the rebellion in Cabul, thanks to the good management of General Nott, in spite of numerous attempts of the Ghilzais to gain the city, the English remained masters until the 8th of August, 1842, when, in obedience to instructions from home, Nott evacuated it, and marched on Cabul. Since then it has often changed hands, but finally was captured for Shere Ali by his unfortunate though gallant son, Yakub Khan, after the battle of the Helmund, on 1st April, 1868, and has remained the capital of Southern Afghanistan ever since.

WITH GENERAL BURROWS—MUTINY OF WALI'S TROOPS.

Camp Kushk-i-Nakhud, July 18.

SINCE I last wrote to you, after our first day's march from Kandahar, our troops have covered a great deal of ground, and, I must honestly confess, to little purpose, if our object has been to measure swords with Ayub Khan, a general who certainly is a strategist of no mean order. Our first day's march was to Kokeran, about six miles from Kandahar, and situated on the left bank of the Argandab. The road was picturesque, and our march an extremely pleasant one, all our fellows being in high spirits and delighted at the near prospect of a brush with so celebrated a foe as the young Prince

Ayub, whose early achievements are the theme of many an Afghan poet's verse. The march was through orchards, villages, across canals and streams, where temporary bridges and ramp had been constructed under the supervision of Colonel John Hills, our head Engineer, and his lieutenants, Blackwood, Osborne, Heath, and Maclean, who, although belonging to the sister scientific branch, the Artillery, placed their services at his disposal, and proved their skill in road and bridge-making. An enemy retiring after a defeat by this road would find it an easy task to greatly obstruct a pursuing foe, by scarping these ramps and by blowing up the bridges we have made. Our next march was but five miles, to Sunguri, across the river Argandab, and through a more difficult piece of country. The ford has a good sound bottom, and at this period of the year the water is not deep, while the width of the river is about forty feet. After reaching the opposite bank without any accident to man, horse, mule, or camel, we had to cross no less than six unbridged canals, where our small pontoon train was found of considerable assistance. Many of the ramps were made last year by General Biddulph, whose notes and itinerary of the route traversed have been of much use to us..

The valley through which we passed after crossing the Argandab is covered with villages, and full of trees of all kinds and luxuriant cultivation. The date, the palm, the mango, and the cocoa-tree abound, and some fine well-tended vines near the villages showed the industry of the inhabitants of this favoured oasis in the desert. We found the village people friendly, civil, and exceedingly communicative, and gleaned from some of the headmen intelligence which corroborated our reports of Ayub's movements.   These were to the effect that the Prince marched from Herat with the existing Herat force on the 20th of June last, his force consisting of 4000 regular infantry, 1000 cavalry, and 37 guns, besides a force of about 3000 irregular horse, which formed his advanced and rear guards. His artillery, we are told, is of various kinds, large and small, and principally of Afghan manufacture.   To these may be added one battery of European-made 4-pounder guns of the latest pattern.

Ayub has issued a proclamation to his troops, worded somewhat as follows :—'Soldiers of the true faith!—We march to the conquest of our city of Kandahar, now in possession of our bitter enemy the Feringhi, whom we will drive hence with our steel, and win back the capital of the south.   The garrison is weak, and we are strong ; besides, we are fighting for our homes and our land, and our foe is not prepared for us with either food or ammunition for a siege.   The bazaars of the city are full of English gold, and this shall be the prize of the conqueror when we have chased away the invader from our soil.   Let us march on, then, day by day, with the determination to conquer or to die!' Copies of this address were sent forward to the villages and the tribes between this place and Herat, with a view, no doubt, of inciting the Ghazis and fanatics to join in this modern crusade.   Ayub, we hear, was at Farah on the 21st of June, and on the 9th of July had pushed forward his cavalry outposts as far as Washin, where they were seen by the advanced horsemen of the Wali, who had effected his junction with us at Girishk on the 9th.   From Sunguri to Hoaz-i-Madad Khan is about fourteen miles, and the canal runs parallel to the road the whole way ; the road consequently is level, and crosses a wide plain, where our column was deployed into line by the General, and in that formation continued our march. The effect of this advance in line was most picturesque and gratifying to a soldier's eye. The artillery on either flank, protected by escorts of cavalry, the six companies of the 66th, 'the Old Berks,' in the centre, and the 1st Bombay Grenadiers and the 19th Bombay Infantry on either flank next the guns ; while the baggage-train and pioneers brought up the rear, the latter ready to move through and take the lead as soon as the column formation was renewed. Here and there along the plain we saw various kinds of game, and I managed to knock over some couples of teal, having taken the precaution of bringing with me a favourite little 12-bore gun, that has seen considerable campaigning out here, and which has helped not a little to assist our commissariat on the march. About a quarter of a mile in advance of our line a squadron of our cavalry covered our front, moving forward in extended order, and sending back messengers when anything of note was seen. As we moved along I could not avoid noticing and contrasting the difference as regards the number of officers between the 66th and the native regiments, the former having as a rule three officers to each company, and the latter about five officers to each regiment. This system of under-officering the Indian corps is one of the most pernicious things in the present *régime*, and is undoubtedly a matter that calls for reform. For years past army reformers have been pointing out the evil, and with no effect. If these two Bombay regiments go into action so short of officers their commanders will be placed in a position of considerable difficulty. If the military authorities do not and cannot be brought to see the necesssity of increasing the number of European officers with native regiments, they will only discover their mistake when some disaster has taught the lesson. I rode part of the day's march with the 19th Bombay Regiment N.I., under the temporary command of Major Walter Jacob, who came out here last winter from furlough, and the only other officers with the corps were Major Trench and Lieuts. Stevenson, Melville, and Steyner. Not one captain! The other native corps with our column is not much better off, as there are only Colonel Heathcote, Lieut.-Colonel Griffith, Captain Grant, and Lieuts. Hinde, Aslett, Daunt, and Whitby.

This day's march was fourteen miles, and soon after crossing the plains the road passes over a small kotal, the gradient nowhere being very steep. From the top of this pass we had a splendid view of the range of hills towards Kushk-i-Nakhud, and the panorama before us was very fine. To the north the splendid line of mountains was lit up by the bright morning sun, which was commencing to pierce through the mists rising from the valleys beneath. To the south range upon range of hills could be seen as far as the eye could reach. It was certainly the finest view we have seen even in this land of splendid scenery. The weather, too, was not quite so hot as on our first day's march. There was not a cloud in the sky, and the sun was doing its best to make up for lost time. After a brief halt of half an hour for refreshment and rest, and after we had thoroughly enjoyed the view, we descended the western side of the kotal, and after an uneventful march for the rest of our road we reached our camp at Hoaz-i-Madad Khan. General Burrows is a man who rises

early, and likes to finish his day's march about the time
that most Londoners are taking their breakfast. By
this means we avoid the hottest part of the day and the
danger of sunstroke. Every morning we are in the
saddle by six, and usually reach our fresh camping-
ground by 10.30 a.m. In order to start at that hour your
servants must be up at four a.m., and you have to be
dressed and out of your tent by half-past five a.m., or your
baggage will be all behindhand; which would mean that
your servants would have to perform the journey without the proper guard, thus running the risk of being cut
off and possibly cut up.

The following day we marched from our camping-
ground at Hoaz-i-Madad Khan to Kushk-i-Nakhud,
a distance little short of sixteen miles. No water was
obtainable during the march, although the road passes
over several watercourses. These, however, are dry
at this season. The march this day took us over an
undulating plain with but few villages, the soil seeming
to yield only an endless crop of stones, making it difficult for our artillery and baggage to get along. On
nearing our fresh camping-ground we left the river
some distance to our left, and ascended a steep slope
which led to our new camp at Kushk-i-Nakhud. Here
we received intelligence from General Nuttall and our
cavalry two days' march in advance of us. He reported
that he had effected a junction with the Wali at the
Helmund on the 9th inst., Colonel St. John being with
him at the time. We had every reason to believe that
the Wali Shere Ali would do his best to keep his
native contingents true to us, but events have proved
his inability to do so. From conversation I have had
with him I should say he was of more than ordinary

intelligence, and well versed in Afghan political affairs. He is a man of about fifty-six, with features of the Jewish type and a nose of a coarse aquiline cast, and an expression of countenance most pleasant and genial. He is very chatty and fond of gossiping freely about Afghan affairs, and talks much of the late Ameer, Shere Ali, and his son Yakub Khan. He is, perhaps, the only Sirdar of late years who ventured to give his namesake the Ameer, when consulted by him, his own honest opinion. His knowledge of Afghan affairs has been gained by his having, as he told me, acted as governor of every province of Afghanistan except Jellalabad. Like all governors, he has been accused of being hard and exacting ; but I believe this arose more from the necessity of his position towards his master than from his natural disposition.

Kushk-i-Nakhud, where we encamped on the 9th July, our cavalry and artillery having preceded us on the 7th, has been termed the 'Key to Kandahar,' and from its strategic advantages may well deserve that appellation. It is well supplied with water, and has every requisite for a good camping-ground for all arms of a small or large column. The camp at Kushk-i-Nakhud was pitched on a small tributary of the Argandab, and as nearly as possible forty miles from Girishk and forty-one from Kandahar, and I made the following notes of the surrounding country for a report to be sent back to General Primrose at Kandahar. Beginning at the Helmund and looking southwards the plain as far as Kushk-i-Nakhud becomes more undulating, and culminating at one point is changed into elevations which bound the southern side of the valley. These hills are rugged, barren, and abrupt, and though difficult would not be

impassable for any arm, but would certainly be awkward
for cavalry.   From here to Hoaz-i-Madad Khan the
plain smooths down by degrees, and here and there a
little cultivation may be seen, and at last develops into
continuous patches of green, making a vivid contrast to
the sandy belt around.   I noticed a number of remarkably fine vineyards, more especially on the lower slopes
of the hills, and also that these vineyards are all enclosed·
by a low stone wall; while the vines are planted in parallel
trenches, seven and eight feet asunder, each trench being
three feet wide and four feet deep, the excavated mould
making a sort of bank in the middle, thus affording a
most perfect entrenched cover for infantry skirmishing.
For some miles after leaving the Helmund the ground
on either side is an extensive stony plain, bounded on
the north by a large chain of hills running parallel to
the road, from which several spurs shoot outwards, approaching more and more to the road until they enclose
the valley of Kushk-i-Nakhud on the east and west.
Towards the centre of the valley, but a little to the right,
and about half a mile from the road, we saw the tomb
of some Mussulman saint or holy man, at the corner of
a large and well-kept vineyard, and easily marked on
account of three magnificent cypress trees, distinguish-
able a long way off by their dark green foliage and
massive shadows.   Away towards the eastern slope,
and under the shadow of the last eminence, we found
the ruins of an old fortification, and on the south side
of the road a square walled enclosure with walls twenty
feet high, while along the inner sides, and built against
them, was a row of round-topped Afghan huts, evidently·
showing that an outpost had once been here.   General
Burrows and Colonel Galbraith, who were with me, re-

minded Major Oliver and myself that it was at this same spot last year that our friends Malcolmson and Tanner, of the 2nd Beloochees, took up their position for the night, when they gave a most signal thrashing to the unruly marauding Zemindawar tribes, who attempted to take our troops by surprise. The only other salient feature of the valley I thought worthy of record was that in the various deep undulations of the plain or valley, so sharply defined, are large hollows, where considerable masses of cavalry might be ambushed and concealed until an enemy had actually arrived within charging distance. This I pointed out to the General, who agreed with me in thinking that this topographical feature materially detracts from the strategic importance of Kushk-i-Nakhud as a position to be held.

On the following morning I received an invitation from the General to ride over with him to confer with Brigadier Nuttall and the Wali at Girishk, and after a hasty *chota hazree*, or light breakfast, we jumped into our saddles, and with a small cavalry escort of some fifty lances were soon on the road, while orders were left that the column should follow us during the day. Meanwhile our chief had left orders that detached outposts and patrols should be sent up and down both banks of the river, to keep us *au courant* with any approach of the enemy, while our head-quarters would be outside Girishk. We had not gone more than two miles on our road when I noticed a small cloud of dust moving rapidly along the plain in our front, and we at once knew, or rather guessed, that this was a messenger or messengers bringing us tidings from the front. Our surmise proved correct, and in a few moments we could distinguish the well-known face of Mustaphi, the orderly of General Nuttall, who, with a couple of Lancers, came to us at a swinging gallop, bearing despatches of the utmost importance, and giving the following items of intelligence ; namely, the Wali, with his levies, was on the west bank of the river, that nearest to Kandahar, and, having reason to suspect his regiments of a design to desert *en masse*, he had sent to us, requesting immediate assistance in case of any treachery being practised, or any mutinous disposition being thought of. Colonel St. John, the Political Officer, had also written to the same effect, and matters seemed so urgent that I suggested that I should ride back to our camp to hasten the march of our column to support the Wali. General Burrows approved of my offer, and, as my horse was quite fresh, I undertook to deliver the message and overtake the General at his first halt at Khan-i-Chopan, nine miles five furlongs nearer to Girishk. I happened to have with me a little Arab entire horse, called ' Peter Simple,' whose galloping and staying powers have won me many a silver cup at our small garrison meetings, and I knew that Peter could do the distance under the time I mentioned to rejoin the General, so I and the orderly started at once.

On reaching the camp I gave the General's order, and, without dismounting, returned to overtake the escort, which had not gone more than a mile or two. We reached the west bank of the Helmund on the 10th, and found the Wali with his levies encamped there, while General Nuttall had chosen an excellent position on the Girishk side for his cavalry and artillery, with outposts up and down the river. Opposite Girishk the bank forms an elevated plateau commanding the valley, 175 feet above the river, while it slopes away somewhat like a glacis towards the town of Bost and Abbaza, affording admirable positions for defence and observation.　Bost, once a fortified city, still maintains its strategic importance, as it commands the entrance of the valley and the road to Kandahar, as well as the junction of the two rivers, the Doab and the Helmund.

On the 13th Colonel St. John, our Political Officer, obtained reliable information that a mutinous spirit pervaded the Wali's regiments, and that Ayub's emissaries had gained many adherents amongst these troops.　The following day, therefore, General Burrows issued an order that the Wali should shift his camp from the west bank, and move over the river in proximity to the English troops.　This order was given out on parade at daybreak on the 14th, and was the immediate signal for revolt. The ranks were broken in a moment, and a rush was made towards the Wali's artillery of six guns and the waggons containing the reserve ammunition.　The guns were limbered up, the horses harnessed to the waggons, and the mutineers, with loud shouts of vengeance against the Wali and his staff, commenced their march along the river bank in the direction of Herat, in order to meet Ayub.　While this was taking place messengers had been sent by the Wali to our advanced camp, about a mile up the river ; and General Nuttall was at once ordered by General Burrows to sound ' boot and saddle,' and with all available cavalry to intercept the mutineers, while a strong detachment of the 66th was held in readiness to pursue.　The idea was splendidly carried out by our dashing Brigadier, who most skilfully detached the 3rd Bombay Cavalry to make a circuit round the hills on the right, and then hold the Cabul regiments in check until our artillery came within their range.　In less time than it takes to tell the 3rd were across the ford, and speeding along the opposite bank at

a swinging gallop in a direction parallel to the mutineers. From the elevated plateau where our camp
was pitched we could see all that passed, and the excitement amongst our men was intense as the interval
between pursuer and pursued decreased. Meanwhile
Blackwood with his guns was not idle, and in less than
five minutes was dashing along the east bank with his
battery to choose a piece of vantage ground whence he
could shell the enemy, who now seemed to be moving in
great disorder, and more like an undisciplined mob than
a body of soldiers. The cavalry now wheel into line
and a troop are dismounted to act as skirmishers, every
third man holding three horses. A long ledge of rock
affords capital cover, and fair practice is made upon the
enemy's masses with the carbines of our horsemen, who,
under their leader, Major Currie, have well carried out
the Brigadier's orders. Meanwhile Colonel Malcolmson
with two squadrons of his corps, the Scinde Horse, is
manœuvring on the other flank, and has opened a cross-
fire which we can see is demoralising in its effect. 'Shall
I give them a shell or two, sir?' inquires Blackwood of
the General, who is riding with the battery. ' By all
means,' replies our chief; ' but be careful of our own
people.' The guns now take ' action right,' are in position, unlimbered, and ready for the word, and in another
moment a shell is dropped into the column of the mutineers, who still, however, manage to retire along the
plain, though harassed and galled on every side. Two
or three daring and most effective charges made by our
cavalry now compel them to form square, and this enables our shells to do more execution. For more than
an hour these tactics were repeated. A dropping carbine fire, an occasional shell from our Horse Artillery,

and now and then, when the ground admitted, a brilliant rush of turbaned horsemen upon the seething and broken masses of the unfortunate wretches, whose situation was now desperate. The knowledge that one or more of these regiments were part of the Cabul garrison last autumn, and probably shared in the massacre of our brave Cavagnari, took away, however, any feelings approaching to commiseration and pity, and more than one exclamation of delight came from our gunners as the firing went on, and became more deadly as we came to closer range. It was now a little after ten o'clock, and a combined charge, made by Colonel Malcolmson and Major Currie, broke up the enemy's columns, and, abandoning the guns and ammunition, '*Sauve qui peut!*' was the order of the day, each Sepoy racing for life, while hotly pressed by sabre and lance and an occasional shrapnel shell.

The loss we inflicted upon the mutineers was not particularly heavy, but this may be accounted for by the nature and configuration of the ground, which afforded cover as they retired, and caused much ammunition to be expended without much effect. However, our object was gained, as we recovered all the guns and ammunition, while getting rid of and dispersing a dangerous foe, whose defection in the actual hour of battle with Ayub would have been far more disastrous than their present flight to his standard.

On the day following these matters the General determined, to our terrible disappointment, to fall back upon his old position at Kushk-i-Nakhud; but whether this retrograde movement was made in obedience to 'higher authority' or not I cannot say. In all respects Abbaza, on the left bank of the Helmund, where we were encamped, is superior in strategic position to Kushk-i-Nakhud ; while commanding the principal ford and the road to Herat, and being exactly opposite to the town and fort of Girishk, where supplies are abundant, it offered many advantages as a dépôt and base. One reason for General Burrows' change of position and retirement upon Kushk-i-Nakhud may possibly have been the present state of the Helmund, and the facilities afforded to an advancing foe by the numerous fords, which at this season of the year are available for all arms. Still, the moral effect of a retrograde movement in the face of an advancing enemy, and above all an Asiatic enemy, is not to be gainsayed, and I thoroughly wish we had held our ground at Abbaza.

I have not said much of the loss inflicted on the mutineers by our people on the 14th, because we marched the next day, and I had too much to attend to to go into statistics ; but on the field where we overtook them I counted more than fifty bodies, and could see that in their hurried flight many of the wounded were placed on camels and carried away. I have since heard their loss estimated at 150. Five companies 66th came up soon after the action began, but what share they took in the affair I did not see, as I was continually carrying messages to and from the General. Our own loss on this eventful day consisted of only three of the 66th wounded and a few horses killed, while all the guns, baggage, and treasure of the Wali, were recovered.

IN KANDAHAR AFTER THE MUTINY—MILITARY SITUATION.

Kandahar, July 20.

SINCE I wrote to you, in perhaps a gloomy strain, on the 3rd of this month, the gravity of our situation has deepened in its tone, and I am fain to confess that an act not quite contemplated by the authors of the Afghan drama may at this moment be preparing by the enemy. Items of menace seem collecting on all sides, and in whatever direction we look the horizon indicates storm rather than calm. On the 14th inst. an event not wholly unforeseen came to pass on the banks of the classic Helmund, where some days previously General Burrows had overtaken and effected a junction with the Wali Shere Ali; and this event is ominous, being no less than a mutiny and desertion *en masse* of all Shere Ali's troops. The Wali, as doubtless you are aware, was sent forward by General Primrose as far as Girishk the moment we heard of Ayub's positive advance to Farah, and the former had with him somewhere about 4000 regular troops, including two Cabul regiments. I was present at their final parade here, and was much struck with their villainous, though, I must own, workmanlike appearance. They were fine, slashing, big, truculent-looking ruffians, dressed mostly after the Sepoy fashion, and armed principally with weapons of European make, while with them was a fairly-turned-out battery of six guns. Why these men were sent away to the very place where Ayub's proximity would tempt them to desert I cannot for my life understand, but the result has been most unfortunate to us and to Gen. Burrows, who not only loses 4000 of his command, but will probably see in a very few days this body of deserters swelling the ranks of his opponent. For some little time nothing was heard of Gen. Burrows' movements, as, for some strange and unaccountable reason, all telegrams were kept private except to the staff, and the consequences were that we lived entirely upon rumour.

The immediate cause of this desertion may undoubtedly be attributed to a proclamation addressed by Ayub to the former soldiers of Shere Ali Khan, in which their patriotism and love of plunder were alike invoked, while the sacking of Kandahar was held out as a reward. It is satisfactory to know that, although the principal portion of the Wali's men got away, all his artillery, stores, and treasure, were recaptured by our troops, while a couple of hundred of the mutineers were placed *hors de combat* by our lead and steel. The next day, however, General Burrows, to the great disappointment of his troops, retraced his steps to Kushk-i-Nakhud; a position, to my mind, in every way inferior to the Helmund, where his cavalry could have kept a watchful eye upon the various fords, which, even at this dry season, are not very easy to cross, at least under an enemy's fire. Another question, strongly mentioned in the letters I have this morning received from Kushk-i-Nakhud, is that of the harass and worry undergone by our troops in this march and counter-march. The 66th, who left here in the most enthusiastic spirits, in the hope and with the prospect of being soon 'yardarm to yardarm' with Ayub, are, my correspondent cannot deny, dispirited and disheartened at retiring before an enemy, even though that enemy greatly outnumbers them. Marching in Europe and marching in India are, I need not say, very different matters. In General Burrows' case, having but one road upon which to move, he would necessarily be much longer *en route* than if he could move on several. Large bodies of soldiers marching on one road are not supposed to do more than $2\frac{1}{4}$ miles an hour, which, of course, will include an occasional short halt ; and, consequently, I am told that when the head of his column moved off at six a.m. for a march of fifteen or sixteen miles, the rear-guard did not come in till late in the forenoon, at a time when the sun was dangerous to man and beast. If a night-march was chosen, the mules and mountain-batteries had to be considered; and much confusion resulted, I am informed, when there was no moon. My experiences of Indian and Afghan marches are anything but pleasant to look back upon, and the horrors of the hour or hour and a half preparing for the road will not easily be forgotten. The discordant bellowing of the overloaded camel, and the *débris* caused by an elephant who has quarrelled with his mahout, the screams of the native drivers, and the objurgations of the English soldier, make an *Inferno* worthy of a modern Dante. All these discomforts have our poor friends the 'Berkshires' suffered, and though they have not openly grumbled, yet, in mutual confidence, one Thomas Atkins has told his 'towny' beyond all doubt that he would rather have three days' fighting than twenty-four hours' marching, especially when he has to cross and recross the same road.

Kushk-i-Nakhud, where General Burrows now is, I know well, having sketched the ground on more than one occasion, and having been fortunate enough to be with Malcolmson when we thrashed the tribes there last year. It is as nearly as possible half-way between the Helmund and Kandahar, and exactly at the junction of the routes from Girishk and Hyderabad, by either of which, or by both, Ayub may advance as soon as he has, being now unopposed, crossed the Helmund. From what I remember of the place, it is simply a military rat-trap, where a clever and artful enemy knowing the country could give or refuse an attack at discretion. The ground when I saw it last year was cut up with small canals, watercourses, small but frequent stone walls, gardens, vineyards, and ruined houses, affording every facility for a sudden attack, and placing the attacking party, from the scattered nature of these obstacles, on a complete equality with the defenders.

Now, as I had something to do with the drilling and rifle practice of the Wali's troops, and helped in the tuition of many of his artillery officers, who doubtless are now using their lessons in the service of Ayub, I cannot but consider that this defection of 4000 well-armed, well-disciplined men, may be a serious matter to Burrows, with his now attenuated column of certainly not more than 1600 bayonets, 500 sabres, and ten guns ; while Ayub has now, I hear, 4000 regular infantry, 4000 Ghazis, and 4000 horsemen. If, as we believe, there are not wanting Ruski officers to point the Afghan guns and Ruski experience to choose position, we must allow that our present pilot at the helm of Indian affairs has somewhat miscalculated the tidal wave which now threatens to wipe out the Gundamuck Treaty, obtained with England's best blood and treasure.

Since the news of the defection of our quondam allies, I need scarcely tell you that every joint in our armour has been examined by our chief, who with Colonel Hills has minutely inspected the villages—our greatest danger, as we cannot afford to occupy them as outposts—the city, its suburbs, and, above all, the *arg*, or citadel. From the gap towards the west Kandahar, last evening, when the sun was setting, and the horizon around was bathed in gold and purple, almost realised to the eye those glorious Eastern landscapes which the pencil of Stansfield, Grieve, or Beverley, gave to the stage in spectacular dramas. The fading light, bathing in its warm tints the surrounding verdure and the glint of many small streams, shone upon the white walls of citadel and mosque, and imparted a fairylike grandeur to the scene.

We have been since the 15th hard at work pulling down and blowing up houses too near the ramparts, while the gates have been all strengthened by flanking works, and the trenches and gaps in each wall have been repaired. As I have already described at some length the actual capabilities, defensive and real, of the outer walls of the city, I will not dwell again upon them, though I may say that much has been improved since I wrote three weeks ago. But it is in the citadel that our Engineers have toiled, and here the result has exceeded expectation.

The citadel of Kandahar would be made short work of by a siege train, but from the calibre of such guns as Ayub is known to possess we need not apprehend any great disaster. The citadel is in a square form, each side being 800 feet long, and formed by a mud wall twenty feet high, and averaging a thickness of sixteen feet, while it is flanked by stoutish-looking bastions at each angle, as well as by intermediate bastions on each side (except the side facing south). Facing the city to the south, as you will see by my sketch, a duplicate of which goes home to ' W. O.' is the ' keep,' a building of solid granite, of considerable strength, and salient enough to form an hexagonal bastion, which bastion, in the olden days, was used as the principal entrance to the fort. On the walls is a parapet, which old reports tell us was once seven feet high by two feet in thickness, and carefully loopholed for matchlock men ; but this work we found required much renovation, and in addition to a good brick *revêtement* we have largely employed sandbags instead of loopholes. Our heaviest task, and where undoubtedly most malt refreshment was used by all ranks, the General giving the order for a double allowance to be served out, was on the east and west faces, where decay and ruin had added to the picturesque, but seriously detracted from the useful. The ' magic and the poetry in the ruined battlement,' so feelingly portrayed by the author of *Childe Harold*, did not strike us when we thought of a night assault with scaling-ladders by Ayub ; and a judicious employment of the spade, the trowel, and a little mortar, have made these ruins less æsthetic but more practical. Six entrances existed to the citadel when we commenced operations, but these have been diminished, while the remainder have been strengthened by strong flanking works.

In regard to supplies, I may say we have an abundance, as well as of ammunition, but water will have to be seen to. There are plenty of tanks, and we have fatigue parties all day and night employed in cleaning them. This water, as I before said, is supplied by the outside canals, and can be at any moment cut off. This may be our weak point. The inside of the citadel is made up of courtyards and squares, affording not only ample room for our garrison, but a means of final defence in case of assault. We have had them all repaired, and used for building hut and tent accommodation for our officers. Underneath, in case of bombardment, are a number of underground passages, called *tykhanas*, which we use for stores and ammunition. Our relative position to the city is as follows :—An extensive open space enclosed by the city wall and a second partition wall face to the north, while on the west side are a number of flat-topped houses and narrow alleys, which perhaps we may demolish. A large open square also lies to the south, which is defensible on all sides by rows of barracks of dome-like shape, used by us as Sepoy lines, and in part for hospital accommodation. On the east we have our commissariat enclosures, extending about 700 yards from the city walls, but unfortunately commanded by neighbouring houses. Such is our position, and if Burrows and his brigade could be at once recalled we could hold the town and citadel against all comers till reliefs were sent. Meanwhile we are anxiously looking out for news from Kushk-i-Nakhud, while working day and night in case of a reverse in *la fortune de la guerre.* Our troops, as I write this, are four guns, C B., 2nd B.; 5th B., 11 B., R. A., ten guns; the Poona Horse; 7th Fusiliers; 19th and 29th Bombay Native Infantry, and amount to a little over 3000 men, but reinforcements are daily expected. Sick-list small, and all in good spirits, and confident of result.

WITH GENERAL BURROWS—CAVALRY RECONNAISSANCE BEFORE THE BATTLE.

Camp Kushk-i-Nakhud, July 25.

I WROTE to you from this place on the 18th, exactly a week ago, and here we are still without any fighting, although, from intelligence just brought in, we learn that Ayub has crossed the Helmund at Hyderabad, and has been joined by a large gathering of Ghazis, whose impetuosity will compel him to attack us on the first opportunity. The mutiny among the Wali's troops has naturally given Ayub great confidence, and it is pretty well certain that his scouts and spies have made him thoroughly acquainted with our strength, or I should perhaps say our weakness. The loss we inflicted on the mutineers on the 14th was, I find, much greater than I at first set down in my letter to you of the 18th. Our spies report that forty-six bodies were buried by the villagers after our departure for this place. Altogether we placed, I should say, including the wounded, about 200 *hors de combat*, and amongst these were one colonel of artillery and two captains of the Cabul regiments. In saying that we have had no fighting I was wrong, as on Thursday last we sent out a cavalry reconnaissance, consisting of two guns E battery Royal Horse Artillery, with Captain Ramsay Slade and Lieut. Hector Maclaine, one squadron of the 3rd (Queen's Own) Light Cavalry with Major Corrie and Captain Willoughby, and a squadron of the 3rd Scinde Horse under Captain Gordon and Lieut. Monteith, in all a couple of guns and 200 sabres. Without much difficulty I succeeded in obtaining permission to accompany this force, and as all the officers I have named are special chums of mine, I looked forward to the expedition as a delightful relief to the enforced dull monotony of camp life at Kushk-i-Nakhud. As the service upon which we were going was important, and as there was every prospect of our coming into contact with some of Ayub's cavalry, known to be in our neighbourhood, Major Corrie, who was detailed to command the reconnaissance, requested that the troopers should be all picked men, well mounted, and good swordsmen.

A morning parade of both our cavalry regiments

was therefore ordered on the 20th, and the two corps turned out as strong as possible. Few prettier sights have I seen than the early morning parade of these smart native squadrons. Would that we had more of them! The men were splendid-looking specimens of the race from which they came ; long-limbed, lean, and sinewy, with not an ounce of superfluous weight, and a muscle well developed by constant lance and sword exercise in the *manège*. Their uniforms struck me as singularly neat and effective, handsome yet workman-like, and well fitting, but allowing full scope for every movement of the limbs and body. The men were, as a rule, uncommonly well mounted, and I was surprised to see such an evidence of breeding, as well as sub-stance, although few of the animals were up to much weight. Most of the horses had small, intelligent, well-set-on heads, sloping powerful shoulders, strong and wide hips, and backs as my friend Galbraith said, ' like feather beds.' Their thighs and gaskins were strongly developed, and their hips, though ragged, showed evidence of galloping power. The men, as a rule, ride well, depending, however, less upon balance than our English troopers, and riding more with the knees and calf, while I particularly noticed that they did not hang on to the bridle. They ride with a moderately short stirrup, with the knee upon the padded part of the saddle-flap, and rather in front of the stirrup leather, the heel well down and the foot pointing nearly straight forward. The weight of the body, I noticed, was well forward on the saddle—a great point in military equitation—with the fork close on the pommel. The bamboo lance in the hands of these fellows is a most deadly weapon, and their constant practice at tent-pegging has made them as certain of their mark as a well-aimed bullet from a rifle. Most of these men are far better swordsmen than our own troopers, whose cumbersome sabres, that won't cut and cannot point, with their heavy steel scabbards, are not to be compared with the native tulwar, whose keen, razor-like edge, enables its owner to lop off a head or a limb as easily as cutting a cabbage. Our English regulation scabbards should most certainly be altered, as they are heavy, difficult to clean, glisten in the sun and moonlight, blunt the sword, and rust if water gets inside, while they make such a rattle that a secret reconnaissance with them is impossible. These sowars have scabbards of solid brown leather, lined thinly with wood, such as is used for carbine buckets, and these are tipped with metal.

Another advantage our native cavalry regiments have over our European troopers is in the matter of equipment, which, for active service, crushes a light cavalry horse. Each sowar carries a spare flannel shirt, a pair of woollen socks, one clothes brush, one boot brush, a towel, sponge, and rubber, with a knife and spoon, while the whole of this kit does not weigh four pounds. All these articles are carried in the wallets, while the cloak replaces the valise on the cantle. The horses have no blankets, and as they receive no grooming but what can be given with a good wisp, they are well able to stand rain and cold. I was much pleased at the manner in which these men drilled, and more particularly in respect to their dismounting to skirmish on foot. The men were formed in squadrons of 100 rank and file each, formed in single rank, and each squadron was told off into four divisions and into fours. The divisions and the sections of fours always consisted of the same men. No. 3 of each section of fours held the other three horses, two on his right and one on his left, an arrangement which allowed him to gallop quickly to the rear out of fire when the squadron dismounted for action. Each squadron and each division had its own leader, and in dismounted service the squadron leader was on foot with his men, while the senior division leader remained mounted with the led horses.

As soon as the parade was over I was sent for to go over to General Burrows' tent, and there I found two of our native spies, who had just come in from the Helmund, where they had been able to carefully observe a body of Ayub's cavalry reconnoitring the roads and villages. These men had, however, a narrow escape of being caught by a troop of the Afghan cavalry, which, coming from an opposite direction to their main body, appeared suddenly at the angle formed by two roads leading from the Helmund to Kushk-i-Nakhud. The spies, Hashim and Abdulla, are Ghilzais, and were formerly in the service of our quondam friend, Padishah Khan, who sent them to us as useful messengers and trustworthy adherents. The Ghilzais are, as doubtless you are aware, the best soldiers the country can produce, and the few we have been able to enlist have certainly remained true to their salt. Both Hashim and Abdulla are splendid runners, and to this accomplishment they undoubtedly owe their lives, as they were chased by half-a-dozen Afghan horsemen for more than a mile. Fortunately they were able to lead their pursuers over some very broken ground, along the banks of the river, until they came to a place where the banks were steep, and so scarped that horses could not descend. A friendly piece of rock jutting out over the stream afforded cover,

and Abdulla, who is a capital shot, resting his short
rifled carbine upon a piece of stone, took a steady aim,
and brought down the leader of the party. Meanwhile
Hashim handed his loaded weapon to Abdulla, receiving
the empty one in exchange to re-load, and by this means
a rapid and continuous fire was kept up, and was so
effective that two more of the enemy were place *hors
de combat.* Hashim and his comrade now shouted an
imaginary word of command as loudly as possible :—
'Run along the bank and take them in the rear!'—and
this was so well done that the pursuers, although reinforced by several more horsemen, imagined that they
had been led into an ambuscade, and hastily retired,
leaving their dead comrade but carrying off their
wounded. Our scouts now cautiously approached the
body of the dead Afghan, and fortunate it was that they
did so, as a leather despatch-bag was found upon him
containing papers, which have now been handed to
General Burrows. These I may not give in detail, but
I may tell you they are of great importance, being
despatches from Ayub to chiefs now in our camp!
Not being able to read did not prevent Abdulla and
Hashim from guessing that the papers were important,
and they at once secured their prize and came back here
in a marvellously short space of time.

This report was to the effect that Ayub's advanced
guard had crossed the Helmund in force on the 20th,
and that on the day following 500 of his cavalry re-
connoitred as far as Sanghar, fourteen miles this side of
the river. There they met a small body of Ghazis, who
reported that 4000 horsemen were on their way to join
Ayub. These items of news were gleaned from the
villagers, who had been requisitioned to provide supplies

for the Herat forces. On the 21st Ayub's main body crossed at Hyderabad, and encamped on the east bank, and 500 horsemen were sent on to reconnoitre our present position.

This news decided our chief to organize and send out our cavalry reconnaissance, and arrangements were at once made to carry out the necessary orders. On the 22nd, at two a.m., we paraded in light order, but each man carrying two days' biscuit ration and a double supply of ammunition. We moved out of camp by the fitful and somewhat misty rays that came now and then through the flying scud which a high wind was driving before it. We sent on a small advanced guard under the guidance of Hashim, who, with Abdulla, had requested permission to come with us. Our guns were in the centre, and, as the result proved, were of much use to us. After a long march we halted about four miles from Sanghar, and, posting vedettes, allowed the men to prepare their breakfast in a splendid mango tope, which not only gave us excellent cover, but admirable shelter from the hot morning sun. In half an hour more we were again in the saddle, and had not proceeded more than a mile when we saw with our field-glasses a large body of horsemen moving slowly across the plain. Instantly wheeling to the left, our commander obtained the cover of a small hillock, intervening between us and the enemy, who came on in perfect unconsciousness of our approach. At the end of the hillock was a deep and wooded ravine, where the rocks were strewn about in a manner that would have rendered artillery impossible, and to avoid this we had to make a rather wide détour, which, however, brought us suddenly in sight of our foes, and within carbine range of them. They at once threw out a cloud of skirmishers, who advanced across the plain, firing rapidly and randomly from the saddle. Major Corrie replied to this move by checking the enemy most neatly, as he made our troops dismount and skirmish on foot in the manner I have described. We remained with our main body ready to charge should opportunity occur, while our guns moved rapidly to the right to gain a crest of the hill, which would command and enable them to enfilade the Afghans. Ping! ping! ping! went the enemy's bullets, all out of range, as they advanced at a walk, while our fellows, taking advantage of every bush and stone, got nearer to their quarry, while we could see now and then a wounded man or horse taken to the rear. Meanwhile, in the front of their main body, composed of about 300 horsemen, rode a tall officer, mounted on a grey horse of remarkable size and splendid action. With our glasses we could see him snatch the standard, or *guidon*, from the standard-bearer, and evidently exhort his men to follow him. At this juncture a shell, well aimed from Slade's gun, dropped within a yard or two of the front rank. This was enough, for the Afghan line of skirmishers wheeled suddenly round like one man and galloped madly to the rear. They seemed to demoralise the main body, for they in turn went 'fours about,' apparently without any word of command, and cantered towards the river, where, fortunately for us, Slade's good glasses enabled us to see a large body of infantry, and several guns in position. We managed, during the hurried retreat of the enemy, to drop one or two shells into the column, but the killed or wounded, if any, were carried away, and the only trophies we obtained were some tulwars dropped by wounded men. As nothing more could be done, and the day was getting towards evening, we were ordered to collect stragglers and march for our camp, which we reached without casualty at nine p.m., having been twenty-one hours in the saddle.

I need not tell you that we daily expect a battle, and that day and night a vigilant look-out is kept. Still I regret our former position on the Helmund. There we commanded the only ford near, and could not be outflanked or taken in the rear, as is possible in this place. As I write, news has come in that two of our men, sowars of the Scinde Horse, have been surprised and killed on outpost duty. This looks like business and close quarters.

CHAPTER III.

THE BATTLE AND DEFEAT OF MAIWAND.

Kandahar, July 30.

How our fellows frustrated the attempt of the Wali's troops to carry off the guns and ammunition you have already heard, and you also know the severe loss we inflicted on them ; but I may tell you now that fully 2000 of these mutineers, with their arms and ammunition, succeeded in getting away to swell the ranks of Ayub Khan, who was then at a place called Lar, two days' march from Girishk. This important acquisition to the Khan, and equivalent loss to us, enabled him to advance with greater confidence to our vicinity. Day by day, through our patrols, our scouts, and our spies, we heard of the Prince's cavalry at Bakwa, Dilarum, Shorah, and other points on the road from Farah to Girishk. The Afghan cavalry were, indeed, well handled, and in whatever direction our patrols were sent, there they were sure to come across some of those marvellous horsemen, whose ubiquity astounded our reconnoitring parties. From Daman, Lar, and Zarak, and many places further north, their horses were foraged and their supplies were obtained. We commenced our retreat upon Kushk-i-Nakhud on the 15th, and great was the dissatisfaction amongst all ranks at the retrograde movement, which we believe is not wholly due to the opinions of our chief, but rather to suggestions made by the Viceroy.

You must bear in mind that the advance to the Helmund was accompanied by much privation and discomfort, yet undertaken and carried out with the greatest enthusiasm by the artillery, cavalry, 66th, and the native corps, who neither murmured at the heat, the short rations, or the night marches. At Girishk we had a very strong position, overlooking the river, where on three sides the hill was scarped, and on the fourth very steep. Supplies, so far from being scarce, were in abundance, and fish and game were to be had in plenty through the guns and rods of our chickarees. Besides, when we retired from the river Ayub was halted two days' march only from us, and it was only, we now learn, on the news of our retreat that he was emboldened to come on. We left the Helmund, as I said, on the 15th, and five days later its banks were lined by Afghan cavalry, while their standards floated in the breeze at all the fords we had abandoned. On the 20th Ayub halted his main body on the Helmund, and, after three days' preparation (three days in which we could have attacked him at advantage) he crossed the river on the 23rd, twelve miles north of Girishk, and took up a position at the village of Hyderabad, where he was joined day by day by a large proportion of the discontented tribes, tempted by our retreat and the prospect of the sack of Kandahar. Affairs were now assuming a warm aspect. Ayub's cavalry, vastly outnumbering ours, were constantly met around the country, and several very smart skirmishes took place between the Afghan horse and our own Scinde regiments. These outpost affairs might have taught us our weakness in *l'arme blanche*, as on more than one occasion our people were surprised, and only managed to get off with loss in men and horses. On the 22nd some of our Scinde Horse were surprised, and lost two of their number. On the day following the enemy's horsemen came reconnoitring in immediate proximity to our camp, but on the 24th we managed to catch them *en flagrant délit*, and after a pretty little affair, of which I sent you an account, made an example of our rivals.

General Burrows meanwhile again struck his camp on the 19th, and moved three miles nearer to the enemy, who, however, remained perfectly stationary until the 22nd, when his ranks were augmented to about 13,000 fighting men by the addition of the predatory villagers of the district. On the 23rd Ayub had pushed forward his horsemen to Sanghar, not more than fourteen miles from our camp, and at last General Burrows seemed to apprehend danger, for he shifted and then entrenched his camp, and made use of the enclosed buildings I have mentioned to shelter his sick, baggage animals, and stores. Our position was now as follows:—Kushk-i-Nakhud, on the main road from Girishk to Kandahar, and as nearly as possible thirty miles from the former place ; the village is upon a plain, much cut up with watercourses, vineyards, and stone walls, while it is masked and commanded on three sides, east, west, and north, by spurs of hills running from the main chain. By crossing the Helmund at Hyderabad Ayub was enabled to march unseen and unheard of behind the spur of hills to the north of our camp, and while our outposts were watching the main road his cavalry was pushing forward behind the treacherous screen of hills which covered his advance, and which, through a friendly opening at the angle of the plain, enabled him to debouch on to the plain and to deploy his squadrons on our right flank. According to Colonel St. John's information, Ayub on the 23rd was still at Hyderabad, but between

that date and the 27th he had unseen worked his way
steadily on the northward slopes of the range of hills
bounding our plain until he reached Maiwand, only three
miles from our camp at Kushk-i-Nakhud, whence he
was enabled to deliver his attack, and with such fatal
result.

I have alluded to the deep undulations of the ground
on our right flank and also in our front, and I have
explained that in these hollows, admirably suited to give
complete cover to whole regiments or batteries, Ayub
was enabled to mass and conceal his columns until the
time came to strike upon our front and flanks, to enfilade our people with his superior armament, and to turn
our flank with his desperate charges of horsemen. On
the morning of the 23rd we had a severe brush with the
advanced guard of the enemy, who pushed his horsemen,
supported by two guns and 2000 infantry. Our cavalry
and a couple of guns went at them in fine style, and as
they evidently wanted more to ' feel ' us, they retired in
capital order, skirmishing and firing as we drove them
back.

On the morning of the 27th inst. Ayub's horsemen
were reported as being advancing towards our camp
from the direction of Maiwand, and through the valley
or opening in the hills of that name. Bearing in mind
the description I have given you, you will see that
as they debouched from this valley on to the plain
their left would somewhat outflank our right wing, and
enable their artillery to bring an enfilade fire upon us.
Without being taken by surprise, I may at once say that
on the previous evening no one in our camp had the
smallest idea of the proximity of our antagonists, whose
flank march screened by the hills to the north showed

strategy of no mean order, while on our side the unguarded portal and the pathway left on our right are faults that have yet to be explained. I had not slept during the night, and about an hour before daylight I was taking advantage of the cool morning breeze to refresh myself in front of my tent, when Galbraith and another 66th officer came over to join me. We discussed the position of our camp, and noticed how admirably it was situated for defence had we double the number of troops to enable us to place entrenched outworks at the head of the valley leading to Hyderabad. Even while we were speaking it is more than possible that Ayub's skirmishers were silently creeping along the valley and seeking cover in the vineyards to their right. Of this I am tolerably convinced, as from these vineyards later on came a galling fire of rifles as well as artillery.

As the day began to break orderlies were sent round to get the men under arms, scouts having come in to say that patrols had been seen on the hills near Maiwand, and also to the left of the valley. Our regiments were accordingly formed in contiguous columns, and breakfast was served out to them in the ranks, while the cavalry were dismounted and the infantry piled arms to eat their frugal meal. Other messengers now came in to say that Ayub's advanced guard had occupied Maiwand.

General Burrows at once decided to advance and meet them, and at 8.30 a.m. two of our guns and the 3rd Scinde Horse were sent out to feel them, and by nine o'clock were engaged in an artillery duel with a portion of Ayub's forces. Our position, had we remained where we were encamped, was, I believe, a much stronger one than that we subsequently took up; as the undulating ground in our front gave every cover and shelter from our fire, while their guns, superior in number, were posted on the heights, in front and on our flank, and told with terrible effect upon our troops. Still our own guns made capital practice as the Afghan cavalry advanced, and succeeded for a time in checking them; but the enemy continued to push forward, and as they came out of the mouth of the valley Ayub deployed regiment after regiment into line, showing six batteries of well-handled guns in front, seven regiments of infantry in centre, three others in reserve, 2000 cavalry on their right, 400 mounted men and 2000 Ghazis and irregular infantry on left, more cavalry and infantry in reserve, and guns judiciously placed upon every piece of vantage ground on the slopes of the hills around.

Meanwhile our own formation was as follows :—Five of our guns, commanded by Major Blackwood, were placed at intervals along our front; while on our extreme left we had five companies of Jacob's Rifles, under Colonel Mainwaring, and next to them the 66th, under my poor friend Galbraith, who, with his majors, Oliver and Ready, had been identified since boyhood with the regiment. Then on our right we had the 1st Bombay Grenadiers, commanded by Colonel Anderson, as popular a leader as ever served; while our slender force of cavalry were drawn up in rear of our line and told to keep as much as possible out of fire. Major Currie commanded 300 sabres of the 3rd Light Cavalry, while Colonel Malcolmson had charge of 200 sabres of the 3rd Scinde Horse. In front of our line rode General Burrows, attended by Colonel St. John, the Nawab Hasan Ali Khan, Major Blackwood, commanding R.A., and a small staff; with whom were Captain M'Math, Brigade-Major; Captain Harris, D.A.Q.G.; Brigadier Hogg, commanding Cavalry Brigade, with his brigade-major, Hogg, and his orderly-officer, Lieut. Monteith.

Our position, I must honestly own, was faulty in the extreme; but it was made worse by our slight entrenchments and the old Afghan outpost, of which a handful of resolute men could have made a second Houguemont. Kushk-i-Nakhud, a ruined village, but offering a splendid *point d'appui* in front of our camp, should have been held by the native regiments, as the place could have been entrenched in an hour, and was flanked on the right by the ruined Afghan fort of which I have already spoken, and which in its turn was again commanded by the spur of hill on our right, and which coign of vantage, had we posted a couple of guns there, would have commanded the road to Kandahar and secured us at least a safe means of retreat.

What followed I will briefly relate, although it is impossible not to draw a parallel between our fearful disaster and that of Isandlana,—the same overweening confidence in our invincibility, the same contempt of an unknown foe, the same attempt at scientific strategy, when the simplest old-fashioned British tactics would have won the day.

At half-past eight the enemy's cavalry, accompanied by some guns, made a feigned demonstration upon our right front, which would have been perfectly innocuous had we remained in our first position. Unfortunately, however, the *ruse* was not detected; and our already too weak force was further attenuated by the despatch of two guns and a squadron of our cavalry, which were drawn away by the enemy's retreat and eventually captured. Now, as at an early hour on the morning of this most fatal Tuesday, I took the messenger round to Colonel St. John's tent with the important news that Ayub's advanced guard had seized and occupied Maiwand, only three miles from our camp at Kushk-i-Nakhud, I naturally concluded that immediate orders would be given to further entrench by earthworks and abattis the not unfavourable position we held, and which consisted of the old Afghan outpost building as a sort of citadel and shelter for our baggage, stores, and wounded, flanked on our right by the range of hills running from the Kandahar road due north, and assisted by the old Afghan fort on the sides sloping westward into the plain. This position was further strengthened by the few earthworks thrown up by our Sappers, whose commanding officer was most anxious to complete the works he had so cleverly begun. Instead of this the General at once gave the order to advance against the enemy; and quitting our fairly good position, our cavalry—consisting of the 3rd Bombay Light Cavalry, two squadrons of the 3rd Scinde Horse, and 200 of the E B battery—pushed on, regardless of all the true principles of war, to the *cul-de-sac* prepared for them by the enemy, who in enormous force was feeling his way westward along the slope of the hills.

It was now about 11 o'clock, and we had been under fire for a couple of hours, but the range was too great for this artillery duel to be effective on either side. At the commencement of the action we were tolerably well posted, having, as I before remarked, the village of Kushk-i-Nakhud as a sort of advanced redoubt in our front, with our right resting on and protected by the old Afghan fort and the hills between it; while on our left was an open plain gradually increasing in undulation until it reached our village, and where our cavalry could have been employed with good effect. Here, with our camp entrenched, we could have fought an enemy ten times our strength. Our guns, well posted on the slopes on our right, would have commanded the main road to Kandahar, while at the same time they would have enfiladed any body of the enemy advancing across the plain. Our cavalry, under Nuttall, should have operated on the left, where the ground, although stony in parts, was practicable for cleverly handled horsemen.

All these advantages were, however, for some inexplicable reason, thrown away, and the order was given for our line to advance and support the two guns and squadron which had been already lured into the narrow valley leading to the Maiwand plain. Here, again, an obvious error was committed, for our rifled nine-pounders, although few in number, had a superiority in range and accuracy of fire over the smooth-bores of the Afghan artillery, and this was all thrown away when we had decreased the range from 2000 to 1000 yards. While the enemy's concentrated fire now began to tell upon our men and horses, our own rifles made splendid practice upon the dense masses of Ayub's infantry. This was at once noticed by the Sirdar, who, pushing forward some bodies of Ghazi irregulars to distract our attention, led some regiments in column to within three quarters of a mile of the left of our camp (where our cavalry should have been), and then, taking advantage of the undulating ground when sufficiently near to us, suddenly deployed his men into line, and appeared upon the crest of the ridge.

General Burrows at once saw this manœuvre, but too

late to counteract its effects. ' Tell Colonel Mainwaring to throw back his left companies, or he will be
outflanked, and send him a troop of the Scinde Horse in
support,' said the General, as he shut his field-glasses
and galloped to the right of our line, where another
danger was to be encountered. Ayub, seeing how
heavily our rifles told upon his centre, began to push
back our right by swarms of skirmishers, continually fed
by supports and assisted by three of his lighter guns,
which he managed, under cover of his infantry fire, to
place in position upon the ridge we should have occupied on our right. The contest was now fiercely
maintained on both sides. Two of our guns were taken
and retaken, while a desperate stand was gallantly made
by Jacob's Rifles, but they were forced back, step by
step, by the weight of superior numbers, until one of our
guns was permanently captured and turned upon our
people. But this was not effected without one of the
bloodiest hand-to-hand struggles it has ever been my lot
to witness, or, I may say, to share in, as my duty called
me to that part of the field at this juncture, and I only
escaped death by the daring and devotion of poor young
Osborne, who fought his gun to the last. Even then I
noticed that many of the enemy were killed within
twenty yards of the muzzles of our guns.

Though this withering fire covered the space of
ground in our immediate front with the dying and the
dead, and though the thirsty sand became red with blood,
still these desperate *enfans perdus* came recklessly on.
Their plan of selecting the tallest and bravest fanatics as
standard-bearers served them on this occasion in good
stead, and our men were literally carried off their feet by
the desperate rush. In the *mêlée* Osborne had been till

now dismounted and fighting his guns on foot, but seeing Major Blackwood and myself surrounded by half-a-dozen Ghazis slashing at us with their tulwars, he called to his orderly for his horse, a big and powerful charger, flung himself into the saddle, and dashed to our rescue, and where the fight seemed the thickest. The impetus of his charge burst through the living wall of turbaned swordsmen surrounding us, and as Osborne slashed his way through the mass our gun was limbered up, and hurriedly galloped two hundred or more yards to the rear, where, upon a knoll, it reopened fire with effect, while a random shot struck down the young gallant gunner as he was wheeling round to rescue the other gun.

Meanwhile the 66th, in our centre, had alternately been ordered to advance and lie down, thus pushing back the enemy, and then escaping the *mitraille* that rained from the Afghan shells. In the rear of the centre of their line rode Galbraith, keeping his men well in hand, and giving now and then a cheering word to his gallant fellows, who were moving as steadily as if on parade.

' Spare your ammunition, my lads!' cried the Colonel, conspicuous, unfortunately, on an iron-grey Arab, and dressed in his full uniform. ' Fire low and steadily, and presently the cold steel !' A sudden charge upon our right centre was now checked by Captain Ready, commanding the flank company, by his bringing up his ' left shoulders ' and delivering a volley at 200 yards. With great difficulty Ready prevented his men, elated by success, from dashing after the Afghan infantry sent to support their horsemen. But this success was, unfortunately, but a momentary one. When our centre was again ordered to advance, it should have been evident to a practised eye that the retreat of the enemy in our front was merely a *ruse* to lure us on to a position where our flanks could be threatened on either side. Meanwhile, as our centre moved forward, our right and left flanks were weakened and compelled to fall back, and our position became that of a two-sided angle, the apex being the 66th, and the sides the native regiments, already terribly galled from the artillery which Ayub had succeeded in placing on the hills right and left. These heights were now bristling with armed men, and a heavy fire was opened upon us from every salient point (which we ourselves should have occupied and held). It was to no purpose that General Burrows now threw out flanking parties to skirmish up the hills and to dislodge the enemy, who, well supported by his guns in good position, could not be driven away. Moving swiftly along the ridges the irregulars of the enemy suddenly swooped down upon our baggage-guard, holding the walled enclosure of which I have spoken, and consisting of one company from each infantry regiment. Suddenly appearing in great numbers, these Ghazis fell furiously upon our rear guard, and for a time our people, being suddenly assailed, were in considerable disorder. But the presence of the company of the 'Old Berkshires' fortunately brought back the native troops to a sense of duty, and restored the confidence which for a little while had forsaken the Grenadiers and Jacob's Rifles. Roberts and Lynch, 66th, rallied their men so energetically that for a time our baggage and stores were saved, although more than 100 men were killed and wounded, including Captain Roberts, who fell sword in hand over the bodies of half-a-dozen fanatics he had cut or shot down.

It was now two o'clock, and the British centre remained unshaken, but at the same time unsupported on either flank. Galbraith was still encouraging his men and keeping them steady with their fire, which we could see told with effect upon the Afghan centre, which was now nearly pierced. Within five minutes the Colonel had received three bullets from the rifles of the foe, who seemed to mark him out for special attack. One rifle ball had cut the crupper of his saddle, and another had passed through his horse's mane, close behind the ears. I had at this time been sent by General Burrows with a message to Colonel Galbraith, just as his adjutant had called his attention to these shots, and was begging him to dismount. Galbraith replied, ' No, my dear fellow ; duty tells me my men should see their colonel, as they always see him on parade, mounted and conspicuous, not only to his men but to the enemy.'

I have said how Ayub saw the weak point in our armour, and how he at once brought round a couple of guns to enfilade us (supported by his horsemen) on our right, and how his picked regiments of infantry had been moved up behind the cover of these guns to make a dash upon our weakest flank. Galbraith, early on the day of this hour of tarnished glory to our arms, had seen this error on our part, and had begged to be allowed to send a couple of companies of his regiment and two guns to hold this important point. But all was in vain. The ground we should have held was abandoned to the foe, and our men were assailed from the very point where we should have galled and thrown back the enemy. While this manœuvre was being carried out by Ayub, our cavalry and artillery — being, I must own, somewhat badly posted—suffered severely, while

Galbraith, an officer of much Indian experience, made his men again lie down to avoid the terribly hot fire, which now from rifle and smooth-bore, from nine and twelve-pounders, poured its shells upon us. At this time, half-past two, all I could see of our position was as follows :—Our cavalry and artillery were doing but little, being in both cases terribly outnumbered by the enemy, who rained shot and shell upon us until the horrors of Sedan seemed again on a smaller scale to be revived. We had been lured from our entrenchments ; not alto-gether, however, by the impetuosity of our young troops, but I must say by the express orders of our own General, who, brave as a lion under fire, and excellent to perfec-tion as a despatch writer and an office man, was certainly not the man for this terrible crisis.

'Oh, for one hour of Roberts !' cried out one of the subalterns, as, with boy-like *insouciance*, he lit a cigarette and felt his six-shooter and his sword. 'We are in a mess ; but a man who could handle troops like old Oakes, or Sayer, or Val. Baker, would soon get us out of this rat-trap !'

'Right you are, Jemmy!' said his comrade ; 'it's low water with us now !'

'Come, my lads, limber up, and move her ten or twelve paces to the right ; let's have another round or two before they come at us !'

Thus said my little friend, a gunner, whose name I will not mention, as he is now missing, and we hope may come in.

About three p.m., the enemy having lured our General on as far as he conceived necessary, delivered, I must say with judgment, his final attack. The 66th alone of all our force had from the first not only held their own, but had pushed steadily on, piercing like a Spartan or Theban phalanx the clouds of horse and foot that yelled and shouted on all sides. Galbraith on the gallant grey horse, his helmet dashed off by the warded blow of a tulwar, whose owner paid dearly for the abortive stroke, cheering on his men with the same full ringing voice that encouraged the regimental pack of beagles to follow up 'poor pussy' in English country quarters; long 'Tom Oliver,' master of the revels at many a festive gathering in English or Indian garrison; 'Ready, always Ready,' as he was called by Sir Hope Grant; and all the young subs whose highest ambition was to live and die in the 'Berkshires;'—all were forcing the gallant old corps, 'shoulder to shoulder' and 'touch to touch,' through the dense mass of turbaned Ghazis and the lurid light of blazing gunpowder that lit up the terrible slopes from which so few would return.

Once more General Burrows did all that a defeated man could do to retrieve the day, and had one more English battalion been near at hand fortune might have changed to our side. Galbraith and Oliver, finding themselves alone with their four companies on this terrible ridge, swept from right to left with thirty guns, pointed and placed I may say by no Afghan gunners, saw that their only chance was to retire upon what had been our camp. In the midst of a *feu d'enfer* and a galling fire from 4000 rifles, fortunately ill aimed and worse sighted, these splendid 400 bayonets commenced to retire, and this was done by the old manœuvre of alternate wings, the Colonel commanding one and Major Oliver the second. Twice did Ayub's cavalry come at them. Twice did those cheery accents ring out, 'On the centre sections! form square! Prepare for cavalry!'

'Ready!' 'Ay!' Ready it was, and as the sheet of flame glistened forth from the low line of bronzed level tubes many a proud and glittering horseman bit the dust, and gnawed the earth in death agony in front of those adamantine squares! Twice was I sent by the General to the 66th, and twice had I barely time to gallop to the bristling shelter of our 'Berkshire bayonets,' as the Colonel jocosely called my haven.

But the day wore on, and our men were falling fast. Our whole force was now ordered (too late) to retreat towards our camp; the left, where Jacob's Rifles and our two guns were posted, was in complete disorder, and the 66th alone checked the fury of our assailants, but the skeleton companies of the fine old corps alone came back. Galbraith fell leading on the rear guard while covering a glorious retreat against overwhelming odds. Oliver was badly hit. Ready was struck in the side, and a dozen more are still missing, whom we dare scarce hope to see again. After we had fallen back about half a mile from the fatal ridge the enemy further developed his attack, advancing not only on our flanks but on all sides, although the rifles of the 66th still told heavily. But a force held in reserve came suddenly from behind the hills, and, being supported by the Ghazis in front and by Ayub's infantry on our left, Jacob's Rifles, which were guarding that flank, were completely rolled up, and retreated in rear of the 66th, carrying in their rush the band and colours of the regiment.

'For Heaven's sake, my children, form square and steadily!' cried out Colonel Anderson of the Grenadiers. 'Keep steady, and it will all be right,' he added in Hindostani.

But this was too late. 'Too late!' The Grenadiers

scarcely hear their leader's cry. They are borne back by the wave of battle and the shields of the Ghazis upon the still unbroken ranks of the 66th, whose colonel was last seen galloping the gallant grey upon the swords and bayonets of the Afghan corps in his front! Oliver, the major, still remained, and as we were borne away by the tide of our horsemen, who now swooped down upon us, we could see the remnants of the 66th, Jacob's Rifles, and the Grenadiers, making a desperate rally in the walled enclosure where we had left our sick and stores (fortunately moved early in the action). Our infantry had now become separated from the cavalry and artillery, and were followed into the walled enclosure and the vineyards, where some desperate hand - to - hand fighting took place. The cavalry, which had been so uselessly decoyed away in the morning, now came back, but could do nothing to aid us, as the retreat had become general, and only our remaining guns and horsemen were enabled to keep any sort of formation. Of the horrors of that night I will tell you to-morrow, if my arm will allow.

AFTER THE BATTLE—HORRORS OF THE NIGHT RETREAT.

Hospital, Kandahar, July 31.

IN my hurriedly written letter of yesterday I endeavoured to describe what I saw during our disastrous engagement of the 27th, and in my version I ventured to point out the causes which, in the opinion of those who were actors in the scene, led to the terrible disgrace thrown upon our arms, a reverse so discreditable

to our military history perhaps unparalleled in army records. To say that our brigade was 'annihilated,' for
such was the term employed in the first telegrams sent
away from here, would perhaps be somewhat of an exaggeration, but I may distinctly say that never was a
defeat more crushing or more complete, and it is impossible to deny the bitter fact that from first to last we
were out-manœuvred by Ayub, who not only chose a
position we should have occupied, but lured us from the
one we had taken into an ambush, where his guns had
the best of ours, where his cavalry had the advantage,
and where his infantry were better handled than our own.
These are sad and humiliating truths, but it would be
idle and useless to try to extenuate their existence.

At about half-past three o'clock in the afternoon our
defeat was complete, and the survivors of our brigade—
that is to say, the remnants of our three infantry and
two cavalry regiments—were hurled into a confused mass
of fugitives, endeavouring to gain the shelter of the
walled enclosure, where in the morning our sick,
wounded, and stores were placed. This place I have
described to you as an oblong walled enclosure, about
80 yards long by 60 broad, and with stoutly built mud
walls some 20 feet in height. Here Major Oliver made
an attempt to rally his men, while General Burrows, with
great gallantry, tried to collect and form the handful of
our Sepoy regiments who had not fled from the field.
Here Colonel Anderson, of the Grenadiers, made a
desperate effort, with half-a-dozen brave fellows of his
corps, to hold the gateway to the enclosure; while
Captain Dick, who had charge of the commissariat
stores, had made a sort of *banquette* of wooden cases and
casks, from which our men were enabled to fire over the

walls. To this piece of forethought I believe we owe the short and partly effective stand we made at this building, for it enabled us to check the advance of our pursuers, while the scattered *débris* of our battalions were making some formation inside. Here at least were the colours of the 66th, and those of the Bombay Grenadiers, still intact, and here were Colonel Mainwaring, Colonel Griffiths, Major Oliver, Lieuts. Whittuck and Lynch, Captain Mayne, and Lieut. Reid, all, or nearly all, wounded, but gallantly getting their men to rally and re-form and cover the retreat. Outside this species of 'laager' some of the cavalry were still maintaining a hand-to-hand fight with the Afghan horsemen, who with fierce yells dashed themselves upon the thinned files of our men. In the midst of this confused mass of turbaned horsemen we could see the white helmet and streaming puggaree of Geoghegan, of the 3rd Cavalry, with two officers, whose faces were so blackened by powder that we could not distinguish them, and these gallant fellows, with a mere handful of their men, were making a desperate attempt to cut through their assailants, while we dared not fire in their direction lest we might injure our own people.

Meanwhile our ammunition was fast failing, and by the General's orders we slackened our fire, only delivering a shot or two when the enemy became massed and near enough to afford a certain mark for our rifles. Flaunting their standards, and with frantic yells and demoniac gestures, the standard-bearers ran in front of the serried masses of our foes, whom, however, we still managed to hold in check with our feeble fire.

'Had we but a couple of guns *en barbette*, and plenty of shrapnel, we could hold them at bay for a time,' said a voice close to my ear, as a shell was thrown short of our range, and which burst outside, killing some of our enemies. I turned and saw the speaker, a lad only lately joined from Woolwich; and even as he spoke, while loading a carbine he had picked up, he fell back, shot through the shoulder, into my arms! The *banquette*, so well improvised by our thoughtful commissariat officer, was invaluable to us at this juncture, as it enabled our men to fire well over the wall without being much exposed to the fire of the enemy. Inside a portion of the faces, however, were here and there some round-topped native huts, probably used in former times as barrack accommodation for the soldiers of the outpost.

'If a ditch and parapet had been thrown up in front of this place, and we had held it as the centre of our position,' said Oliver, 'we could have licked these fellows!'

Meanwhile the Afghan horsemen swarmed in increased masses over the hills, and their leaders saw the remnants of our infantry cut off from our place of refuge in the laager. Their squadrons were on the hills skirting one side of the pass, while a few of our cavalry still held the opposite declivity. Currie, with a few files of his gallant Scinde horse, sees the Afghan cavalry forming to attack, and, thank Heaven! casts behind him all thought of shunning the encounter. At the head of his small band of sturdy horsemen, few, indeed, in number, but splendidly mounted, he 'goes for' his enemy. The Afghan leader, a tall, gold-embroidered fellow, evidently of high rank, accepts the challenge. At his side rides the bearer of the blue and gold standard we had so often noticed during the day. Suddenly reining in his horse he tears the white lunghi from his head, stands erect in his stirrups, and points to Currie's devoted little band —' Follow me !' we can almost hear him cry, as slowly, but steadily, our Scinde horsemen advance. The English officers lead on the men as steadily as on parade, while we can see the *serrefiles* in rear, keeping the line from wavering as they descend the slopes. Currie increases his pace from a trot to a gallop, and then, at the proper moment, his trumpet rings out the charge.

'Well done ! Well done !' we shout from our walls, as we see the white line of Afghan horsemen pierced like a paper wall by our gallant soldiers and rolled over by scores in the *mêlée !*

'*Shabash ! Shabash ! Chi Roostmany !*' ('Bravo ! bravo ! Worthy of Roostum himself !') our Sepoys shout as they see the splendid charge of their comrades. For a short time the progress of the struggle was lost to sight by the gazers from our wall, but soon the quick rattle of musketry, the booming of heavy artillery, and the clouds of dust against the clear sky, told that the Afghan infantry had covered the retreat of their horsemen. The tide of victory still flowed on with the Afghan troops, although a charge was now and then still made by our horse to check their pursuit, and enable our refugees to cross the plain and gain the road. Meanwhile the Afghan cavalry in increased masses issued from the hollows in the ground where they had lain in ambush, and spreading themselves over the open country chased our flying infantry across the plain, while the few unfortunate wretches who had taken refuge towards the centre of the valley, and 800 yards from the road, at the musjid, or tomb of an

Afghan saint, were surrounded and slaughtered to a man. Wherever a few of our soldiers, European or Indian, appeared, the terrible Afghan horse streamed across the plain and swept upon their quarry. Meanwhile, as our own fire was obliged to slacken from scarcity of ammunition, that of the enemy, upon the hills overlooking our enclosed building, now became hot and galling, and General Burrows determined to make one final effort to bring off the shattered remnants of what once was a brigade; but our fire having slackened, the Ghazis were emboldened to try conclusions at close quarters, and about half-past four a determined rush was made upon the northern and eastern faces of our building, and a desperate hand-to-hand struggle inside our walls took place. Our officers stood upon the walls like brave men, and as the Ghazis attempted to carry our position by storm they hurled down upon them huge masses of stone from the tops of the walls. Still on they came, and in a few moments we were grappling these lithe and sinewy fanatics by their throats and beards, and knives and bayonets contended in deadly clash. Twice did we beat them back, hurling their bodies alive and dead over our shelter walls, while the shouts of defiance given by our men were met by yells of rage from our assailing hordes. But suddenly a ray of hope gleamed upon us when we saw that one of our guns had escaped, and with its detachment had mounted to a position overlooking our road, and was about to open fire upon the Afghans below. Here it so happened the enemy had no artillery, and our one gun, nobly worked, told for a time with terrible effect upon the masses beneath. But after a few rounds poured in as quickly us the piece could be loaded, the vent became so heated by continued firing that it became unserviceable. As soon, therefore, as the firing ceased the gallant gunners were compelled to abandon their weapon, which with its companion fell into the hands of our enemy.

I have said that the nature of the ground was most unfavourable to our people, as between us and the brow of the hill there were undulations and rising ground which prevented us from seeing the movements of the foe. But from our walls we could now see a party of Ghazis crawling from the gorge up the hillside, ready to rush down with fury upon our entrenchment. This unexpected danger seemed to strike a panic into the heart of our Sepoys, who now clamoured to be led forth and no longer to be penned in for slaughter. General Burrows—who, whatever may be said of his merits or demerits as a leader in the moment of danger, behaved like an English officer, and stood with iron courage in the midst of the thickest fire—vainly called on these men to take example by the 66th and remain steady. Finding the panic increasing, and deeming it possible it might communicate to the 66th, the General decided to make a retreat along the road to Kandahar at all hazards, rather than we should be cut down where we stood.

Nothing, however, could now infuse courage into the panic-stricken native regiments, and their efforts to get first through the gateway partially defeated our General's attempt to restore some sort of order into our retreat. Our cavalry, however, outside still charged the enemy, and the artillerymen still stuck to their single gun. Two we saw cut down beside it; a third had his brains blown out by a matchlock; a fourth, when the Ghazis rushed

upon it, clung to the wheels to prevent it being carried
off, and only escaped death by the bravery of his officer,
Major Blackwood, at that time badly wounded, and
than whom not a better soldier or a braver man ever
served the Queen.   The gun was lost, and then all was
confused and disastrous flight.   All, however, was not
yet lost.   General Burrows ordered the halt to be
sounded, and part of the flying regiment had the sense
to see that their only hope of safety was in keeping
together and fighting their way through the foe.   The
few remaining officers reformed them, and the Ghazis
for a time shrunk from the aspect of the 66th bayonets.

Meanwhile the enemy's cavalry on the plain had
been thrown into some confusion by the fall of their
leader.   How or when he fell I cannot say, but it was
generally believed that he was killed by a shot from our
gun ; but at all events his loss seemed for a time to
paralyse the movements of his horsemen, who allowed
us, almost unmolested, to march as far as the road,
along which our retreat was again covered by two
brilliant charges of our cavalry, who thereby, however,
lost considerably.   At this moment we believed we
should be able to bring off the remnant of our force
with something like order, but the lull was not for long.
The enemy returned from looting our camp, recruited
by fresh hordes whom they met coming over the hills,
and again this increasing mass poured itself upon our
little column, and once more a wave of furious Ghazis
burst through our ranks and scattered our men like
sheep.   Even the 66th now began to lose heart, and to
cower between the fire of the jezails.   Again the Afghan
horse, seizing the opportunity, dashed upon our retreating force, and in a short time friend and foe, Sepoy

and Afghan, were mixed up in inextricable confusion. In one confused mass European and native, officer and private, old and young, brave and coward, fled rapidly along the road. The General and his staff watched their flight with dismay, and strove in vain to stay it and to rally the fugitives. The enemy at one part of the causeway were so completely mixed up with our men that their guns, fortunately for us, ceased to fire, and the conflict was confined to knife and bayonet, sword and lance. With some considerable difficulty, General Burrows, assisted by Major Oliver, formed some sort of advanced and rear guard, and placed some of the camels and baggage in the centre of our column, with orders to keep the formation, and allow no one to fall out or impede the march. It was necessary to protect the camels, mules, and ponies, on account of the assistance they could afford to the wounded. The main body, under General Burrows, with its string of baggage-laden cattle, then began to move out along the road, while the rear guard, under Major Oliver, manned the walls of the bazaar, and looked down upon a scene of uproar and confusion such as no imagination can conceive. The enemy, however, were not idle, and, whenever an opportunity occurred, dashed in among the baggage, cutting down the helpless camp-followers and helping themselves to whatever they could.

The road was soon slippery with blood. From the opening in the enclosure we had left to the small causeway built across the watercourse by the road streamed one long tide of endless humanity, from which arose shouts, yells, and oaths, the bellowings of the camels, the curses of the mule-drivers, the lamentations of the Sepoys, and the savage yells of the Ghazis, rising loud above all.   By some terrible fatality the road indicated by the General—the upper one—was not taken, and the lower, or ' main road,' as it is called, which was followed, is utterly without water at this season of the year.   All our efforts to turn them away from this route were unavailing, and the consequences were even worse than we anticipated.

Not until two hours after we had started from our entrenchments did we commence to realise the helpless nature of our condition.   We had been under arms since daylight, about four a.m., and it was now six p.m.   We had been marching and fighting against an overwhelming enemy since nine a.m., and had been thoroughly beaten, leaving about one half of our force killed upon the field, with two of our guns lost, and the colours of the 66th and Bombay Grenadiers taken.   Nearly all our ammunition was captured; in fact, all that was saved was what the men were enabled to carry with them from the field. We had been savagely attacked on leaving our entrenchments, and how we escaped annihilation is yet a mystery. In two hours we had only accomplished about six miles of our wretched journey, as we had to face about and defend ourselves at every bend or turn of the road, and it was impossible not to see and foretell in the horrors that we saw around us the fate that might yet be in store for ourselves.

In the front, most of their horses bleeding and wounded, rode Colonel Mainwaring, commanding the advanced guard, Major River, and Colonel Griffith; while in the centre was General Burrows, doing all he could to cheer and keep up the courage of the men. With him were Lieut. Lynch, wounded ; Captain Grant, wounded ; Major Vench, and Drs. Burrows and Eaton, while Colonel St. John overtook us further on. With the rear guard, if such it could be called, were Brigadier Nuttall and the remnants of his cavalry, Lieut. Whittuck, Lieut. Geoghegan, and Major River. Finding it impossible to turn back the confused mass of fugitives from the road they had chosen, General Burrows decided that it was better to stay with them than to divide the force, although he knew that the want of water would add terribly to their pitiable position on the march. As we moved silently and sadly along the road soon became strewn with dying wretches worn out by fatigue and devoured by a burning thirst that added frenzy to their sufferings. Strong men and weak lads alike abandoned themselves to despair, and lay themselves down rather than attempt a further struggle with the ruthless foe. Had we known more of the locality, it would have been better to have kept more to our right, and in a few miles we should have struck across the Argandab river, where we could have, perhaps, crossed and obtained refuge from the enemy and water for our people and cattle. But it was fated otherwise, and we were obliged to follow the stream. Meanwhile we longed for safety and darkness of the night, but when it came it was one of suffering and horror. Order and method became less and less as we advanced through the gloom ; corps and regiments were mixed up anyhow and anywhere. Soldiers and camp-followers were huddled together, when, for a few uneasy moments, we halted in one inextricable mass of moaning and agonised humanity. Horses, mostly wounded or lame, with their tongues fevered and blistering with thirst, camels, baggage-ponies, and mules, were mixed up confusedly together. Nothing could be done to restore order or arrangement, and the wounded and weary wretches, man and brute, lay down to sleep, never, in most cases, to rise again.

After two very brief halts during the night, on both of which we were overtaken and attacked by the Afghan horse, we reached Hoaz-i-Madad Khan, a distance little short of sixteen miles from our fatal battle-ground at Kushk-i-Nakhud. As we marched, or rather draggled, through the villages of this district, the enemy, taking advantage of the dawn just breaking again, pressed down upon our rear and flanks, and here Nuttall delivered a splendid charge with the few sabres he had left. Hearing the sound of hoofs along the road in our rear he took advantage of some friendly vineyards skirting the path, and posted fifty of his best men on the least tired horses in ambush to fall upon our pursuers. The plot answered capitally, for, as the Afghans sighted our last retreating file and a lagging camel or two laden with baggage, they quickened the pace to a gallop and came at us. To their utter astonishment our files opened and let them pass, and then as the last horseman went through we drew up, front rank kneeling, across the road, which was bounded on either side by high rocks impassable for cavalry, and, having fixed bayonets, gave them a volley. As they attempted to get away by the flank towards the vineyards they were suddenly charged by Nuttall and his fifty horsemen, and cut down almost to a man. But this was only a temporary success, as five miles further on, where we debouched into a plain, the enemy again overtook us in the open, and pressed hardly upon our rear, seizing most of our baggage and cutting up the wretched camp-followers, who were too overcome with fatigue and thirst to fly. Our soldiers, however, even now weary almost unto death, feeble, wounded, famished, and driven almost mad with thirst, still made a gallant stand against the fierce charge of the Afghan horsemen.

Still the pursuit continued, and as our people became more enfeebled and despondent the confusion around far exceeded that of the previous night—men, horses, camels, ponies, without shelter from the guns and tulwars of the enemy, without water, without food, without ammunition! The road over which we passed was covered with plundered and torn baggage, with dead cattle, and with stiffened corpses. My spirit of discipline was indeed shocked to see that our men were becoming more like wild beasts than human beings. Worn out myself with fatigue, covered with blood, and suffering severe pain from my wound received early in the day, I should have fallen from my horse had not the wounded man I was carrying *en croupe* caught me in his arms. Ten miles from Kandahar the General, with two of the staff, rode on to report the disaster to General Primrose, and from the time he started we suffered no further molestation from our pursuers, who probably thought that a force might be sent from Kandahar to help us on our way. When we reached the walls of the city on the morning of the 28th the following officers were killed or missing:— Colonel Galbraith, Captain M'Wrath, Captain Garrett, Captain Cullen, Captain Roberts, Major Blackwood, Captain Heath, Lieutenants Hen, Rayner, Chute, Honeywood, Barr, Osborne, Owen, Hinde, Whitby, Justice, Cole, Astlett, Maclaine (we have since heard taken prisoner); while our wounded were—Dr. Preston, Colonel Anderson, Major Iredell, Captains Mayne, Grant, and Lieutenants Lynch, Fowell, and Reid. Those who reached Kandahar I have already named.

Meanwhile my wound is going on favourably, though at first amputation was suggested, but, thanks to a good doctor and a capital soldier-nurse, I am in a fair way to be in the saddle, they tell me, in a fortnight or three weeks. I may say, in conclusion, that neither General Haines nor General Primrose had any share in General Burrows' ill-starred expedition. It was planned and devised at Simla, and *hinc illæ lachrymæ*. Playing chess by telegraph may succeed, but making war and planning a campaign on the Helmund from the cool shades of breezy Simla is an experiment which will not, I hope, be repeated.

STATE OF THE KANDAHAR GARRISON AFTER MAIWAND.

Kandahar, Aug. 7.

IN my despatch to you of the 30th ult. I had barely time to tell you some of the horrors we witnessed and endured during the night after the battle of the 27th. On comparing notes with several of my comrades who survived the slaughter—for I can call it nothing else—I find that what I witnessed was but a part of the terrors of the pursuit. In describing the battle I find, on comparing my account with that of others who fought in different portions of the field, that I have made a few omissions which I can now supply. I have stated, on what I believe to be the best authority, that General Burrows, before the battle, was in almost daily receipt of telegraphic orders, which left him little freedom of independent judgment; and I now know that he was so trammelled by instructions of a contradictory nature that he had much excuse for the indecision he displayed, and the ignorance under which he laboured as to the movements and position of his enemy, who should never have been allowed to cross the Helmund. The retreat from that river, where a formidable position could have been held by our troops, was ordered by telegram, and in consequence we lost all clue to Ayub's movements, until too late to meet him, except, as it proved, to disadvantage and defeat. At the Helmund, and after our retreat therefrom, our cavalry made daily patrols over a circuit of fifteen or twenty miles ; but these were, for some cause or another, discontinued, and while Ayub, through his spies in the villages, was day by day kept *au courant* with our movements, we remained completely in the dark as to his. Even after our retreat from the Helmund we had the choice of several splendid positions near Maiwand, three miles from Kushk-i-Nakhud, but none of these were taken, and we were encamped in a sort of *cul-de-sac*, surrounded on three sides by eminences affording every concealment to our enemy, who was thus enabled to mask his attack and enfilade us with his superior artillery. Of the gallantry of General Burrows I have not sufficiently spoken. Wherever the fighting was most desperate there he was to be found, and while two horses were shot under him he escaped without a wound, and was enabled, during the terrible night retreat, to save more than one wounded man by placing him *en croupe* upon his horse.

I am glad to correct my first account of our losses by telling you that stragglers kept coming in from time to time during the days following the fight, who have considerably reduced the number of our casualties,

which may now be set down about one third less than
at first stated. I have so frequently alluded to the
paucity of officers in our native regiments that I need
not dwell upon this want, but the action of the 27th
clearly demonstrates the folly of the present staff-corps
system. Had Jacob's Rifles been officered up to their
full complement, there is every reason to believe they
would have made a better stand in front of the foe. As
it was, they, having lost their leaders, gave way to panic,
and, being completely demoralised, were driven in confusion upon the flank of the 66th, who up to that time
were gallantly holding the enemy in check. Seven miles
west of Kandahar, on the Herat road, is Kokeran, and
here a small force, fortunately for us, had come out from
Kandahar to meet and succour our fugitives, and with
their assistance our further retreat was covered, until,
almost dead with fatigue and thirst, we managed to
reach the Herat gate of the city.

Meanwhile along the road between Kokeran and
Kandahar the sun rose upon a long string of stiffened
corpses, and the ghastly remains of those who had fallen
out from sheer exhaustion. One paramount desire to
escape death animated those who still pressed on, though
all order was lost, and soldiers and camp-followers, men
and officers, mules and baggage - animals, guns and
ammunition-carts, pushed on confusedly to the front.
Surging backwards and forwards, this seething, bleeding,
dust-stained mass of humanity, made up principally of
the miserable crowd of camp-followers, who, in their
agony and terror, overwhelmed the handful of the 66th,
who were still showing a bold front, gave a mark to
the enemy, which they took advantage of with their
long jezails from the neighbouring cliffs.

On the arrival of the first batch of our broken column at Kandahar, principally, I may say, composed of native camp-followers, their terror-stricken faces and their accounts of the disaster spread a panic through the city, and in the confusion that ensued sentries deserted their posts, men ran away from their guard-rooms, public offices and stores were abandoned, and the impression gained ground that the foe was at the gates of the city. 250 of our cavalry, and two guns of our horse artillery meanwhile protected our rear, under Generals Burrows and Nuttall, who used all their energies to save the wounded stragglers by placing them, as they fell exhausted, on the guns and baggage-ponies which were left.

It was well for us that Burrows and Nuttall behaved as they did, and sought to retrieve with the sacrifice of their own lives the fortunes of this piteous day. A large body of Ghazis had climbed to a crag overlooking the portion of the road where our rear guard determined to make their last stand. On the summit of this almost inaccessible crag they had got one of their lighter guns in position. Large bodies of these fanatics, each with a distinguishing standard, and each under a different leader, continued to swarm along these heights, which in a measure formed a sort of amphitheatre to the road where our men were halted. Their shells crashed into our disordered masses, inflicting terrible loss, while we were utterly unable to return their fire, as a deep ravine protected them from our rifles. At all hazards it was determined to dislodge the foe, and Major Oliver, of the 66th, volunteered to attempt this feat. Taking but fifty men, he gallantly ascended the heights, the nature of the ground preventing his being seen until he had gained a footing with his devoted band not more than 200 yards from the unprepared mob who were firing upon us. In spite of the hot fire from their jezails, our men still held the angle of the road, and found sufficient cover in an old half-ruined fort to make arrangements for the carriage of the wounded on baggage-ponies and the few mules we had now left.

Oliver and his men had meanwhile crowned the heights, and got a lodgment behind some rocks which formed the key of the enemy's position. All had rushed after their leader with the most impetuous gallantry, and eager to avenge the loss of their favourite Colonel, killed on the previous evening. As the caps of our 'Berkshires' appeared upon the ledge of rocks to the right of where the enemy was posted, and as they dashed at the Ghazi standards, a ringing cheer, such as Britons alone can give, went forth from our stormers, whose hearts were evidently in their work, and who would take no denial to what they had resolved to achieve. The loud cheer of our British infantry seemed to carry dismay into the Ghazi ranks, and as our fellows went at them like greyhounds, with a line of living steel, they turned, and would not face our bayonets. Our stormers still dashed on, the standards were captured, and the spot which they considered a stronghold almost inaccessible was in our possession, and enabled the scanty remnants of our shattered brigade to continue their march almost unmolested. In this last encounter, General Burrows was seen galloping to that portion of the road wherever the fire seemed hottest—twice, thrice, did I see men struck down at his side by the bullets of the enemy; and while our chief was behaving in this gallant and noble manner, General Nuttall was getting together the fragments of what in the morning was a fine brigade of sabres, to dash themselves once more against the pursuing horsemen of the enemy, who, in spite of their numbers, still kept a respectful distance. Dr. Harvey, Dr. Eaton, Major River, and Colonel St. John (whose horse was here shot under him), all distinguished themselves by conspicuous gallantry, saving many lives at the risk of their own.

Our entrance to the old cantonments of Kandahar was pitiable and deplorable in the extreme. The most fearful rumours had preceded our arrival, and, bad as matters were with us, they had been fearfully exaggerated by the first arrivals from the field of slaughter. These old cantonments are about a mile and a half to the west of Kandahar on the road to Kokeran, and consist of three blocks of barracks built north-east and south-west, with an enclosure of forty-three acres, called ' The Sappers' Garden,' on the left. Here last year were stationed the 59th Regiment, G-4 R.A., 6-11 R.A., and 11-11 R.A., 2-60th, and D-2 R.A., and 25th P.N.I. Here on the right of the first block, and immediately fronting our hospital, were our Horse Artillery quarters, and here were waiting, in the most intense anxiety, the menaced officers who had been left at Kandahar, and who had heard with dismay of our loss of guns and colours. Our Brigadier's staff and our Artillery officers are in another block to the right, and a little behind, while their horses and mules are picketed in rear of the building. In rear of the right centre block are the Engineer park and stores, while the guns are parked between the barrack squares. Behind these are the quarters of the 7th Royal Fusiliers and the 66th. Again in the rear we have the enclosure known as 'Mahomed Amin's Garden,' where

General Primrose has his head-quarters. At about 450 yards away to the right are the three villages till recently occupied by our cavalry.

This cantonment is not less than forty years old. It is built in blocks about 150 yards long by 140 deep, and about 200 yards apart. The barrack-rooms extend all round the quadrangle, leaving a clear space of about twenty feet between walls of sun-dried bricks and mud at least five feet thick. The roofing of these buildings is curious, being composed of a series of arched ribs, with vaulting between. These arched roofs are ingeniously constructed, and are of great strength. In building them a centre-piece of wood, the thickness of one brick, is set up in two pieces, with the feet resting upon a sun-burnt brick, supported by a couple of nails driven into the wall, about six feet from the floor, the ribs being joined at the apex, lashed firmly together, and steadied by a guy-pole. Bricks are then placed on the edge resting on the centre rib, and the work is carried on from both sides, what is called the ' gach,' a sort of plaster, being freely applied by hand.

I mention these cantonments, as we shall have to give them up, and, it is said, retire into the citadel, should the city be closely invested, and our garrison be found unequal to the task of defending the walls I have described. In such a case these buildings would form an admirable coign of vantage to an investing force, and a picked body of riflemen could terribly gall our men in the citadel.

Meanwhile there was no time for idling, or even for the rest we all so much required. The worst cases of the wounded were sent at once to the hospital, while those who were but slightly hit requested to be allowed to remain at duty, and to assist in the task before us. A council of war was held at three p.m. on the 28th, and the commissariat officers made their reports as to the state of our supplies, which, it is said, are sufficient for thirty days. Preparations for the defence were at once commenced, and all hands were pressed into service to demolish all useless buildings, and to renovate the dilapidated walls of the citadel and outworks. We have in round numbers about 3000 men as a garrison, and with this force we feel confident we can hold the place until relief comes from either Phayre or Roberts. We have four guns C B. 2nd B, and 6 guns 5 B. 11 B, the Poona Horse, 7th Fusiliers, and the 19th and 29th B.N.I. These with the remainder of the 66th, Jacob's Rifles, and the Bombay Grenadiers, make up our little force. Our immediate help, we imagine, should come from General Phayre, whose force, however, is much scattered on detachment and small posts along the Quetta line. He has at Quetta, Sibi, Thal Chotiali, and other posts, the 2nd Light Cavalry, 1st and 2nd Scinde Horse, three companies of Sappers, 14 B., 9 B., R.A., No. 2 Mountain. Battery, and the 5th, 10th, 16th, 23rd, 27th, and 28th Regiments B.N.I. These, we hear, will be pushed on to us at once, while their places will be taken by the Bombay Reserve.

Our anxiety for the safety of the small garrison of Khelat-i-Ghilzai is very great. Colonel Tanner is in command, and has with him one regiment Bombay Infantry, two companies 66th, and small detachments of artillery and cavalry. We know that Ayub wrote as far back as the 16th July to the villages around the fort ordering them, on pain of destruction, not to furnish supplies of any sort, and telling them that he was about to drive the English hence. The tribes in the neighbourhood had been troublesome even before the battle, and now are in a most excited state. The most formidable enemy in the neighbourhood is a Ghilzai chief, named Mahomed Aslam Khan, and he is known to be in communication with Ayub. In compensation for this, we hear, however, that the Khan of Khelat is reliable, and will afford us all the assistance he can in men, camels, and supplies.

All the buildings outside our walls are being blown up or pulled down by our Engineers, whose commanding officer, Colonel Hills, has no spare time on his hands. While I write, runners have just come in to say that Ayub Khan has advanced, *viâ* Singuri, as far as Kokeran, and that he has made the latter village his head-quarters. He has a useful ally there named Nur Mahomed, the sirtip, or cavalry commander, who made in the late campaign a good fight against a portion of General Stewart's force. From Kokeran, Ayub will advance in all probability by the two roads to Kandahar, one of which leads to the Herat Gate and the other to the Topkhand Gate. From Kokeran the road leads almost due east to Kandahar, having on the right flank a stony range throwing out long spurs, and on the left a broad belt of cultivated plain, descending with a gentle slope to the Argandab river, and covered with orchards of peaches, nectarines, plums, and other fruits, and here and there delightful halting-places shaded by avenues of fine mulberry-trees. There are a number of watercourses here, but they have been ramped and bridged over by our Engineers, so they would present no obstacle to artillery or cavalry. Indian corn, barley, lucerne, clover, mulberry and poplar-groves, red rose-bushes, cultivated in rare perfection, adorn the landscape, which is now looking its best.

From the 27th July to this day, 7th August, the movements of Ayub have been made known to us by our scouts, spies, and patrols, and the latter have had some slight but successful skirmishes with his pickets in the villages around our city. On the night of the 27th the Afghan leader did not pursue with his main body, but left that to his cavalry and the fanatic Ghazis, while he bivouacked on the field he had won at Maiwand. On the 28th he halted to recruit his men, and to divide the spoil amongst his soldiers, adding, we are told, considerable presents from his own military chests, and then during the following week he came on by deliberate and easy stages to Kokeran, which was occupied by his cavalry on the 4th and by his main body on the following day. The reason for this slow advance was undoubtedly caused by the motley nature of his levies, swelling in numbers each day as he came on, and as the news of his success became talked of in the villages. Another cause of this apparent delay in advance is said to be shortness of ammunition, as in pushing forward rapidly from the Helmund he came as lightly freighted as possible. I said that it was contemplated to abandon our cantonment and retire within the *arg*, or citadel. This, I am happy to say, has not been as yet necessary, for we hold our cantonment ready mined, and with the option of blowing it up should the investment become a blockade. In case Ayub tries a bombardment he no doubt would find our cantonment walls, if left standing, an excellent position for his batteries to obtain cover; but, on the other hand, he would be within 2500 yards' range of our guns mounted on the citadel. The present state of our fortifications leaves, I must own, much to be desired ; but, under the superintendence of Colonel Hills, wonders have been achieved in the short space of time we have had. The works consist of an outer wall 10 feet high and 18 feet thick, with a *chemin des rondes* 18 feet wide and a main parapet 20 feet high, and averaging 15 feet in thickness at its centre. This again has a top wall 6 feet high, and a covered way 30 feet wide, with a space between it and the houses.

When we marched into Kandahar last year all was in sad disrepair, and in a state of filth baffling description. Prothero, assistant political to Colonel St. John, undertook the sanitary arrangements of the city, while the citadel was taken charge of by the Engineer officer, Oliver. In the bazaars gangs of labourers were at once employed to clean out the open drains in front of the shops, and the refuse was carried away by relays of donkeys, so that in a short space of time the 'Shah' bazaar and the Alizai quarters, once the dirtiest part of the town, were thoroughly clean, walls had been removed, and spaces cleared for latrines. All the lanes were swept each day, and in a short time the Populzai and Barukzai quarters were put to the same test. The city is divided into four quarters, and each is a little more than half a mile long and half a mile wide. The main lanes run, as a rule, at right angles, and the spaces intervening are formed into squares, while mosques, gardens, public buildings, and bazaars, fill up the intervals. Running water is plentiful, and could not be easily cut off by an enemy, as the canals are well commanded by our guns. The houses are low and mud built, and not laid out, as with us, in streets, but in irregular blocks, and such blocks separated from each other by narrow lanes, or what in

Edinburgh would be called 'wynds,' varying in width from ten to two feet. Most of the roofs are flat, and have a sort of breastwork parapet, from which an uncommonly effective defence might be made, as most of these walls are solidly built of mud and sun-dried bricks, and are crenellated and loopholed. Our principal hospital is at Mir Afsul's old dwelling, not far from the Herat gate.

The place has been wonderfully improved of late, and fortunately so, as it is now so full of sick and wounded, most of whom, however, are doing well. There is a large, well-tended garden in front, with a splendid mulberrry-tree giving agreeable shelter to the convalescents, while a mass of rose-trees in fullest bloom light up the place in a wonderful manner. Some of these rose-trees are fifteen feet high, and the same in diameter, while the branches are kept from falling by supports which form them into delightful arbours. The great domed bazaar is in the centre of the town, and from it there are streets leading to the four principal gates of the city. The citadel street is the principal thoroughfare, and thronged at all hours by fruit and vegetable sellers, while all day long there is a never-ceasing traffic of camels, mules, donkeys, cows, and foot-passengers. Watercourses run through the street, gardeners are washing lettuces, blacksmiths' shops. coppersmiths' shops, crowded with men and boys at work, while the front of the shop is crowded with vessels for sale—huge cooking-pots, salvers, tea-urns, washing-basins, candlesticks, all engraved with letters and texts from the Koran : leather-curriers, tailors making sheep-skin coats, shoe-shops, sellers of rosaries, carpet-sellers, ornamental saddle-cloths ; and a motley crew of men, women, and children, moving incessantly up and down, giving little indication that we are in a state of siege.

The citadel has been so often described that I will merely call attention to one remarkable feature, and that is the vast underground accommodation we possess in its admirably built vaults, which are shell and bomb-proof, and which we can use as magazines, storehouses, hospital, stables, as they are cool, water-tight, with high-domed roof, and well-fitted solid stable furniture. Here we have placed a greater portion of our cavalry, and men and horses are rapidly recovering from the fatigue and wounds received on the 27th.

These native horsemen are fine fellows, and as a rule will follow their officers anywhere. On the 27th, however, the ground was unfavourable, and they were terribly demoralised by the *feu d'enfer* of Ayub's thirty-six guns. Their horses are tethered by double head and heel-ropes, which on the march is carried from the lower ring of the headstall to a ring in front of the saddle. The sowar now carries a Snider carbine, a curved sword, sharp as a razor, and a lance. The uniform is an indigo blue *pugri*, or turban, around a red-wadded skull-cap, a blue serge *koorta* (frock), red cummerbund, loose yellow pyjamas, and long boots, while his belt and appointments are black, with silver fittings. His pouch-belt and pouch carry twenty rounds, and his waist-belt is broad, with a blue and white pennon to his lance. These men get twenty-seven rupees a-month, and on this they find horse, *tatoo* (pony), and all. It is a great pity we have not more of these fellows, as Ayub is exceptionally strong in cavalry, and we are now unable to make a reconnaisance in force.

A large number of the Pathan population were expelled yesterday, and although this may seem a harsh measure, it has been a necessary one. They have all friends and relations in the neighbouring villages, and were allowed to store any property they could not carry in the citadel. With plenty of ammunition, sufficient provisions to last a month on full rations, and a really close investment almost impossible, I can see no reason why we should have the smallest anxiety as to the result. Meanwhile, not an hour passes but some addition to our defences is made, and every day of inaction on Ayub's part makes his chances of success more remote : the only fear we have is that he may not wait to fight our relieving force.

CHAPTER IV.

VALEDICTORY VISITS IN CABUL—ABDURRAHMAN.

Cantonment of the Bala Hissar, July 26.

A FÉW days ago I, by the merest chance, had the opportunity of conversing for some considerable period with Abdurrahman Khan, the ruler elect, and as such acknowledged by our representatives. Before I enter into delails I may as well put you *au courant* with the state of affairs previous to the Ameer's recognition by our Government.

In the first place we had been instructed, before the late English Ministry went out of office, that, before our troops retired to the new scientific frontier, a strong and capable Governor should, if possible, be found to carry on the government of Cabul and its district. As far back as March last Lord Lytton was in communication with more than one royal Sirdar, but with Abdurrahman in particular, whom the Viceroy looked upon as the chief, the most popular, and the most likely to win the suffrages of the Sirdars and the people of this most difficult country. The delays which took place in the progress of these negotiations are perhaps to be accounted for through their delicate nature, as Lord Lytton was careful to promise little, while Abdurrahman was too astute and cautious a politician to pledge himself until he felt his footing tolerably secure. Then we must remember how great is the distance between Turkestan and Cabul ; while Abdurrahman no doubt felt some distrust of an offer so apparently disinterested and unselfish on Lord Lytton's part. Beyond this was his desire to be called to the throne of his ancestors more by the will of the people than as the nominee of a victorious invader; and this, of course, compelled him to conciliate the jealousy of the Sirdars by not showing himself too ready to meet our overtures. While matters were in this halting state the Conservatives went out and Lord Ripon become Viceroy, and he wisely decided to carry on the negotiations inaugurated by his predecessor.

In the meanwhile Abdurrahman advanced towards Cabul, and passing through Kohistan, came on to Charikar, a few marches from Cabul, at which place, being in the neighbourhood, I had the honour of a somewhat protracted interview. As my visit was purely unofficial, and in fact almost the result of accident, I made a point of touching as lightly as possible upon political matters; but I found that my reticence had one advantage, and this was, that it placed my host and interlocutor at his ease, and caused him to express himself with much more frankness than I could have anticipated.

I had been deer-shooting in the neighbourhood of Charikar for several days, and with such indifferent success that I determined to give the order to my people to prepare for our return to Sherpur, when one evening tidings were brought me by the headman of a neighbouring village that the advanced guard of Abdurrahman's escort had arrived there in the morning with orders to prepare supplies for the following day, when the prince himself was expected to arrive, and halt for one or two days. I accordingly countermanded my orders to return, and determined to stay and pay my respects to his Highness should he arrive the next day. With this intent I caused to be unpacked some clothing of less sporting and *chikar* a nature than what I was wearing, and found I possessed a suit not altogether military, and yet sufficiently such to denote that I was not a civilian.

At daybreak the following morning I was aroused by the sound of an Afghan gong, such as is used to denote the arrival of some person of rank, and while I was finishing my *al fresco* bath my orderly rushed in with the news that the Sirdar Abdurrahman had arrived, and had pitched his camp near a grove of mango-trees half a mile from the village, where part of his troops were located. Making a very hasty toilet and a still hastier breakfast, I despatched my orderly to the captain of the Sirdar's body-guard with a note in Persian, asking permission to pay my respects to his Highness; and in about half an hour my messenger returned with a very civil message from Abdurrahman's secretary, assuring me of a cordial welcome. At noon, therefore, I mounted my best horse, and taking two of my smartest attendants with me I started for the Ameer's camp, which I found was situated on the banks of a very picturesque little stream running at the foot of some hills, and affording irrigation to the cultivation around.

The Ameer's tent was somewhat in the shape of a marquee, but it had three poles and a double lining, while it was divided and subdivided into ante-chamber, audience-hall, dining-room, and bedchamber ; the whole being tastefully draped with shawls, and carpeted with Afghan rugs woven with the most delicate and harmonious colours. Around on all sides were the ruder tents of hides and blankets, occupied by the Ameer's soldiers, who, to avoid the midday sun, were lounging about under the shade of the date, mango, and cocoa-trees around. As I rode through the rows of tents it was evident that my visit was expected, and that my nationality and military rank were known, for all the groups lying or lounging about separated and came to a standing position, saluting me as I passed. This considerably astonished me, as most of these men I could see were Turkestan and mercenaries, whose abomination of the infidel is proverbial. About 200 of these fellows appeared to compose a sort of guard round the Sirdar's tent, and these were not only clothed but armed in every conceivable way. Swords of various Asiatic makes, lances of various lengths, battle-axes, shields of hide and of metal, matchlocks, Minié-patterned rifles, Martinis and Chassepots, all were there ; while some were cleaning their arms and others preparing their midday meal.

On arriving at the Ameer's tent I was courteously received by two officers of high rank, who wore Persian uniforms of a costly nature, and who invited me politely to dismount and enter, as his Highness, they said, had been anxiously waiting to see me. After handing over my horses to the attendants told off to receive and take care of them I was ushered into the ante-room, and, after a few moments' delay, into the audience-chamber of the tent. Seated on a *musnud,* slightly elevated above the floor, the new Ameer received me with dignity and cordiality. He then desired me to seat myself on a carpet laid out near to his own seat ; and after a short pause commenced our conference by asking after Sir Donald Stewart's health and my own.

Abdurrahman's appearance is much in his favour,

and he has an open frank look about his eyes not at all usual among his countrymen. His age seemed to be about fifty, and his face had more roundness of contour than is customary with the Afghan type; while a certain heaviness of limb gave little indication of his well-known active habits. Abdurrahman, with whom I now conversed, spoke frankly of the past times—to him almost as eventful as the present; and gave me many hints as to the future possibilities of his rule, which is a problem we none of us can venture to solve.

'I believe,' said he, stroking his long beard with an air of calm dignity, 'in the English Government, and in their wise and just policy, although my enemies have taunted me with being a pensioner of Russia. I was their guest, not their tool, and treated with much honour and respect. In 1866 I saw the mistaken course pursued by Shere Ali; and, in conjunction with my uncle Azim, I determined to strike hard and to strike promptly. Cabul was taken from Ibrahim; Shere Ali's second son, Shekhabad, followed; and the result was the release of my father and the capture of Ghuzni. The crowning victory of Khelat-i-Ghilzai gave my father the recognition of Ameer from the British Government. What followed I could not prevent; and when our cause was hopeless I gave in my allegiance to my uncle, Shere Ali, suppressing all personal feelings.'

We spoke of education, and the Ameer said:—

'As a nation, it would not be going too far to say the Afghans are very illiterate; few besides the priests can write their own or any other language. For this, I may observe, there is some explanation in the fact of the Pushtu being for the most a spoken language—comparatively few books being written in it. The literature of the country is for the most part in the Persian language, and is confined to the priesthood and the wealthy classes. Correspondence, business transactions, and the work of Government, are also carried on through the medium of Persian. The books written in Pushtu by Afghan authors are chiefly on theology, poetical romances, and on history; but the number of authors is few, and the copies of their works are confined to a very limited circulation. In their marriage ceremonies the Afghans, as a rule, follow the customs of other Mohammedan nations, but (and especially among the nomad tribes) it is not an uncommon custom for the suitor to serve the girl's father for a stipulated period, in order to win her as his wife. Among the Afghans it is considered incumbent on a man to marry his deceased brother's widow, and this custom is so strongly insisted on that any departure from it is considered a scandal and a blot upon the parties concerned.'

On my asking his opinion as to the Afghan religion, he replied: 'The Afghans are very proud of the devotion to Islam, or the Mohammedan religion, and affect a scrupulous adherence to its precepts. But I cannot say that by their conduct they maintain either the credit of the religion they profess or their own character for sincerity, for though they punish the blasphemer and apostate by stoning to death— which, among this people, as among the Israelites of old, is the peculiar punishment for this sort of crime—they do not scruple to depart from, or act in direct opposition to, the most binding or important of their religious laws when, by so doing, they can attain the object of their desires without personal risk or detriment to their interests.

The Cabul population is made up of such varying elements that the customs and morals of the inhabitants of each quarter of district or the town differ as widely as the races from which they derive. Speaking generally, the people one sees about the streets are either Cabulees or visitors, and the latter may be again divided into dwellers in tents and dwellers in houses; the former occupying themselves, when at peace, with rearing flocks and herds, which they bring to the towns to sell, and the latter engaged in commerce and agriculture. The Afghan shepherds who come in here with sheep and cattle live in tents made of coarse black stuff, and are fond, like all Orientals, of smoking and story-telling, fairy tales or romantic histories of the loves and battles of their kings forming the favourite themes.'

Two days after the interview I had with Abdurrahman a formal meeting was arranged between the Ameer and Sir Donald Stewart, and for this ceremony a spot was selected a short distance west of Sherpur; and close to this locality we placed a couple of large mess marquees together, so as to form one large audience hall, while a guard of honour of 200 men with their regimental and Queen's colours was drawn up at the entrance. As the gong sounded the hour of meeting our chief and his moderate *cortége* rode on to the space set apart for the meeting in front of the canvas pavilion. A peal of trumpets and a royal salute from the guard of honour shortly afterwards announced the advent of Abdurrahman, who rode in regal style and with a right royal mien. I must own his appearance gave assurance of a man, and not a puppet. Simultaneously Sir Donald and the Ameer halted their chargers and most courteously saluted, as the band played the opening eight bars of the National Anthem. Our chief then dismounted and hastened forward to hold the stirrup of his Highness, a mark of respect and etiquette still preserved in the Persian and the Russian Courts. Abdurrahman seemed greatly impressed with this mark of respect, and cordially shook hands *à l'Anglaise* with Sir Donald, with whom he then entered the marquees. About two dozen seats were placed for the chief actors in this impressive scene, and Mr. Lepel Griffin was in attendance as interpreter, although our friends Cunningham and Hills had to be called upon for assistance in that language. The conversation was purely composed of diplomatic platitudes, and would not in the least interest any one; but one portion of the Ameer's speech certainly deserves mention, and this was when, with great feeling, he said as follows:—'An exile for fifteen years, I now see again my native mountains, and have re-gained, through God and my right, my hereditary birthright—the throne of my fathers. But the means by which this success has been achieved are due to my English friends and to the Empress, whose cause is always just. On my right I see the General to whose generous diplomacy I owe my present position, and ungrateful should I be were I not now to express my regard and esteem to one who, like myself, is a soldier more than a politician.'

After this we were all in due course presented. The Ameer took particular notice of General Hills, V.C., of Mutiny fame, and of General Gough.

I start directly for India with General Hills' division, and shall probably write to you from our next halt. We expect no resistance. Yet, though,

of course, glad to see our friends there; we have taken
odds we march before long again to Cabul.

IN CABUL—THE NEWS FROM KANDAHAR—THE RELIEVING
COLUMN.

Racecourse Camp, Siah Sung Ridge, Cabul, Aug. 5.

I HAVE this moment returned from an official and non-
official visit to the most successful soldier in India, I
might almost say in the British army, General Sir
Frederick Sleigh Roberts, V.C., K.C.B., whose name
has just been notified in orders as the commander-in-
chief of a relieving column of no less than 10,000 picked
men, to march on Sunday for Kandahar. As the late
and inimitable Charles Mathews said, 'We live quick in
these days, and in all professions, civilian or soldier, we
must crop the harvest whether it be ripe or not.' But
the harvest awaiting our husbandmen is ripe for the
sickle, and our General, we feel certain, will not tarry by
the way, lest it should be lost or gathered by another
hand.

When the first brief but panic-stricken telegrams
containing the news of a grievous disaster to our troops
on the Helmund came to this city from the Governor of
Bombay, the gravity of the misfortune which had be-
fallen the Kandahar division of our arms was not underrated in Cabul, but, at the same time, it was believed
that the reports were much exaggerated, and that the
details which appeared in the Indian native papers were
considerably embellished by the imaginations of the
writers. Our position, moreover, at Cabul has been less

unfavourably influenced by our defeat on the Helmund than might have been expected, and although the excitement at first was very great, it has now, in a great measure, subsided. Most of the intelligent Sirdars with whom I have conversed are of opinion that the British Government will promptly wipe out the disgrace their colours have suffered at Ayub's hands, and believe at the same time that the Khan in attacking a British force, instead of husbanding his entire strength to confront Abdurrahman, has ruined all his chances of the throne.

On Tuesday last, the 3rd, orders came to us from Simla, to the effect that a force of 10,000 men were to march at once to the relief of Kandahar, that General Sir Frederick Roberts was to have the chief command, and likewise the selection of the troops composing his division. When the above order came I was riding, as usual, with the General, and as the orderly overtook us and placed the despatch in his hand a glow of pride and delight came over the General's face as he cried out, 'At last, at last, our orders have arrived, and our work is cut out for us!' A short canter brought us quickly back to the General's tent, and while the necessary staff officers were summoned, and the morning field-state sent for, the General marked on his map the halts he should have to make between Maidan and Ghuzni, and, from the notes he had already prepared, the localities where supplies could be obtained. The forces at the disposal of General Roberts at Cabul and its neighbourhood consisted of his own division, ready to start for India, of 14,000 men; that of General Hills, of 10,000 men; and that of General Gough, on the Khyber line, of 6000 men. With these forces it was not a difficult task to select as fine a division as ever marched under British colours, and it did not take our General long to make out the list. Two Highland corps, both renowned in song and story, the gallant and stalwart 72nd and 92nd, with the 60th Rifles, made up a strength of 1800 bayonets, and these were all picked men, passed by the surgeons, and pronounced medically fit for the march. Three of the best Sikh regiments, viz. the 2nd, 3rd, and 10th; the 2nd, three picked Goorkha battalions, the 2nd, 4th, and 5th; and the 23rd Pioneers; the 24th and 25th Native Infantry. These brigades were commanded by Colonels Macpherson, Baker, and Macgregor. Then the cavalry brigade, under General Hugh Gough, comprised as fine a mass of horsemen as any army could produce. Sir Hope Grant's fine old corps, the 9th Lancers, where the memory of that *beau sabreur* and thorough musician is still as green and fresh as the souvenir of poor 'Bill' Clayton, the introducer of polo into the army, and its victim by a random blow, with their fiery little horses, caparisoned, broken, and groomed to perfection, the 3rd Bengal Cavalry, the 3rd Punjabi Cavalry, and the Central India Horse, troopers recruited nearly all in the north-western border of India, with tall, lean, muscular-looking fellows, whose sabres and bamboo-lances have ploughed through many an Afghan squadron, and made many a turbaned foe bite the dust in the shock of the *mêlée*. These are led by one whose family name and renown are well maintained by its present representative in Afghanistan. Coming to the Artillery, we have three mountain batteries of seven-pounders, carried on mules, but no wheeled guns, making up altogether 274 British officers, 2562 British troops, and 7159 native troops, or a total of 9993 men, of which

1615 are cavalry, 318 being British cavalry. Our combatant portion of the division was arranged with the most complete detail, under the personal supervision of General Roberts, by the morning following the receipt of the order from Simla, but the transport arrangements and the question of supplies were deferred till a conference of the Generals and the staff was held. This took place at Sir Donald Stewart's head-quarters, where there were present Sir Donald, Sir Frederick Roberts and his brigadiers, General Hills, and the general staff. The official requisitions were then produced by General Roberts, and approved of by the Commander-in-chief, and were as follows :—For transport, 8307 animals of various kinds, with an addition of 2138 litter-bearers, and 266 riding animals of all kinds, for the conveyance of the sick and wounded. The ammunition carried by the ordnance park will be 236 rounds per gun and 100 rounds per rifle, the remainder being in regimental charge, while the small Engineer park will be carried by 80 mules ; 30 days' rum, tea, and sugar ; five days' flour for the Europeans, and the same proportion of rice for the natives, as well as 23,000 lbs. of attah and 28,000 lbs. of grain—the attah for the men and the grain for the animals.

These figures, having been carefully calculated, were then submitted to the political, supply, and transport officers who were present, and they assured Sir Donald and Sir Frederick that all these items should be forthcoming. General Roberts then said to Sir Donald that he had ascertained that the autumn crops of Indian corn in the Logar Valley were at this season well grown, and would, in all probability, be sufficient to supply what green forage was required on the march.

'I see that the Logar route is one march longer,' said Sir Donald, looking at the map.

'You are right, Sir Donald,' replied our General; 'but our chances of obtaining supplies in it are far stronger than if we went by Argandab and Maidan, as the latter route has been heavily drained by our troops and those of the enemy.'

It was in consequence of the Logar route being chosen by Sir Frederick that no wheeled artillery or 9-pounders were taken, the mule-batteries being more fitted to cope with the difficulties of the southern end of the valley, which is shut in by a rugged mountainous ridge, almost impassable to wheels. Where the Logar river enters the valley, the ridge in question, I remember from last year's march, crosses the Zamburra Pass, a steep of 900 feet, where it is met by the Wardek Glen, a defile in the mountain through which our troops must pass.

The next question discussed at this important conference was whether or not a base of operations should be retained for General Roberts, and the latter strenuously urged that under the present circumstances such would hamper instead of aiding him, while it would considerably weaken Sir Donald Stewart.

'A base of operations,' said General Roberts, 'where I could have magazines, provisions, ammunition, and recruits, and to which I could send back my sick and wounded men and horses, would imply an amount of transport which it would take a month to supply; and, moreover, I have every confidence in our being able to for once discard such dépôt, as our commissariat and political officers are assured by the Ameer that supplies will be readily forthcoming on the route.'

'Besides,' said Sir Donald, 'Ghuzni is but seven marches from Cabul, and at this time of the year the country from here to there, by the villages of Zargun Shahr, in the Logar Valley, Hissarak, Shekhabad, Hyder · Khal, Haftasia, and Shahgao, is through rich and cultivated valleys, studded with prosperous villages, whose people cultivate all sorts of grain, fruit, and vegetables.'

'All these villages, Sir Donald,' added our General, 'will, I believe, be only too glad to afford us supplies when they see how well we pay for them ; and if we can depend upon the agents of the Ameer being sent on well in advance of our column, I do not anticipate any difficulty, as the season of the year is so favourable.'

'I have every confidence,' said Sir Donald, 'that you can do now what I did in marching from Kandahar to Cabul, and what Nott did when he abandoned his base at Kandahar and marched to Ghuzni in 1842.'

Since the above conference constant communications have been passing between Sir Donald Stewart and the Ameer Abdurrahman, who has, in all that lay in his power, most loyally and energetically carried out his promises of help in supplies and transport. Every exertion has been made by his agents to produce carriage for our several columns, and it was with intense astonishment that we were made acquainted with the resources of the country round Cabul. Sir Donald has thrown his heart into the work, and so has General Roberts, as each sees how much depends on this requisite, and the success or failure of the expedition must in a great measure, if not wholly, depend on the result of their efforts in this direction.

With regard to the Ameer, his co-operation and

willingness to aid us are easily comprehended, as he naturally sees that the departure of our troops will not only in all probability extinguish a somewhat formidable rival in his cousin Ayub, but will leave him a king and not a puppet in the capital of his ancestors. It has, therefore, so happened, that in a few days there was a sufficiency of cattle and grain at Sir Donald's disposal to warrant his deciding on letting General Roberts march boldly, without any base, and *en l'air*.

The services rendered by our transport and commissariat officers have been highly and publicly commended by Sir Frederick, who has not lost an opportunity of expressing his gratitude for the assistance he has received from the exertions of these officers. Aware of the difficulty of obtaining camels in sufficient number, letters were written by the commissariat staff to the headmen of every village, calling upon them to purchase as many mules and ponies as they could procure in their various districts, and these letters, being endorsed and forwarded by the Minister of Abdurrahman, succeeded in obtaining us all we required.

It has been fortunate for our Government, and for our country, that the Viceroy has had to deal with such men as Donald Stewart and Frederick Sleigh Roberts, men who care more for the honour of England than for their own personal safety, and who do not shrink from a responsibility like the present, if by incurring it they can confer great and lasting benefit in restoring the prestige of our army in the eyes of the Afghan nation. In regard to the abandonment of a base of operations, whatever may have been the amount of responsibility cast upon the two Generals, neither Stewart nor Roberts have shrunk from it. They cheerfully took up the burden and placed it upon their own shoulders. They had no doubt as to the ability of their troops to carry everything before them. Cattle had been supplied, or were being supplied, sufficient for their movements, and it was only necessary that they should act in concert with each other in apportioning fairly the transport coming in, and so combine their operations as to move about the same time.

After a second Council of War had been held, and at which several of the Ameer's chief officers were present, further reports from the outlying villages were made to the General, and these were in the highest degree satisfactory. The Sirdar Mahmoud, an intelligent official and a man who has had considerable experience in obtaining supplies for Shere Ali's soldiers, was introduced while we were sitting, and on being questioned in Persian by the General said,—

'Excellency, I have come to you from the Ameer to say that no pains have been spared to carry out your views in regard to supplies and transport. Forage, consisting of barley, bhoosa (chaff), grain, and grass, will be at all the villages for your first six days' march, and in the quantities you have named to the Ameer. Atta, dhall, rice, and other grain for the native soldiers and camp-followers, are now being collected and stored. Potatoes in moderate quantities can also be had ; vegetables will not be wanting, and sheep have been requisitioned. They are of the Dhoomba species, and are numerous in the Ghilzai villages.'

The General then said, 'We shall want bearers to carry our sick in khujawahs, doolies, and dandies ; can you get them in any quantity ? I mean men who will not desert on the road.'

'I can send your Excellency 500 or 1000,' replied Mahmoud; 'men who will not fail when the Ameer orders.'

I may explain that a khujawah is one of the most horrible modes of locomotion ever invented. It is simply a long wooden or wicker framework, covered with canvas or cloth, with seats for two wounded men or invalids, and can be either carried on each side of a camel or on poles by bearers; six bearers are required for one of these doolies.

After the interview was over we adjourned to General Roberts' tent, where he explained to me at some length full details of his proposed march.

'I hope, should all go well,' said he, 'and we can start on Saturday, the 7th, to be at Ghuzni on the 15th, at Khelat-i-Ghilzai on the 23rd, and Kandahar on the 31st. We shall be lightly equipped, no man to carry more than 30 lbs., no wheeled vehicles, perhaps no sick or wounded; the hardest lot will fall, I fear, on our poor camp-followers and our animals, but I know the troops are full of enthusiasm, and will follow me anywhere.'

In reply, I told the General that the whole garrison were delighted at his good fortune in having been once more selected when an arduous task had to be performed. The General then gave me the draft of his order, which will be issued to the troops to-morrow :—

'It has been decided by the Government of India that a force shall proceed with all possible despatch from Cabul towards Khelat-i-Ghilzai and Kandahar for the relief of the British garrisons in those places, now threatened by a large army under the leadership of the Sirdar Mahomed Ayub Khan. Sir Frederick Roberts feels sure that the troops placed under his command for this important duty will cheerfully respond to the call made upon them, notwithstanding the privations and hardships inseparable from a long march through a hostile country. The Lieut.-General wishes to impress upon both officers and men the necessity of preserving the same strict discipline which has been so successfully and uniformly maintained since the commencement of the war, and to treat all the people who may be well disposed towards the British troops with justice and forbearance. Sir Frederick Roberts looks confidently forward to the successful accomplishment of the object of this expedition, convinced as he is, that all ranks are animated with the proud feeling that to them is entrusted the duty and the privilege of relieving their fellow-soldiers and restoring the prestige of the British arms.'

Such were the few simple yet soldier-like words addressed by the most popular and successful General in our army to the men who, European and native, would and will make any sacrifice for their leader, a leader who, like Bayard, is *sans peur et sans reproche.*

On taking leave of our young chief, he informed me that the Ameer had sent all his Turkestani camels and baggage-animals to our camp, and is at the same time forwarding all kinds of useful supplies. He has appointed governors to Ghuzni, Jellalabad, and Bamian, and the Governor of Ghuzni has received orders to assist and accompany our column when it arrives near his jurisdiction. The headman of the Wardek, Hazara, and Southern Ghilzai tribes, from whom we expected hostility, have, on the contrary, been sent on to collect supplies and to conciliate the people. 'And, in fact, I may say,' concluded the General, 'that if, under all these favourable conditions, and with soldiers such as mine, we do not achieve success, we will do more— deserve it!'

K.

BANQUET TO GENERAL ROBERTS—THE NEW AMEER—THE MARCH.

Head-Quarters Camp, Hissarak, Logar Valley, Aug. 10.

I HAD just finished my despatch to you of the 5th inst., when my orderly reminded me of the banquet to be given in honour of Sir Frederick Roberts that same evening, and to which I had the honour of a special invitation. *Grande tenue* out here is a very different affair from full dress at home; and although uniform is rigidly a *sine quâ non,* its various modifications suitable to the climate render it a costume perhaps as comfortable as the most inveterate lover of mufti could desire. White jean patrol jackets, deftly starched and glazed by the wily native washerman, a waistcoat and overalls of the same, and a pith helmet with white and gold puggaree, form the usual regimental and staff attire of all ranks, and give us a costume at once cool and comfortable, and yet neat and soldier-like. On duty a white pouch belt, and for evening a gold one, with patent leather boots and gilt spurs, complete the 'get-up;' and in this latter attire some thirty of us assembled on the evening of the 5th, to give a valedictory entertainment and farewell symposium to one who has earned and won the goodwill of all ranks—European and native—out here.

The dinner was inaugurated by Mr. Lepel Griffin and our political staff, and presided over by the former gentleman, than whom a better chairman it would be difficult to select. It took place in the same marquee formerly used by Yakub Khan, and in which Mr. Lepel Griffin a few days ago received the Ameer Abdurrahman. Amongst the invited guests the principal were Sir Donald Stewart, our Commander-in-chief; Generals Hills and Ross; and Brigadiers Macpherson, Baker,

Macgregor, and Gough ; as well as Colonel A. C. Johnson, R.A., and the very numerous staff allotted to the relieving column.

The tent was most artistically decorated with flags, trophies of arms, and wreaths of beautiful flowers, while over the President's chair a floral device was hung, with the words, 'God Speed,' in large letters. As the dinner hour drew near the portion of the marquee partitioned off to form an ante-room began to fill, and conversation became general. Greetings were interchanged, and warm wishes for success were proffered by the unfortunates to be left behind to their more lucky brethren selected for the expedition. The *menu* was in excellent taste, and had been entrusted to General Hills (and two other officers), whose reputation at the Bengal Club as a host can have suffered no loss by his efforts on this occasion. Soups, fish, roast, boiled, stewed, broiled, and curried meats, poultry and game, pastry, jellies, blancmange, &c., were there; while one *plat* was specially commended by the *cognoscenti*, being a dish, I subsequently ascertained, of rice, split peas, fried onions, chillies, small raisins, and curried fowl. Instead of lamb we had kid— the flesh of the young goat—which dish is much esteemed, as being small, tender, and nutritious, whether roasted or cut up into cutlets. But England supplied us with many a dish not procurable in Cabul ; and our friends at home who fancy we live on ration beef and mutton will perhaps be gratified to learn that we are sufficiently Sybaritic to procure here from the mother country such articles as York and Westphalia hams, reindeer tongues, cheese of all kinds, hermetically sealed vegetables and fish, anchovies and sardines, potted meats, German sausages, pickles, preserved fruits ; and indeed all those delicacies, called here technically 'Europe,' which can be obtained from those soldiers' friends, Fortnum and Mason.

Never shall I forget the pleasure of this farewell banquet ; never cease to remember the brilliant character of the conversation, the stories that were told, the speeches that were made, and the songs that were sung. Everybody was in the highest spirits ; and although, doubtless, it was impossible for a little *soupçon* of envy not to creep into the breasts of those who had no prospect of sharing in the dangers and glories of the march, yet this feeling, I feel sure, was but momentary, and soon driven away by more generous sympathy for the parting guests. After an excellent dinner, washed down by the generous vintage of Moët and Roederer, the Chairman gave, as usual, 'The Queen,' drank upstanding and most enthusiastically; and then, after a short pause, the health of the guest of the evening—Sir Frederick Roberts,—and with it, 'Success, and a speedy return with honour! May my lips be never again moistened with a glass of this Roederer if in my thoughts I associate the Kandahar column with aught but honour, glory, and success, a force commanded by the most brilliant and dashing leader of our day, and composed of the flower and the pick of our Indian army. His first march over the Peiwar Kotal and the Shutargardan will long be remembered in history, and will, I feel sure, be paralleled by his present march to Kandahar.'

General Roberts in his reply was, as befitting his nature, manly, terse, soldier-like, and modest; attributing his past successes to the materials placed at his disposal, and the character and quality of his men and officers.

I have given you some particulars of Abdurrahman, the new Ameer, in a former letter describing my private interview with him, while I was on leave upon a shooting expedition; and since then I was fortunate enough to accompany Mr. Lepel Griffin to the long-expected meeting which took place at the picturesque little village called Zernina, about ten miles from Cabul. Zernina is the very type of an Afghan village, surrounded by groves of mulberry, date, and palm-trees, built on the banks of a clear running stream, which is admirably utilised to irrigate the crops of Indian corn, maize, and other products of the soil. The houses are one-storied, with flat roofs and scarcely any ventilation, and are inhabited by a hard-working, industrious class of people, whose prosperity is amply evidenced by their flocks of sheep and other cattle. Pine-apples, custard-apples, mangoe,—the latter as a mere tree being very valuable, and affording by its shade, dense and dark, a grateful shelter to the horses of the escort—were in profusion; while thc teak, palm, banyan, bamboo, and the taliput, grew over the plain.

Our escort consisted of three squadrons of cavalry, made up from the 9th Lancers, 3rd Bombay Cavalry, and the 3rd Punjab Cavalry, and our advent to the village, which took place about seven a.m., induced a crowd of men, women, and children, to come out and look at us. The men seemed a handsome, manly-looking race; and what struck me mostly was the dignified air they assumed as they saluted our political officer and his staff. The dresses of the women were handsome and picturesque, and such as I had not seen in Cabul. Their attire consisted of a pair of gay-coloured silk trowsers, edged in some cases with silver or gold lace, so long as only to afford an occasional glimpse of the rich anklets, strung with small bells, which encircle the legs. Their toes were covered with rings, and a broad flat chain was passed across the foot. Over the trowsers a petticoat of some rich stuff was worn, containing at least twelve breadths, profusely trimmed, having broad silver or gold borders, finished with deep fringes of the same. The vest is of the usual dimensions, but it is almost hidden by an immense veil, crossing the bosom several times, and hanging down in front and at the back in broad ends, either trimmed to match the petticoat, or, in the case of a rich man's wife, composed of still more costly materials. The hands, arms, and necks of many of these women were covered with jewels—some, indeed, of considerable value; and it speaks most highly for our troops that cases of robbery or violence have been unknown, or almost unknown, when we have found occasion to occupy these villages.

One woman had her hair braided with silver ribbons and confined with bodkins of beautiful workmanship, while her ears were pierced round the top and furnished with a fringe-like series of rings; and the diameter of the nose-ring was as large as that of a crown-piece; it was of gold wire, and very thin. A pearl and two other gems were strung together over the mouth, much disfiguring the countenance. With the exception of this hideous article of decoration the dress of these women was, when they were young and handsome, and when they did not adopt the too prevalent custom of blackening their faces, not only rich, but becoming; and in the case of those with tall and graceful figures, most picturesque.

After passing through the village we reached the open space near a tope, or grove of mangoes, where the tents were pitched; and here our Political Agent dismounted, and sent two of his staff on to apprise his

Highness of our visit. In a few moments we saw the curtains of the Ameer's tent thrown back, and his Highness appeared, leaning on the arm of one of his ministers. He was dressed in a costume somewhat resembling our own—that is to say, a coat made of white linen, and cut in the European fashion, but plentifully embroidered with gold lace, while his blue cloth trowsers—made somewhat like knickerbockers—were tucked Yankee fashion into high boots made of patent leather. Upon his head he wore a sort of turban-shaped cap of some rich fur, and he also wore a couple of massive gold chains around his neck and across his chest, carrying at the same time a splendidly mounted gold-hilted sword, presented to him, I was afterwards told, by his friend General Kaufmann. The Ameer advanced midway between the two tents, and graciously saluted Mr. Lepel Griffin, to whom he offered his arm, and thus conducted our envoy to the larger marquee, where tea, coffee, sherbet, and pipes, were handed round by handsomely dressed attendants.

Abdurrahman having courteously invited our 'Political' to be seated on the couch near to him, commenced the conversation by the usual inquiries after our health and the health of our General. He struck me as a better-looking man than I considered him at my last interview, and his countenance indicated honesty of purpose and an expression of candour and *bonhomie* not characteristic of his race. He is a powerfully built man, with rather a full face and a large heavy beard, somewhat grizzled, but trimmed with care. After the usual compliments had been exchanged and the presents sent by our General had been examined most minutely, a conversation ensued on an infinite variety of topics, the Ameer passing from one topic to another with the greatest rapidity.   The conversation naturally turned upon recent events, and Abdurrahman spoke freely about the late defeat of General Burrows, which he characterised as unaccountable and almost excusable.

'What,' said the Ameer, 'was your General doing so far from Kandahar, with a force of little more than 2000 men ? and why did he not entrench his position and wait to be attacked, instead of giving all the advantage to Ayub ?'

I explained to his Highness that both General Primrose and General Burrows were acting under a higher authority than their own, and were, therefore, not free agents.

'In that case,' said the Ameer, 'your General should have assumed responsibility and retired carefully upon Kandahar, or at least sufficiently near to it to be supported by General Primrose.'

The Ameer then suggested that the conference should be continued in a more private manner, and consequently, upon a signal, all but the immediate staffs of Abdurrahman and Mr. Lepel Griffin retired into the outer tent. The Ameer then continued the conversation in a less formal manner, and expressed his warm gratitude to Sir Donald Stewart and Mr. Griffin for the manner in which all negotiations had been conducted. This was fluently spoken, and taken down in shorthand by our interpreter, who then translated most excellently the letter sent by Sir Donald to Abdurrahman. To this letter, enumerating certain details in the convention, the Ameer listened most attentively, only interrupting the speaker now and then to express his concurrence with, and complete satisfaction at, the proposals made by our Government.

'Two courses,' said the Ameer, 'are now before my

cousin, Ayub Khan,—to evade General Roberts and endeavour to march upon Cabul, or to await your General and give battle to his army. From what I know of him and the chiefs with him, he will, I believe, choose the latter course; and although he may fight well, he will be defeated.'

He spoke of the Afghans as a nation, and the Ameer dwelt with feeling upon their better qualities, which he said only required a just and firm rule to develop.

'The towns,' said he, 'in this country are few and far between, and the kingdom is but thinly populated; while the people, instead of a united race, are rather a group of races. They are brave, independent, and turbulent, at all times vindictive, and given to a constant succession of internal feuds. Amongst such a people war perpetuates itself, and blood is always crying for blood. Every Afghan is trained to arms, and, from his habits and the conditions of his life, becomes more or less a soldier.'

'But in the villages,' said our Envoy, 'I have noticed a different side to the picture, and I have seen that the inhabitants are hospitable and generous, entertaining us without stint, and coming into our camps with cheerful faces and courteous manners.'

'To see them at their best,' said the Ameer, 'you should visit the villages, not the towns, where, as soldiers, husbandmen, and shepherds, they are the very antithesis of the traders or shopkeepers of Cabul or Kandahar. In the evening, when the toils of the day are over, the headmen of the village are to be seen smoking and telling stories to their children in their gardens, or singing old Afghan ballads of love and war. They are, as a rule, kindly and considerate to their dependants, and in no Eastern country that I have seen is less of tyranny exercised over the slaves of the household or the dwellers in the Zenana. I do not anticipate much difficulty in my government, provided I can retain the friendship of the English ; and I trust I may live to see peace in the land, and wealth and prosperity in our marts and bazaars.'

The conversation then turned upon political matters, and lasted for more than three hours. Both our Envoy and the Ameer seem very much pleased with each other.

Sir Frederick Roberts' splendid column was to have assembled for a day or two in the Maidan Valley, previous to its final departure for Kandahar ; but as soon as the Logar Valley route was decided upon the force was reviewed outside Sherpur, where an immense crowd of Cabul people as well as many from the neighbouring villages came to look on. I consider the review that was held a most politic measure, as never in the history of Cabul had a finer military display been set before the Afghans. This review took place on Saturday, the 7th, and Sunday was given as a day of rest, so that the actual march did not commence till Monday morning at daylight, when even at that early hour a large multitude came forth to see us depart.

First of all, the whole force was formed outside the Sherpur cautonment in line of contiguous columns, having the cavalry and guns on either flank, and the whole of the baggage in rear. Soon after the line had been formed Sir Frederick Roberts rode on to the ground with Sir Donald Stewart, who purposed accompanying us part of our first day's march. The most minute medical investigation had been made, so that every man with the slightest complaint was excluded and left behind. Of our commissariat arrangements I have already given you details in my letter of last week; and I need only add that the mule and pony carriage of these supplies is so thoroughly complete that we shall be able, the General thinks, to make an average of seventeen or eighteen miles a-day. At 5.30 a.m. the orderlies galloped along the line of columns to say that all officers commanding corps and batteries were required by the General; and in the space of a minute or two Sir Frederick and General Stewart were surrounded by these officers, and received from him the following instructions :—

' Gentlemen, by the desire of Sir Donald Stewart I have sent for you to thank you for the admirable manner in which all my instructions have been carried out, and for the perfect state in which your men have appeared this day. The march of a division of 10,000 men over 300 miles of an enemy's country in a given time is a task which I have undertaken, and which I feel confident I can carry out; relying, as I do, upon the zeal and devotion of those who are now under my command. Our march will doubtless be watched with anxiety by our friends in Kandahar and by those belonging to us at home. We must, therefore, show that British soldiers can now accomplish what our forefathers achieved in old times ; and that upon an occasion like the present we can make any sacrifices to carry out the task set before us.'

Precisely at six o'clock all was ready, and the final order was given to move off by column of fours in successive brigades from the right. An advanced guard, composed of a squadron of the 9th Lancers and two mountain guns, were sent on at the usual distance in front, while a similar force formed the rear guard. The column then moved off by brigades as follows:— Cavalry Brigade, under Brigadier-General Gough, V.C., C.B.—9th Lancers, 3rd Punjab Cavalry, 3rd Bengal Cavalry, Central India Horse, and 50 volunteers 1st and 2nd Punjab Cavalry. Artillery—1, 2, 3 mountain batteries, under Colonel A. C. Johnson, R.A. First Brigade, Colonel Macpherson—92nd Highlanders, 2nd Goorkhas, 23rd Pioneers, 24th Native Infantry. Second Brigade, Colonel Baker—72nd Highlanders, 5th Goorkhas, 2nd Sikhs, and 3rd Sikhs. Third Brigade, Colonel Macgregor—60th Rifles, 15th Sikhs, 4th Goorkhas, and 25th Native Infantry. Amongst the very numerous staff the principal are Lieut.-Colonel Chapman, D.Q.M.G.; Major G. de C. Morton, A.A.G.; Major R. G. Kennedy, A.Q.M.G.; Major Badcock, Deputy Commissary-General; Captain Rynd, Lieut. Fitzgerald, Lieut. Montgomery, Lieut. Hawkes, Commissariat officers; Colonel Perkins, commanding R.E.; Major Cowie, Commissary of Ordnance; Colonel Low, Director of Transport; Lieut. Booth, staff officer Transport; Lieut. Fisher, Transport officer Cavalry Brigade; Lieut. Wilson, Transport officer 1st Brigade; Captain G. H. Elliott, Transport officer 2nd Brigade; Captain Macgregor, Transport officer 3rd Brigade; Captain Stratton, Superintendent of Signalling; Major Goshaw, Deputy Judge Advocate; and the Rev. J. H. Adams, chaplain, and Father Browne, Roman Catholic chaplain.

In a military sense Cabul may bé said to lie in a *cul-de-sac*, as, although 6000 feet above the sea, it is enclosed on three sides by mountain ranges, and has a succession of minor hills and rocky eminences, from which crowds of the inhabitants were now watching our movement across the plain. On our north lay the village of Behmaru, and on the low range of hills of the same name were also numbers of spectators observing our march. On the south-west angle of the city walls, and commanding the plain through which runs the Kandahar, Kohistan, and Bamian roads, stand the ruins of Mahomed Shah's fort ; and here again a large gathering of villagers and townspeople had collected. The sun had been early in the morning somewhat obscured by dark clouds and the mist rising from the Cabul river ; but now its rays came out in splendour, and lit up the glittering mass of armed men that swept across the plain in close and compact order.

The transport arrangements reflect great credit upon Colonel Low and those under him; and the subdivision of duties, each brigade and each regiment having its own staff, works admirably. Of course we are as lightly equipped as possible ; and great care has been taken to assign the most moderate loads to the ponies and mules, which form our only transport. I have on many recent occasions made excursions on horseback over the plains outside Cabul, and could not but be struck with the wonderful fertility of the district and its great capacity for agricultural operations. In the valley of the Cabul river and as far as the Logar there is really no unproductive soil ; corn and all the fruits and flowers of Europe growing there in abundance. The numerous streams which intersect this part of the country, rising from the snows of the Sufed Koh, and which discharge their waters into the Cabul river, are utilised by the inhabitants of the villages they pass for irrigation. In the neighbourhood around as we passed we noticed fields of wheat and barley and other cereals growing in luxuriance, and the whole length of the valley seemed one smiling garden.

Leaving the Maidan road on our right, we kept to the lower route leading to Sufed Sang, our first day's halt; but our 1st Brigade and our Engineer park with its eighty mules pushed on as far as Zargun Shahr in the Logar Valley, in both of which places there is good camping ground, with plenty of wood and water. Yesterday's march brought us through a fertile district to the village of Hissarak, where our camp was pitched in a splendid position on the slopes of the hills, which now became more steep and difficult. To-morrow we march for Shekhabad, where it is possible we may have some little opposition, as reports of a gathering of tribes have been brought to us. As far as we have yet come all has gone well. The men are in splendid trim for marching, and each regiment vies with the others in enthusiasm and eagerness to push on; indeed, were the opinions of 'Thomas Atkins' to be considered, our marches would be thirty miles a-day instead of sixteen. However, General Roberts is too good a soldier to hurry his men or to risk knocking up the weaker pedestrians: and his idea is to increase the length of our march as the men get into training. Thus after Ghuzni is passed we may probably do twenty miles a-day instead of our present rate. A tough day's work awaits us at the southern end of the Logar Valley, where the baggage animals will have to ascend a steep ridge over the Zamburra Pass, 900 feet, after which the road descends towards Ghuzni.

Our mules and ponies carry only two maunds, equal to about 160 lbs., and 430 of these useful animals have been told off for our thirty days' supply of European articles, to be husbanded as much as possible. Our men, however, receive their full ration of 1 lb meat; 1¼ lb. bread, or biscuit, rice, or flour ; 4 ozs. sugar ; tea, ¾ oz. ; salt, ⅔ oz. ; potatoes or vegetables, 10 ozs.; rum, 1 dram ; and the natives, attah, 2 lbs. ; dhall, ¼ lb. ; ghee, ⅛ lb.; salt, ⅔ oz.: while our horses are allowed, grain, 8 lbs., grass, 12 lbs.; and our mules, grain, 4 lbs., grass, 8 lbs. The commissariat arrangements work so well that these supplies are always ready for issue when the brigades arrive, and no man is kept waiting a moment for his daily ration. The length of our column is necessarily great, and yesterday it was computed to be six miles from van to rear.

CHAPTER V.

ON THE LINE OF MARCH WITH THE RELIEVING COLUMN.

Ghuzni, Aug. 15.

MY last letter to you from our camp at Hissarak, in the Logar Valley, gave you, I believe, full details of the magnificent force now under General Roberts' command, and I can now supplement my account by telling you how admirably our hopes have been fulfilled as regards the marching powers of our men. Leaving Cabul on the 7th, our marches were through a smiling and fertile country, *viâ* Zargun Shahr, Hissarak, Shekhabad, Hyder Khel, Haftasia, and Shashgao. We crossed without difficulty the steep mountain ridge which closes in the southern end of the Logar Valley by the Zamburra Pass and the Wardek defile. Here the road becomes difficult, and we had some little delay with our mountain batteries; but fortunately we have no wheeled carriages, and all obstacles were surmounted. In specifying our force of mountain batteries, I omitted to tell you that we are fortunate in possessing in 6–8 some of the new 7-pounder 'jointed guns,' due to the invention of Colonel C. B. Le Mesurier, R.A. The ordinary mountain gun, you are no doubt aware, was limited in its weight to 200 lbs., and this limit enabled it to be carried by one mule; but Colonel Le Mesurier conceived the happy idea of increasing the length and weight of the weapon, by making the muzzle and breech in two portions, to screw together by means of what is called 'a trunnion hoop.' Each of these portions weighs about 200 lbs., and the gun can therefore be carried by a couple of mules.

General Roberts has impressed upon all ranks the necessity for strict rule and obedience on the line of march, and at every halt a careful inspection of men, horses, mules, and cattle, is made. Sore backs, foot-sores, galls, and accidents, are at once reported, and all ranks are divided into squads for greater convenience in issuing supplies and detecting casualties. The wisdom of choosing the Logar Valley route has been fully justified by our present rapid and successful advance, for had we marched by the Maidan and Argandab road we should have found great difficulties in obtaining supplies. Fortunate for us the autumn crops in the valley have been unusually fine, and the Indian corn especially, being well grown, has supplied us with plenty of green forage. As we have with us 8307 animals of all kinds, you can imagine what an important element is forage and grain. The ordinary rate of marching in Europe is allowed to be not more than two and a quarter miles an hour—this, of course, to include short halts at the end of each hour—but, from the calculations I have made, I see that our average has been within a fraction of three miles an hour, which, considering the heat, is, to say the least, wonderful. For a division of all arms, again, it is laid down that twelve or fifteen miles a-day is a fair march; but we have exceeded this, as our average has been sixteen miles a-day. As Sir Frederick's division numbers 274 British officers, 2562 British troops, 7157 native troops, in all 9993 men, the daily supply in round numbers, on our full rations, comes to no less than 70 country sheep, 900 4 lb. loaves, or 25 cwt. of biscuit, besides rice, sugar, tea, salt, and vegetables.   These commissariat difficulties, however, have been gallantly overcome by the energy of our supply officers and the exertions of the native Gomastahs, or commissariat agents, sent on from village to village by the Ameer.   In case of accident, however, and to insure men and animals not missing their rations, each man and each animal has always carried one day's supply.   These rations are consumed during the day, and replaced at every evening's halt.   But we are not, of course, dependent upon the villages for our supplies, as we carry with us plenty of cases of cooked corned beef, 28 tins in a box, weighing 1 lb. $10\frac{1}{2}$ ozs. each, plain boiled beef in boxes of 12 tins of 4 lbs. each, preserved potatoes in boxes of two tins, 56 lbs. each, compressed vegetables, in boxes of three tins, 16 lbs. each, and rock cocoa in boxes of 56 lbs.

Nothing can exceed the beauty of the Logar Valley, and many were the artistic sketches made by our fellows at our various halts.   The views on either side of the Logar River were charmingly varied.   The moisture of the climate and the nature of the soil concur in preserving a perpetual verdure most refreshing to the eye, after the dusty and parched regions we had quitted. Even at the hottest period of the day, and when the sun poured down with so fierce a light that it seemed as if its scorching influence were sufficient to dry up every blade of grass, the whole earth seemed covered with a rich carpet ; while the moment the sun sets a refreshing coolness fills the air, and our eyes revel upon the richest luxuriance.   The diversity occasioned by the wood, sometimes in small clumps, sometimes spreading to groves, and at others thickening into forests, and at all times profusely scattered, takes away all monotony from the scene. The banks of the Logar are in some places so high, especially at some of the sharper angles of the stream, that they assume the character of promontories, and most of these are wooded to the top. Nothing, I repeat, can exceed the beauty of the foliage which waves over this favoured valley; the bamboo, flinging its long branches down with willow-like grace, the varied species of palms rising in regal majesty above, and the fine feathery foliage of both, relieved by the bright masses of the neem, the peepul, and a host of others, many bearing flowers of a thousand dyes. The magnolia is common in the valley, and amidst a vast number of the acacia tribe there is one of peculiar beauty called the Cabool. It is covered with a flower tufted like a ball of a golden colour, which gives out so delicious a perfume, that one will scent a whole garden. Here and there the summits of the more striking elevations are crowned by mosques or tombs of some Afghan hero. Most of these buildings have the round flattened dome usual with Mussulman temples, while the stairs, which are very handsome, are not unfrequently strewn from top to bottom with fresh flowers of the most beautiful description. Long garlands of the Afghan jessamine, a large, white, double blossom, with a rich but heavy perfume, or of a large scarlet or yellow flower, hang over the rails, as these followers of Mahomet have so far adopted the custom of their heathen neighbours as to spread flowers upon the tombs of their departed friends.

At five o'clock on the morning of the 10th I accompanied General Roberts, with his escort of 50 Lancers, in advance of the cavalry brigade, from Zargun Shahr towards Hissarak. Messages had been sent back from us to the Ameer at Cabul, in order that General Stewart might be kept *au courant* with our progress. Soon after moving off we passed a grove of neem trees more extensive than any I had seen, and at a small distance a large but ruinous village ; and thence on, came to a country much wilder, worse cultivated, and seemingly less peopled than the districts we had left. What cultivation there was seemed principally of maize, growing very tall, but sadly burnt by the recent drought. This, however, was only in patches, and the greater part of the prospect consisted of small woods, scattered in a very picturesque manner over a champaign country, with few signs of habitation, and those only in ruins.

Every traveller whom we met, even the common people going to market, had either swords or shields, spears or matchlock guns, and some, indeed, had bows and arrows. The road was now rugged, and nothing could be more unfounded than the statements we had heard that horse artillery could have passed easily. Both the sides of the road were walled in in places by high scarp rocks, where our flanking parties had considerable difficulty in getting along. By driving slowly no doubt it would have been possible to get a 9-pounder along, but it would have been a difficult task to take wheels along a track which, when beaten, was so dented by the feet of horses and cattle, and so hardened by the sun, as to resemble a frozen farm-yard ; while whenever we forsook the road we encountered cracks deep enough to break any ordinary gun-wheel. Sir Frederick and I were about a mile in front of the head of our first brigade. We had a couple of sowars in front at a couple of hundred yards' distance, and vedettes on either flank, while connecting files kept us in communication with our main body. We occasionally passed a few villagers on the road, who seemed to manifest no surprise at the military display we afforded. Both men and women whom we met I thought taller and fairer people than the Cabulese. Some of the women whom we passed were of complexions so little darker than our own, that as they approached they might have passed for Europeans. Instead of the softness and gentleness so apparent in our own Sepoys, these men have a proud step, a stern eye, and a rough and loud voice, such as might indeed be expected from a people living almost entirely in the open air, and in a country where, as a rule, no man is sure that he may not at any moment be compelled to fight for his life or land.

Judging from those I have seen, I should say the Afghans of the Logar Valley are remarkably handsome and athletic, with fair complexions, flowing beards, and highly aquiline features. Their limbs are muscular, though perhaps not stout, and they are capable of enduring great hardships in their own country. They are fond of hunting, hawking, and all kinds of field sports; are capital horsemen and unerring marksmen with the rifle, and nearly as true in their aim with a stone thrown from the hand. Among themselves they are humorous and convivial. In the presence of strangers, however, they are proud of their nationality, and especially of the 'Nang-i-Puckhtana' or 'Pukhtun honour,' and assume an air of integrity which is but ill supported by the other traits of their character. I have found them, as a rule, vain, bigoted in religious matters and national or tribal prejudices, revengeful of real or imaginary injuries, avaricious and penurious in the extreme, prone to deception, which, however, they fail to conceal, and very often wanting in courage and perseverance. But with all this they assume a frankness and affability of manner which, coupled with their apparent hospitality, is very apt to deceive and disarm the unwary. They are, moreover, by nature and profession, a race of robbers, and never fail to practise this peculiarly national calling on any and every available opportunity. Among themselves the Logar Afghans, I have noticed, are quarrelsome, intriguing, and distrustful of each other, and by their neighbours they are considered faithless and intractable.

By ordinary stages, and *viâ* Maidan, Ghuzni is seven marches from Cabul, but by the lower road and the Logar Valley it is one march longer. Passing under a range of low hills, the columns crossed the Cabul river, which at this season is not a formidable obstacle, being not more than twenty-five yards in breadth and two feet deep. Zargun and Hissarak are the first two halts by the lower road, as Magandah, Maidan, and Shekhabad would be on the upper route. After passing Zargun Shahr and Hissarak, the lower road inclines to the right, and tends towards Saidabad and Shekhabad; while another branch leads through a richly cultivated country to Hyder Kheyl and Haftasia. Shekhabad is eighteen miles from Maidan, and one brigade of our force went by that road, effecting a junction with us at Haftasia. After passing Shekhabad we crossed the Logar by a narrow bridge, and marched through a smiling and richly cultivated landscape for about eleven miles, which brought us to Hyder Kheyl, ten miles from Shekhabad; and marching through the richest part of the valley, where thriving villages were seen, another eleven miles brought us to Haftasia, where we halted on the 12th.

Marching from Haftasia on the morning of the 13th we had to pass several short defiles, where the road was so narrow that, although the cliffs on either side rose to several hundred feet, our flanking parties could converse with each other as they advanced along the rocks towards Shashgao, which we found to have an elevation of 8700 feet.

The nights under canvas were now delightful, and nothing could exceed the comfort of our cotton dwellings. The authorities, of course by General Roberts' desire, have placed us on the shortest possible baggage allowance; but this has not made us in the least uncomfortable, and will, I trust, lead to many reforms in the absurd *impedimenta* usual to an Indian army on a march. The mess tents serve as dwelling tents, and instead of the small-pattern Cabul tent the ends open right from top to bottom down the centre, and both ends are 'porched,' that is, the porches fastened to the inner not the outer fly. Even then the weights run rather heavy for the camels, and are as follows :— Outer fly, 15 lbs.; inner ditto, 30 lbs.; 3 poles, 15 lbs.; mallet, 9 lbs.; suleetah and peg bag, 7 lbs.; pegs of iron, 30 lbs.: total, 99 lbs. These tents give accommodation to 15 men or 10 officers, and to each mess are assigned cooking utensils amounting to 10 lbs.—with mess stores 40 lbs.—viz. four copper handis, four copper talis, two tin flour-pots, one large spoon, one knife ; and for each person table utensils as follows :— one drinking-cup, one cup and saucer, three iron enamelled plates, one pair of tin muffineer plates, two teaspoons, one dessert and one tablespoon, two small knives and forks, weighing in all 7 lbs.

The mess stores are 1 tin of 30 portions soup, 2 packages dried vegetables, 4½ tins Huntley and Palmer's meat wafers, 6 small pots of Liebig's extract, 3 1 lb. tins of 'Erbswurst' pea sausage (each tin sufficient for four people), 12 bags meat cabbage, 3 1lb. tins Romford soup, 12 tins Effner's condensed eggs (containing 6 eggs each), Dalby's compressed tea, 2 tins condensed milk, 2 lbs. condiments, 5 lbs. corn flour, arrowroot, sugar, 6 lbs. candles and lantern 8 lbs., making in all 40 lbs.; 640 dinners of 'Erbswurst'—two maunds—can be carried on one mule. Our camp followers are allowed 10 lbs. each, and the horses 15 lbs. each, the latter consisting of waterproof hood, 2 horse-blankets, fore-shackle and rope, brush, comb, hand-glove, two cloths, knee-pads, and blinds, zine bucket, tobia (grain bag), and 1 kit bag.

To those who imagine we are undergoing the hardships of the mutiny, or the privations of a Siberian campaign, I will merely say that our march up to the present time has been a veritable picnic, not unaccompanied by a rubber of whist in the afternoon, and not divested of that little duck and quail slaughter which, in a measure, consoles our youngsters for the banishment from Hurlingham and the fierce delights of an English *battue.* Wild duck are plentiful, and although the *tanks* are not so large as those I have shot over in Mysore or the Carnatic, the sport has been excellent. The General, as an Irishman, is naturally a sportsman, and gives every encouragement to our youngsters to add to our mess ration a toothsome relish of teal and other wild fowl. Yesterday I had the pleasure of making, in company with our chief, a very fair bag of snipe and teal, but I must say the work was hard even for a man in severe training. The walking was bad enough on dry land and bog alternately, and then one has to retrieve one's birds oneself by wading in after the wounded ones through a mass of long weeds, which have a knack of knotting round one's legs in a most dangerous manner.

After passing Shashgao, eight and a half miles from Haftasia, we found that, leaving an elevation of 8700 feet, the road undulated through a gloriously cultivated piece of country leading us to the celebrated Pass of Sher-i-dana, over 9000 feet high, and in the vicinity of which is the tomb of Sultan Mahmoud. This monument is in tolerable repair, and is in a grave and solemn style of architecture, being a square tower pierced on each front with elegantly formed doorways. A grove of noble trees under which General Roberts' tents were pitched, and where our horses, camels, and bullocks, were disposed in different clusters ; the marquees, tents, fires, baskets of fruit, rice, ghee, &c., brought for sale by the villagers, and the varied and picturesque costumes of the crowd assembled to stare at the Feringhi, the white garments of our camp followers and servants, the long veils and silver ornaments of the female villagers, and the dark mantles, dark beards, and naked limbs of the native peasantry, gave the whole scene of our encampment an animated and interesting effect. For the latter part of our way up this magnificent defile we saw our immense and sinuous column, like some leviathan monster, winding its way up the steep hills,.and amid mountain scenery of great magnificence. The rocks on the summit had all the appearance of fortresses, and the deception was in one instance singularly heightened by the circumstance of one of the creepers I have mentioned having thrown itself across the chasm, just below the walls of an imaginary fortress, like a drawbridge. This spot, if held by a resolute foe with a few pieces of cannon, might have stopped us for a considerable time, but, fortunately for us, no Afghan tribe had seen its value. The valleys between these hills are well cultivated with rice, and I was told that enormous quantities are grown. The verdure of the young rice is particularly fine, and the fields are really a beautiful sight when surrounded, as on this occasion, with magnificent mountain scenery. About two thirds of the way up the pass we halted to breakfast at a spot of singular and romantic beauty, and here we were met by some of the headmen of Sher-i-dana, who accompanied us part of our way on horseback. The road, which must have been constructed with immense labour, winds up the side of a mountain covered with thick jungle and magnificent forest trees, amongst which are the ebony, the iron, and the 'thief' trees—the former with a tall, black, slender stem, spotted with white ; the iron tree, black and hard, as its name denotes ; and the last, rising with a straight white stem to a great height, singularly contrasting with the deep verdure around it. I have a vague hope that our messengers may reach with these letters; but the packets are now closing, so I must reserve my account of Ghuzni till my next. Meanwhile all well and in high spirits.

At Hissarak the Logar is a narrow and sluggish stream, and one of our camps was pitched on a piece of ploughed ground between the village and the river. The stream has a firm, pebbly bed, but at this season is of no particular depth, and consequently easily fordable. In a month or so, and during the rains, however, matters change, and the volume of water greatly increases. On the western bank of the river the surface is curtailed by low stony hills, with scarcely any vegetation excepting a few scattered specimens of the 'khingak,' which are dotted here and there over the surface. On either side of the Logar river the country for, perhaps, an average breadth of three or four miles, is densely populated, and, I noticed, is laid out in one mass of vineyards, orchards, and corn-fields, in the midst of which, in close proximity to each other, are scattered the numerous little fort-enclosed villages of the inhabitants. Logar is, I need hardly repeat, a cultivated valley, and densely populated by several different tribes, who are generally at enmity with each other, and this will account for the bellicose appearance of most of the men we met. The district, fortunately for our contractors, produces corn in great abundance, and, in fact, with Ghuzni may be called one of the principal granaries of Cabul. It also produces vast quantities of fruit, and its apricots and grapes are extensively exported to Hindostan. Here, instead of being grown in deep trenches, and their branches supported by intervening ridges of earth, or on frameworks of wood, the vines are planted in regular rows, and trained like bushes, by clipping and pruning their branches and tendrils. The grapes are chiefly known as the varieties of 'Hussaini' and 'Shaikh-Khalli.' They are gathered before they are quite ripe, and packed in 'drums' of poplar wood, between layers of cotton wool, and in this manner are exported to Hindostan.

But besides these fruits are vegetables, of which we have partaken of almost every variety, including the potato, which, however, is of recent introduction. The people seem, for the most part, occupied with the care of their flocks and herds, and, as a mass, have a healthy and robust appearance ; but I hear that during the greater part of the autumn months numbers of them are laid up with a malarious fever.

In some of the villages we were shown manufacturers of a coarse material from the wool of the 'baira,' or sheep, while in other districts they are celebrated as the makers of a sort of earthenware water-jug, called a 'surahi.' These we found very useful, as they keep water cool by means of evaporation.

The Logar population, though so often at enmity with each other, go for the most part about their fields unarmed, and in this respect contrast wonderfully with some of the other villages beyond the valley. They have been, on the whole, more than disposed to be friendly with our men, who have, as a rule, freely fraternised with them.

From Tangi Wardak to Hyder Kheyl the distance is twelve miles, and beyond Tangi the Logar Valley narrows into a defile flanked by low hills of bare rock. The hills are of very irregular outline, and in some parts hardly a couple of hundred yards apart. From Tangi the road led through part of this defile along a watercourse that was cut in the slope of the hilly ridge that bounded the valley towards the north, and the banks of which were flanked by rows of willow-trees and 'sangits.' The latter is a very handsome tree with silvery leaves and a sweet-scented flower, very diminutive and growing in clusters. Although at Tangi the valley is narrow, it is covered nevertheless with a mass of villages and cultivation. Many of the former are fortified, and built with great regularity. Beyond the Tangi defile the road passes over a series of ascents and descents, and conducts to the high table-land of Ghuzni.

Now our halt is at the village of Shekhabad, where

it joins the main road between the cities of Cabul and Ghuzni. From Hyder Kheyl to Swara is fifteen miles, by a gradual and easy ascent all the way, along a fair military road that traverses the brow of a long and regular mountain ridge. On the east and left of the road the country slopes away by an easy ascent for about a couple of miles, and then rises in low hills or peaked eminences. Immense flocks of goats and sheep, herds of cattle and camels, ploughed lands regularly mapped out with lovely looking villages, corn-fields, fruit - gardens irrigated by numerous streams coming from the high lands above, and an abundance of grain, assured us that, if we were not in a land of milk and honey, we should not perish of starvation.

Ghuzni, where we arrived to-day, is one of the principal cities in the Afghan empire. It is eighty-eight miles west of Cabul, on the main road to Kandahar, which is 233 miles off. There are many roads hence to India, the principal being by the Kuram route, by Urgunj and Khost, by the Jadran country and Dawar, by the Gomal to Dera Ismail Khan.

It is situated on the left bank of the Ghuznee river, on the level ground between the river and the termination of a spur jutting out from the Gulkoh range. The city spreads out to the south and east of the spur, at the extremity of which the citadel is built. The town is an irregular square, each side being about a quarter of a mile in length, and is surrounded by a high wall built partly of stone, partly of brick. The wall is flanked by lofty towers, and is surrounded by a deep ditch, except across the spur where the citadel stands. The city is composed of dirty, irregular streets of houses, several stories high. They are very irregular, and will not bear any comparison with the bazaars of Cabul and Kandahar. The population, who are mostly Afghans, with the exception of about 200 families of Hindu shopkeepers, number close on 10,000.

They have a look of wretchedness and poverty, and are remarkable only for their ignorance and superstition. The chief trade of the city is in corn, fruit, madder, wool, and camels'-hair cloth. The only manufacture is that of sheepskin coats. The neighbouring country is very fertile, the orchards being especially renowned ; the fruit of these are largely exported to Hindostan. Tobacco and corn are grown only for home use ; also the castor-oil plant.

On our taking the place in 1839, we found half a million pounds of wheat and barley and 80,000 pounds of flour in the bazaar.

The weather still continues most favourable for marching, and the men have not suffered ; but the climate of Ghuznee is very severe in the winter—it is said to be the coldest place in Afghanistan ; as a rule, snow lies on the ground from November to February. In the summer the heat is very disagreeable, and storms being of constant occurrence it is very unhealthy, owing probably to its bad drainage and the dirty condition of the inhabitants.

Until the present war Ghuzni was comparatively unknown, as no Europeans, to our knowledge, had visited the place since Nott destroyed it, so we are ignorant of its defences ; but in 1842 all the Engineers were of opinion that, though admirably calculated to defy the implements of war in use at the time of its construction, its defences would not be sufficient to detain an army provided with a siege train for three days before its walls. Some scientific authorities give it as their opinion that its situation, as well as its construction, is totally defective; others, in location, position, construction, and condition, consider it useless. Durand, on the contrary, deemed it a spot, situated on the line of communication between Cabul and Kandahar, commanding access to the Gomal Pass, of great strategical value, and the question of strengthening it of great importance. There can be no doubt that he is right.

THE SORTIE FROM KANDAHAR—VILLAGE OF DEH KWAJA.

Kandahar, Aug. 20.

WE have been in such a state of worry and excitement since the disastrous affair of the 27th, and we have had so much work to do in regard to pulling down buildings and cutting down trees, to place obstacles on the roads and in front of our gates, that I have allowed two opportunities for the despatch of letters to escape. In war, as in other matters mundane, misfortunes seldom come alone; and now I have to chronicle a disaster almost equal in intensity to the sad story of which I told you in my last.

At the instance of Brigadier-General Brooke, who strongly advised General Primrose to the attempt, an ill-judged, ill-devised, and foolish sortie, was attempted by us four days ago. We have been much annoyed by an irritating rifle fire upon our ramparts from a village called Deh Kwaja, which lies within range of and towards the east face of our citadel. We knew that the main position of the Afghan Prince faced east. Our spies have brought us intelligence that Ayub had with him thirteen regiments of regular infantry, thirty-eight guns—many of them rifled,—a very numerous array of cavalry, and a large body of fanatical Ghazis. General Brooke himself demanded permission to lead the sortie, stipulating however—or, I should say, suggesting—that our very weak artillery should bombard the village. Poor Vandeleur was with me on the night of the 15th; and although he had specially requested to serve as a volunteer, he pointed out that his knowledge of the locality, gained from frequent quail shooting in the neighbourhood, made him certain that the village we deemed so easy of assault would be found an extremely difficult, hard nut to crack. Several of our men and camp followers have from time to time been murdered by these villagers, who are known to be most bitterly hostile to the wealthier traders of Kandahar and the Kizilbashi merchants, who are friendly to us. With Vandeleur in my tent were two other officers, who had been in the habit of quail and duck shooting on the plains near the village, and they also were strongly of opinion that a simple bombardment, instead of a rush at the village, would be more prudent. However, as we had not the ordering of the affair, nor the control of events, matters were allowed to take their own course.

Before I give you full particulars of the sortie, I may tell you that Brigadier-General Brooke most gallantly led the assault, and was cut to pieces while endeavouring to carry off his wounded comrade and my old friend, Major Cruickshank, our field engineer. Amongst the killed were Colonel Newport, 28th Bombay N.I.; Le Poer Trench, 19th Bombay N.I.; and young Charley Stayner, of the same corps; Poor Teddy Marsh, 7th Fusiliers; young Phil Wood, of the same; and our popular and zealous chaplain, the Rev. J. Gordon—for many years connected with the Church Missionary Society.

About two hours before daylight our force, in two columns, was drawn out in front of the Cabul gate. The night was somewhat misty, but the moon now and then came through the clouds and lit up the bronzed faces of our Sepoys, many of whom, to say the truth, seemed not particularly elated at the prospect of our venture. The innumerable watercourses that interlace, as it were, the plain that intervenes between our citadel and the village seriously interfered with the order of our march and the movements of our field guns. Prior to the sortie, I have omitted to inform you Ayub had occupied the cantonments, which we had, I think, imprudently abandoned. This occupation, however, afforded considerable amusement, combined with some very excellent artillery practice to our gunners, who, at 900 yards from the Cabul gate, were not long in shelling out the forces posted there by the Afghan general. The latter on the 7th of the month detached a couple of brigades to a strong position on the Herat road, almost between the Mir Bazaar and the Argandab river ; while his cavalry and right flank were placed on a steep prominence not far from the ruins of the old Kandahar city. It would be difficult to describe how unusually strong and strategically chosen was this front, enfilading the village, whose approach was watered by many deep canals and irrigation channels, which could be crossed only at few points.

On the morning of the 9th General Primrose ordered some field guns to take up a position on the Picket Hill overlooking our cantonment, and these guns during several days made excellent practice upon the loopholed walls of Deh Kwaja. Ayub, it was known, had posted a strong body of irregulars in the smaller villages to the right and left of Deh Kwaja ; and we were given to understand that, should an opportunity occur, a night attack would be made upon our Cabul and Durani gates. As I have said, the walls of the village are honeycombed with loopholes, and approachable only through a mass of orchards and considerably broken ground. Our cavalry were carefully selected, and consisted of 300 of picked sabres, in equal proportions of lancers and *l'arme blanche.* To these were added 900 bayonets, furnished respectively by the 7th Fusiliers, and 19th and 28th Native Infantry.

At the first approach of dawn our guns opened fire upon the village, which we could see was very strongly occupied and reinforced from the neighbouring hamlets. Deploying one half of his infantry into line, with 100 of our cavalry on either flank extended in skirmishing order, General Brooke moved steadily across the plain, taking advantage of whatever cover we could obtain in the gardens and orchards through which we passed. Some 200 yards from the Cabul gate there is a rather deep nullah, behind which there is a mass of rock, the whole forming a most perfect ditch and parapet. Here we came to our first obstacle, namely, some 500 well-posted rifles, who inflicted considerable loss upon our men. Here Colonel Malcolmson, of the Scinde Horse, had his charger shot under him, being himself badly hit through the sword arm. Major Cruickshank, with fifty men, was then ordered to move round to the left, with the intention of outflanking the enemy ; while Colonel Shewell made a very gallant charge on the other flank. The nullah did not suffice to stop our gallant Scinde horsemen, who charged it in brilliant style with but few casualties.

Here, however, one of our guns became entangled, and for a short time had to be abandoned. Lieut. Wood of the Transport, and Lieut.-Colonel Nimmo, 28th Native Infantry, and two other officers, made the most desperate efforts to prevent the Ghazis from carrying off the gun. Here one of the best hand-to-hand combats that has ever been witnessed between our Sepoys and the Afghans took place; and, after several repulses, one final rush of a company of the 7th drove the enemy from his vantage ground. Our loss, however, I am sorry to say, was not slight; and considerable delay was experienced from the necessity of carrying back to the shelter of our ramparts our wounded comrades, who would otherwise have been massacred and mutilated by the villagers, whom we could see collecting in the distance.

Experience in Afghan warfare and in a difficult country is the prosecution of an art under the most trying circumstances to 'Thomas Atkins' when led by inexperienced generals. In our case we had certain advantages, which were counterbalanced by telegraphic instructions from civilian authorities. All the ordinary obstructions to a successful defence or to an effective sortie accumulated upon us in an aggravated form. Whether in climbing steep ridges, crossing the Kandahar watercourses, forcing rocky defiles, or attacking villages encompassed by loopholed walls, all the knowledge of locality was, unfortunately for us, entirely in favour of the enemy. In my previous letter, written more than a month ago, I gave you some short sketch of Ayub's training in the grim school of war. Ten years younger than his cousin, Abdurrahman, the present Ameer, whom we have placed upon the throne, he has, whether from Russian tuition or intuitive knowledge, evinced a capability of handling troops in his own country and on his own ground which makes him at all times a formidable antagonist to any red-tapist school to which he may be opposed. He knows how to hold all the commanding points of the difficult country, and he of necessity is well acquainted with the peculiarly strong adaptations of the villagers who can assist him in his method of irregular fighting. Simple and abstemious in their living, inured from childhood to the use of arms, careless and reckless of life and blood, having as a rule that air and exercise on their mountain-sides which inure them to hardships, these men are capable of physical exertion such as our well-fed recruits, on the other hand, toiling wearily over unwonted difficulties, cannot pretend to ; and they fight with overwhelming numbers. which far overbalance the ordinary conditions of our more regular formations aud severe drill. He well understands the difficulties we have to experience in moving regularly organized bodies of men over an almost pathless country. His devoted adherents and innumerable spies in all the villages—in fact, in all the districts—make him well acquainted with our efforts to supply transport required for the carriage of food, ammunition, clothing, medical stores, and the almost countless details which have to meet the artificial wants of a European force. Our long lines of elephants, camels, bullocks, carts, transporting huge tents, together with tables, chairs, waterproof clothing, tinned meats, and other unwieldy and unnecessary—so we think—items of our military equipment, give him enormous advantages in our present struggle. But when to these *impedi-menta* we add the hordes of native followers, out-numbering, by a large percentage, our actual fighting men, vast allowances must be made for any mistake which a well-meaning, but not brilliant, English leader may commit.

The enemy, who had, as I before stated, taken ad-vantage of the natural defences of the deep nullah, with its rocky breastwork behind, and who were in consider-able strength in the hamlets and villages beyond, without any doubt had gained reliable intelligence of our intended attack.

Our troops, on the morning of the 16th, were scarcely in position outside the Cabul and Kandahar gates, when a strong force of their cavalry, admirably led by the chief who was so conspicuous in his brilliant charges at Maiwand, rushed down the steep slopes of the mountain above, and with loud shouts attacked our advanced skirmishers and our unsupported guns. Nothing but the steadiness of one company of the 7th Fusiliers, who had been posted in a hollow, would have checked the onslaught, and all their efforts to dislodge this picket failed against the determined handful of men which the General had sent forward.

The peculiar manner in which an Afghan village is constructed, and the skill which their simple engineering and knowledge of field fortification display, ought perhaps to have suggested a night instead of a day attack, a mode of fighting which former frontier ex-periences tell us is always objectionable to these hardy combatants. In that case the smallness of our force would have been unknown, and a desperate attack hardly pressed would, in all probability, have effected our object without the loss and bloodshed which daylight enabled superior numbers to inflict.

While the fierce struggle was taking place at the nullah I have described, and whilst the echoes were ringing with the shouts of the combatants and the booming of our covering artillery, General Brooke was sitting on horseback with his field-glasses in hand behind a small breastwork of which we had taken possession on the left flank of the village. From this we saw a strong force, composed of swordsmen and matchlock men, advancing boldly to the attack, charging across the plateau in our front in the most determined manner, and following their standard-bearer with a red and gold lunghi steadily.

It was now seven o'clock, and we were still some hundred yards from the village. The fire from these men was uncommonly steady, and our efforts, both with musketry and occasional charges of horsemen, for a time were unsuccessful. Their swordsmen at intervals endeavoured to rush upon our flanks, but here we were advantageously posted, and our mountain guns moving to a neighbouring hillock, with an effective fire at short range, threw their masses into disorder. A general advance was now ordered, but our losses were now heavy, our infantry suffering most, as the nature of the ground gave cover to our foe while we were in the open. General Brooke, Colonel Newport, Major Trench, and Lieutenants Stayner, Marsh, and Wood, were all badly hit, but still seemed in the thickest of the fight. At this juncture messengers arrived from the city with instructions, if possible, to retire, but I fear that a point of honour deterred our chief from accepting this alternative. Our leading companies, moreover, were now at the walls of the village, and we could see that practically they were in a position to be cut off if not supported. Under these circumstances our General sent back word that he could not with safety retire, and galloping in front of a squadron of Scinde Horse the main street of the village was carried. Here Major Cruickshank, with his Sappers, had effected a lodgment in a ruined building surrounded by a large compound, and held at bay the increasing forces of the enemy, who were now swarming in from the neighbouring hamlets ; but a ball from one of the matchlock men struck him in the groin, and as he fell from his horse half-a-dozen swordsmen rushed to despatch him. General Brooke saw his plight, and generously endeavoured to save him by assisting him with his stirrup. In the *mêlée* which ensued both were carried away by the rush. Colonel Newport, who was riding with Colonel Malcolmson, of the Scinde Horse, now gave the order to retire, and the street was held by the 7th Fusiliers and a detachment of the Sappers while the movement was effected.

If any satisfaction can be experienced at this disastrous and unsuccessful day, it lies in the fact that our ill-advised attempt upon the position of Deh Kwaja resulted in a far greater loss to the enemy than to our people, while the *morale* of the affair has had beyond all doubt a vast effect upon the besieged and the besiegers. The conduct of our native troops in this sanguinary tussle has, we all think, greatly redeemed, if not atoned for the demoralisation of our Sepoys and Sowars at Kushk-i-Nakhud, and the fate of the brave young officers who led their men to the assault at the village, and who were struck down sword and revolver in hand, has taught both the Afghan Ghazi and the Indian

Sepoy that the race of Clive, Wellesley, Havelock, and Outram is not extinct. One native officer I particularly noticed who tried to save his colonel (Newport), and who gave up his life in the attempt. He not only stood over his commanding officer when struck down, but remained to defend him, while the conspicuous gallantry of a havildar was noticeable, as, rushing ten paces in front of his company, he cut down a standard-bearer and captured his standard.

Our retreat, I need scarcely say, was not unmolested, and had it not been for Malcolmson's Horse, and the brilliant manner in which they wheeled about to charge across our flanks, the day would have been even more disastrous than it was. They not only drove off the pursuing enemy who now swarmed along the rocky knolls, which gave so many coigns of vantage to our foe, but chased them precipitously along the ridges, and forced them back in confusion into the valley. While this was being effected, our Sappers and half a company of the 7th Fusiliers had thrown up a low breastwork across the rear of our column, and this being flanked by a couple of mountain guns, and held with unflinching tenacity, enabled our disordered infantry to retire in something not approaching to actual flight. The combat during the retreat was perhaps even more desperate than during our assault. These desperate Ghazis and bold mountaineers, ignorant of discipline or any regular art of war, and armed only with rude matchlocks, short swords, and axes of native manufacture, had by a sort of natural instinct discovered at once our weak points, and, by feints upon our centre, and furious assaults upon our flanks during the whole of our retreat across the plain, not only inflicted a tremendous loss upon us, but at one period seriously endangered our position. Our losses are out of all comparison with the number of forces engaged, and may be set down at the very least at 200, including General Brooke, who was last seen endeavouring to save his old friend Cruickshank. Colonel Newport was three times wounded, and was last seen with Colonel Shewell trying to save an injured man. Our chaplain, Mr. Gordon, with the greatest devotion, returned from the Cabul gate to a spot outside the walls, where five men were lying, and in trying to assist the dhoolie bearers to save them was, with several of our men, shot down by a volley of musketry. Poor Vandeleur, who was badly hit early in the day, has since died, and our hospital is now full to overflowing. Meanwhile we know that Roberts is not more than two or three marches from Khelat-i-Ghilzai, and should be with us in a week. Our wounded are doing well. Our provisions and ammunition, if not abundant, are sufficient, and our greatest anxiety now is that we may measure swords with Ayub, and wipe out the inglorious 27th of July.

CHAPTER VI.

WITH GENERAL HILLS IN CABUL—INTERVIEW WITH THE AMEER—
EVACUATION OF THE CITY BY GENERAL STEWART.

Jellalabad, Aug. 23.

THE division to which I am attached is under the command of Major-General Hills, V.C., C.B., and is composed of three brigades, led respectively by Brigadier Charles Gough, with the 9th Regiment, 28th Punjab N.I., 45th Sikhs, three troops 1st Punjab Cavalry, the Guides Cavalry, four guns of the 11th B, 11th B, R.A., and half a company of Sappers. Brigadier Hughes commands the 2nd Brigade, with the 59th Regiment, the Guides Infantry, 3rd Goorkhas, one squadron 2nd Punjab Cavalry, and two guns of 11th B, 11th B, R.A. The 3rd Brigade, under command of Brigadier Daunt, has the 67th Regiment, 5th Punjab Infantry, three troops 1st Punjab Cavalry, and G battery, 4th Brigade, Royal Artillery. Our whole combatant strength does not exceed 7500 fighting men, while our artillery consists of twelve guns; but what with camp followers, refugees, pilgrims, and others, who are taking advantage of our escort to flee from the anarchy they believe is in store, our columns cannot be less than 30,000 men, with about 20,000 beasts of burthen. Roberts, on the contrary, had with him 10,000 fighting men, and as little *impedimenta* as possible; while to our care are left the sick, the wounded, the lame, the halt, and the blind!

The great event of the week of our departure was, naturally, the formal meeting which took place between

Abdurrahman and our chief, and the announcement in divisional orders that such would happen caused no inconsiderable surprise in camp and quarters. The first refusal of the new Ameer to meet Sir Donald was, of course, attributed—and, I believe, justly—to motives of policy and prudence in not wishing to offend the sirdars and moulahs, who are inimical to the English ; but these scruples were eventually overcome, and all arrangements were concluded most satisfactorily.

On the morning of the 12th the whole of our division had been judiciously withdrawn outside the cantonments, and the city was in virtual possession of the Ameer. This was a wise arrangement, and prevented any wounded susceptibilities on the part of the Ameer and his advisers. It was impossible not to feel a little humiliation at the inroad made upon the Sherpur cantonment by the filthy rabble who came like vultures to prey and rob before we had well quitted the walls. An aspect of desolation is invariable in an abandoned camp, and ours was certainly no exception to the rule. Jews, Arabs, Mussulmans, Budmashr of all kinds, swarmed around our men as they were getting our baggage, stores, and ammunition ready for the march. Theft and barter, the latter strongly the more prominent, reigned on all sides, and it needed all the vigilance of our sentries to keep off the ruffians who pressed on all sides.

It was arranged that the meeting between the Ameer, Mr. Lepel Griffin, and the English Commander-in-Chief, should be held in a couple of marquee tents placed end on to end on at a spot some short distance from the western wall of the Sherpur cantonment, and at the appointed hour, at this point, the tents were pitched for a few chairs for the principals to the interview. The

Ameer's troops were massed in considerable numbers on the plain, but the actual *cortége* did not number more than fifty horsemen, including, however, the principal sirdars and the palace officials, all attired in gorgeously trimmed robes. The costumes worn by the higher officers of the Court were really very handsome—a loose shirt with wide sleeves, and trowsers equally large, the latter fastened round the ankle; over this the 'chogo,' a garment worn even during the hot season. This is made (for the higher ranks) of the finest camel or goat's wool, and dyed with the richest and most varied colours. Some of the sirdars, however, had adopted the more modern fashion of wearing a 'chogo' made of English broad-cloth. The 'chogo' is a graceful garment, giving dignity to a tall or well-made figure—a loose cloak, worn open in the front, and reaching from the neck to the ankles. The sleeves are wide and loose above, and are made much longer than the arm, but narrow and close-fitting below, so as to clasp the wrist. Some-times the loose folds of the 'chogo' are gathered in round the waist by the cummerbund, which is usually from fifteen to eighteen feet in length, of rich material, and four to six feet in breadth. Shawl materials are usually chosen by the rich, and coarse cotton by the poor. Most of the nobles wore the 'charah,' a for-midable Afghan knife, while a few carried in the folds of the waistband the 'peshkabs,' or Persian knife, a smaller and more convenient dagger for close quarters. The head-dresses were various, but all the elder chiefs had the close-fitting skull-cap, gold embroidered, and padded with cotton-wool. This, of course, is worn on the closely shaven head, and then round it the richly embroidered 'lunghi,' or turban. Most of the chiefs had flowing beards and moustaches, which, with their fine, well-cut, Oriental profiles, gave a nobility of mien.

As the Ameer and Sir Donald came within a dozen yards of each other, each dismounted and shook hands, and, followed by their respective retinues, walked side by side into the tents. Sir Donald conducted the Ameer through the length of the canvas hall, which was decorated with boughs and flowers, and hung with coloured drapery, until the seats of honour were reached, and placing Abdurrahman on the highest, placed himself on the right, Mr. Lepel Griffin and General Hills being on the left ; while, standing around on the borders of the rich rugs, were about a dozen of the more friendly sirdars, who were politic enough to 'assist' at the ceremony. The Sirdar, Abdul Raman, or Abdurrahman Khan, is a good-looking, but somewhat unwieldy, personage, with rather open and pleasing features, of a strongly developed Jewish cast. His age is about fifty ; but care and campaigns, battles and prisons, have not failed to leave their mark upon his face. Mr. Lepel Griffin, General Hills, and Mr. Cunningham, acted as interpreters, and the conversation did not flag in the least. Sir Donald said,—

'I have the honour to welcome your Highness to your ancestral city and your throne, and trust your journey hither has not fatigued you.'

. To this good opening the Ameer responded,—

'I desire, General, before expressing my thanks for all you have done for me and mine, to wish you long life, health, and prosperity in your noble profession.' His Highness then said,—'The joy, the delight I feel at returning, after fourteen years of exile, to my home and throne, is enhanced by the interview we now have, where. instead of writing, I can express my gratitude by my tongue to you and to your political officers, whose correspondence has shown so much friendly courtesy.'

Sir Donald then wished the Ameer a long and happy reign, and said how proud he felt at in any manner aiding to place the Prince upon the throne. The conversation then turned upon less formal subjects, and the General requested permission to present us to his Highness, to which he most graciously assented. As we passed in rotation according to our relative positions more than according to our rank, the Ameer, as we bowed, responded by half rising from his seat. We now moved outside the tent, to allow the Ameer, our ' Political,' and the Chief, to be alone ; and while we were waiting our orders to join our brigades we amused ourselves by watching, with considerable interest, the proceedings of a detachment of Gazailchis (probably Ghilzais), who were marching in to relieve our main guard. These fellows numbered about 250 men, and looked a wild, but serviceable lot, stepping over the ground as I have seen some of the little Chasseurs de Vincennes step years ago, and marching with that quick, jaunty air so characteristic of French or Irish regiments. They marched to the sounds of their ' sarnai ' and ' niggarah,' pipe and drum, whose piercing strains made the hills re-echo, while the spirits of the men, excited no doubt by our departure, every now and then caused them to burst out into shrill yells and fantastic capers worthy of Donnybrook or a Highland wedding.

Ten minutes after the interview we had commenced our march from Cabul. As we moved across the plain we saw on our right and left detachments of the Ameer's army marching in to take possession of our late cantonments, and to guard the stores left behind by General Stewart as a present to the Ameer. The infantry seemed a fine set of young men, and appeared more orderly than those from whom we had just parted. They were clad in uniforms of a European pattern, but of a drab colour, and evidently made from 'barak' (sheep's wool) or 'shuturi' (camels' hair). Then came straggling bodies of cavalry, whose appearance betokened a set of savage marauders, and their cruelty and violence to the villagers around has already engaged the Ameer's attention. These men are the curse of the country they are supposed to protect. They take what they want from the villagers without any recompense, and commit the most lawless excesses without any fear of retribution, for their officers, as a rule, share the spoil wherever they go.

Our advanced guard, some of artillery and cavalry, had moved away before daybreak, but we did not get away till after the interview was over and the formal handing over of the keys had taken place. Along the hills, under which our troops moved in the closest possible order, we could see with our field-glasses predatory bands of mountaineers watching us in impotent rage,—these men, of small stature, wild air, and of squalid clothing, creeping along from rock to rock.

Cabul, as I have before said, in a military sense, lies in a *cul-de-sac*, inasmuch as, although it is situated 6000 feet above the sea level, it is enclosed on three sides by the mountain ranges. It is approached on the east by a pass only 200 yards wide, where the road crosses the river by a stone bridge and enters the city by a fortified gate. On the north lies the village of Bemaru ('Without a husband'), which, with a low range of hills bearing the same name, is called after a virgin who was buried there. These mountain ranges, from which artillery could be brought to bear at every point, afforded so many coigns of vantage for the mob' of fanatics and hill-robbers who now came to gloat over our departure. The heights around our camp were already in possession of these people, and they amused themselves with a succession of war-dances, accompanied by a constant beating of drums, while working themselves up to the wildest excitement as they saw us march. Scattered parties on the hill-tops around followed each other with a succession of shouts and yells of the most demoniac description. All this time we could hear a chorus of 'Wo-ho, hah-ha,' the slowly repeated syllables of which were echoed back in a confused reverberation from the crags above. It is almost impossible to describe the excited appearance of these men and the wild antics they performed, while it was wonderful that they did not wound each other in their intricate and rapid evolutions with unsheathed knives. Some of them were almost nude, while others wore a sort of loose shirt and trowsers of cotton dyed red or blue. Round the waist were suspended by leather straps powder-flasks of uncured sheepskin, with other paraphernalia of the usual jezail slung across the shoulder. Those who had not the rifle carried the 'charia,' the sheath of which was stuck into the folds of the waistband, while the blade was flourished about in the air in the most insolent and defiant air, and with grotesque antics and grimaces. As we moved along, these ruffians, having failed to irritate our men into retaliatory measures, sought to provoke our fellows by their taunts and jeers, but eventually gradually quieted down, leaving us, however, in full expectation of a night attack when we should encamp. The forbearance of our men, and the manner in which they obeyed their orders, deserve every commendation. Of course we were under no apprehensions of anything beyond plunder, or the murder of some of our camp followers, but at this juncture General Hills was most anxious to carry out his instructions, which were to put up with everything except actual hostilities. Two friendly sirdars, whose names I had better not mention, rode with me several miles on our first morning's march, and, while deeply incensed at the conduct of these hillmen, explained that they were exceptionally lawless, and opposed to the Barukzai rule.

'They do not know,' said one of my interlocutors, a fine, manly young Barukzai chief, 'all the good qualities of my cousin, Abdurrahman, but he will soon regain his popularity in the districts over which he ruled for many years. In Turkestan his influence is considerable, and from Balkh to Badakshan his name ranks high as a just man and a good administrator, while as a popular governor he has no rival. Under these circumstances, I believe we have not made a false step in giving him the chance of a probationary Ameership, without any positive guarantee of future assistance should his rule not be accepted by the majority of the Afghan people.'

Said I, 'The address of Mr. Lepel Griffin in April last admirably sets forth the reasons for our choice of the new Ameer. It was to this effect :—"The course of events having placed the Sirdar Abdurrahman in a position which fulfils the expectations of the Government of her Majesty the Queen-Empress, they are pleased to announce that they publicly recognise the Sirdar Abdurrahman Khan, grandson of the illustrious

Dost Mohammad Khan, as Ameer of Cabul. It is to the Government a source of satisfaction that the tribes and chiefs have preferred a distinguished member of the Barukzai family, who is a renowned soldier, wise and experienced, with sentiments most friendly to the British Government ; and so long as his rule shows that he is animated by these sentiments he cannot fail to receive our support." '

WITH SIR FREDERICK ROBERTS—ARRIVAL AT KANDAHAR.

Head-quarters Camp, Karez Hill, Night of 31st Aug.

TO-DAY has been an eventful one in the annals of our march from Cabul to Kandahar, for not only has our gallant young chief arrived some days before his estimated time, but he has, with the able assistance of General Hugh Gough, felt the enemy's position, and made all preparations for to-morrow's attack. Before I tell of to-day's proceedings and our effective reconnaisance, I perhaps had better take up some portion of my broken story, dating from my last despatch of the 23rd ; and when our friends at the military clubs are envying our fortunate stars in serving under such a chief as ours, they must not forget that in fourteen marches we have covered 235 miles, namely, from Cabul to Khelat-i-Ghilzai, and that the remaining distance has been accomplished at the same average per diem —roughly speaking, sixteen miles a-day. To see the way in which all ranks vied with each other in putting up with the fierce blaze of an Afghan August sun, the hardy resolution of our English soldiers, stimulated by the example of their officers, both young and old, and nobly emulated by our gallant Sepoys, would have gladdened the eyes and warmed the heart of a Wellesley, a Gough, a Clyde, or a Napier, still household words in our native ranks. Almost within a month of the Maiwand defeat we now stand face to face with the foe; ready—nay, I may say certain—to inflict one of those terrible lessons of the game of war which our little army is compelled now and then to teach.

The month of August, although trying in the midday sun, is singularly favourable to the march of an army in this portion of Afghanistan, in regard to supplies of all kinds ; and the assistance afforded to us by the headmen of the villages favourable to the new Ameer, the strict discipline enjoined and carried out by our General, and the ample recompense made in money payments for what we consumed, have caused our troops to be fed, as our subalterns observe, 'like fighting-cocks.' The country through which we have passed is at this period of the year in its most smiling mood. Nature seems to revel in corn and wine, and plenty. Flocks and herds have come in in abundance, and our men declare they have never been better fed.

Between Cabul and Khelat-i-Ghilzai I told you in one of my letters how wonderful was the system of irrigation. The country has not such a cultivated look, but this may be accounted for by the neglected water-channels, whose remains show that in former years the Afghan husbandman was more diligent or more provident than in our present day. After the close valleys and cramped defiles leading out of the Logar Valley, it was a delightful relief to come upon ground near Ghuzni where wide and open plains enabled our General to deploy his brigades and to march in line, thus saving valuable time and allowing our baggage to come up in reasonable time. On arrival at Ghuzni we found that Sirdar Hashim Khan had made the best of his way hence but a few days before, and the buildings and barracks in the citadel and city gave ample indication of the recent occupation of his troops.

Ghuzni has been so often described that I need only say we were agreeably disappointed by its appearance ; and much pleased during our hasty halt at being enabled to look at its various historical landmarks still extant, and reminding one of the old struggles between the British and Afghan troops. The landscape round the citadel and the neighbouring villages showed signs of assiduous cultivation, and afforded us many welcome delicacies in früit and vegetables ; while the pleasant waters of the small river enabled some of us to have an impromptu swim, to the great astonishment of the native inhabitants.

On leaving Ghuzni a few miles brought us to the scene of General Stewart's fight at Ahmed Khel, where several of my friends were engaged last April ; and here, as we passed, we could see many traces of the battle, notably in the graves of our soldiers and those of the enemy. The district and the villages through which we passed were friendly, and most of the headmen came in to our camp to offer supplies and to converse with us. Here we obtained some excellent sheep of the fat-tailed breed, and more than one chief explained to us what a delicacy these tails were considered, dished either as kabobs or pillau. On marching onwards from Khelat-i-Ghilzai, I should have mentioned that General Roberts decided to take with him the garrison under Colonel

Tanner, whose delight and that of his officers and men at the chance of sharing in our fight with Ayub were beyond all expression. I may tell you that to Colonel Tanner's courtesy in keeping the communications open I and my brother-officers are indebted for the opportunities we have had of sending letters on the march to our friends in England. Colonel Tanner's contingent was by no means an inefficient factor in our military strength, consisting as it did of two guns of C.B., 2nd B., a Belooch corps, and about 170 men of the 66th. The old fort has been handed over by the General to the Sirdar, and we are thus free from all present anxiety.

Our hour of march has usually been from 2 to 2.30 a.m., and this necessitates a parade of an hour beforehand. Our camel loss, as I before said, was at first heavy, but since we left Ghuzni matters have gone better, as the country was more suited and the loads were much lighter, mules and a few country ponies having been obtained at the villages. During our last week's marches the scenery has been exquisite in its variety, displaying a singular combination of romantic wildness with charming fertility. One day our columns would wind through luxurious valleys, interspersed with hamlets, vineyards, and flower-gardens ; and the next we found ourselves struggling up mountain ridges and forcing our path through alp-like passes, overhung with toppling cliffs, looking as though some terrific convulsion of nature had rifted the hillside asunder, and scarped the precipice more regularly than could be effected by the hand of the cleverest engineer. Sometimes looking below we saw streams rippling in the moonlit and misty dells, and above us rose naked rocks and splintered precipices, while the varied uniforms of

our moving stream of soldiers, their glittering arms—
now seen, now lost amidst the windings of our route—
gave a moving and panoramic character to the *ensemble*
that would make the fortune of an artist if reproduced
on the painter's canvas.

Some smart skirmishing occurred during our march
about five days back, when part of our rear guard was
attacked as it was coming into the camp ; but the affair
ended without any loss of men or baggage to us, while
we shot down some dozen or more fanatical robbers who
thought they would loot our mule train.

The spot where the attack was made was a wild and
romantic valley on the banks of a bright and rapid
stream. Our leading brigade had encamped here the
preceding afternoon, and it was chosen for our rear
guard on account of its defensive position, having excellent points of vantage and observation on the rocks
above for our sentries and vedettes. It is wonderful
how quickly, after a little practice, our fellows arrange
their resting-places after a halt. Within half an hour
from the halt of the advanced guard our rearmost mules
were up, the baggage unladen, the fires lighted, and
dinner prepared. No delay is ever seen at these important operations ; every man has his place, and there are
no idlers, for every man is told off for some employment.
Here a party are unloading mules, there another are
carrying wood, some men are watching the camp-kettles,
others are mending harness. All are busy, while ' chaff,'
smoking, and laughter, lighten each toil.

But to our skirmish. There is always to a soldier
considerable satisfaction in fighting under the eyes of a
favourite commander, and on the occasion of which I
speak our rear guard had that gratification, for General

Roberts, with a few of his staff, happened to be in the rear of our last column. Although the ground was most unfavourable for a surprise on the part of the enemy, they attempted and managed to catch a Tartar. The road by which we were passing was, it is true, rugged, steep, and narrow ; but, at the same time, it was overhung with crags and underwood which the General had carefully occupied early in the morning of the attempted surprise. A mountain stream protected our rear, and increased the difficulty of an attack in that direction. The enemy, however, had established a breastwork of their own on our right, and this was concealed by some tall brushwood which grew luxuriantly in front of their work.

General Roberts has ridden frequently to hounds with me in Lord Waterford's country, and has, as I well remember, an inimitable eye for country. The quiver of a blade of grass, the rustle, the 'frou-frou' of a leaf, or the slightest footfall in his neighbourhood, are to him a language that a soldier or a sportsman can understand. Sir Frederick, moreover, on this occasion had other reasons, which he kept most carefully to himself, for believing that our rear and baggage guards would be attacked about this time, and in some locality near this day's march. The rear guard, much to the astonishment of its worthy commandant, was therefore somewhat reinforced, and the most stringent orders were given to keep a sharp look-out during the day. Every precaution, I need scarcely tell you, was taken on this occasion. The sick, or rather those who, although not exactly on our surgeons' list, were at all 'done up' or 'a little seedy' from sun or footsores, were carefully sent to the centre of our column, and were replaced by well-selected fellows, whose marching and athletic powers were known. The steep slopes on either side were occupied by strong pickets, except where the enemy's breastwork had been formed, which we did not discover till later on. These were flanked and supported by a couple of guns, and under such conditions we entered what was intended to be our trap. Still, our position was not all we could have wished. Our length of column was of necessity far extended, and might have been attacked at any point. Our flankers were extended far up the mountain-sides, and any help sent to them could only reach them after considerable delay and a fatiguing ascent. Our extreme picket on the left stood on a rocky and projecting crag, commanding part of our line of march, and, indeed, dominating, as it towered up towards the sky, the road below. On our front, a little off the road, was another pinnacle, almost equally commanding, and sparsely clothed with pines. Both these coigns of vantage were invaluable, and helped us to defeat the foe, for they entirely overlooked our lower defences. But, high as these positions were, they had other ridges and dominant positions still again far above them, where our enemies could gather unknown to us and pour upon us, at their own choice of time, a fire from their long jezails and our captured rifles.

The mode of fighting of these hillmen has been so often described by older and more experienced hands than mine, that I will merely say that their usual plan of attack is carried out on the same simple and uniform system. Taking up a position under cover, and, if possible, within short range, and with only the muzzles of their matchlocks appearing above the sheltering rocks, they, at a given signal, open up a brisk fire upon their enemy, and thus compel our men to seek shelter by coming to close quarters. Then their wonderful swordsmen rush to the attack, and are only too glad to have a hand-to-hand fight against a man armed only with a bayonet. These men are armed with the terrible Afghan short sword, which they know so well how to use, and which has lopped off the limbs of so many of the Kaffir race. Collecting for a moment to regain their breath, and to prepare for their final rush, while showers of stone and vast splinters of rock are hurled at us from above, the hillmen, with terrible and unearthly yells, 'go for' our young and hardly full-grown lads.

Is it then a wonder that, now and then, our battle prestige of conquest is tarnished, and in actual hand-to-hand combat, where a knowledge of the 'manual and platoon' is no match for the rude cunning of the tulwar, we occasionally see demoralisation and a hitherto unknown feeling of terror in our ranks? It is, even to me, a wonder that, marching for days and nights through a difficult country, with an unfriendly population, and under conditions to which 'Thomas Atkins' has never been accustomed, our 'boys' (for really many of them are no more) bear up so bravely, and think so much of England and so little of themselves.

On the morning of the 26th we were one day's march from Khelat-i-Ghilzai, and encamped on the banks of the Tarnuk, which graceful little stream has yielded us capital supplies of excellent water. This river has its origin in some fine springs we passed near Makier, a village some eight or nine marches from Cabul. We did not march from our camping-ground till rather later than usual, as there was no moon and the night was cloudy, with fitful gusts of rain. But about one a.m. it became clear and starry, although there was no moon, and the dark masses of mountain, occupied by our enemy, were visible for many a mile. Waiting for us on those hills above were, our General knew, some thousands of Afghans thirsting for our blood. Few sounds were there in the night except the challenge of our sentries, the Highlanders, 'Wha gaes thar?' or the Sepoys, 'Woo-go-da?' as our chief and two of his staff go round. Then we heard the ripple of the waters, and saw in their reflections a myriad stars, reminding us of nights, perhaps less bright, but more dear, at home. Away in the distance were the occasional watch-fires of our men, for as our force was of such magnitude, it would have been idle and useless to have attempted to conceal our camps.

Our leading columns moved off quietly and unmolested at four a.m., and not until our rear guard approached the defile I have attempted to describe were we attacked. Our last brigade was scarcely clear of the pass when a heavy and rattling fire, although ill aimed, came from the concealed breastwork I have named. A dear young friend with whom I was riding cried out with all the ardour of a schoolboy, 'By George, the chief *was* right! There *is* a wasp's nest here!

Our conversation was curtailed, as the General galloped up to find an officer to take a message. Fortunately I was chosen, and putting spurs into the old bay Arab, from whose saddle many a pig has been smitten, I galloped up the side of the kotal to give the General's order to young P—— who held the picket.

Meanwhile our baggage was clear of the pass, and all we had to do was to keep these human vultures off and give our mules and camels time enough to obtain protection from our columns. The rocks I have named on our flanks were held by some Highlanders and some native troops, chiefly chosen marksmen, and these had been until now unseen by the enemy. Our concealed foe, as I have said, had constructed a small breastwork on the rock to our right, but did not know that it was dominated by our detachments hidden higher among the tall crags. The Afghans, seeing our preparations for attack, gladly accepted the challenge. We had no sooner commenced to fire at them with our mountain guns, with shrapnel, common shell, and shot, than they rushed down the slopes of the hills, climbing, or rather jumping, over places which no one but a born cragsman could face ; then they with loud cries dashed upon our pickets above. Our shrapnel fire had checked them from advancing direct upon us, and drove them on to the muzzles and bayonets of our concealed pickets. The latter, I must say, were attacked with the greatest determination, while two of the enemy's standards were carried in front by leaders who evidently did not belong to the village. All the efforts of our enemy to dislodge our pickets proved unavailing, and about an hour after the combat had begun a larger body of men, who had hitherto fired only an occasional shot, commenced to move upon us from their position, their jezail and matchlock men posting themselves most advantageously in the pine wood, and opening a fire upon us which, with better marksmen, would have been galling in the extreme. The steady *mitraille*, however, from our rifles, with which they they were received, rendered their gallant attempt abortive, and we drove them back up the hill, leaving the ground marked here and there by a few dead men, who had fought bravely to the last, and who, doubtless, thought more of their faith than of their lives.

Of our reconnaissance to-day and preparations for to-morrow I would fain tell you, but I am sent for by a staff officer, and must close my bag, unless the mail be delayed. At all events, I may say that Gough this day has done good work. His news after his skirmish was important, and to the following effect :—The head-quarters of Ayub are now at Mazra, where nearly all his best forces are with him. He has been endeavouring to break up the roads leading from Kandahar to his position with gunpowder, but, we hear, without much success. This afternoon, therefore, Gough went out with the 3rd Bengal Cavalry, 15th Sikhs, and a couple of mountain guns, and made a most successful reconnaissance towards the enemy on the Herat road. Of this, as I obtained permission to go, I will tell you to-morrow, if I 'keep the number of my watch,' for to-morrow we fight, as Ayub cannot escape, and, to do him justice, I do not think he would, flushed as he must be with the bloody records of Maiwand.

CAVALRY RECONNAISSANCE BEFORE THE BATTLE.

Head-quarters Camp, Karez Hill, Night of 31st Aug.

YESTERDAY afternoon General Roberts sent for Generals Macpherson, Hugh Gough, Macgregor, and Colonel Chapman, chief of the staff, and explained to them his wish for a cavalry reconnaissance, and to utilise the same by clearing the low hills beyond our old cantonments, as these were held by the enemy in force, and commanded our water supply in that direction. Indeed, the supply for the use of the garrison had already been cut off, and great was the rejoicing thereat by Ayub's people. At first it was thought only necessary to drive these fellows from the hills, whence they were occasionally dropping shells into our camp, but second considerations induced the General to make the reconnaissance in force, and, if necessary, convert it into a serious attack. The position of the enemy on the morning of the 31st was as follows :—His main camp was on the Baba Wali range and Kotal, standing on the right bank of the river, and extending about thirty miles from east to west, and at its topmost ridges not less than 5000 feet high. Its sides are for the most part steep, bare, and rugged, the higher summits being fringed with forests of fir, and in the winter capped with snow. There are, however, various small villages belonging to the tribes, amongst which the principal is called Gundi-Moola-Sahibdab. Here and there dense forests run down to the plains. The roads are few and bad—in fact, mere tracks for mules between the villages. To the north-west of the Baba Wali Kotal is a higher and more precipitous range, through which there is only one pass, called Murcha Kotal, and this lies almost due north of Kandahar. The mountain on the eastern side is very abrupt, and is divided by the Argandab, while all along its southern slopes lie the plains of Pir Paimal. The scenery from the crest of the Pir Paimal Kotal is very varied, and contains, in many respects, elements of grandeur. To the south-west the vast plains of Kandahar stretch away in endless expanse—at least, such is the effect produced by the mists rising in the valleys. The Argandab, after leaving the foot of the mountain, widens considerably in its southern course, and at certain seasons attains the proportions of a lake. Just before reaching the highest range of hills it joins the Helmund, flowing in the valley of that name, and then, passing along by many villages, it rushes through a narrow gorge, and is lost to sight. Whilst the chief characteristics of the southern view are those of a vast cultivated plain, watered by numerous rivers, and dotted here and there with peaceful villages, the aspect to the north is of an entirely different character. At the very foot of the northern slopes lies the sheltered narrow valley of Mazra, and here Ayub had made his head-quarters.

As many details had to be settled, our force did not parade as early as originally intended, but by ten a.m. the following troops were paraded :—3rd Bengal Cavalry, two mountain guns, the 15th Sikhs, and a few of Macpherson's Brigade. We moved quietly out of camp, the cavalry and guns bearing away under some low hills to our right, while Macpherson took his infantry steadily to the front. Our plan was to drive the enemy from the first range of low hills, which acted as a sort of glacis to the Pir Paimal range to the south-west of Kandahar, while Gough and Chapman took their handful of cavalry along the Herat road, in the hope of getting the enemy to show his strength in that direction. All turned out admirably. But little resistance was made at first to Macpherson, whose men did not fire more than twenty shots before the fellows placed as outlying pickets on the hills bolted in front of our men. At first they seemed inclined to make a stand ; but when they saw Macpherson's well-known grey charger, and heard the ringing tones of his word of command, they would not wait for the levelled bayonets. At the foot of the range Macpherson dismounted, and giving his horse to his orderly, deliberately formed his men in skirmishing order, with two supports right and left, and a small reserve in rear. Sending a company of the Sikhs to the left to turn the enemy's flank, he placed himself in the centre of his skirmishers, telling his men to keep in a line with him, and advance according to his pace. In this manner he proceeded to march up the height as calmly as if he was executing the same manœuvre at Aldershot or the Phœnix. The Afghans have shown us what they can do, and of what stuff they are made when opposed to Native troops, however good ; but they were not quite prepared for the direct assault of a Highland regiment, which in open day, with its colonel at its head, was steadily climbing a steep ascent, and would infallibly try conclusions with the bayonet in a few moments. The Afghans, therefore, retired as we advanced ; an occasional shot from both sides being all the mischief done. Our troops pursued them along the ridges, and here several were overtaken by the sturdy Highlanders, whose mountain training was now of value in the race.

Meanwhile another strong body of the enemy were descending in great numbers to the hollow in our front, which in half an hour was full of them. Here they were held in check by the gallant 15th Sikhs, who broke into yells of defiance as they advanced in masses to the attack. We allowed them to approach to within 200 yards, and then Macpherson, bringing his line of skirmishers ' right shoulders forward,' while he closed in upon his left files, until he came in front of the new enemy, opened a rapid and well-sustained fire along the front, which we believe did great execution, and drove them once more into cover, some to the broken and wooded ground to the left, and the remainder to the ravine below us. Half an hour now elapsed while we were waiting to see Gough's sabres on our right. We could not see any sign of his coming, but we did see the walled enclosures of the villages now swarming with Afghans, who opened a smart fire upon us, while supported by their guns on the ridge above. These latter made tolerably good shell practice. Another half hour and no sign of Gough, who, by-the-by, we discovered afterwards, was hotly engaged on our right, where with his mountain guns he was holding at bay about 5000 Afghans. Time after time they rallied, and, with increased numbers, rushed again to the attack—sometimes assaulting on his front, sometimes on his left. As they came on in masses, shrapnel was poured into them from the guns, and as soon as they were shaken Gough dashed at them with his horsemen, cutting them down like sheep, driving them again to the crags and rocky ground, where he could not follow.

Meanwhile we were not idle. General Macpherson called for his charger, mounted, and with his brigade-major, Jarvis, and a bugler, rode away to the crest on our right, and, adjusting his glasses, could distinctly make out Gough's critical position. We had with us of Macpherson's fine brigade contingents from the 92nd (Gordon Highlanders), 23rd (Pioneers), 24th B.N.I., and the 2nd (Sirmur) Goorkha Regiment, making in all not more than 400 bayonets, as it was deemed advisable to keep the main portion of the brigade fresh in case we attacked Ayub to-morrow. In view of strengthening Gough's position, General Macpherson determined on abandoning the ground we had won, as we had practically attained our object, and drew back his left flank, concentrating his force on the right. Our new position was now as follows :—Our right was in the bed of a rocky stream, a tributary of the Argandab ; our centre in the mouth of a narrow pass ; and our left on the steep slopes of the mountains we had just quitted. These mountains were clothed with forests of fir of large growth, whilst here and there open spaces and rocky knolls formed convenient spots for our pickets. In our front the pass gradually widened and merged into the Argandab Valley, which we could see was well cultivated, and with small streams and canals flowing through it.

'It seems to me, gentlemen,' said the General, shutting his glasses, and offering us from his wallet a flask and sandwich-case, 'that our position here is not a desirable one to hold for any length of time, and my intention is to get out of it as soon as we can.'

We were in fact drawn up in a deep gorge with huge mountains on either side, in front of a narrow defile nine miles long, blocked up, we could see, by a powerful enemy, well posted on the crags above, and hoping we could be induced to enter, so that they might hurl upon us the huge pieces of rock they had already loosened in anticipation. On our left a wing of Ayub's army, ready to enfilade us should we move that way ; and the night gradually closing in.

' Let the brigade move down to the right, and see if we cannot join hands with Gough to the left of the Karez,' said the General.

The road we had now to traverse certainly presented considerable difficulties for troops. The track lay up the bed of a stream encumbered with boulders and large masses of rock, and was overgrown with low trees and jungle. The hills on either side rose to some height, but for the most part with a gradual slope, so that our flankers ascended them without much difficulty, notwithstanding the obstacle presented by the thick jungle. Our progress was consequently slow, as in one or two parts our men were compelled to move in single file. Our men by this time were getting much fatigued, but the plentiful stream of water flowing through the pass prevented any suffering from thirst. Hardly had we cleared the pass and arrived within a few hundred yards of the base of the next range of hills, when a heavy fire was opened upon our advanced guard, and suddenly from the broken ground and ravines several hundreds of men, who looked like and probably were Ghazis, rushed out sword in hand and furiously attacked the Goorkhas who were leading, but rallied by General Macpherson himself, who at once formed squares in *échelon*, and supported by the 92nd, the two regiments poured in a volley, and then commenced file-firing from the right of faces. This staggered the enemy, who broke and fled. The Goorkhas were allowed to pursue, and with their long knives made short work of the unfortunate wretches they overtook.

At this juncture, and while our commanders were re-forming their ranks, the well-known sound of a cavalry trumpet rings out on our right, and sweeping round the base of the nearest hill we see with delight the pennons of Gough's lancers, a squadron of whom are led on by their brigadier. Nothing could be better timed; nothing could be more opportune for both. We had been nearly all day working on the arc of a circle to effect a junction, but the nature of the ground, the intervening villages, loopholed, barricaded, and defended with *abatis* of felled trees, while full of Ayub's people, had made that circle wider than we intended. As the enemy fled from our little Goorkhas the avenging lancers of Gough dealt death swiftly amongst them ; but, turning at bay, these brave fellows refused all quarter, and died fighting to the last.

The several regiments of the cavalry and infantry brigades as they came up were formed under shelter of the broken ground, the infantry being in the centre and the cavalry with one gun on either flank. When all was ready General Macpherson directed the advance to be sounded from the centre of the line. At that signal our little array of about 1000 men rose up from their cover, and advanced against the villages in the plain. Immediately in our front stood the small but strongly fortified village of Chuzireæ, and a few hundred yards to its proper left one of the great spurs running up the valley, terminating in a lofty peak dominating the whole ridge. On this natural stronghold the Afghans had established themselves in great force, flying their standards over the mountain top, and prepared for our attack. They had increased the ordinary difficulties of the place by occasional breastworks, so that it was a most formidable position to take by assault. Our skirmishers, who were spread across our front, had easily driven in the outlying bands of the enemy, and were halted about 500 yards from the village while waiting the arrival of our two brigades and the mule batteries, which soon unlimbered and opened fire.

It took but a few seconds for us to cross the open ground, and then the steep ascent began, our men having to climb from rock to rock, and our regular formation being necessarily much broken. Foremost among the many there could be distinguished the gallant Colonel of the 92nd, who led on his men ten yards in front, steadily breasting the mountain, and with his gallant countrymen carrying each successive defence at the point of the bayonet, the enemy's standards dropping as their outworks fell. Nothing could withstand the impetuosity of the assault, and although many of the Pathans stood their ground well and fell at their posts, their gallantry was of no avail, and before many minutes had elapsed the village and its peak were in our hands. In the meantime the guns had been brought from the flanks to the front, and shelled the heights crowded with fugitives, while across the plain, sweeping along our former front, came Gough's pursuing squadrons, their fiery little horses covered with foam and the gay pennons of each lance red with the foeman's blood.

Our object was now gained ; we had, with comparatively slight loss to ourselves, mastered the key of Ayub's position. We had drawn out a considerable portion of his force, he doubtless being under the impression that we were about to push home our attack. The Khan's principal camp we now knew was behind a ridge of hills between Mazra and Baba Wali, with canals and the Argandab in his rear. To attack him, General Roberts would have to turn his flank by occupying the village of Goondegaum and the adjoining hills, while Gough with his cavalry watched the Murcha Pass, and worked down past it to the Argandab to cut off the enemy's retreat. The Picket Hill was to be held with a strong force, while our 40-pounders engaged Ayub's guns on the Baba Wali Kotal. Our main body of three brigades were to be massed in rear of Picket Hill, and deliver the real attack by clearing the gardens, storming the village of Gundi-Moola-Sahibdab in front, and then to work around the Pir Paimal Kotal and take the Baba Wali Kotal in rear and Ayub's position at Mazra in flank. All these memoranda, with a sketch of the ground we had worked over, were handed to General Roberts, who met us on our return at dusk, when we encamped, or rather bivouacked, for the night on a position covering the Karez Hill. To-morrow, then, we hope to win back all that was lost at Maiwand, and to inflict such a blow upon Ayub that he will no longer trouble us in this part of Afghanistan. I am just starting to attend the General on his nightly round, and will close my letter by hoping that next mail I may be able to tell you how the Queen's troops can fight when led by a commander they regard as we do our present chief.

CHAPTER VII.

THE VICTORY OF BABA WALI.

Kandahar, Sept. 5.

As I mentioned in my last, General Hugh Gough's admirable reconnaissance of the 31st had put us completely *au fait* with the position and distribution of the Sirdar Ayub's forces; and, pity it is to say, had the same use of his cavalry been made by General Burrows, in all probability Maiwand would have been a victory instead of defeat. The 'eyes and ears' of an army, as *l'arme blanche* has been termed, have peculiar opportunities for distinction in a country like Afghanistan, where the native horsemen opposed to us are so numerous, and, as a rule, so well handled. Of this fact no one can be better aware than General Roberts; and we have only to go back to his cautious, yet brilliant tactics, during the three days occupied in reconnoitring and capturing the Peiwar Kotal, to see what good use he can make of this arm of the service. The reconnaissance I have described showed that our enemy was posted in great strength behind the Baba Wali Kotal, that he had taken up a strong position on the Pir Paimal ridge, extending about a mile and a half south-west of the Baba Wali, and that his camp at Mazra was strongly entrenched.

I do not think that many of our officers thought of sleep on the night of the 31st. I know that neither Sir Frederick nor any of his staff took any rest save what could be obtained stretched in a cloak in front of a camp fire. With our men it was different, and our General is too old a soldier to allow a talkative and noisy camp in front of an enemy's position. Nothing could be more picturesque than our encampment. For more than half a mile along our extended lines of occupation our tents, crowning the heights or studding the plains, showed the Afghans what manner of array the Feringhi could put into the field. As the night came on, as the moon rose, silvering the tall palms and the mangoe groves in the valley, and as, one by one, each bright star appeared, the bark of the wild dog and the ghastly howl of the jackal, the half-whispered challenge of the sentry, and the scream of some wandering night bird, met the ear, and came to us more distinctly as the hum of human voices died away in our camp.

Orders had been sent round during the evening that the officers commanding brigades, together with our principal staff officers, should meet at the General-in-Chief's quarters at half-past five on the morning of the first. The Chief's *état major* was at the building in the Sapper Gardens, and at the appointed time came Sir Frederick and his A.D.C., Prettyman; Colonel Chapman, Chief of the Staff; Deputy-Surgeon-General Hanbury, Captain Straton, Signal Superintendent; Major Cowie, Commissary of Ordnance; Colonel Perkins; Colonel Hills, R.E.; Colonel Johnson, commanding R.A.; General Hugh Gough, commanding the Cavalry Brigade; Captain Brabazon, 10th Hussars, Brigade-Major; commanding officers of the 9th Lancers, 3rd Bengal Cavalry, 3rd Punjaub Cavalry, 1st Central India Horse, 2nd Central India Horse; Major-General J. Ross, commanding Infantry Division; Captain Mansel,

A.D.C. ; Brigadier - General Macpherson, V.C., C.B., commanding 1st Brigade ; Captain Jarvis, Brigade-Major; Brigadier-General Baker, C.B., commanding 2nd Brigade ; Captain Farwell, Brigade-Major ; Brigadier-General Macgregor, C.B., commanding 3rd Brigade ; Captain Chalmer, 60th Rifles, Brigade-Major ; and all the commanders of infantry corps.

While this somewhat large gathering was collecting, coffee, biscuits, cigars, and other refreshments, were handed round ; men split up into groups, and conversation was carried on, as it were, in detachments. The scene reminded me of a hunting breakfast at a large country house, where ' coffee-house ' gossip whiles away the impatient half-hour which intervenes between breakfast and the signal to horse.

As soon as all were reported present complete silence reigned, and Sir Frederick very briefly, but clearly, pointed out the day's programme ; some officers taking notes, and others trusting to their memory. The last to arrive was General Primrose; but he had previously conferred with Sir Frederick, and had been all the morning engaged upon other duties.

' I have sent for you, gentlemen,' said our chief, ' not to call a council of war, which implies a difficulty or a doubt in regard to action, but to point out to you my plans for the attack I purpose making this morning. From the report made to me yesterday evening by my chief of the staff, Colonel Chapman, I find that Ayub's position is as follows :—Their camps are situated on the range of hills extending from the Argandab westerly to the Pir Paimal. To pass this ridge there are, as doubtless you may be aware, two openings from Kandahar— the Baba Wali and the Morcha. The latter is the most difficult, but the former is more strongly held by the enemy, who has several guns on its crest. The Morcha Pass is covered by several half-dried-up canals, which General Gough and Colonel Chapman consider as formidable obstacles. Then, in rear of this position there is, you will find, a detached hill, marked here on the map, and connected with the outer ridge by a number of detached orchards and gardens. I purpose, therefore, attacking the south-west portion of the ridge with three brigades of infantry, massed in the rear of Picket Hill, while our 40-pounders, on the extreme right of the hill, supported by the 7th Fusiliers and Rifles, engage and silence Ayub's guns on the Baba Wali. The Kandahar garrison will meanwhile watch and be ready to operate on the Morcha Pass, while part of General Gough's cavalry will act independently on the left, and, if possible, cut off any fugitives on that flank. The real attack will therefore be made, first by clearing the gardens in front of Gundi-Moola-Sahibdab, then by storming that village in front, then by turning the Paimal hill, and, finally, taking the Baba Wali in reverse and the Sirdar's camp at Mazra in flank. I feel convinced, gentlemen, that if the villages and ridge of Pir Paimal can be turned, the Baba Wali Kotal would be untenable. I look, gentlemen, to you to carry out my instructions, and I leave the details to you.' Such was the simple yet scientific plan set forth in clear and unmistakable terms by our chief, and I can only tell you that it was carried out to the very letter, and precisely with the results anticipated by the General.

It was now only half-past six o'clock, and the General advised all the Brigadiers to see that their men had a good breakfast, with the day's meat and biscuit ration in each haversack, together with the water-bottles properly filled. General parade was ordered for half-past eight, and this gave ample time for these instructions to be carried out. Meanwhile the brigades were already in their respective positions, and ready to take their breakfasts as they stood in order of battle; but the cavalry dismounted, and the infantry with arms piled. At seven all the trumpets sounded the welcome 'breakfast call,' and a very amusing and comforting sight was it to observe the different nationalities as denoted by this morning meal, and the manner in which it was partaken of. At eight a.m. I rode along our position, which was as follows :—The troops of the Kandahar garrison, under General Primrose, had, as I have said, a special task to perform,—to attack the batteries on the Baba Wali with our 40-pounders, and to make a feigned attack on that pass, while the 1st and 2nd Brigades made their real attack on the left and worked round the enemy's right. General Primrose had with him for this duty four companies of the 2-7th Fusiliers, and the 19th N.I., behind the walls of the cavalry lines, the 4th Rifles, Goorkhas, two companies 1st Grenadiers, four companies 66th, and two companies 28th N.I. These regiments held the line you will see marked in my map from the canal at Hyder Khan, on the right to the Picket Hill, and Karez Hill on the left. Admirably posted between Karez Hill and Picket Hill was a battery of artillery, covering the advance of our real attack upon Gundi-Moola-Sahibdab, while behind Karez Hill and Picket Hill were the 1st and 2nd Infantry Brigades, under Macpherson and Baker. To the left of Karez, and in a splendid position to cover the advance of these brigades, was the screw battery of mountain guns I told you of when we left Cabul; while still more to the left, and commanding the Gandigan village, was the E B. Royal Horse Artillery. All these troops, as I rode past, were enjoying their morning meal, and seemed to be in excellent spirits, the delight of coming face to face with the boasted and boasting Ayub more than repaying them for the toils of the road and the privations of the march.

It was impossible not to be struck with the splendid appearance and peculiarly fine physique of the Highland regiments. Their chest measurement, muscular development, and the bronzed hues of sun and wind, giving them a martial appearance beyond all the other corps. I stopped with the friend with whom I was riding at the 92nd (Gordon) Highland column to exchange greetings with an old comrade, and was glad to partake of some of the national dish, oatmeal porridge, excellently cooked and evidently highly appreciated by these hardy North Britons, whose only grievance, it is said, is that it does not always rain out here. As the screw battery was close at hand we went on and partook of some excellent coffee, made from Branson's extract. This, with a little goat's milk boiled over a camp fire, and a ration biscuit, was most acceptable after our matutinal peregrinations.

Ayub, it cannot be denied, had admirably chosen his ground and cleverly concealed his men. Before yesterday's reconnaissance St. John, with whom I had been conversing, was positive that the Sirdar's strongest position was at Mazra, where he had his head-quarters and his military chest. But for the reconnaissance this belief might have led us into a trap where, even if we were successful, we might have lost heavily.

A long valley, over which we had to cross, intersected

in all directions by obstacles, watercourses, canals, stone-wall enclosures, and loopholed villages full of armed men ; the ground unequal, and backed, defiladed, by higher points, crowned with cannon, and breastworks placed on the crests of an acclivity that required the attacking force to halt frequently for breathing-time— a General inclined to fight never had a field, I believe, that offered more advantages, and a leader less skilful than our own might have easily been forgiven had he failed in his attack. I have noticed the positions of our various columns and guns, and I may as well describe those of our enemy. On the Baba Wali Kotal Ayub had placed three guns, namely, one of our 9-pounders taken at Kushk-i-Nakhud and two of his own Armstrong breechloaders. This position was indeed a strong one, as on all sides it is scarped in a most precipitous manner, while only two narrow winding footpaths a few feet wide lead up to it. These guns were *en barbette*, but traverses and épaulements had been thrown up for their protection. Near Pir Paimal Ayub had five guns in position, and his remaining artillery was distributed along the front and flanks of his position.

At nine a.m. General Roberts threw away a half-finished cigar, mounted his well-known chestnut Arab, pulled out his watch, and made a signal to his chief of the staff, and in one moment our four 40-pounders of 5-11 R.A. were booming with their first fire. Some changes had been made, and the battery was now escorted and supported by General Nuttall's Kandahar Cavalry Brigade, four companies of the 66th, and two native regiments. This portion of the field was confided to General Burrows. These arms were well placed on the right position of Picket Hill, and left of the old cavalry lines to Hyder Khan. C 2 R.A. battery, placed on the right of the Karez Hill, took up the signal, and soon got the range of the village in front of Gundi-Moola-Sahibdab, and the little screw battery, on the left of Karez and resting on the canal, at once followed suit. General Roberts at this moment rode up to see how the ranges were, and if the guns could be better placed, but finding no fault, and having, on the contrary, to praise one of our latest joined youngsters from Woolwich, said, as he commended the successful shot, 'This is better fun than even Woolwich—eh? Tell them to stop the screw battery till the troops advance,' added the General. 'They are only wasting their ammunition at that range.'

The General now rode to a splendid position on the centre of the Karez crest, where he could see almost every position of the field.

'Tell General Gough to wait awhile,' said he. 'Let him not move his brigade until Gandigan is cleared by Macpherson. He'll not keep him long waiting.'

'I beg your pardon, sir, you ordered the 2nd, General Baker's brigade, to take Gandigan,' said Colonel Chapman.

'You are quite right, and you see he has commenced,' answered the chief, looking anxiously through his glasses. 'Too soon, I fear; too soon; a few more rounds would have cleared the way.'

'No, sir, I think they're all right,' said Colonel Johnson. 'E Battery have peppered them, and they are beginning to bolt to the next village.'

'It is so,' said the chief; 'and Baker is after them like a greyhound out of leash !'

Major Tillard, who commanded the Horse Artillery

battery in front of Gandigan, now moved his guns where he could fire over the heads of Baker's brigade as it advanced in skirmishing order across the plain. A check here occurred, for a wooded knoll dominated the village, and a well-kept-up fire was opened on our advancing companies, who were ordered to lie down until reinforced.

Meanwhile the General ordered the screw battery to reopen fire in support of C 2 Battery at Gundi-Moola-Sahibdab, which we could see was the Houguemont of the position, and which was held by a large body of Afghans, who fired remarkably well. General Roberts now despatched an orderly to General Baker to tell him to work more to his left flank, so as to be out of range of Gundi-Moola, which could otherwise gall him on his right flank while moving on towards Gandigan. At this moment it appeared as though the enemy were abandoning Gundi-Moola, as a number of horsemen and some infantry were seen escaping towards Pir Paimal, and General Macpherson sent forward his Goorkha regiment at the village. The Goorkhas were advancing splendidly in skirmishing order on the left, the 92nd Highlanders on the right, and the remainder in reserve, when, as the former drew near to the gardens on the left, a hot fire was poured at them from the windows of the houses, showing that the place was still held in force. Still our two batteries, C 2 and the screw, poured in shell in a terrific manner, a perfect *feu d'enfer*, which must have made the garrison anything but comfortable. The Goorkhas now advanced and lay down alternately, waiting for the 92nd to come up on their right. They had not long to wait, for the gallant Highlanders, finding a garden wall on the right, made a rush for it, and obtained cover while the stragglers came up. The Colonel now wisely detached a company away to make a diversion on the right, and as soon as this was done rushed in front with his bugler sounding the 'advance,' and then the 'double.' From our hill we could see them plainly, and our gunners being told to cease fire, we had the delight of seeing the gallant little Goorkhas rise from their cover on the left, dash through some orchards, which for a moment hid them from our view, and reappear simultaneously at the village with the 92nd on the other side. The principal portion of the enemy here we could see were Ghazis, and while many got away towards Pir Paimal, others remained concealed in the houses and died at bay. Some splendid hand-to-hand fighting, I was told, occurred. The 92nd fellows would not be denied, and in many cases the combatants were well matched, the one fighting for duty, the other for life, and both for their country.

Meanwhile we had not ceased, with our glasses, to follow the fortunes of General Baker, who had a much larger circuit to make, but who had been equally successful in his attack.

'Nothing,' said General Roberts, 'could be finer than the rush made by those two regiments, the 92nd and the Goorkhas, and how well the 23rd and 24th worked in support!'

But we can see that the fighting still continues. The village was taken, by my watch, at 10.30; but hours after that fighting went on, and fanatical Ghazis, having shut themselves up, could not be dislodged. Here poor old Stewart was wounded in the first attack, and here Menzies was cut down.

Meanwhile Baker and Gough, assisted by E B.,

R.H.A., were steadily making good their ground. In the first line of this gallant brigade were the 72nd and the 2nd Sikhs, with the 5th Goorkhas and the 3rd Sikhs in immediate support, and having as a reserve the 2nd Beloochees on their left rear. The fighting on this side, and among the orchards and walled enclosures, was even more desperate than on the other flank. The Ghazis did not always wait to be attacked, but whenever opportunity occurred dashed forward with terrible valour upon our bayonets, their shields ringing against our barrels, and their faces smeared with gunpowder and blood. Ill betide the man that day who flinched or wavered in his place!

Seeing the fiery valour of these fanatics, General Baker drew in his skirmishers, and made his men advance shoulder to shoulder, in the good old fashion that won so many victories long ago, before Flanders and the Peninsula. On several occasions these fellows, undeterred by our volleys, came right up to the ranks and tried to wrest the bayonets from our men, and one tall turbaned warrior actually clove one of our men through his helmet before he could be cut down!

The right wing of the 72nd had the hardest ground to move on, cut up in all directions by watercoures and nullahs, loopholed walls affording shelter and defence, and here and there a garden full of Ghazis blazing at our flanks. Here, at one of the walled enclosures, fell Colonel Brownlow while in the act of giving an order to his men.

While this was happening the left of the 72nd, 3rd Sikhs, 5th Goorkhas, and 2nd Beloochees, were pushed round by the Brigadier away to the left, to endeavour to find better ground and take the enemy in flank. In

executing this movement, however, they were exposed
to a galling fire from a masked battery on the slopes of
the Pir Paimal basin. Pushing on, however, these were
carried with a rush, and at that moment the bugle calls
of the 1st Brigade were heard on the right. The Colonel
of the 92nd (Parker) saw his advantage, and making a
splendid forward movement at a swift run, the two
brigades were enabled to join hands and attack the Pir
Paimal in front, flank, and rear.

'Send on your battery at once in support, Sir!'
shouted the chief, as he galloped quickly to this part of
the field.

The guns were rapidly limbered up, and went
forward at a rapid pace, coming to action right at a
favourable spot, and terribly shaking the dense masses of
the enemy, who were now driven in on both flanks.

The position was now as follows :—The 92nd, under
Parker, and a couple of companies of the 2nd Goorkhas,
under my old friend Beecher, were hugging the slope of
the Pir Paimal, with the screw battery on an eminence
above, pouring shells upon the enemy. Major White,
with a wing of the regiment, was now detached round
the south-western edge of the ridge, and found himself
in close proximity to the main body of the Afghans in
the open. They were here in great strength, and scattered along the northern slope of the Pir Paimal as far
as the Baba Wali.

General Ross now galloped to the front and directed
all operations, and as we had pushed the enemy from
his splendid position and our flanks were secure, he
directed Major White and Captain Beecher with their
men to go straight at the enemy in front. Here, I
believe, was the heaviest hand-to-hand fighting of the

day.   Here I came up with General Roberts and the reserve brigade, commanded by General Macgregor, and even the sight of this strong reinforcement did not appal the gallant foe opposed to us. But again the screw battery is moved.

'Where, Sir?' said the officer in command to the General, who was sitting calmly on the Arab looking for Baker's brigade over towards the Mazra basin, hidden from our view by the intervening ridge.

'Follow me, Sir!' said the General, and, with the trained eye of a gunner, showing the very spot where the guns should be placed. 'Now, get your range and let them have it, my boy,' said our chief; and as the first shell fell amongst the broken masses of the already routed foe, we saw the puggareed helmets of Baker's men topping the low ridgea bove Mazra, where Ayub's camp now lay at our mercy.

'Meanwhile, where is our old friend Gough?' Gough had carried out his instructions, but could not get through the village of Gandigan, although he made some desperate attempts. He accordingly made a much wider *détour*, and, rather late in the day, managed to get his men across the Argandab, and then, making up for lost time, pushed rapidly on in rear of the Pir Paimal and Mazra, just in time to intercept numerous detached bodies of fugitives who were endeavouring to escape in that direction. But in the meanwhile General Roberts, seeing no sign of Gough, made the best of it by sending for General Nuttall, and detaching him, with the 3rd Bombay Cavalry and the 3rd Scinde Horse, towards the front of the Baba Wali Pass as far as Mazra, with orders to carry on the pursuit for fifteen miles. Some distance along the road Nuttall and Gough met, and together continued the pursuit, killing 500 of the enemy, of whom 300 fell to the lances and sabres of Gough's men and 200 to those of Nuttall. The Cavalry did not get back till ten o'clock, and many of the horses were quite knocked up. Our casualties are about 240; namely, 33 killed, 196 wounded; our loss in officers being Colonel Brownlow and Captain Frome, both of the 72nd, and poor dear Stratton of the 22nd. Our wounded officers are Captain Murray and Lieut. Munroe, 72nd; Lieuts. Menzies and Stewart, 92nd; Lieut.-Colonel Battye, 2nd Goorkhas; and Major Slater of the 2nd Sikhs.

Of course, you will have heard of the sad fate of poor Maclaine, taken prisoner at Maiwand. I heard the story from two of our sowars taken prisoners at the same time. They tell me, that up to the day of our battle Maclaine was well treated by Ayub, who doubtless intended to exchange him for some of his relatives in our hands. But, unfortunately, the defeat was so sudden on the 1st, and the Prince's flight so desperate, that he neglected to give any special orders for the prisoner's safety. The ruffians who were guarding him, when they saw their camp about to be captured by the Feringhi, in a moment of frenzy summoned him from his tent and deliberately cut his throat. His body was not yet cold when we found him.

The whole of Ayub's camp fell into our hands, with standards, 27 guns (including the two lost by us at Maiwand), stores, uniforms, tents, camp equipage, and odds and ends too numerous to mention. At the end of the action, at half-past one, our General rode up to the head of each regiment, and personally thanked them for their conduct on that day; and I do not think that

Mr. John Bright would have grudged those few kindly, homely, honest, and welcome words, valued by our soldiers more deeply than any cross of valour or other distinction won in honour for Old England.

———

AFTER THE BATTLE—CAVALRY PURSUIT—BURIAL OF THE DEAD.

Kandahar, Sept. 7.

ON the day following the battle I rode with General Roberts over the principal portions of the field, and was even more astonished than before at the strength of Ayub's position. It was evident, however, to a military eye, that he had weakened himself by covering too much ground, and thus allowed himself to be treated in detail. Had he, instead of extending his front along the whole length of the Baba Wali range, confined himself to holding Gandigan and Gundi-Moola-Sahibdab, the keys to Pir Paimal, in force, and at the same time so disposed his troops that the position should not be taken in reverse, he would undoubtedly have made a better stand against our attack. The first village we came to was Gundi-Moola-Sahibdab, and here the carnage had been more than we could have expected. The road was strewn with the stark bodies of the mangled dead, while the sickening smell of blood rose from the corpses through which the General and his staff guided their horses. Although during the whole of the previous night fatigue parties had been working to bring in the wounded, still here and there, as we passed, we heard the groan of some unfortunate and shattered wretch whose life was hanging in the balance of life and death. Dead horses, and others frightfully mutilated and struggling pitiably where they lay, were to be seen, while others, wounded and unwounded, wandered through the enclosures searching for food and water. Broken tulwars, fragments of turbans, rifles, pistols, lances, and shields, were littered around. The stream which ran through the village was almost choked with fragments of these things, while the mud of the streets was black with gunpowder, and splinters of shell lay in all directions. Here and there under the orchard-walls we came to a cluster of corpses, while the dark pool near them gave gastly evidence of their end. On the hillside north of the village, where Ayub's cavalry had charged our troops, we saw the ground covered with dead men and horses, and in one place I noticed no less than six Ghazis huddled together in death, evidently struck down by the same shell.

Decomposition had not set in, for but a day had passed. It was singular to note the difference of expression between those who had been killed by the bayonet and those who had met their death by the bullet. In the case of the former the features were, as a rule, distorted in agony, while in the latter they seemed composed, and, in some cases, even smiling. In whatever direction we turned we saw the same havoc and ruin. In the houses the same sights met the eye—dead men singly and in groups, shattered walls, smouldering doors, and carrion-birds hovering about. Here it was that Battye's splendid little Goorkhas taught the immense Afghan Ghazis what pluck and the bayonet can do even against the most skilful swordsman, and here in the clusters of dead around were to be seen the evidences of their prowess. The Goorkha fights capitally with the bayonet, but if in any doubt or difficulty as to the result, invariably dashes himself upon his adversary and finishes with the knife, a curved weapon about twice the size of an ordinary bowie. In this and other villages, even after their capture by our troops, numbers of Ghazis had shut themselves up in the underground chambers of the various houses, and fought there till nightfall. I counted more than 150 bodies, but many had already been carried away by the burying-parties we had sent out.

My friend Menzies had rather a narrow escape at Gundi-Moola-Sahibdab. In leading on his company to capture a walled enclosure he found himself suddenly opposed to about 300 Ghazis who were lying in ambush, and their leader, a tall, stalwart fanatic, rushed at him with a terrific yell, brandishing his tulwar and waving a standard in his left hand. Menzies accepted the challenge and rushed half way to meet him, and as the Afghan raised his tulwar to give the terrific backstroke at the neck which is said to be so difficult to parry, the young officer, with lightning-like quickness, by a straight thrust in tierce ran his enemy through the heart. Before, however, he could extricate his weapon, a real Andrea Ferrara, he was cut down by two fellows behind him, who in their turn were despatched by a corporal of the 72nd. As his wound, although severe, was not mortal, Menzies was placed by his sergeant, for shelter and safety, in an empty room, and left; but no sooner had our men quitted the house than a Ghazi, concealed in the veranda, crept through the window and stabbed him in the shoulder. Fortunately a Goorkha sentry left at the door saw the act, and at once despatched the fanatic with his knife.

Here I was presented with the knife with which the

ruffian attacked my friend. It is called a 'peshkabs,' a peculiar sort of weapon worn by the Ghazis. The handle is of ivory, though occasionally I have seen them made of horn. The blade is long, with a straight, strong back, and a curved edge running to a point. Such a ' toothpick can inflict a fearful wound ; and they are often heavily tipped, to enable the point to go through armour. The hilt is very handsomely ornamented and the blade tastefully damascened.

A karez stream runs through the village, and seems to supply the inhabitants with plenty of good water, as well as to irrigate the gardens and orchards of the neighbourhood. The karez is a subterranean aqueduct connecting several wells, and conducting their waters, when united in one stream at a lower level, to the surface of the earth. The object of this arrangement is to do away with the loss caused by evaporation, which, if the stream were to flow for any distance over the open surface, would be so great that it would be almost dissipated before it reached the fields it was to supply with water. To make one of these karezha the following plan is usually adopted :—

On the slope of a neighbouring hill, or any rising ground where underground springs are supposed to exist, a large well or shaft is sunk until it opens on one of the springs. Then, if there be signs of a sufficiency of water, the construction of the karez for its conveyance is determined upon, and the work is commenced on the site where it is intended that the water shall issue to the surface. Here a shaft three or four feet in depth is sunk, and, at regular intervals of twenty or thirty paces from this, in the direction of the hill or other site, where the former shaft had been sunk, a series of similar shafts or wells are sunk, and these are all connected by tunnels bored from the bottom of one shaft to the base of the one next above it, and so on up to the shaft first sunk over the spring from which the water is to be drawn away. The depth of the shafts gradually increases with their distance from the one near the spot at which the stream is to issue to the surface, and in proportion to the slope of the ground and the number of the shafts. The length of the karez depends, of course, upon the supply of water obtained, and the distance of the spring from the site selected for cultivation or habitation. I noticed that from the shaft sunk near the land to be irrigated the water is conducted into the fields through a tunnel, which, commencing at the base of the shaft, opens on the surface at the base of a small aperture at about twenty or thirty feet distance, and from this point onwards the water flows in a narrow and shallow stream along a superficial trench that winds through the fields. The position of the shafts was marked by circular heaps of earth excavated from them, and collected on the surface around their openings, which are usually closed over by a roofing of leaves and matting covered with earth. These coverings are removed at intervals of a couple of years or more, according to circumstances, for the purpose of clearing out the shafts and tunnels, which are mere excavations of the soil, with bricks or mortar, and which in time naturally become coated with a deposit more or less thick of earthy matter from the streams flowing through them. Some karezha (plural for karez) have afforded a constant stream of water for ages, while some, on the other hand, have become exhausted ere they have yielded a return commensurate with the cost of their construction. The oldest karez in Afghanistan is the one we saw at Ghuzni, said to have been constructed by the Sultan Mahmud Ghuzni, whose name it bears. This karez is more than twenty miles in length, and is now nearly eight centuries old.

Leaving Gundi-Moola-Sahibdab, where our fatigue parties and dhoolie bearers were carrying away and burying the dead, we rode through the orchards and wall enclosures where yesterday the fighting was so severe. Here the traces of the conflict were most apparent, and here we were enabled to save several wounded men who had managed to crawl under the topes of the mulberry-trees for shelter during the night. One poor fellow seemed to imagine that he was about to be despatched, and although unable to rise, as both his legs were shattered, he attempted to seize his jezail in defence the moment our doctor approached.

'Be not alarmed, my friend,' said the General; 'we shall take care of you.'

'*Ba aman i Khuda*—May God protect you!' replied the man, a fine specimen of the Afghan mountaineer, whose bold bearing and frank manner to the General much impressed us in his favour. While the doctor was probing the wound for the bullet he never even winced, and there was a savage fierceness in his looks, heightened by the fire of his piercing eyes, that declared him to be a merciless ruffian upon his native soil and out of the hands of the Feringhi power.

We also brought away a party of five of our own men, Sepoys, who had been left overnight wounded. They had become separated from our columns during the attack, and were not able to get back to our camp. These men were all more or less wounded with the charàh, or Afghan knife, and the wounds, although frightful to look at, are seldom mortal, or even of a very serious nature. This may be accounted for by the way the Afghans use the terrible charàh. They never employ this weapon except for direct blows, which are usually aimed at the outer side of the limbs, where, although they produce enormous gashes, the larger vessels and nerves, being inside, generally escape injury, and the wounds are deprived of much of their otherwise dangerous character. An Afghan has no idea of thrusting with the charàh, and I have always found it successful to keep him at bay until an opportunity occurred to give point. Any good pupil of Grisier, of Angelo, or of Roland, should be able to hold his own against the best Afghan swordsman. One of these unfortunate fellows, a man of the 3rd Sikhs, had his arm completely lopped off above the elbow by a blow from a charàh, but his antagonist was lying dead beside him, a little Goorkha having nearly cut his head off with his knife as he was attacking the Sikh.

The Colonel of the 2nd Goorkhas told General Roberts rather a good story this morning. When the village was about to be assaulted, as a compliment to the regiment, the Brigadier ordered that the Goorkhas should lead the way, supported by the 92nd; and when the village had been carried by a rush at half-past ten, one of Colonel Battye's Goorkhas raced with a 92nd Highlander for a gun which the Afghan gunners were endeavouring to carry off. The Goorkha managed to get up first, cut the mule-traces, cut down the drivers, and jump upon the captured weapon, shouting, 'This for the honour of my regiment! The 2nd Goorkhas! The Prince of Wales's!' As Colonel Battye saw the incident I can vouch for its authenticity.

Leaving Gundi - Moola - Sahibdab, we cantered on through the walled gardens, and along the banks of the canal by the road taken the previous day by the 1st Brigade. As we advanced every portion of the way was marked with the *débris* of the fight. Guns, swords, belts, Afghan drums, pouch-boxes, broken-down ammunition-carts, dead mules and horses, and innumerable human corpses, marked the progress of our attack. Here and there, striving to reach the canal, we saw some wretched horse, with shattered limbs and parched tongue, unable to drag itself away from the body of its late rider, who lay with cleft skull and staring eyeballs, apparently watching us as we passed. The roads here converge as well as the three canals, and here it was that the screw battery played upon the flying masses of the enemy as we drove them out of the orchards and vineyards into the open plain. Here, or at least a little farther on, it was that Baker and Macpherson joined hands, and, after a tough struggle, drove the flower of Ayub's infantry into the basin behind the low ridge that hid the Mazra camp, and here the avenging shells of Tillard's guns enfiladed them as they fled. Rounding the base of the hills, we came to the village and crest of Pir Paimal, and to the Prince's first camp, still standing, and occupied by a portion of Baker's brigade, while Macpherson held the Mazra camp.

Leaving the village of Baba Wali on our left, the General pushed on to Ayub's camp in front of Mazra and in rear of the hills. The tents extended for more than a mile, and were about half that distance in width. They were well and regularly pitched, and, except in the matter of cleanliness, would have been no discredit to a European army. Everything was, however, in the utmost disorder, showing how ill-prepared the Afghan prince was for his defeat, and how completely '*Sauve qui peut!*' must have been the order of the day.   Ayub's tent was still standing, and we carefully inspected it. Sentries had been placed on the previous evening by Colonel Parker, so that nothing had been looted or removed. A couch of rich damask, covered with matting of the finest description, and with some large leopard skins as a counterpane, shaded and curtained by rich shawls draped above the bed, a number of costly weapons hanging from the hooks of the tent-poles, a double-barrelled rifle of English make (Lancaster), with an inscription in Persian, showing it to be a Russian general's gift, pipes of all kinds, handsome chogas, pagris (turbans), and other articles of dress, evidently lately in use, lay about, and gave a lifelike look to the scene.

'I cannot help feeling sorry for the poor fellow,' said the General, smiling at the curiosity of some of our staff, who were minutely examining every article. 'How comfortable he must have been here!'

'And now galloping for his life to Herat,' said Colonel Chapman.

Round the Sirdar's tent, and within easy call, were various smaller tents for the use of guards, attendants, &c., and on entering these we could see the remains of food partly cooked, and evidently intended for the Prince. Here was a delicate 'pallao,' consisting of rice stewed up with fowl, and deluged with melted fat from the tail of the sheep, and coloured with turmeric powder, sweetened with sugar, and flavoured with almonds and raisins. There was also a kid roasted whole, and stuffed with a mixture of rice, almonds, raisins, and pistachio nuts. This is called the 'mallanjan pallao,' and, I can

say from experience, is a tasty dish, as we have more
than once tried it at our mess. A chess-board, several
Persian books, and a curiously shaped musical instrument, something between a banjo and a guitar, showed
the Prince's tastes to be not by any means barbaric.
Orders were given by the General that every article in
the tent should be carefully labelled and packed away—
that all the other tents should be cleared of rubbish and
placed ready for removal or destruction. Many of them
looked so dirty that our Scotch surgeon observed,
'They're unco' filthy, an' wad breed a pestilence in our
camp!' an opinion in which I cordially agreed. In the
soldiers' tents were half-cooked rations, showing how
unexpected must have been our attack, and how ill-
prepared were they for the dashing energy of our commander. Wheat, maize, millet, and various vegetables,
cooked generally in the form of a pottage, with dried
pulse or raisins, mutton, fowls, camel's flesh, goat and
buffalo, were here, but always accompanied by melted
fat or butter, not considered eatable unless rancid.
Another favourite dish I noticed, and this is 'krut,' a
sort of essence of cheese. This is esteemed a great
delicacy, as it has a flavour of rancid cheese and sour
butter combined.

On the 2nd I had a long conversation with General
Gough, who gave me all the details of his pursuit, and I
find that, so far from being inactive, he was engaged,
although out of our sight, nearly the whole of the day.
Gough left the camp with his splendid little ' clump of
spears ' at 8 a.m., with a sort of skeleton instruction
from the chief, but with *carte blanche* to use his own
discretion as events came on. First of all, there was no
opportunity to utilise cavalry on our left, as the village

of Gandigan was only assailable by infantry, the ground intervening being one mass of jungle, nullahs, water-courses, and other impediments, where cavalry are practically out of place and useless. Gough, as I before said, had with him Brabazon, of the 10th Hussars—as good a man across country as I know—as brigade-major, and the following fine corps of horsemen :—The 9th (Queen's Royal) Lancers, 3rd Bengal Cavalry, 3rd Punjab Cavalry, and two squadrons each of the 1st Central India Horse and the 2nd Central India Horse. These may be taken roughly to represent not more than 1000 sabres, but the quality of the troops was unexceptionable. Gough had been over some of the ground the day before, and knew that, at one period of the day, he might have lost many men but for Macpherson's flank movement to his assistance, and he also knew that to waste cavalry amongst stone walls, jungle, orchards, gardens, vineyards, nullahs, and every kind of obstacle, would be an unpardonable fault in a commander. He determined, then, to give Baker sufficient time to clear the village of Gandigan, and formed his brigade up under the shelter of the Chuzina range, and on the right of the E B. R.H.A., ready to move forward at the proper time, and when Gandigan was cleared by Baker's brigade.

'Tell General Baker that I am waiting on him and shall keep touch with him, if possible, all day,' said the Brigadier to his adjutant, who put spurs into his horse and dashed across the plain to give the order. Baker, as I told you in my last, was considerably delayed at Gandigan, and although Gough three times made demonstrations against the village, it was found that the ground was hopeless for either guns or cavalry. M Battery, B Brigade R.A., was then moved down to the right of the canal, and shelled the village for some time without any perceptible effect, and after more than an hour's delay Baker sent back to ask Gough to act independently.

'By making a wider *détour* to the left, and leaving Gandigan to me, you can get across the Argandab, and work round to the reverse of Baba Wali,' wrote Baker on a leaf of his pocket-book, which he sent by his orderly to Gough. The latter at once adopted the suggestion, and this will account for the non-appearance of his brigade during the earlier period of the action.

Gough accordingly moved along the Herat road to the left of Gandigan, and after a good deal of skirmishing through the villages came to Kokeran, which he found strongly defended. Dismounting a portion of a regiment to act as infantry, he attacked and soon cleared the village by a charge of the 9th, and then pushed on to the Argandab, which, at about eleven o'clock, was crossed a little below the Sirtip's house.

'It was most irritating,' said the Brigadier, as we discussed the matter, 'that you should have all the fun, whilst we were unseen, fighting our way over fearful ground and under great difficulties to shake hands with you on our right.'

However, as it turned out, all went, well for by eleven o'clock Gundi-Moola-Sahibdab was in Macpherson's hands, and the fugitives were streaming away across the Argandab, just in time to be met by Gough's squadrons lying *perdu* for them on the right bank. Gough's presence on the right of the Argandab at this juncture was most opportune, and enabled General Roberts to drive home his principal attack upon the Pir Paimal and the three camps; while Nuttall, working steadily towards the Murcha Pass and along the hills in front of Baba Wali, completed the chain or web woven round Ayub's force. Had it not been for the mass of enclosures peculiar to the country on the banks of the Argandab, Gough's Lancers would have given a better account of the enemy; but, as it was, they had no reason to be dissatisfied with the day's work. Recrossing the river by a ford in rear of Baba Wali, Gough had scarcely formed his leading squadrons on the bank when he was assailed by two guns posted on a ridge, and a heavy mass of Afghan horse, who came on with wild yells till they heard in ringing tones from the Brigadier the command, 'In column of squadrons! Walk! march! gallop! charge!' In one moment he had burst through the swarm of Afghan horsemen, and drove a number of them into the river, where, even with the water up to the girths, a hand-to-hand combat took place. Re-forming his column, the charge was continued until Nuttall's trumpets were heard through the Murcha Pass, when the two brigadiers joined hands, and continued the pursuit till nightfall—with what results I have already said.

———

AFTER BABA WALI—A NIGHT RIDE WITH GOUGH IN PURSUIT OF THE ENEMY.

Cavalry Lines, Kandahar, Sept. 7.

'WHAT were your fellows doing all day, during and after Baba Wali?' Such is the query put to me wherever I go, and, for the sake of our friends at home, I have just jotted down roughly what I for one saw of the fight, and what share our brigade had in it. Cavalry service is undoubtedly very pleasant, and when all goes well, and we can get at our enemy, we come in for our share of praise; but, on the contrary, when fortune and opportunity fail, small allowance too often is made for our apparent inaction. On the eventful day of Baba Wali we breakfasted in high glee at half-past six; our horses had on this occasion a double feed of grain, and each trooper carried a day's forage.

Previous to moving from our own lines General Gough had a careful inspection of the 9th Lancers, 3rd Bengal Cavalry, 3rd Punjab Cavalry, and the Central India Horse, and he was pleased to say that he never wished to ride in front of a better lot of horsemen. During the march from Cabul to Kandahar I have had many opportunities of studying the interior economy of these Native Cavalry regiments,- and I have been greatly impressed with the eminently workmanlike manner in which all details are carried out. Arms, horse equipment, saddlery, uniform and drill, are excellent, and even our own cavalry might take an occasional hint from the system employed by these turbaned spearmen. In looking over the horse appointments of my orderly, a 3rd Punjabi, the other day, I found that the headstall of his bridle is now like our own cavalry, having the bit and bridoon detachable when in the stable or in lines, each being separately fitted. The horses used to be tethered fore and after by a double fore-shackle and heel-ropes, which added much to the weight; but this has been altered, and the new plan, introduced some years ago by the 17th Lancers, is adopted. That is to say, the animal is tethered by a single fore-tackle and a single heel-rope; the latter even might be abolished,

Q

and the horse, being tethered only by the fore-leg, could turn round at will and avoid either sun or rain. On the march these head-ropes are carried from the lower ring of the head-stall to a ring in front of the saddle. Formerly the sowar carried a pistol in his wallet, but now these are available for spare kit or provisions, as a beneficent Government issues to him a Snider carbine! In addition to this weapon he carries a curved and uncommonly sharp sword and a lance. His uniform consists of a dark-blue *lunghi*, or turban, wound deftly round a red wadded skull-cap; his frock, or *koorta*, of coarse blue serge, shaped something like a Norfolk shirt, and bound into the waist by a red cummerbund; wide, yellow pyjamas, tucked into long boots of brown untanned leather; brown leather pouch and sword-belt, the former carrying twenty rounds, and a very long bamboo lance with bright steel point and blue and white pennon; make up a neat, workmanlike, and most picturesque set of 'fixins,' as an American gentleman, Colonel and Journalist, called them. The sowar would, of course, be incomplete without his *choga* (cloak), and this he carries strapped over his wallet, while he has a lance-socket at each stirrup, a grain-bag on the near side behind the saddle, with the horse's blanket and pegs fastened behind. On the off-side is the carbine in its bucket, as also his shot-case. A single leather girth and surcingle to make all secure complete his equipment. These men are, for this country, the perfection of light cavalry; they have taken kindly to the Snider, and, since its issue, some of them make excellent practice. They have also been taught the English cavalry system of signalling, and the approach of an enemy is at once notified to the column forming their head-quarters in rear by the chain of scouts that connect them with it. These fellows are allowed twenty-seven rupees a-month, and for this each man finds his horse and tatoo pony. Government finds a small tent to every two men, but they provide the tatoo which carries it, as well as all their spare belongings.

Thanking my friend, Major Anderson of the 3rd Punjab Cavalry, for all the above information, which he gave me as we smoked our first cheroot, I rode over to the 9th Lancers, and had a chat with old Stewart Mackenzie and MacMuir of that fine old polo corps, and they showed me all their Colonel's newest inventions. Some of the saddles, to my astonishment, had no numdah (felt saddle-cloths), only leather pannels. The wallets carry a pair of high-lows and his brushes, and the cloak is buckled in front. The shot-case is on the off-side behind, 'with the carbine-bucket for the Martini over it, and strapped to surcingle; while the mess-tin is over cloak on off-side. The feed-bag is fastened to a D behind on near side, and looped to prevent feed escaping. Pegs, heel-rope, and shackles, strapped behind the cape on the cantle. The rider then has to carry on his person his sword, haversack, water-bottle, and pouch-belt; pouch, with twenty rounds, on waist-belt. Of course, as a rule, a Lancer does not carry a carbine; but this is an experiment, and the innovation may, I think, with advantage be adopted. The horse-blanket is carried on the tatoo, and one tatoo is allowed to every two horses.

I need not tell you that the 9th keep up their old reputation for smartness, and that Sir Hope Grant's favourite corps are at present as near perfection as a regiment can be. Each troop is more like a family than a conglomeration of horsemen, and each captain is looked upon as a friend as well as a commander. The regiment itself is a clan, and *esprit de corps*, the life and soul of our army, reigns supreme. Great care is taken as to recruiting, and consequently the troopers are pretty much of a size, and not too big for their horses. It is a great mistake to send big regiments to India, as it is impossible to mount them ; and when we remember that the regulation height for a cavalry horse out here is only 14–2, it will easily be understood that a six-foot man and big in proportion would look as though he were riding a pony.

The 9th were having a sort of second breakfast when I came up, and I was rather astonished to find myself invited to share in a number of luxuries I little expected at such a time and place. Apperley had actually a small spirit-lamp in his wallet, and made me some capital tea with sugar and preserved milk! Gough (not the General, but the Captain) had a lot of kabobs, which we warmed, and Stewart Mackenzie supplied some excellent German sausage from an enormous tin case. These, with a small *chasse* from a flask and a capital cheroot, rendered the time less heavy on our hands. Meanwhile the men, having finished their morning meal some time before, were carefully overhauling their saddlery, shoes, and weapons. Girths were examined, buckles adjusted, and the horses' feet carefully looked over by the farriers, and all was reported as correct to the Brigadier, who, with Brabazon, his brigade-major, was sitting near his charger carefully studying the rough sketch-map he had made the day before. Talking of maps, I may warn you in regard to one or two I have been shown here, and which possibly may find their way to England. Some of these are fairly drawn, and the distances are in proportion, but they have the simple fault of being 'partly upside down;' that is to say, the north is where the west should be, and *vice versâ:* the consequence being that, judging from them as they are drawn, you would get a totally erroneous idea of the position of the Argandab, and the various ridges over which we fought.

At eight o'clock an orderly galloped over to us from General Roberts with a note in pencil for our Brigadier, who immediately gave the word, 'Stand by your horses!' What a change from the buzz and chatter in the ranks to the deathlike silence that discipline enjoins! Cigars and pipes were hurriedly put away, mess-tins were reclosed, biscuits, kabobs, cold meat, sausages, &c., are hurriedly relegated to haversack or wallet, and grim and stark at the sharp word of command stand our troops as contiguous columns of squadrons, ready for the next word, 'Prepare to mount!' 'Mount!' And a thousand horsemen swing into the saddle as lightly and as deftly as in the *manège!* At five minutes past eight the General moved us on to Ahasabad, where, for a short time, we were again dismounted, so as to give the infantry brigades time to initiate their attack on Gundi-Moola-Sahibdab. Here we were to wait until the time came to advance through the village of Gandigan, push across the Argandab river at Kokeran, and pursue the enemy along the road to Sheurin. To the south of the road which leads past the Baba Wali Kotal to the Argandab are the three villages of Kalach-i-Haidar, and although these were purchased by Colonel St. John for our use more than a year ago (in May last), General Primrose had to abandon them when Ayub advanced to Kokeran. They were now, we believed, held in force by the enemy, and strongly fortified by the villagers.

From the Herat gate to Kokeran is seven miles, and from the peculiar nature of the ground, and the numbers of villages and walled enclosures, we had to move with the utmost precaution. On our left front we had the ruins of old Kandahar, and here Ayub might have posted a strong body of men to resist our advance, and open upon us with a flanking fire from a gun placed *en cavalier*. But this was obviated by Sir Frederick Roberts, whose first care on the 31st was to post a strong detachment with two guns at the Chuzina Canal, which commands the road to the ruins.

At nine o'clock the 40-pounder battery placed on the right crest of Picket Hill opened on Ayub's guns on the Baba Wali Kotal; and this was our signal to move. Just as our chief was about to give the word we heard the rattle of gun-carriages on our right, and we turned and saw, to our great delight, Tillard with his splendid battery of Horse Artillery sent to join us.

'Are we to have the pleasure of your company during the day?' said the General to the Major, who galloped up and saluted.

'Yes, sir,' said the latter. 'The General says the ground is difficult by Gandigan, but he thinks, where Cavalry can go Horse Artillery ought to go.'

'So much the better,' replied the Brigadier. 'You can shell the villages for us.'

The order was now given to move off by sections from the right, with the guns divided on either flank, two squadrons thrown out in open order in front, and the usual flanking parties. The firing had now become general, and the infantry, we could see, had commenced to skirmish through the gardens and over the numerous watercourses which impeded our way. Soon after we were in motion we came to some splendid groves of mulberry - trees and poplars, watered by one of the numerous canals which irrigate the plain. Here our advanced skirmishers were fired at, but dashing forward at a gallop our fellows cleared the wall of the enclosure in splendid style, and sabred about half-a-dozen Ghazis, while the remainder bolted on to the nearest village.

The ground was now cut up by enclosures and fields of Indian corn, barley, lucerne, clover, with here and there patches of red rose-bushes, as well as more clumps of mulberries. Watercourses, or rather the beds of such, ran in all directions, and these were quite deep enough to considerably delay our artillery. After much difficulty with the guns, we had pushed forward about a mile across the plain, exchanging a shot now and then as we pushed forward our first line of skirmishers through the enclosures. Here we came to two villages right and left, and as we could see they were loopholed, Major Tillard, who rode in front with our Brigadier, suggested a few shells to clear the way. While this was being carried out, half a troop of the Central India Horse was dismounted and sent forward to seize an avenue of fine mulberry-trees, which would give us some cover while attacking the villages.

The manner in which these men skirmished was admirable, taking advantage of every bit of cover afforded by the numerous clumps of tangled ' bhendi,' a sort of cucumber with a yellow flower, interspersed with the more formidable cactus and prickly pear. While these men were picking off the Ghazis who lined the walls of the orchard, Tillard with his guns was making capital practice in the mulberry tope. To have carried the villages by a charge would have been quite practicable, but our object was more to hold the enemy in check until our first and second brigades had forced their way through the orchards and gardens on our right, than to make good our position at a heavy loss of men and horses. Step by step, however, we pushed on our skirmishers, until we drove the Ghazis from one village into another ; and at this juncture General Gough, taking advantage of an open piece of ground, deployed one of his regiments to the left, and, pivoting on his right, swept round until the village was almost surrounded.

The 9th Lancers were now detached to outflank the enemy's position, and this they did by prolonging our line to the left until we almost touched the river in that direction. It was half-past ten o'clock ; we had cleared the villages which had given us so much trouble, and we were enabled to bring round our right shoulders and advance towards Kokeran. On our right hand was a broad plain of cultivated ground, sloping away towards the Argandab river and divided by enclosures into gardens, orchards, and vineyards, where peach, apricot, nectarine, and vines, were cultivated. On our left was a long barren range, covered with fragments of rock, boulders, and the *débris* of innumerable storms. Behind this ridge Tillard was moving his guns in a line parallel to our advance, and with him were the 9th Lancers. This movement was ordered by General Gough in case the enemy, driven from the slopes of the Pir Paimal, should endeavour to break away towards Girishk. About the middle of this ridge are two high points, about a thousand feet above the bed of the river, and on one of these used to be the heliographic signal-station where messages were flashed to Kandahar while we held the city.

The road as we advanced became more steep, and we had to cross more watercourses and to pass by narrow paths winding along the face of the mountain, where, in the distance, we could see some of the chiefs of the tribes and villages in the vicinity. These with their principal adherents, on horseback, were drawn up the crest of the mountain, while their followers sprang like demons from rock to rock, yelling uncouthly, and, although out of range, firing their matchlocks at us as we passed. The scene was most singular. On our left a rugged and steep precipice, on the summit of which were these creatures with ragged clothes, yet robust figures, howling defiance at us, and firing in impotent rage, while on our right our eyes were cheered by the sight of rich fields, where corn and wine, wild myrtle and roses, were in profusion, clear rivulets, date and mulberry-plantations, flowers, and birds of song—Man, in all his savage nature, on the other side!

Meanwhile Generals Gough and Baker had agreed that the cavalry should make a very wide *détour*, leaving Gandigan to be carried at the point of the bayonet by the latter officer, as it was important that the Argandab should be crossed by our cavalry and its right bank held by us. We could now see how well Baker, with the 2nd Sikhs, 3rd Sikhs, and 5th Goorkhas, was doing his work; but a mounted orderly overtook our column about eleven o'clock to tell us that Gandigan was carried in gallant style, and that three guns were captured by Colonel Monny with the 3rd Sikhs. The orderly also told us that Baker and Macpherson had joined hands, having carried Gundi-Moola-Sahibdab and Gandigan, and were now reinforced by the 3rd Brigade, and about to storm the Pir Paimal village and crest.

'This is good news, gentlemen,' said our Brigadier, as he tied a silk handkerchief round his head, finding his helmet rather heavy. 'I think, Major Tillard, that you had better come on with us to Kokeran, and when you've assisted us to take it you can get your battery back along the Herat and Kandahar road a short distance, and come up in rear and to the left of the infantry. You'll be able then to take the Baba Wali in reverse, which is what the General wants, while we cross the river and cut off those who retreat towards Jul Sabor, Niaz Mahomed, Shuin, and even Khanan Gharcaro.'

'I see what you mean,' said Tillard. 'You want to prevent them getting into the Khakrez Valley, where the villages are all friendly to Ayub. Come along!'

It is as well to note these names, as I have carefully marked them on the map I send you, and Hills has scaled them, and finds the distances tolerably correct. You can thus see the admirable understanding which exists between Sir Frederick and his lieutenants, and how well his ideas are developed in detail by them. This portion of our march, although almost unmolested, was difficult, on account of the guns, as we got entangled in a lot of nullahs, and although at this season of the year there was nothing in the way of water to stop any troops, yet a mile or two in the bed of a nullah with high, steep banks, is enough to try the wheels and spokes of even a gun-carriage. On getting out of this difficulty our route lay past some plains, broken by hillocks more or less bare and rocky, and with few houses or dwellings of any kind. The fields ran parallel to the numerous watercourses, and were but sparsely cultivated.

We came at length to a better road, and the General deployed to make as wide a front as we could, and as soon as the plain widened sufficiently the halt was sounded, and we moved along in line of contiguous columns, with guns upon either flank. On rounding the spur of one of the hills we bore away to the right, and came in sight of the village of Kokeran, seven miles west of Kandahar and six south-west from Baba Wali. Kokeran is a village, guarded as usual by mud walls, and close to it is the dwelling of Nur Mahomed, the Sartip, or commander of cavalry, whose son was so active against us last May, and who himself attempted at that time to oppose General Stewart's advance on Kandahar.

As we neared the walls our guns galloped to the front, and sent a couple of shells purposely over the village and into the river, as the Brigadier did not wish to injure the inhabitants should no opposition be offered. A few horsemen were seen galloping down to the ford and escaping, but not a shot was fired, and two squadrons swept through the village, and with two of Tillard's guns secured the ford.

It was now half-past eleven, and no time was to be lost, as already we heard less firing, and we concluded that Pir Paimal was won, and that our infantry were pushing on to Baba Wali and the camps between it and Mazra. By-the-by, I saw in a sketch-map sent home from Kandahar that Mazra is marked on the right bank of the Argandab. Such is not the case. It is in the Argandab Valley, on the left bank, and is separated from the river by several canals, as I have marked it for you.

As soon as we were well across the river Major

Tillard's men gave us a cheer, and, limbering up, went away towards Baba Wali at a speed that would have made a nervous person quake. '*Au revoir! au revoir!*' cried our chief, waving his sword to them as they galloped away. 'And now, gentlemen, it is our turn,' added the General; 'we have been out of sight all day, and they will wonder where we have been hiding.'

What a change of ground we now found! Smooth, sound, galloping ground, a little sandy here and there, but delightful in comparison to the place we had ridden over during the morning.

As we drew away from a low range of hills on the left bank, which hid Baba Wali from our sight, we began to get glimpses of what was going on on our flank. Now and then these hills dipped until almost level with the plain, and as the left bank of the river now began to rise we could occasionally see the smoke from our guns and those of Ayub as the slopes of the Pir Paimal were contested, and the conflict drew nearer and nearer to us.

'I wonder if they can see us?' said Colonel Cracroft of the 3rd Bengal Cavalry to his major (Willock), as they cantered along over the sandy plain.

'I think not,' said the Major: 'there is too much smoke to begin with, and they are too much occupied themselves to look this way.'

At this moment the Brigadier sounded the halt, and ordered the men to dismount to breathe their horses, and we took advantage of this to ride up a little knoll commanding the river and a portion of the Argandab Valley. Every glass was out in an instant, and we were soon rewarded for our pains. Imagine a rich, fair valley stretching away from the angle made by the river at Kokeran, up in a north-easterly direction towards Fattah Khan and Sher Ahmad, met by the Baba Wali range, running parallel to it almost due north of Kandahar city. Imagine two gaps, seemingly cut shield-shape out of this range, the one called Murcher Kotal and the other Baba Wali Kotal, and in this four batteries of guns, manned by Afghan soldiers, sworn to defend the position and exterminate the infidel. Then look across the intervening space between the river and these defences, and see what resembles three long serpents belching forth flame and smoke as they wind their sinuous course up the reverse slopes of this position.

It is high noon, and the sun, till lately hidden by light and fleecy clouds, rising over the green and flowery valley, burst out in increased splendour as we watch our gallant fellows marching up the heights, regardless of the well-served guns that still continued to play from Ayub's well-placed batteries. Ever and anon we could see a mass of Afghans come down with a rush at our fellows, and then the sun glanced on the glittering and terrible steel barrier which met and stopped their career.

'Look! look! there goes the screw battery at them!' exclaimed Egerton of the 3rd, as he handed Anderson, his major, his glass.

'What a pity that the river and three miles intervene!' said the General. 'However, they *have* got cavalry, and *we* must account for them. 'Stand to your horses!' 'Prepare to mount!' 'Mount!' 'Colonel Cracroft, be good enough to take two squadrons of your regiment on to the second ford, which is at Niaz Mahomed; I need not tell you what to do when you get there.'

'Major Willock, you will take the remaining squadron, and hold the nearest ford at Jul Lahor. If General Nuttall's people are where they should be, on the left bank, we shall astonish them. Major Anderson, let Captain Macpherson take about a dozen or more vedettes along the ridge to move parallel to us, as signal to us as we move along in the other. Major Buller, take a wing of the Central Horse, and keep half a mile in front, with a few connecting files to signal. And Major Colledge can do the same in rear.'

But action came on sooner than we had expected, and it was well that the General had taken these precautions. The dash of our infantry, and especially the Highlanders, up the slopes of Pir Paimal and the Baba Wali was more than the Sirdar's mercenaries or Ghazis could stand. The splendid advance of the screw battery and Tillard's fortunate arrival with the R. H. A. drove the Afghans headlong from their strong positions. There is nothing an Afghan soldier dreads more than to be taken in flank, unless it be to be attacked in reverse, and on this occasion both were accomplished. As our men ran up the slopes like deer the guns were abandoned, random volleys were fired, their defensive camps were abandoned, and a mass of fugitives made for the river and the fords. Before the Brigadier's orders could be carried out a strong body of Herati horsemen had managed to get across the Niaz Mahomed ford, and were making their way by a road which led to the Khakrez Valley on our left. General Gough saw this just as it was signalled to him, and at once sounded the halt. All at once an orderly galloped up to our column, where the General was riding in front of the 9th Lancers, and informed us that Colonel Cracroft was engaged with a large cavalry force of the enemy, and was driving them back into the river.

'Walk! March! Trot! Draw swords! Form squadrons!' (the plain would not allow a wider front), were given by the commanders in obedience to the chief, who had told them to take the time and pace from him. In about seven or eight minutes we were in the plain, and on fairly good ground. We saw on our right Cracroft having a very pretty little 'mill' with about 300 Heratis. Our fellows, it seems, were hidden in a mango tope, and, allowing them to cross the ford, had caught them in flank and *en flagrant délit*, as they were coming up the bank in column. However, they managed to wheel into line, and took the initiative, charging down upon Cracroft's handful of sabres, as they knew it was their only chance. As fast as each man reached the bank he galloped after his comrades, and the two lines met at a good pace about 300 yards from the bank. Our fellows, however, were better under hand, and having the impetus, went through them with unbroken files, rolling the Afghan horsemen down the hill and many of them into the river. A hand-to-hand encounter then ensued, our men laying their lances in the socket and taking to their swords. Meanwhile we had no idle time. A much larger body of horsemen had crossed at a ford we knew not of, and came round the brow of a small hillock on our right. Fortunately for us the ground was in our favour, and General Gough, leaving the 9th in reserve to cover us if necessary, formed his remaining men in column of squadrons, and went steadily at them.

'Advance in column of squadrons! Walk! March! Trot! Canter! Gallop! Steady, men! the pace from me ! Charge !' As the trumpeter rings out the welcome sound we are into their ranks, and down they go like ninepins. Now the avenging lances of the 9th come 'pricking o'er the plain,' not quite a 'thousand spears in rest,' but a poor 300, and woe to the poor wretch who does not cast away his weapon and cry for quarter ! We must have chased them for more than two miles, and while capturing several standards and a number of prisoners, one or two of high rank, our sabres and lances must have cut down a couple of hundred. Still numbers got away into the villages, and of course, hiding their arms and uniforms, escaped.

Getting his men together, and leaving detachments at every ford, General Gough pushed on for fifteen miles, occasionally coming up with small parties of infantry, who as a rule died hard and would not accept quarter. Ten miles on, near Shuin, we met Nuttall, who had been doing good execution on the other bank. It was now dark, and we were much encumbered with prisoners, but we lashed them on their horses, and fastened the latter in strings together, placing twenty or thirty in the middle of a troop. In this manner, and with our own nags almost dead beat, we reached our lines at Kandahar about 11 p.m. Our friends were much exercised to know where we had been all day, but when General Gough's report was made, and General Nuttall gave in his, Sir Frederick said, 'Gentlemen, you could not have done better!' At a rough estimate we must have put some 500 *hors-de-combat*, but doubtless many of them are now being banded in the villages.

THE SITUATION IN KANDAHAR—PEACE, HONOURS, AND REWARDS —BREAKING UP OF THE KANDAHAR FIELD FORCE— RETIRE- MENT TO INDIA.

Kandahar, Sept. 11.

THE victory of the 1st has, I need scarcely tell you, made glorious summer out of the five weeks' winter of discontent which came between Maiwand and Baba Wali. Pessimists who inundated our mail-bags with long tirades against that time-honoured field-officer, General Incapacity, are now vigorous and ardent ad- mirers of the heroes of the hour, and every excuse is sought for to condone what at first was set down as an unpardonable series of military faults. Perhaps in the long run, deferred, if not posthumous criticism, will turn out the most true; and Time, the great physician, may award the true and just balance of praise and blame to those who caused our defeat and those who retrieved our hidden, if not lost, prestige. Sir Frederick Roberts' own account of the battle of the 1st September may always be quoted as a model of terse and clearly worded despatch writing; and, like the great Cæsar, he has certainly the gift of the pen as well as of the sword.

On the occasion, a day or two since, of the presenta- tion of the distinguished service medals to the soldiers of the 72nd and 92nd Highlanders, and my little friends the gallant 5th Goorkhas, Sir Frederick ordered a general parade of all arms, and made use of the opportunity by addressing a few eloquent and welcome words of com- mendation to the regiments on the ground. As his speech has been most imperfectly reported, I will give you the text as it was copied into our general order-book. After the General had ridden on to the ground where the whole garrison was drawn up on three sides of a square in close columns facing inwards, and a general salute had been given, Sir Frederick raised his helmet in acknowledgment, and spoke as follows :—

'I need scarcely tell you, Soldiers of the Kandahar Field Force, how pleased I am to have this opportunity of giving to the men of the 72nd and 92nd Highlanders, and the 5th Goorkhas, the medals for distinguished conduct on the field, which they have so deservedly earned and won. I say this, from my experience as a soldier, that no men with whom I ever served could have better deserved these rewards; and it is an additional pleasure to me to have seen the other day of what material my Highlanders and Goorkhas are made. I can but hope that it may be my good fortune to have such good soldiers by my side when next I go into action. The 72nd have, I grieve to say, to mourn the loss of their Colonel, as fine a leader of men as I have ever seen, and with him fell an equally gallant spirit, Captain Frome, and many brave men, amongst whom, I grieve to say, Sergeant Cameron, a grand specimen of a Highland soldier! But the 92nd had also a heavy loss, Colour-Sergeant Fraser, and other good soldiers, being amongst the slain. On the 2nd of September no less than fourteen gallant fellows were laid in one grave, and many of their comrades are now lying wounded in our hospital. But in all this you have a British soldier's consolation, that of knowing that you did your duty nobly. I believe, in my day, I have seen some hard knocks given and received, but never do I remember noticing a greater look of determination to win a battle than I observed on your faces on that morning of the 1st of September.

'Not even the bravest of the Afghans could stand

against such a bold attack. Yes! You beat them at Cabul and you have beaten them at Kandahar; and now, as you are about leaving the country, you may feel assured that the very last troops the Afghans ever wish to meet in the field are Highlanders and Goorkhas. You have indeed made for yourselves a name in this country, and as you will not be forgotten in Afghanistan, so you may rest assured you will never be forgotten by me.'

General Roberts has an admirable presence. His seat on horseback is perfect, and his voice is clear and well pitched, while his charm of manner is proverbial. At the close of these few well-chosen sentences there was a short pause, but only for a moment, for the enthusiasm of the Highlanders was contagious; and led by them, three ringing British cheers were given, echoing and re-echoing far away into the city and the heights above Sherpur.

Although not yet officially announced in orders, I hear on the best authority that General Roberts, as well as Sir Donald Stewart, are to have the higher grace of the Bath, while the former will succeed General Sir Neville Chamberlain as Commander-in-Chief of the Madras Army in February next. But more remains behind. These rewards have been already earned in the winter of 1879 in Cabul and in Sherpur, and for the wondrous march of 318 miles in twenty days, and the battle and relief of Kandahar, a peerage and the thanks of Parliament, we think, are not too much!

Few, if any officer of our General's age, have such a record of good and successful service to show. From the mutiny of 1857 to the battle at Mazra, what a long bead-roll of glory! The siege and capture of Delhi (wounded badly, and horse shot under him) ; the affairs of Bulundshuhur (horse shot), Allygunge, Agra, Kanoug (horse sabred) to Bundhera, where he was nearly captured while on reconnaissance ; from the relief of Lucknow by Lord Clyde, the operations at Cawnpore, the defeat of the Gwalior contingent, the battle of Khodnagunge, the retaking of Futtehghur, the storming of Meangunge, the skirmish at Koorsee, and the various actions which ended with our taking of Lucknow (thanked by the Governor - General, Victoria Cross, Brevet Majority, and Medal with three clasps) to the period when he was employed on special service with the expedition of 1863 against the tribes on the north-western frontier of India ; from the Abyssinian campaign of 1868 (Assistant Quarter-Master-General, and bearer of Sir Robert Napier's final despatches ; Brevet of Lieutenant - Colonel and Medal) ; from the Looshai expeditionary force in 1871 to the capture of the Khobel villages, the attack on the Northlang Range, and the burning of Taikoom ; from the Afghan campaign of 1878, with the actions of the Peiwar Kotal, Saperi Pass, Khost expedition, the action of Malun (thanks of Parliament, and K.C.B. ; the outbreak and massacre at Cabul in September, 1879, the second command of the Kurram field force, and passage of Shuturgardan ; the defeat of the Afghan army at Charasaiah ; the reoccupation of Cabul and defence of Sherpur ; the final defeat of the enemy on 23rd December, down to the famous march and the crowning victory of Baba Wali ;—where can a more glorious calendar of success be shown in so short a space of time ?

Since I wrote to you on the 7th our time has been fully occupied. The whole of Ayub's guns have been brought in—thirty-two, including the two we had to abandon after Maiwand, but not the six presented to the Wali. These are said to be somewhere on the Girishk road, and we shall probably get them before long, as our cavalry are scouring the country in all directions.

Meanwhile, immediately after the battle on 1st, Ayub fled towards Khakrez, *en route* to Herat, where it is doubtful what sort of a reception, as a beaten man, he will receive. He had with him, we learn, no baggage, and but a couple of hundred Herati horsemen. His Khakrez-Cabuli infantry fled without attempting to make a stand, and were cut down in numbers as they retired up the Argandab Valley. Day by day we continue to receive additional particulars of Ayub's loss, which is now found to be much more severe than at first estimated. As forage is very scarce here it was decided on the 2nd that Gough should march his cavalry brigade to Kokeran, where supplies of all kinds are plentiful, and where the position is of high strategic value. Our total casualties on 31st and 1st are now ascertained to be 248, including two officers not before mentioned, viz. Rowcroft of the 4th Goorkhas and young Chesney of the 23rd Pioneers.

As soon as we have full reports from Gough as to the state of the country we shall send a strong column to Kushk-i-Nakhud, to bury the dead and open out the district, which is most fertile for supplies. Kokeran is not more than eight miles from Kandahar; it has a walled village and a fort, and during our early occupation of Kandahar we had a considerable detachment of our garrison stationed there, and if these had not been we should not have been so painfully in the dark as to Ayub's movements.

Some three months ago I was sent out towards the Helmund to report upon Kokeran and the neighbouring village of Khalacha-i-Hyder, and found them in all respects amply suited to the requirements of a strong brigade. Chinar and mulberry-trees, the date, the plantain, the cocoanut, the vine, and almost every species of grain and fruit, abound. The walnut-trees were finer than any I had yet seen, except, perhaps, in the Kurram Valley, many of them being upwards of ten and some seventeen feet in height. Apricots, plums, apples, pears, grapes, peaches, quinces, pomegranates, and almonds abound, while mulberries are grown for feeding silkworms. Wheat, barley, field peas, turnips, lucerne, and Indian corn, are grown round the villages, and in the rivers are trout and barbel, although not of large size. I have caught them with a worm, not a fly, up to two pounds weight. Teal also, in the season, were to be got, but only in the spring and autumn; while in the cold weather there are large flocks of blue pigeons, making a welcome addition to our mess bill of fare. Sheep of the dumba, or broad-tailed breed, are plentiful, browsing along the sides of the valleys, where they thrive upon the aromatic herbs; and on the hills north-ward of the Helmund there are wild sheep and goats, while the *chikore*, or hill partridge, can be shot in the gulleys to the south. Gough, with whom I rode out on the day of his march, has taken with him a whole battery of weapons of the fire-arm persuasion, and has sent us in numerous delicacies in the *genre* of fish, flesh, and fowl.

On the 3rd, the day after our arrival at Kokeran, we organized an expedition, partly to reconnoitre and partly to shoot, as far as Sangeri, which is on the further side of the Argandab, and my description of Kokeran will apply very much to it. As we were told by the Kazi of Kokeran last summer that September and October were the two best months for shooting chikor (hill partridge), as in August they are not full grown, we determined to combine pleasure with business, and see some sport while we surveyed the line of country. The chikor very much resembles in colour and size the French red-legged partridge, with the exception that the latter appeared to be darker about the throat and more brown on the back and wings than the former. The call of the birds is, moreover, very much alike, and its name, 'chikor,' given to it by the natives, is the exact sound of its cry.

Taking some cold meat and biscuits in our haversacks, and accompanied by a small escort of Gough's native cavalry, we made an early start on the morning of the 3rd, and before the sun was over the horizon were well upon our way. There is a peculiar formation of the three plateaus near the villages of Kokeran and Khalacha-i-Hyder, owing to the drainage of the river, and these plateaus make consequently splendid camping-grounds, with much purer air than at Kandahar. From the right bank of the Argandab, opposite Kokeran, a capital view of the village is obtained. The village lay beneath us, on the banks of the river we saw winding away in the distance, with other small villages dotted about its banks, and surrounded by green rice-fields and orchards. Chehul Dokteran stands to our left, while the gardens of Rahmedil and Ameen Kans are glowing with colour and fertility. To the north-east we saw the Pir Paimal and Baba Wali range, black and frowning, and with but scanty vegetation on its lower spurs, while nearly the whole range beyond lay before us, its many spurs running out in all directions, and taking various hues, lit up here, shadow there. Again, on our right, we looked upon Haaz Madat Khan and the wooded ranges which gave to each kotal such a variety of tints in the colour of their foliage. All this neighbourhood is well cultivated, rich in barley, rich in rice, the villages surrounded by fruit-trees, and most of the fields watered by a most elaborate system of irrigation from the Argandab.

About half-past six we were crossing the steep slope of a rocky ledge, and having left our escort in the plain below, with instructions to choose a good camping-ground with wood and water, as well, of course, as a position where we could keep a good look-out, we could hear by the peculiar call of the birds that we should have some sport. Not a whisper did we indulge in as we wended along our toilsome ascent, where it was with difficulty we were enabled to balance ourselves. This was evidently the place for chikor in the early morning, and we soon saw one, two, three, and more coveys driven down from the hills above by our markers, whom we had sent on. A chikor comes whizzing down the hill, and, making at the same time a tremendous curve, offers a most difficult shot, while I manage to bowl him over with the right barrel.

After getting a few brace of birds and driving the first covey about we lost sight of them, and my friend, a gunner, who is a most excellent mentor, advised us to sit down quietly above, where we had an idea the birds were, and in a few minutes, as the covey had been split up, one of the lost tribe ascended a piece of rock, and began to call his fellows with all his throat power. The silence once broken, every bird in the covey joined in, and we thus became aware where each one was, and were enabled to pick them nearly all up in succession. The chikor is one of the best Indian partridges for the table, and we did full justice to those we bagged.

I stayed with my friends, the Sirdars, at Kokeran for three days. until General Roberts' first brigade began its march for Quetta, and I accompanied several search parties of our cavalry to the various villages about here, where we picked up a number of Ayub's wounded, and sent them to our hospitals in Kandahar. These men gave us many particulars of the action, and told us, I believe truly, that their loss on the Pir Paimal was infinitely greater than we imagined,

General Phayre's advanced brigades reached Kandahar on the 6th, and on the 8th General Macgregor, with his brigades of the Cabul Kandahar forces, marched for Killa Abdulla. General Roberts went with it to see after transport and supplies, and when he has seen his men well out of Afghanistan he goes home on short leave to England. Meanwhile a brigade under General Daubeny marches to-day to bury the dead at Maiwand, and to search the villages not visited by Gough for arms and prisoners.

'Are we to retain Kandahar?' Such is the question we ask each other every day, and no one can give a positive answer. The victory we have achieved under Roberts has undoubtedly restored our name and prestige, and we shall, I believe, lose all the honour gained by the battle if we at once withdraw. The argument which formerly applied to the possession of Kandahar now no longer exists. The railway to Sibi alone has brought us so near to the southern capital that we can hold it with ease with a moderate garrison, while the completion of the line to Quettah would make the Durani city our strongest and most natural outpost.

My young friend, our host, to whom I interpreted many expressions of English good will, seemed greatly pleased at the compliments paid by our Government to the head of his house, and as we were then joined by his friend, the Sirdar General Gholam Hyder Khan, just appointed by the Ameer as Governor of the Bala Hissar, he translated my remarks, to the evident gratification of the older soldier and an intelligent lad who rode with him.

Transport and commissariat difficulties, and that 'unspiritual god, Circumstance,' have, as usual, compelled our General to alter his arrangements, and to move by separate brigades instead of in one compact column. On the rough road map and itinerary I send you will see the difficulties, from the immense extent of our columns, we had to encounter, and that we did manage to surmount them so far may be attributed in a great measure to the good fortune we have experienced than to the providence of the Government, who have had now three years' experience of transport difficulties, and still grudge the necessary money required to overcome them.

Leaving Cabul as I have said at an early hour on the morning of Wednesday, the 11th, and with the Siah Pung hills occupied by villagers more or less hostile on our left, here, along the base of which lay the road between the Bala Hissar and the cantonments, was the spot so fatal to the British force in 1841; and here it was that Akbar Khan, at the last moment, declared that it would be impossible to restrain the Ghilzai robbers. Here it was on the 6th of January, 1842, the army commanded by General Elphinstone, which had for sixty-five days endured such humiliation as a British force had never perhaps suffered, prepared to abandon its possession, and, leaving the trophies of war in the hands of a semi-savage enemy, commenced a retreat which has scarcely a parallel in horror and disgrace! We could not avoid these thoughts as we moved along at a fearfully slow pace, and after four days marching only reached Seh-i-Babi, the whole of Saturday being taken up in ascending the Lataband Pass, an ascent of 8000 feet. On the 14th our first brigade halted at Seh-i-Babi, while our other two moved on to Jagdallak, to which place the first placed followed by the 15th.

Of the passage of the Lataband I will speak in my next, but I may tell you that our transport difficulties commenced, and from the fearful heat, the steepness of the road, and the bad condition of the camels, our loss in these animals was immense. The view from the summit of this celebrated mountain defile is magnificent, and our huge columns winding slowly along the range, while the morning sun lit up the accoutrements and white trappings of our cavalry, gave a picturesque and life-like feature to the scene. Towards the distant west stretched a maze of misty network of valleys, in lovely contrast to the wild and tangled crags that formed our foreground. Nearer to ourselves rose in wild grandeur a confused mass of mountain peaks, already fast parting with their green mantle, and exposing to view a bare, craggy surface, almost destitute of vegetation. These hid from us the distant view towards the south and west, and immediately below the position we occupied, at a depth of some 1500 feet, wound the long, narrow, tortuous gorge, through which lay our road, and down which we descended on the almost perpendicular side of the mountain. Winding along this for some distance, and passing between rocks overhanging from the sides of precipices fearful to look upon, and which appeared so insecurely held as to threaten all who passed with annihilation by their fall, we passed through a lot of natural gateways to the pass, formed by the approximation of the opposite sides of the valley, and leading us into a wider and more open gorge, the scenery of which was no less wildly grand than that over the one from which we had just emerged.

Through this natural gateway, as regularly made by Nature's hand as if it had been artificially built through the solid rock, as if to unite the two gorges, flowed away to the west a little rivulet, whose course we had followed through the gorge above the pass. Varied in hues of porphyry and syenite pebbles, that formed its bed, and fragments of which showed the path, its waters sparkled with the most delightful hues.

All of this pass consists of a single mountain road, where our camps were situated on rocky mountain beds such as I have endeavoured to describe.

The heat in the tents, even at night, is great, and our loss in camels has been great. The secret we should learn if possible, from this, in any future war, the mule should be the only transport animal. If well bred and well chosen he will live, while a camel, unless fed on his own species of rations, will perish. From Lalaband to Gundamuck is twenty miles, and this we accomplished in two days. All our brigades reached Gundamuck on the 18th, and Jellalabad to-day. No time to say more till to-morrow.

LONDON:

Printed by STRANGEWAYS & SONS, Tower Street, Upper St. Martin's Lane.

A CATALOGUE

OF WORKS ON

Science and Art,
Natural History,

AND

General Literature

PUBLISHED BY

DAVID BOGUE.

LONDON:

3, ST. MARTIN'S PLACE, TRAFALGAR SQUARE.

OCTOBER, 1880.

INDEX OF SUBJECTS.

ANGLING.—*See* Dick.

ANIMALS.—*See* Lankester (E.), Wood.

ANTHROPOLOGY.—*See* Bonwick.

ANTIQUARIAN.—*See* Jewitt, Walford.

AQUARIUM.—*See* Science Gossip, Taylor.

ART.—*See* Bayliss, British Painters, Heaphy, Zerffi.

ASTRONOMY.—*See* Darby. Herschel, Popular Science Review, Proctor.

ATHLETIC TRAINING.—*See* Exercise, Michod.

BEES.—*See* Hunter, Jardine, Ribeaucourt.

BIOGRAPHY.—*See* Dramatic List, Kaye.

BIRDS.—*See* Ornithology.

BIRTHDAY BOOKS.—*See* Byron, Time's Footprints.

BOTANY.—*See* Braithwaite, Carrington, Cooke, De Crespigny, Edgeworth, Hooker, Lankester (Mrs.), London, Messer, Midland Naturalist, Nave, Notes on Collecting, Popular Science Review, Robson, Schleiden, Science Gossip, Smith (J.), Smith (W.), Sowerby, Sprague, Taylor, Trimen.

CHEMISTRY.—*See* Brande and Taylor, Popular Science Review, Ralfe.

CHILDREN'S BOOKS.—*See* Æsop, Keene, Letters, Wordsworth.

CONCHOLOGY.—*See* Conchology (Journal of). Notes on Collecting, Rimmer.

CRUIKSHANK.—*See* Chamisso.

DEVOTIONAL. — *See* Aids to Prayer, Alford, Personal Piety, Sunday Evening Book.

DOGS.—*See* Smith (C. H.)

DRAMATIC.—*See* Dramatic, Shakspere.

EDUCATION.—*See* Pascoe.

ELECTRIC LIGHTING.—*See* Shoolbred.

ENTOMOLOGY. — *See* Duncan, Midland Naturalist, Naturalist's Library, Newman, Notes on Collecting, Science Gossip.

EYE (THE).—*See* Angell, Dudgeon.

FABLES.—*See* Æsop, Keene.

FERNS. — *See* Eaton, Hooker, Lankester (Mrs.), Smith (J.)

FICTION.—*See* Alcott, Author of " Schonberg-Cotta Family."

FISH.—*See* ICHTHYOLOGY.

FOLK-LORE.—*See* Dyer.

FOOD.—*See* Johnson, Lankester.

GENEALOGY.—*See* Walford.

GEOLOGY.—*See* Ansted, Croll, Geologist, Kinahan, Midland Naturalist, Notes on Collecting, Reade, Science Gossip, Symonds, Taylor.

HISTORY.—*See* Kaye, Mangnall.

HORSE AND RIDING.—*See* Howden, Waite.

AUTHOR OF "THE SCHÖNBERG-COTTA FAMILY."

AGAINST THE STREAM. The Story of an Heroic Age in England. With Illustrations. Fifth Edition. Post 8vo, cloth, 6s. 6d.

THE BERTRAM FAMILY. With Illustrations. Post 8vo, cloth, 6s. 6d.

CONQUERING AND TO CONQUER. A Story of Rome in the Days of St. Jerome. With Illustrations. Crown 8vo, cloth, 5s.

LAPSED, BUT NOT LOST. A Story of Roman Carthage. Crown 8vo, cloth, 5s.

SELECTIONS FROM THE WRITINGS OF THE Author of "The Schönberg-Cotta Family." Post 8vo, cloth, 6s. 6d.

BARCLAY, H. D.

ORPHEUS AND EURYDICE, ENDYMION, and other Poems. With Illustrations by EDGAR BARCLAY. Crown 8vo, cloth gilt, 5s.

BARETTI.

A NEW DICTIONARY of the ITALIAN and ENGLISH LANGUAGES. Compiled by J. DAVENPORT and G. COMELATI. Two vols., demy 8vo, cloth, 30s.

BARKER, S., M.D.

MANAGEMENT OF CHILDREN in Health and Disease: A Book for Mothers. Demy 8vo, 6s.

BARNARD, H.

ORAL TRAINING LESSONS IN NATURAL SCIENCE AND GENERAL KNOWLEDGE: Embracing the subjects of Astronomy, Anatomy, Physiology, Chemistry, Mathematics and Geography. Crown 8vo, 2s. 6d.

BATHS AND BATHING. Fifth Thousand. Royal 16mo, cloth, price 1s. *See* Health Primers, page 29.

BAYLISS, WYKE.

THE WITNESS OF ART, OR THE LEGEND OF BEAUTY. With Illustrations by the Author. Second Edition. Crown 8vo, cloth, 6s.

THE HIGHER LIFE IN ART: With a Chapter on Hobgoblins, by the Great Masters. Crown 8vo, cloth, Illustrated, 6s.

BENNOCH, FRANCIS.
  POEMS, LYRICS, SONGS, AND SONNETS. With
  a Portrait of the Author on Steel. Fcap. 8vo, cloth, 7*s.* 6*d.*
  A few copies on Large Paper, fcap. 4to, cloth, 12*s.* 6*d.*

BENTON, SAMUEL, L.R.C.P., M.R.C.S., &c.
  **HOME NURSING, and HOW TO HELP IN CASES
  OF ACCIDENT.** Illustrated with 19 woodcuts. Crown
  8vo, cloth, 2*s.* 6*d.*

BLAKE, EDWARD T., M.D., M.R.C.S., F.B.H.S.
  **SEWAGE POISONING : HOW TO AVOID IT IN
  THE CHEAPEST AND BEST WAY.** Demy 8vo,
  Illustrated, 1*s.*

*BONWICK, JAMES, F.R.G.S., Fellow of the Anthropological
  Institute, London.*
  OUR NATIONALITIES. No. 1. Who are the Irish?
  No. 2. Who are the Scotch? Crown 8vo, sewed, 1*s.* ;
  cloth, 2*s.* each.

BOOK of KNOTS. Illustrated by 172 Examples, showing the
  manner of Making every Knot, Tie, and Splice, by "Tom
  Bowling." Third Edition. Crown 8vo, cloth, 2*s.* 6*d.*

BRAITHWAITE, R., M.D., F.L.S., &c.
  THE SPHAGNACEÆ, or Peat Mosses of Europe and
  North America. Illustrated with 29 Plates, Coloured by Hand.
  Imp. 8vo, cloth, 25*s.*

*BRANDE, Prof., D.C.L., F.R.S.L., and Prof. A. S. TAYLOR,
  M.D., F.R.S., &c.*
  CHEMISTRY. Fcap. 8vo, 900 pages, 12*s.* 6*d.*

*BRISTOWE, J. S., M.D., F.R.C.P. ; Senior Physician and Joint
  Lecturer on Medicine, St. Thomas's Hospital.*

  **THE PHYSIOLOGICAL AND PATHOLOGICAL
  RELATIONS OF THE VOICE AND SPEECH.**
  Demy 8vo, cloth, Illustrated, 7*s.* 6*d.*

**BRITISH PAINTERS OF THE EIGHTEENTH and
  NINETEENTH CENTURIES.** With 80 Examples of
  their Work engraved on Wood. Demy 4to, handsomely bound
  in cloth, gilt, 21*s.*

BURBIDGE, F. W.
  COOL ORCHIDS, and How to Grow Them. With
  Descriptive List of all the best Species in Cultivation.
  Illustrated with numerous Woodcuts and Coloured Figures of
  13 Varieties. Crown 8vo, cloth, 6*s.*

BUTLER, SAMUEL, Author of " Erewhon."

EVOLUTION, OLD AND NEW: Being a Comparison of the Theories of BUFFON, Dr. ERASMUS DARWIN, and LAMARCK, with that of Mr. CHARLES DARWIN. With copious Extracts from the Writings of the first three-named Authors. Crown 8vo, cloth, price 7*s.* 6*d.*

EREWHON; or, Over the Range. Sixth Edition. Crown 8vo, cloth, 5*s.*

THE FAIR HAVEN. Second Edition. Demy 8vo, cloth, 7*s.* 6*d.*

LIFE AND HABIT. Crown 8vo, cloth, 7*s.* 6*d.*

BYRON BIRTHDAY BOOK (THE). Compiled and Edited by JAMES BURROWS. Second Edition, 16mo, morocco, gilt edges, 3*s.* 6*d.*

CAPEL, C. C.

TROUT CULTURE. A Practical Treatise on Spawning, Hatching, and Rearing Trout. Fcap. 8vo, cloth, 2*s.* 6*d.*

CARRINGTON, B., M.D., F.R.S.

BRITISH HEPATICÆ. Containing Descriptions and Figures of the Native Species of Jungermannia, Marchantia, and Anthoceros. Imp. 8vo, sewed, Parts 1 to 4, each 2*s.* 6*d.* plain ; 3*s.* 6*d.* coloured. To be Completed in about 12 Parts.

CHAMISSO, ADALBERT VON.

PETER SCHLEMIHL. Translated by Sir JOHN BOW-RING, LL.D., &c. Illustrations on India paper by GEORGE CRUIKSHANK. Large paper, crown 4to, half-Roxburghe, 10*s.* 6*d.*

CHANGED CROSS (THE). Words by L. P. W. Illuminated by K. K. Square 16mo, with Illuminated Crosses and Border Lines, 6*s.* *See also " Crown of Life."*

CHANGED CROSS (THE). A Large Edition of the above work, printed in outline on best Plate Paper, for Illumination. Fcap. 4to, handsomely bound, cloth gilt, 6*s.*

COLLECTION CATALOGUE for NATURALISTS. A Ruled Book for keeping a permanent Record of Objects in any branch of Natural History, with Appendix for recording interesting particulars, and lettered pages for general Index. Strongly bound, 200 pages, 7*s.* 6*d.* ; 300 pages, 10*s.* ; and 2*s.* 6*d.* extra for every additional 100 pages. Working Catalogues, 1*s.* 6*d.* each.

COMPANION TO THE WRITING DESK. *See "How to Address Titled People."*

CONCHOLOGY, Journal of. *See page* 31.

COOKE, M. C., M.A., LL.D.

A PLAIN and **EASY ACCOUNT** of **THE BRITISH FUNGI.** With especial reference to the Esculent and other Economic Species. With Coloured Plates of 40 Species. Third Edition, revised. Crown 8vo, cloth, 6s.

THE BRITISH REPTILES: A Plain and Easy Account of the Lizards, Snakes, Newts, Toads, Frogs, and Tortoises indigenous to Great Britain. Numerous Illustrations, Coloured by hand. Fcap. 8vo, cloth, 6s.

RUST, SMUT, MILDEW, AND MOULD. An Introduction to the Study of Microscopic Fungi. Illustrated with 269 Coloured Figures by J. E. SOWERBY. Fourth Edition, with Appendix of New Species. Crown 8vo, cloth, 6s.

A MANUAL OF BOTANIC TERMS. New Edition, greatly Enlarged, including the recent Teratological terms. Illustrated with over 300 Woodcuts. Fcap. 8vo, cloth, 2s. 6d.

A MANUAL OF STRUCTURAL BOTANY. Revised Edition, with New Chemical Notation. Illustrated with 200 Woodcuts. Twenty-fifth Thousand. 32mo, cloth, 1s.

COOKE, M. C., M.A., A.L.S., et L. QUELET, M.D., O.A., Inst. et Sorb. Laur.

CLAVIS SYNOPTICA HYMENOMYCETUM EUROPÆORUM. Fcap. 8vo, cloth, 7s. 6d.

CRESSWELL, C. N., of the Inner Temple.

WOMAN, AND HER WORK IN THE WORLD. Crown 8vo, cloth, 3s. 6d.

CROLL, JAMES, LL.D., F.R.S., of Her Majesty's Geological Survey of Scotland.

CLIMATE AND TIME IN THEIR GEOLOGICAL RELATIONS. A Theory of Secular Changes of the Earth's Climate. Illustrated with 8 Coloured Plates and 11 Woodcuts. Demy 8vo, cloth, 577 pp., 24s.

CROWN OF LIFE (THE). By M. Y. W. With elegantly Illuminated Borders from designs by ARTHUR ROBERTSON. Uniform with "*The Changed Cross.*" Fcap. 4to, cloth extra, 6s.

CUVIER, *Baron.*

THE ANIMAL KINGDOM : Arranged after its Organisation, forming a Natural History of Animals, and Introduction to Comparative Anatomy. With considerable Additions by W. B. CARPENTER, M.D., F.R.S., and J. O. WESTWOOD, F.L.S. New Edition, illustrated with 500 Engravings on Wood and 36 Coloured Plates. Imp. 8vo, cloth, 21*s.*

DARBY, *W. A., M.A., F.R.A.S.*

THE ASTRONOMICAL OBSERVER : A Handbook for the Observatory and the Common Telescope. Embracing 965 Nebulæ, Clusters, and Double Stars. Roy. 8vo, cloth, 7*s.* 6*d.*

DAVIES, *THOMAS.*

THE PREPARATION and MOUNTING of MICRO-SCOPIC OBJECTS. New Edition, greatly Enlarged and brought up to the Present Time by JOHN MATTHEWS, M.D., F.R.M.S., Vice-President of the Quekett Microscopical Club. Eleventh Thousand. Fcap. 8vo, cloth, 2*s.* 6*d.*

DE CRESPIGNY, *E.C., M.D.*

A NEW LONDON FLORA ; or, Handbook to the Botanical Localities of the Metropolitan Districts. Compiled from the Latest Authorities and from Personal Observation. Crown 8vo, cloth, 5*s.*

DEWAR, *J., L.R.C.P.E.*

INDIGESTION AND DIET. Crown 8vo, limp cloth, 2*s.*

DICK, *Capt. ST. JOHN.*

FLIES AND FLY FISHING. Illustrated. Crown 8vo, cloth, 4*s.* 6*d.*

DRAMATIC LIST (THE). A Record of the Principal Performances of Living Actors and Actresses of the British Stage. With Criticisms from Contemporary Journals. Compiled and Edited by CHARLES EYRE PASCOE. Second Edition, Revised and Enlarged. Crown 8vo, cloth, 3*s.* 6*d.*

DRAMATIC NOTES. An Illustrated Year Book of the Stage. With Fifty-one Sketches of Scenes and Characters of the Principal Plays of the Year. Published Annually, price 1*s.*

DRURY, *E. J.*

.**CHRONOLOGY AT A GLANCE** : An Epitome of Events from 4000 B.C. to A.D. 1878. Fcap. 8vo, sewed, 1*s.*

DUDGEON, *R. E., M.D.*

THE HUMAN EYE : Its Optical Construction Popularly Explained. Illustrated with 32 Woodcuts. Royal 18mo, cloth, 3*s.* 6*d.*

DUNCAN, JAMES, F.L.S.
INTRODUCTION TO ENTOMOLOGY. With 38 Coloured Plates. Fcap. 8vo, cloth, 4*s.* 6*d.*

BRITISH BUTTERFLIES: A complete Description of the Larvæ and full-grown Insects of our Native Species. With Coloured Figures of Eighty Varieties. Fcap. 8vo, cloth, 4*s.* 6*d.*

BRITISH MOTHS: A complete Description of the Larvæ and full-grown Insects of our Native Species. With Coloured Figures of Eighty Varieties. Fcap. 8vo, cloth, 4*s.* 6*d.*

BEETLES, BRITISH AND FOREIGN. Containing a full description of the more important species. With Coloured Figures of more than One Hundred Varieties. Fcap. 8vo, cloth, 4*s.* 6*d.*

EXOTIC BUTTERFLIES. With 36 Coloured Plates. Fcap. 8vo, cloth, 4*s.* 6*d.*

EXOTIC MOTHS. With 34 Coloured Plates. Fcap. 8vo, cloth, 4*s.* 6*d.*

DYER, Rev. T. F. THISELTON, M.A.
ENGLISH FOLK-LORE. *Contents:*—Trees—Plants—Flowers—The Moon—Birds—Animals—Insects—Reptiles—Charms—Birth—Baptism—Marriage—Death—Days of the Week—The Months and their Weather Lore—Bells—Miscellaneous Folk-Lore. Second Edition. Crown 8vo, cloth, 5*s.*

EATON, Professor D. C., of Yale College.
THE FERNS OF NORTH AMERICA. Illustrated with numerous Coloured Plates by JAMES H. EMERTON. Demy 4to. 27 Parts, price 5*s.* each.

EDGEWORTH, M. P., F.L.S., F.A.S.
POLLEN. Illustrated with 438 Figures. Second Edition, revised and corrected. Demy 8vo, cloth, 7*s.* 6*d.*

EDWARDS, A. M., M.D., C. JOHNSTON, M.D., and H. L. SMITH, LL.D.
DIATOMS: Practical Directions for Collecting, Preserving, Transporting, Preparing and Mounting. Crown 8vo, cloth, 3*s.* 6*d.*

EXERCISE AND TRAINING. Tenth Thousand. Royal 16mo, cloth, illustrated, price 1*s.* *See* Health Primers, page 29.

FLEISCHMANN, A., M.R.C.S.

PLAIN AND PRACTICAL MEDICAL PRECEPTS.
Second Edition, revised and enlarged.   On a large sheet, 4*d.*

FLOWER, W. H., Conservator of the Museum.

CATALOGUE of the **SPECIMENS** Illustrating the **OSTEOLOGY** or **DENTITION** of **VERTEBRATED ANIMALS** in the Museum of the Royal College of Surgeons of England.   Part I. Containing Human Osteology, with Observations upon Cranial Measurements, and Tables for calculating Indices.   Demy 8vo, cloth, 7*s.* 6*d.*

FORBES, URQUHART A., of Lincoln's Inn.

THE LAW RELATING TO TRUSTEE AND POSTOFFICE SAVINGS' BANKS, with Notes of Decisions and Awards made by the Barrister and the Registrar of Friendly Societies.   Demy 12mo, cloth, 7*s.* 6*d.*

FOURNIER, ALFRED, Professeur à la Faculté de Médecine de Paris, Médecin de l'Hôpital Saint Louis, Membre de l'Académie de Médecine.

SYPHILIS AND MARRIAGE : Lectures Delivered at the Hospital of St. Louis.   Translated by ALFRED LINGARD, M.R.C.S.   Demy 8vo, cloth.   [*In the Press.*

FRY, HERBERT.

LONDON IN 1880.   Illustrated with 13 Bird's-Eye Views of the Principal Streets and a Map. Second Edition. Crown 8vo, cloth, 1*s.*

ROYAL GUIDE TO THE LONDON CHARITIES, 1878–81.   Showing, in alphabetical order, their Name, Date of Foundation, Address, Objects, Annual Income, Chief Officials, &c. Seventeenth Annual Edition. Crown 8vo, cloth, 1*s.* 6*d.*

GEOLOGISTS' ASSOCIATION, Proceedings of.   Edited by J. LOGAN LOBLEY, F.G.S.   Demy 8vo, with Illustrations. Published Quarterly.   Vol. I., 8 Parts, 6*d.* each ;   Vol. II., 8 Parts ; Vol. III., 8 Parts ; Vol. IV., 9 Parts ; Vol. V., Parts 1 to 6, 1*s.* 6*d.* each.

GRANVILLE, J. MORTIMER, M.D., L.R.C.P.

THE CARE AND CURE OF THE INSANE : Being the Reports of *The Lancet* Commission on Lunatic Asylums, 1875-6-7, for Middlesex, City of London, and Surrey (republished by permission), with a Digest of the principal records extant, and a Statistical Review of the Work of each Asylum, from the date of its opening to the end of 1875.   Two Vols., demy 8vo, cloth, 36*s.*

GRANVILLE, J. MORTIMER, continued.

COMMON MIND TROUBLES. *Contents :*—Failings—
Defects of Memory—Confusions of Thought—Sleeplessness
—Hesitation and Errors in Speech—Low Spirits—Tempers,
&c. Eighth Thousand. Fcap. 8vo, cloth, 1s.

THE SECRET OF A CLEAR HEAD. *Contents :*—
Temperature—Habit—Time—Pleasure—Self-Importance—
Consistency—Simplicity—A Clear Head. Eleventh Thousand.
Fcap. 8vo, cloth, 1s.

THE SECRET OF A GOOD MEMORY. *Contents :*—
What Memory is, and How it Works—Taking in and Storing
—Ways of Remembering Facts, Figures, Forms, Persons,
Places, Property—The Secret of a Good Memory. Fifth
Thousand. Fcap. 8vo, cloth, 1s.

SLEEP AND SLEEPLESSNESS. *Contents :*—Sleep—
Going to Sleep—Sleeping—Awaking—Sleeplessness—Sleep
and Food. Tenth Thousand. Fcap. 8vo, cloth, 1s.

YOUTH : Its Care and Culture. An Outline of Principles
for Parents and Guardians. *Contents :*—Development and
Improvement—The Eradication of Disease—The Threshold
of Life—Boy-Manhood; in the Early Stage, and in Later
Years—Girl-Womanhood; in the Early Stage, and in Later
Years—Jottings on Detail. Post 8vo, cloth, 2s. 6d.

"CHANGE" AS A MENTAL RESTORATIVE.
Demy 8vo, parchment, 1s.

HAMILTON, R., M.D., F.R.S.

THE NATURAL HISTORY OF BRITISH FISHES.
With 72 Coloured Plates. Two Vols., fcap. 8vo, cloth, 9s.

HAWEIS, H. R., M.A.

MUSIC AND MORALS. Ninth Edition. Crown 8vo,
cloth, Illustrated, 7s. 6d.

WEALTH PRIMERS. *See page* 29.

HEAPHY, THOMAS.

THE LIKENESS OF CHRIST. Being an Enquiry into
the verisimilitude of the received Likeness of our Blessed
Lord. Edited by WYKE BAYLISS, F.S.A. Illustrated with
Twelve Photographs Coloured as Facsimiles, and Fifty Engravings on Wood from original Frescoes, Mosaics, Pateræ,
and other Works of Art of the first Six Centuries. Handsomely bound in cloth gilt, atlas 4to. Price to Subscribers
before issue, £3 3s.

HEART (THE) AND ITS FUNCTIONS. Royal 16mo,
cloth, Illustrated, price 1s. *See* Health Primers, *page* 29.

HERSCHEL, Sir JOHN F. W., Bart., K.H., &c., Member of the Institute of France, &c.

POPULAR LECTURES ON SCIENTIFIC SUBJECTS. Eighth Thousand. Crown 8vo, cloth, 6s.

HOOKER, Sir W. J., F.R.S., and J. G. BAKER, F.L.S.

SYNOPSIS FILICUM; or, A Synopsis of all Known Ferns, including the Osmundaceæ, Schizæaceæ, Marratiaceæ, and Ophioglossaceæ (chiefly derived from the Kew Herbarium), accompanied by Figures representing the essential Characters of each Genus. Second Edition, brought up to the Present Time. 8vo, cloth, Coloured Plates, £1 8s.

HOUSE (THE) AND ITS SURROUNDINGS. Tenth Thousand. Royal 16mo, cloth, price 1s. *See* Health Primers, *page* 29.

HOWDEN, PETER, V.S.

HORSE WARRANTY: A Plain and Comprehensive Guide to the various Points to be noted, showing which are essential and which are unimportant. With Forms of Warranty. Fcap. 8vo, cloth, 3s. 6d.

HOW TO ADDRESS TITLED PEOPLE. With Explanations of over 500 Abbreviations, Academical, Ecclesiastical, Legal, Literary, Masonic, Imperial, and Ancient. Royal 32mo, cloth gilt, 1s.

HOW TO CHOOSE A MICROSCOPE. By a Demonstrator. With 80 Illustrations. Demy 8vo, 1s.

HOW TO USE THE PISTOL. The Pistol as a Weapon of Defence in the House and on the Road : How to Choose it, and How to Use it. Crown 8vo, cloth, 2s. 6d.

HUNTER, J., late Hon. Sec. of the Brit. Bee-keepers' Association.

A MANUAL OF BEE-KEEPING. Containing Practical Information for Rational and Profitable Methods of Bee Management. Full Instructions on Stimulative Feeding, Ligurianizing and Queen-raising, with descriptions of the American Comb Foundation, Sectional Supers, and the best Hives and Apiarian Appliances on all systems. With Illustrations. Third Edition. Crown 8vo, cloth, 3s. 6d.

HUSBAND, H. AUBREY, M.B., F.R.C.S.E., &c.

THE STUDENT'S HANDBOOK OF THE PRACTICE of MEDICINE. Designed for the Use of Students preparing for Examination. Second Edition, Revised and Enlarged. Post 8vo, cloth, 7s. 6d.

HUSBAND, H. AUBREY, continued.
THE STUDENT'S HANDBOOK OF FORENSIC MEDICINE AND MEDICAL POLICE. Third Edition, Enlarged and Improved. Post 8vo, cloth, 10s. 6d.

IDYLS OF THE RINK. Illustrated by G. BOWERS and J. CARLISLE. Royal 16mo, cloth gilt, 2s. 6d.

JARDINE, Sir W., F.L.S., F.R.S.
THE NATURAL HISTORY OF BRITISH BIRDS. With 120 Coloured Plates. 4 vols. Fcap. 8vo, cloth, 18s.

JEWITT, LLEWELLYNN, F.S.A.
HALF-HOURS AMONG ENGLISH ANTIQUITIES. *Contents :* Arms, Armour, Pottery, Brasses, Coins, Church Bells, Glass, Tapestry, Ornaments, Flint Implements, &c. With 304 Illustrations. Second Edition. Crown 8vo, cl., 5s.

JOHNSON, R. LOCKE, L.R.C.P., L.R.C.I., L.S.A., &c.
FOOD CHART, giving the Names, Classification, Composition, Elementary Value, rates of Digestibility, Adulterations, Tests, &c., of the Alimentary substances in general use. In wrapper, 4to, 2s. 6d. ; or on roller, varnished, 6s.

JORDAN, W. L., F.R.G.S.
REMARKS ON THE RECENT OCEANIC EX-PLORATIONS, and the Current-creating Action of Vis-Inertiæ in the Ocean. With 6 Plates. Demy 8vo, cloth, 4s.

THE WINDS, and their Story of the World. Demy 8vo, cloth, 5s.

THE SYSTEM OF THE WORLD CHALLENGE LECTURES. Second Edition. Illustrated with Maps and Diagrams. Demy 8vo, cloth, 4s.

THE ARGENTINE REPUBLIC, A Descriptive and Historical Sketch. Demy 8vo, cloth, 2s.

KAYE, SIR JOHN WILLIAM.
LIVES OF INDIAN OFFICERS. Illustrative of the History of the Civil and Military Service of India. 1st Series : CORNWALLIS, MALCOLM, ELPHINSTONE.—2nd Series : MARTYN, METCALFE, BURNES, CONOLLY, POTTINGER.—3rd Series : TODD, LAWRENCE, NEILL, NICHOLSON. Three Volumes, crown 8vo, cloth, 6s. each.

KEENE, Rev. H. G., Sometime Persian and Arabic Professor of the East Indian College, Halibury, Herts.
THE MODEST RAINDROP, and other Fables for Old and Young. Translated from the Persian. A New Edition, edited by KATHERINE KEENE, with Illustrations by SAMUEL FRY. Square 16mo, cloth, 5s.

*KENT, W. SAVILLE, F.L.S., F.Z.S., F.R.M.S., formerly
Assistant in the Nat. Hist. Department of the British Museum.*
A MANUAL OF THE INFUSORIA. Including a Description of the Flagellate, Ciliate, and Tentaculiferous Protozoa, British and Foreign, and an account of the Organization and Affinities of the Sponges. With numerous Illustrations. Super-royal 8vo, cloth. To be completed in 6 monthly parts, price 10*s*. 6*d*. each. Part I. was published on Oct. 1.

KINAHAN, G. H.
HANDY BOOK OF ROCK NAMES. With Brief Descriptions of the Rocks. Fcap. 8vo, cloth, 4*s*.

LANKESTER, E., M.D., F.R.S., F.L.S.
OUR FOOD : Lectures delivered at the South Kensington Museum. Illustrated. New Edition. Crown 8vo, cloth, 4*s*.

THE USES OF ANIMALS in Relation to the Industry of Man : Lectures delivered at the South Kensington Museum. Illustrated. New Edition. Crown 8vo, cloth, 4*s*.

PRACTICAL PHYSIOLOGY : A School Manual of Health, for the use of Classes and General Reading. Illustrated with numerous Woodcuts. Sixth Edition. Fcap. 8vo, cloth, 2*s*. 6*d*.

HALF - HOURS WITH THE MICROSCOPE : A Popular Guide to the Use of the Instrument. With 250 Illustrations. Sixteenth Thousand, enlarged. Fcap. 8vo, cloth, plain 2*s*. 6*d*. ; coloured 4*s*.

SANITARY INSTRUCTIONS : A Series of Handbills for general Distribution :—1. Management of Infants ; 2. Scarlet Fever, and the best Means of Preventing it ; 3. Typhoid or Drain Fever, and its Prevention ; 4. Small Pox, and its Prevention ; 5. Cholera and Diarrhœa, and its Prevention ; 6. Measles, and their Prevention. Each, 1*d*. ; per dozen, 6*d*. ; per 100, 4*s*. ; per 1,000, 30*s*.

LANKESTER, MRS.
TALKS ABOUT HEALTH : A Book for Boys and Girls ; Being an Explanation of all the Processes by which Life is sustained. Illustrated. Small 8vo, cloth, 1*s*.

A PLAIN and EASY ACCOUNT of BRITISH FERNS. Together with their Classification, Arrangement of Genera, Structures, and Functions, Directions for Out-door and In-door Cultivation, &c. Numerous Coloured Illustrations. *A New Edition in preparation.*

WILD FLOWERS WORTH NOTICE: A Selection of some of our Native Plants which are most attractive for their Beauty, Uses, or Associations. With 108 Coloured Figures by J. E. SOWERBY. New Edition. Crown 8vo, cloth, 5*s.*

LETTERS FROM A CAT. Published by her Mistress, for the Benefit of all Cats and the Amusement of Little Children. Illustrated with numerous Woodcuts and a Frontispiece. Small 4to, cloth, gilt edges, 5*s.*

LONDON CATALOGUE OF BRITISH PLANTS. Published under the direction of the London Botanical Exchange Club, adapted for marking Desiderata in Exchanges of Specimens. Seventh Edition. 8vo, sewed, 6*d.*

LIVING VOICES. Selections chiefly from Recent Poetry. With a Preface by His Grace·the ARCHBISHOP of CANTERBURY. Post 8vo, cloth extra, 4*s.* 6*d.*

LORD, J. KEAST.

 AT HOME IN THE WILDERNESS: What to Do there and How to do it. A Handbook for Travellers and Emigrants. With numerous Illustrations of necessary Baggage, Tents, Tools, &c. &c. Second Edition. Crown 8vo, 5*s.*

MANGNALL'S HISTORICAL & MISCELLANEOUS QUESTIONS. New and improved Edition, carefully Revised and brought up to the Present Time. Well printed and strongly bound. 18mo, cloth boards, 1*s.*

MESSER, FREDERICK A.

 A NEW AND EASY METHOD OF STUDYING BRITISH WILD FLOWERS BY NATURAL ANALYSIS. Being a Complete Series of Illustrations of their Natural Orders and Genera, Analytically Arranged. Demy 8vo, cloth, 10*s.* 6*d.*

MICHOD, C. J., late Secretary of the London Athletic Club.

 GOOD CONDITION: A Guide to Athletic Training, for Amateurs and Professionals. Fourth Thousand. Small 8vo, cloth, 1*s.*

MIDLAND NATURALIST. *See page* 31.

MILNE, ALEXANDER, M.D.

 THE PRINCIPLES AND PRACTICE OF MID-WIFERY, with some of the Diseases of Women. Illustrated with numerous Wood Engravings. Second Edition. Crown 8vo, cloth, 12*s.* 6*d.*

MILNE, ALEXANDER, continued.
**MANUAL OF MATERIA MEDICA AND THERA-
PEUTICS.** Embracing all the Medicines of the British
Pharmacopœia. Fourth Edition, Revised and Enlarged, by
WILLIAM CRAIG, M.D., &c. Post 8vo, cloth, 9*s.*

MILTON, J. L., M.R.C.S.
THE STREAM OF LIFE ON OUR GLOBE: Its
Archives, Traditions, and Laws, as revealed by Modern
Discoveries in Geology and Palæontology. A Sketch in
Untechnical Language of the Beginning and Growth of Life,
and the Physiological Laws which govern its Progress and
Operations. Second Edition. Crown 8vo, cloth, 6*s.*

MIVART, ST. GEORGE, F.R.S., V.P.Z.S.
MAN AND APES: An Exposition of Structural Resem-
blances and Differences bearing upon Questions of Affinity
and Origin. With numerous Illustrations. Crown 8vo, cloth, 6*s.*

MONKHOVEN, D. VAN, Ph.D.
PHOTOGRAPHIC OPTICS, including the description of
Lenses and Enlarging Apparatus. With 200 Woodcuts. Crown
8vo, cloth, 7*s.* 6*d.*

NATURALIST'S LIBRARY (THE). Edited by Sir
WILLIAM JARDINE, F.L.S., F.R.S. Containing numerous
Portraits and Memoirs of Eminent Naturalists. Illustrated
with 1,300 Coloured Plates. Forty-two Volumes, fcap. 8vo,
cloth, gilt tops, £9 9*s.*

THE LIBRARY comprises.—**BIRDS,** 15 Vols. British
Birds, 4 Vols., Sun Birds, Humming Birds, 3 Vols., Game
Birds, Pigeons, Parrots, Birds of Western Africa, 2 Vols.,
Fly-Catchers, Pheasants and Peacocks, &c. **ANIMALS,**
14 Vols. Introduction, Lions and Tigers, British Quadru-
peds, Dogs, 2 Vols., Horses, Ruminating Animals, 2 Vols.,
Elephants, Marsupialia, Seals, Whales, Monkeys, and Man.
INSECTS, 7 Vols. Introduction to Entomology, British
Butterflies and Moths, 2 Vols., Foreign Butterflies and Moths,
2 Vols., Beetles, Bees. **FISHES,** 6 Vols. Introduction
and Foreign Fishes, British Fishes, 2 Vols., Perch Family,
Fishes of Guiana, 2 Vols.

NAVE, JOHANN.
THE COLLECTOR'S HANDY-BOOK of Algæ,
Diatoms, Desmids, Fungi, Lichens, Mosses, &c. With
Instructions for their Preparation and for the Formation of an
Herbarium. Translated and Edited by Rev. W. W. SPICER,
M.A. Illustrated with 114 Woodcuts. Fcap. 8vo, cloth, 2*s.* 6*d.*

NEWMAN, EDWARD, F.Z.S.
**BRITISH BUTTERFLIES AND MOTHS (AN IL-
LUSTRATED NATURAL HISTORY OF).** Con-
taining Life-size Figures from Nature of each Species, and of
the more striking Varieties ; also full descriptions of both the
Perfect Insect and the Caterpillar, together with Dates of
Appearance and Localities where found. With over 800
Illustrations. Super-royal 8vo, cloth gilt, 25*s.*

*The above Work may also be had in Two Volumes, sold separately.
Vol. I., Butterflies, 7s. 6d. ; Vol. II., Moths, 20s.*

NEWMAN, Cardinal.
**MISCELLANIES FROM THE OXFORD SERMONS
OF JOHN HENRY NEWMAN, D.D.** Third Thou-
sand. Crown 8vo, cloth, 6*s.*

NEWTON, JOSEPH, F.R.H.S.
THE LANDSCAPE GARDENER : A Practical Guide
t• the Laying-Out, Planting, and Arrangement of Villa
Gardens, Town Squares, and Open Spaces, from a Quarter
of an Acre to Four Acres. For the use of Practical Gardeners, Amateurs, Architects, and Builders. With 24 Plans.
Fcap. folio, cloth, 12*s.*

**NOTES ON COLLECTING AND PRESERVING
NATURAL HISTORY OBJECTS.** Edited by J. E.
TAYLOR, F.L.S., F.G.S., Editor of " Science Gossip." With
numerous Illustrations. Crown 8vo, cloth, 3*s.* 6*d.*

Contents—Geological Specimens, by the Editor ; Bones, by E. F. ELWIN;
Birds' Eggs, by T. SOUTHWELL, F.Z.S. ; Butterflies, by Dr. KNAGGS;
Beetles, by E. C. RYE, F.Z.S. ; Hymenoptera, by J. B. BRIDGMAN;
Fresh-water Shells, by Prof. RALPH TATE, F.G.S. ; Flowering Plants,
by JAMES BRITTEN, F.L.S. ; Trees and Shrubs, by Prof. BUCKMAN,
F.G.S.; Mosses, by Dr. BRAITHWAITE, F.L.S.; Fungi, by W. G. SMITH,
F.L.S.; Lichens, by Rev. J. CROMBIE ; Seaweeds, by W. GRATTANN.

OUR ACTORS AND ACTRESSES. *See* Dramatic List.

*PARKER, ROBERT WILLIAM, Assistant-Surgeon to the East
London Hospital for Children.*
TRACHEOTOMY IN LARYNGEAL DIPHTHERIA
(Membranous Croup). With Special Reference to After-
treatment. To which are added a few General Remarks on
Diphtheria and its earlier Treatment. Demy 8vo, cloth, 6*s.*

PARKIN, JOHN, F.R.C.P., F.R.C.S.
GOUT : Its Causes, Nature, and Treatment. With
Directions for the Regulation of the Diet. Second Edition.
Demy 8vo, cloth, 5*s.*

PARKIN, JOHN, continued.
THE ANTIDOTAL TREATMENT OF DISEASE.
Part I. Demy 8vo, cloth, 7s. 6d.

EPIDEMIOLOGY; or, The Remote Cause of Epidemic
Diseases in the Animal and in the Vegetable Creation. With
the cause of Hurricanes, and Abnormal Atmospherical Vicissi-
tudes. Part II. Demy 8vo, cloth, 10s. 6d.

PASCOE, CHARLES E.
**SCHOOLS FOR GIRLS AND COLLEGES FOR
WOMEN:** A Handbook of Female Education, chiefly
Designed for the Use of Persons of the Upper Middle Class.
With a Chapter on the Higher Employment of Women.
Crown 8vo, cloth, 5s.

**THE PRINCIPAL PROFESSIONS, A PRACTICAL
HANDBOOK TO.** Compiled from Authentic Sources,
and based on the most recent Regulations concerning Admission to the Navy, Army, and Civil Services (Home and Indian),
the Legal and Medical Professions, the Professions of a Civil
Engineer, Architect and Artist, and the Mercantile Marine.
Crown 8vo, cloth, 3s. 6d.

**PERSONAL APPEARANCES IN HEALTH AND
DISEASE.** Fifth Thousand. Royal 16mo, cloth, Illustrated, price 1s. *See* Health Primers, *page* 29.

PERSONAL PIETY. A Help to Christians to Walk worthy
of their Calling. Twenty-second Thousand. 24mo, cloth, 1s.6d.

PHIN, J., Editor of American Journal of Microscopy.
HOW TO USE THE MICROSCOPE. Practical Hints
on the Selection and Use of the Microscope, intended for
Beginners. Second Edition. Crown 8vo, cloth, 3s. 6d.

POMONA, THE HEREFORDSHIRE. Containing Coloured Figures and Descriptions of all the most esteemed
kinds of Apples and Pears of Great Britain. Edited by
ROBERT HOGG, LL.D., F.L.S. To be completed in SIX
PARTS, 4to. Part I. Illustrated with 22 Coloured Figures
and numerous Woodcuts, price 15s. Part II. Illustrated
with 41 Coloured Figures and numerous Woodcuts, price 21s.

POPULAR SCIENCE REVIEW· A Quarterly Summary
of Scientific Progress and Miscellany of Entertaining and
Instructive Articles on Scientific Subjects, by the Best Writers
of the Day. SECOND SERIES. Edited by W. S. DALLAS,
F.L.S., F.G.S. With high-class Illustrations by first-rate

Artists. The FIRST SERIES, Edited by Dr. HENRY LAWSON, F.R.M.S., is Complete in 15 Volumes, fully Illustrated. Price in Parts, £7 12s. 6d. ; in cloth gilt, £9 2s.; in half-morocco, extra, £11 8s. SECOND SERIES, Vols. 1 to 3, in Numbers, £1 10s.; in cloth gilt, £1 16s.; in half-morocco extra, £2 8s. *See also page* 31.

PREMATURE DEATH : Its Promotion or Prevention. Fifth Thousand. Royal 16mo, cloth, price 1s. *See* Health Primers, *page* 29.

PROCTOR, RICHARD A., B.A., F.R.A.S.
HALF-HOURS WITH THE STARS : A Plain and Easy Guide to the knowledge of the Constellations ; showing, in 12 Maps, the position of the principal Star-groups, night after night throughout the Year, with Introduction and a separate Explanation of each Map. Tenth Thousand. Demy 4to, boards, 5s.

HALF-HOURS WITH THE TELESCOPE : A Popular Guide to the Use of the Telescope as a means of Amusement and Instruction. Seventh Edition, Illustrated. Fcap. 8vo, cloth, 2s. 6d.

QUEKETT MICROSCOPICAL CLUB, Journal of the. *See page* 31.

RALFE, CHARLES HENRY, M.A., M.D. Cantab. ; F.R.C.P. Lond. ; Teacher of Physiological Chemistry, St. George's Hospital, &c., &c.
DEMONSTRATIONS IN PHYSIOLOGICAL AND PATHOLOGICAL CHEMISTRY. Arranged to meet the Requirements for the Practical Examination in these Subjects at the Royal College of Physicians and College of Surgeons. Fcap. 8vo, cloth, 5s.

READE, T. MELLARD, C.E., F.G.S., F.R.I.B.A., &c.
CHEMICAL DENUDATION IN RELATION TO GEOLOGICAL TIME. Demy 8vo, cloth, 2s. 6d.

RIBEAUCOURT, C. DE.
A MANUAL OF RATIONAL BEE-KEEPING. Translated from the French by ARTHUR F. G. LEVESON-GOWER. Fcap. 8vo, cloth, Illustrated, 2s. 6d.

RIMMER, R., F.L.S.
THE LAND AND FRESH WATER SHELLS OF THE BRITISH ISLES. Illustrated with 8 Photographs and 3 Lithographs containing figures of all the principal species. Crown 8vo, cloth, 10s. 6d.

ROBSON, JOHN E.
 BOTANICAL LABELS for Labelling Herbaria, adapted to the names in the London Catalogue of Plants and the Manuals of Prof. BABINGTON and Dr. HOOKER, with Extra Labels for all New Species. 3,576 Labels, with Index. Demy 8vo, 5*s*.

RUSSELL, C.
 THE TANNIN PROCESS. Second Edition, with Appendix. Fcap. 8vo, cloth, 2*s*. 6*d*.

SCHAIBLE, CHARLES H., M.D., Ph.D.
 FIRST HELP IN ACCIDENTS: Being a Surgical Guide in the absence, or before the arrival, of Medical Assistance. Fully Illustrated. 32mo, cloth, 1*s*.

SCHLEIDEN, J. M., M.D.
 THE PRINCIPLES OF SCIENTIFIC BOTANY; or, Botany as an Inductive Science. Translated by Dr. LANKESTER. Numerous Woodcuts, and Six Steel Plates. Demy 8vo, cloth, 10*s*. 6*d*.

SCHMIDT, ADOLPH, assisted by GRUNDLER, GRUNOW, JANECH, &c.
 ATLAS OF THE DIATOMACEÆ. This magnificent work consists of Photographic Reproductions of the various forms of Diatomaceæ, on Folio Plates, with description (in German). Price to Subscribers, for Twelve Parts, payable in advance, £3 12*s*. To be Completed in about 25 Parts. (*Sixteen Parts are now ready.*)

SCIENCE GOSSIP. A Medium of Interchange and Gossip for Students and Lovers of Nature. Edited by J. E. TAYLOR, F.L.S., F.G.S., &c. Published Monthly, with numerous Illustrations. Price Fourpence, or by post Fivepence. 15 Volumes are now published. Price, Vols. I. to XIV., 7*s*. 6*d*. each ; Vol. XV., 5*s*. *See also page* 32.

SHAKSPERE QUARTO FACSIMILES. Photo-lithographed by W. GRIGGS, under the superintendence of E. J. FURNIVALL, M.A. Camb. No. 1, HAMLET, 1603, is now ready. No. 2, HAMLET, 1604, will be ready shortly. Price to Subscribers for the whole Series (35), 7*s*. 6*d*. each ; to Non-subscribers, 10*s*. 6*d*. each.

SHOOLBRED, J. N., Memb. Inst. C.E.
 ELECTRIC LIGHTING, and its Practical Application. With Results from existing Examples. Numerous Illustrations, crown 8vo, cloth, 5*s*.

SHOOTING ON THE WING. Plain Directions for acquiring the art of Shooting on the Wing. With useful Hints concerning all that relates to Guns and Shooting, and particularly in regard to the art of Loading so as to Kill. By an Old Gamekeeper. Crown 8vo, cloth, 3*s.* 6*d.*

SIMMONDS, P. L., Editor of the Journal of Applied Science.

WASTE PRODUCTS AND UNDEVELOPED SUB-STANCES : A Synopsis of Progress made in their Economic Utilization during the last Quarter of a Century, at Home and Abroad. Third Edition. Crown 8vo, cloth, 9*s.*

SCIENCE AND COMMERCE : Their Influence on our Manufactures. Fcap. 8vo, cloth, 6*s.*

SKIN (THE) AND ITS TROUBLES. Fifth Thousand. Royal 16mo, cloth, Illustrated, price 1*s.* *See* Health Primers, *page* 29.

SMITH, J., A.L.S., late Curator of the Royal Gardens, Kew.

FERNS, BRITISH AND FOREIGN : The History, Organography, Classification, and Examination of the Species of Garden Ferns, with a Treatise on their Cultivation, and Directions showing which are the best adapted for the Hothouse, Greenhouse, Open Air Fernery, or Wardian Case. With an Index of Genera, Species, and Synonyms. Fourth Edition, revised and greatly enlarged, with New Figures, &c. Crown 8vo, cloth, 7*s.* 6*d.*

BIBLE PLANTS : Their History. With a Review of the Opinions of Various Writers regarding their Identification. Illustrated with 10 Lithographic Plates by W. H. FITCH, F.L.S. Crown 8vo, cloth, 5*s.*

SMITH, WORTHINGTON, F.L.S.

MUSHROOMS AND TOADSTOOLS : How to Distinguish easily the Difference between Edible and Poisonous Fungi. Two large Sheets, containing Figures of 29 Edible and 31 Poisonous Species, drawn the natural size, and Coloured from Living Specimens. With descriptive letterpress, 6*s.* ; on canvas, in cloth case for pocket, 10*s.* 6*d.* ; on canvas, on rollers and varnished, 10*s.* 6*d.* The letterpress may be had separately, with key-plates of figures, 1*s.*

SOWERBY, J.

ENGLISH BOTANY. Containing a Description and Life-size Drawing of every British Plant. Edited and brought up to the Present Standard of Scientific Knowledge, by T. BOSWELL SYME, LL.D., F.L.S., &c. With Popular Descriptions of the Uses, History, and Traditions of each Plant, by Mrs. LANKESTER. Complete in 11 Volumes, cloth, £22 8*s.* ; half morocco, £24 12*s.* ; whole morocco, £28 3*s.* 6*d.*

SPRAGUE, ISAAC, and GEORGE L. GOODALE, M.D.,
Professor of Botany at Harvard University.

THE WILD FLOWERS OF AMERICA. Illustrated with beautifully Coloured Plates from original Water-Coloured Paintings by ISAAC SPRAGUE. Demy 4to, Parts 1 to 8 now ready, price 5*s.* each.

STANLEY, ARTHUR PENRHYN, D.D., Dean of West-minster.

SCRIPTURE PORTRAITS and other Miscellanies. Crown 8vo, cloth, 6*s.*

STEINMETZ, A.

SMOKER'S GUIDE (THE), PHILOSOPHER AND FRIEND. What to Smoke—What to Smoke with—and the whole "What's What" of Tobacco, Historical, Botanical, Manufactural, Anecdotal, Social, Medical, &c. Eighth Thousand. Royal 32mo, cloth, 1*s.*

SUNDAY EVENING BOOK (THE). Short Papers for Family Reading. By J. HAMILTON, D.D., Dean STANLEY, J. EADIE, D.D., Rev. W. M. PUNSHON, Rev. T. BINNEY, J. R. MACDUFF, D.D. Fourteenth Thousand. 24mo, cloth antique, 1*s.* 6*d.*

SYMONDS, Rev. W. S., Rector of Pendock.

OLD BONES; or, Notes for Young Naturalists. With References to the Typical Specimens in the British Museum. Second Edition, much improved and enlarged. Numerous Illustrations. Fcap. 8vo, cloth, 2*s.* 6*d.*

TAYLOR, J. E., F.L.S., F.G.S., Editor of "Science Gossip."

NATURE'S BYE-PATHS: A Series of Recreative Papers in Natural History. Crown 8vo, cloth, 7*s.* 6*d.* *See* also p. 28.

FLOWERS: Their Origin, Shapes, Perfumes, and Colours. Illustrated with 32 Coloured Figures by SOWERBY, and 161 Woodcuts. Second Edition. Crown 8vo, cloth gilt, 7*s.* 6*d.*

HALF-HOURS IN THE GREEN LANES. A Book for a Country Stroll. Illustrated with 300 Woodcuts. Fifth Edition. Crown 8vo, cloth, 4*s.*

HALF-HOURS AT THE SEA-SIDE; or, Recreations with Marine Objects. Illustrated with 250 Woodcuts. Fourth Edition. Crown 8vo, cloth, 4*s.*

TAYLOR, J. E., continued.

GEOLOGICAL STORIES: A Series of Autobiographies in Chronological Order. Numerous Illustrations. Fourth Edition. Crown 8vo, cloth, 4*s.*

THE AQUARIUM: Its Inhabitants, Structure, and Management. With 238 Woodcuts. Crown 8vo, cloth extra, 6*s.*

See also NOTES ON COLLECTING AND PRESERVING NATURAL HISTORY OBJECTS, *page* 19.

TIME'S FOOTPRINTS: A Birthday Book of Bitter-Sweet. 16mo, cloth gilt, 2*s.* 6*d.*

TREASURY OF CHOICE QUOTATIONS. Selections from more than 300 Eminent Authors. With a complete Index. Crown 8vo, cloth extra, 3*s.* 6*d.*

TRIMEN, H., M.B. (Lond.), F.L.S., and DYER, W. T., B.A.

THE FLORA OF MIDDLESEX: A Topographical and Historical Account of the Plants found in the County. With Sketches of its Physical Geography and Climate, and of the Progress of Middlesex Botany during the last Three Centuries. With a Map of Botanical Districts. Crown 8vo, 12*s.* 6*d.*

TROTTER, M. E.

A METHOD OF TEACHING PLAIN NEEDLE-WORK IN SCHOOLS. Illustrated with Diagrams and Samplers. New Edition, revised and arranged according to Standards. Demy 8vo, cloth, 2*s.* 6*d.*

TURNER, M., and HARRIS, W.

A GUIDE to the INSTITUTIONS and CHARITIES for the BLIND in the United Kingdom. Together with Lists of Books and Appliances for their Use, a Catalogue of Books published upon the subject of the Blind, and a List of Foreign Institutions, &c. Demy 8vo, cloth, 3*s.*

TWINING, THOMAS, F.S.A.

SCIENCE MADE EASY. A Connected and Progressive Course of Ten Familiar Lectures. Six Parts, 4to, price 1*s.* each. *Contents:*—Part I. Introduction, explaining the purpose of the present Course, and its use in Schools, or for Home Study.—Part II. Lecture I. The first Elements of Mechanical Physics. Lecture II. Mechanical Physics *(continued)*.—Part III. Lecture III. Mechanical Physics *(concluded)*. Lecture IV. Chemical Physics. — Part IV. Lecture V.

Inorganic Chemistry. Lecture VI. Organic Chemistry.—Part V. Lecture VII. Outlines of the Mineral and Vegetable Kingdoms. Lecture VIII. . Outlines of the Animal Kingdom.—Part VI. Lecture IX. Human Physiology, with Outlines of Anatomy. Lecture X. Human Physiology *(concluded)*.

A Series of Diagrams illustrating the above has been published, a list of which may be had on application. The price of a Complete Set of Diagrams is £3 ; the cost of the separate sheets varies from 6*d.* to 4*s.*

"For their perspicuity, cheapness and usefulness, we heartily commend this course of Lectures to all primary schools and to very many populous localities where it is desired by influential residents to impart pleasing and instructive information, free from high-class scientific phraseology."—*Journal of Applied Science.*

UP THE RIVER from WESTMINSTER to WINDSOR. A Panorama in Pen and Ink. Illustrated with 81 Engravings and a Map of the Thames. Demy 8vo, 1*s.* 6*d.*

VICTORIA INSTITUTE, or Philosophical Society of Great Britain, Journal of the Transactions of. Edited by the Honorary Secretary, Captain F. W. H. PETRIE, F.R.S.L., F.G.S., &c. Demy 8vo. Vol. XII. Part I. 7*s.* 6*d.* Part II. 3*s.* 6*d.* Vols. I. to XI., cloth, gilt tops, price £1 1*s.* each. Most of the more important articles are published also in pamphlet form. A list of these may be had on application.

WAITE, S. C.
  GRACEFUL RIDING : A Pocket Manual for Equestrians. Illustrated. Fcap. 8vo, cloth, 2*s.* 6*d.*

WALFORD, E., M.A., Late Scholar of Balliol College, Oxford.
  PLEASANT DAYS IN PLEASANT PLACES : *Contents :* Dorney and Burnham—Shanklin—Hadleigh—St. David's—Winchilsea—Sandwich—St. Osyth's Priory—Richborough Castle — Great Yarmouth — Old Moreton Hall—Cumnor—Ightham — Shoreham and Bramber—Beaulieu—Kenilworth—Tattershall Tower—Tower of Essex. Second Edition. Illustrated with numerous Woodcuts. Crown 8vo, cloth extra, 5*s.*

  HOLIDAYS IN HOME COUNTIES. *Contents :* A Pilgrimage to the Birthplace of Nelson—A Summer Day at Chiswick—A Day at Selbourne—Brambletye House—A Pilgrimage to Cheneys—A Summer Day about Dover—Footprints of Wolsey at Esher—A Day at Stoke Pogis—A Visit to Leeds Castle—A Ramble in Search of Thames Head—St. Albans and Gorhambury—An Autumn Day at Chertsey—A Day at Harold's Tomb—A Day at Rochester—A Summer Day at Ely—Halnaker and Boxgrove. Illustrated with numerous Woodcuts. Crown 8vo, cloth extra, 5*s.*

WALFORD, E., continued.

THE SHILLING PEERAGE. Containing an Alphabetical List of the House of Lords, Dates of Creation, Lists of Scotch and Irish Peers, Addresses, &c. 32mo, cloth, 1*s.* Published annually.

THE SHILLING BARONETAGE. Containing an Alphabetical List of the Baronets of the United Kingdom, Short Biographical Notices, Dates of Creation, Addresses, &c. 32mo, cloth, 1*s.* Published annually.

THE SHILLING KNIGHTAGE. Containing an Alphabetical List of the Knights of the United Kingdom, Short Biographical Notices, Dates of Creation, Addresses, &c. 32mo, cloth, 1*s.* Published annually.

THE SHILLING HOUSE OF COMMONS. Containing a List of all the Members of the British Parliament, their Town and Country Addresses, &c. 32mo, cl., 1*s.* Published annually.

THE COMPLETE PEERAGE, BARONETAGE, KNIGHTAGE, AND HOUSE OF COMMONS. In One Volume, royal 32mo, cloth extra, gilt edges, 5*s.* Published annually.

WATFORD NATURAL HISTORY SOCIETY, Transactions of the. Demy 8vo, Illustrated. Vol. I., 10 Parts, 10*s.* 6*d.*; Vol. II., Part I., 1*s.* 6*d.*; Part II., 1*s.* 6*d.*; Part III., 1*s.*; Part IV., 1*s.* 6*d.*

WILBERFORCE, SAMUEL, D.D., Bishop of Winchester.
HEROES OF HEBREW HISTORY. New Edition. Crown 8vo, cloth, 5*s.*

WILSON'S AMERICAN ORNITHOLOGY; or, Natural History of the Birds of the United States; with the Continuation by Prince CHARLES LUCIEN BONAPARTE. New and Enlarged Edition, completed by the insertion of above One Hundred Birds omitted in the original Work, and by valuable Notes and Life of the Author by Sir WILLIAM JARDINE. Three Vols. Large Paper, demy 4to, with Portrait of WILSON, and 103 Plates, exhibiting nearly 400 figures, carefully Coloured by hand, half-Roxburghe, £6 6*s.*

WOOD, The Rev. J. G., M.A., F.L.S., &c.
MAN AND BEAST, HERE AND HEREAFTER. Illustrated by more than 300 original Anecdotes. Fourth Edition. Post 8vo, cloth, 6*s.* 6*d.*

WORDSWORTH'S POEMS FOR THE YOUNG. With 50 Illustrations by JOHN MACWHIRTER and JOHN PETTIE, and a Vignette by J. E. MILLAIS, R.A. Demy 16mo, cloth gilt, 1s. 6d.

WYNTER, ANDREW, M.D., M.R.C.P.

SUBTLE BRAINS AND LISSOM FINGERS : Being some of the Chisel Marks of our Industrial and Scientific Progress. Third Edition, revised and corrected by ANDREW STEINMETZ. Fcap. 8vo, cloth, 3s. 6d.

CURIOSITIES OF CIVILIZATION. Being Essays reprinted from the *Quarterly* and *Edinburgh Reviews.* Crown 8vo, cloth, 6s.

ZERFFI, G. G., Ph.D., F.R.S.L.

MANUAL of the HISTORICAL DEVELOPMENT OF ART—Prehistoric, Ancient, Hebrew, Classic, Early Christian. With special reference to Architecture, Sculpture, Painting, and Ornamentation. Crown 8vo, cloth, 6s.

SPIRITUALISM AND ANIMAL MAGNETISM. A Treatise on Spiritual Manifestations, &c. &c., in which it is shown that these can, by careful study, be traced to Natural Causes. Third Edition. Crown 8vo, sewed, 1s.

NEW WORK BY J. E. TAYLOR, F.L.S., F.G.S.,
Editor of " Science Gossip."

Crown 8vo, cloth, 7s. 6d.

NATURE'S BYE-PATHS.

A Series of Recreative Papers in Natural History.

CONTENTS.

CHAP.
1. Subterranean Mountains.
2. Over an Old-Lane Surface.
3. Submarine Forests.
4. Hunting for Minerals.
5. Soils: their Origin, Renovation, and Decay.
6, 7, 8, 9. A Naturalist on the Tramp.
10. Phosphates: their Origin and Uses.
11. Vulcan's Forge.
12, 13. Geological Dispersion of Animals and Plants.
14. Watery Wastes.

CHAP.
15. Scientific Pilgrims.
16. The Norfolk Broads.
17. Old Wine in New Bottles.
18. The County Palatine.
19. The Story of a Recent Scare.
20. Pike-Fishing in Norfolk.
21. Aquatic Engineers.
22. Vegetable Parasites.
23. The Time of Catkins.
24. The Flowers of the Prime.
25. " Violets Blue."
26. Summer Meadows.
27. Hedge Garlands.

London: DAVID BOGUE, 3, St. Martin's Place, W.C.

Demy 16mo, cloth, Price One Shilling.

HEALTH PRIMERS.

EDITORS:

J. LANGDON DOWN, M.D., F.R.C.P., HENRY POWER, M.B., F.R.C.S.,
J. MORTIMER GRANVILLE, M.D., JOHN TWEEDY, F.R.C.S.

Under this title is being issued a Series of SHILLING PRIMERS on subjects connected with the Preservation of Health, written and edited by eminent medical authorities.

The list of Contributors includes the following names :—

W. H. ALLCHIN, M.B., F.R.C.P., F.R.S.E., G. W. BALFOUR, M.D., F.R.C.P.E., J. CRICHTON BROWNE, M.D., LL.D., F.R.S.E., SIDNEY COUPLAND, M.D., M.R.C.P., JOHN CURNOW, M.D., F.R.C.P., J. LANGDON DOWN, M.D., F.R.C.P., ROBERT FARQUHARSON, M.D. Edin., M.R.C.P., TILBURY FOX, M.D., F.R.C.P., J. MORTIMER GRANVILLE, M.D., F.G.S., F.S.S., W. S. GREENFIELD, M.D., F.R.C.P., C. W. HEATON, F.C.S., HARRY LEACH, M.R.C.P., G. V. POORE, M.D., F.R.C.P., HENRY POWER, M.B., F.R.C.S., W. L. PURVES, M.D., F.R.C.S., J. NETTEN RADCLIFFE, Ex.-Pres. Epidl. Soc., &c., C. H. RALFE, M.A., M.D., F.R.C.P., S. RINGER, M.D., F.R.C.P., JOHN TWEEDY, F.R.C.S., JOHN WILLIAMS, M.D., F.R.C.P.

The following Volumes are now ready :—

Premature Death : Its Promotion or Prevention.
Alcohol : Its Use and Abuse.
Exercise and Training.
The House and its Surroundings.
Personal Appearances in Health and Disease.
Baths and Bathing.
The Skin and its Troubles.
The Heart and its Functions.

To be followed by—

The Nerves.	The Throat and Voice.
The Ear and Hearing.	Temperature in Health and Disease.
The Head.	
Clothing and Dress.	Health of Travellers.
Water.	Health in Schools.
Fatigue and Pain.	Breath Organs.
The Eye and Vision.	Foods and Feeding.

London : DAVID BOGUE, 3, St. Martin's Place, W.C.

3, St. Martin's Place, W.C.

BOGUE'S HALF-HOUR VOLUMES.

THE GREEN LANES : A Book for a Country Stroll. By J. E. TAYLOR, F.L.S., F.G.S. Illustrated with 300 Woodcuts. Fifth Edition. Crown 8vo, cloth, 4*s.*

THE SEA-SIDE ; or, Recreations with Marine Objects. By J. E. TAYLOR, F.L.S., F.G.S. Illustrated with 150 Woodcuts. Fourth Edition. Crown 8vo, cloth, 4*s.*

GEOLOGICAL STORIES : A Series of Autobiographies in Chronological Order. By J. E. TAYLOR, F.L.S., F.G.S. Numerous Illustrations. Fourth Edition. Crown 8vo, cloth, 4*s.*

THE MICROSCOPE : A Popular Guide to the Use of the Instrument. By E. LANKESTER, M.D., F.R.S. With 250 Illustrations. Sixteenth Thousand. Fcap. 8vo, cloth plain, 2*s.* 6*d.* ; coloured, 4*s.*

THE TELESCOPE : A Popular Guide to its Use as a means of Amusement and Instruction . By R. A. PROCTOR, B.A. With numerous Illustrations on Stone and Wood. Seventh Edition. Fcap. 8vo, cloth, 2*s.* 6*d.*

THE STARS : A Plain and Easy Guide to the Constellations. By R. A. PROCTOR, B.A. Illustrated with 12 Maps. Tenth Thousand. Demy 4to, boards, 5*s.*

ENGLISH ANTIQUITIES. By LLEWELLYNN JEWITT, F.S.A. *Contents :—* Barrows, Stone Arches, Cromlechs — Implements of Flint and Stone—Celts and other Instruments of Bronze—Roman Roads, Towns, &c. — Tesselated Pavements, Temples, Altars — Ancient Pottery— Arms and Armour—Sepulchral Slabs and Brasses—Coins—Church Bells— Glass—Stained Glass—Tiles—Tapestry—Personal Ornaments, &c. With 300 Woodcuts. Second Edition. Crown 8vo, cloth extra, 5*s.*

ENGLISH FOLK-LORE. By the Rev. T. F. THISELTON DYER. *Contents :* — Trees — Plants — Flowers — The Moon — Birds — Animals—Insects—Reptiles—Charms—Birth—Baptism — Marriage—Death —Days of the Week—The Months and their Weather Lore —Bells—Miscellaneous Folk-Lore. Second Edition. Crown 8vo, cloth, 5*s.*

PLEASANT DAYS IN PLEASANT PLACES. By EDWARD WALFORD, M.A., late Scholar of Balliol College, Oxford, Editor of "County Families," &c. *Contents :*—Dorney and Burnham—Shanklin —Hadleigh—St. David's—Winchilsea—Sandwich — St. Osyth's Priory— Richborough Castle—Great Yarmouth—Old Moreton Hall — Cumnor— Ightham — Shoreham and Bramber — Beaulieu — Kenilworth — Tattershall Tower—Tower of Essex. Illustrated with numerous Woodcuts. Second Edition. Crown 8vo, cloth extra, 5*s.*

HOLIDAYS IN HOME COUNTIES. By EDWARD WALFORD, M.A. *Contents :* A Pilgrimage to the Birthplace of Nelson—A Summer Day at Chiswick—A Day at Selborne—Brambletye House—A Pilgrimage to Cheneys—A Summer Day about Dover—Footprints of Wolsey at Esher—A Day at Stoke Pogis—A Visit to Leeds Castle—A Ramble in Search of Thames Head—St. Albans and Gorhambury—An Autumn Day at Chertsey—A Day at Harold's Tomb—A Day at Rochester —A Summer Day at Ely—Halnaker and Boxgrove. With numerous Illustrations. Crown 8vo, cloth extra, 5*s.*

Other Volumes in Preparation.

London : DAVID BOGUE, 3, St. Martin's Place, W.C.

PUBLISHED QUARTERLY, Price 2s. 6d.

THE POPULAR SCIENCE REVIEW:

A Quarterly Summary of Scientific Progress and Miscellany of Entertaining and Instructive Articles on Scientific Subjects.

Edited by W. S. DALLAS, F.L.S.,
Assistant Secretary of the Geological Society.

In addition to Articles which are of abiding interest, the POPULAR SCIENCE REVIEW contains a Complete Record of Progress in every Department of Science, including:

ASTRONOMY.	GEOGRAPHY.	MICROSCOPY.
BOTANY.	GEOLOGY.	PHOTOGRAPHY.
CHEMISTRY.	MECHANICS.	PHYSICS.
ETHNOLOGY.	METALLURGY.	ZOOLOGY.

Quarterly, price 2s. 6d. ; Annual Subscription (by post), 10s. 10d.

*Volumes I. to XVIII. may be had, bound in cloth,
price 12s. each.*

PUBLISHED MONTHLY, Price 6d.

THE MIDLAND NATURALIST.

The Journal of the Associated Natural History, Philosophical, and Archæological Societies and Field Clubs of the Midland Counties. Edited by E. W. BADGER, and W. J. HARRISON, F.G.S. Demy 8vo, Illustrated. Vols. I. and II. now ready, cloth, 7s. 6d. each ; Vol. III. commenced January, 1880.

PUBLISHED QUARTERLY, Price 1s.

THE JOURNAL OF CONCHOLOGY.

Containing Original Communications, Descriptions of New Species, &c. Demy 8vo. Vol. I (17 Nos.) 13s., Vol. II. (12 Nos.) 12s., Vol. III. Nos. 1 to 3, 1s. each.

THE JOURNAL OF THE QUEKETT MICROSCOPICAL CLUB.

Demy 8vo, Illustrated. Parts 1 to 44 (Vol. VI., Part 3) are published, 1s. each. A few Sets of Vols. I. to V. may still be had, bound in cloth gilt, price £3 3s.

London : DAVID BOGUE, 3, St. Martin's Place, W.C.

3, St. Martin's Place, W.C.

Monthly, price 4*d.* ; Annual Subscription, 5*s.* (including Postage)

HARDWICKE'S
SCIENCE GOSSIP:

An Illustrated Medium of Interchange and Gossip
for Students and Lovers of Nature.

Edited by J. E. TAYLOR, Ph.D., F.L.S., F.G.S., &c.

NUMEROUS ILLUSTRATIONS.

Vol. XVI. commenced January, 1880.

Among the subjects included in its pages will be found :
AQUARIA, BEES, BEETLES, BIRDS, BUTTERFLIES, FERNS, FISH,
FLIES, FOSSILS, FUNGI, GEOLOGY, LICHENS, MICRO-
SCOPES, MOSSES, MOTHS, REPTILES, SEAWEEDS,
SPIDERS, WILD FLOWERS, WORMS,
&c., &c.

"This is a very pleasant journal, that costs only fourpence a month, and from which the reader who is no naturalist ought to be able to pick up a good fourpenny-worth of pleasant information. It is conducted and contributed to by expert naturalists, who are cheerful companions, as all good naturalists are ; technical enough to make the general reader feel that they are in earnest, and are not insulting him by writing down to his comprehension, but natural enough and direct enough in their records of facts, their questioning and answering each other concerning curiosities of nature. The reader who buys for himself their monthly budget of notes and discussions upon pleasant points in natural history and science, will probably find his curiosity excited and his interest in the world about him taking the form of a little study of some branch of the sort of knowledge that has won his readiest attention. For when the study itself is so delightful, and the enthusiasm it excites so genuine and well-directed, these enthusiasms are contagious. The fault is not with itself, but with the public, if this little magazine be not in favour with a very large circle of readers."—*Examiner.*

London : DAVID BOGUE, 3, St. Martin's Place, W.C.

3, *St. Martin's Place, W.C.* ·

I. OGDEN AND CO., PRINTERS, 172, ST. JOHN STREET, E.C.